Sleep tight, Caitlin. . . .

She struggled against him. His face was masked, invisible. His body was pure darkness.

She sucked in a deep draft of oxygen, and then the cloth was over her nose again, and before she could stop herself she had breathed its fumes.

Cold.

The fumes were sweet-smelling, intoxicating. They made her head spin. The world blurred, everything going double, no clarity anywhere, and she was tired, sleepy.

Far away, his chuckle of triumph. Then his words, low, spoken close to her ear.

"Got you now, C. J."

That voice.

She *knew* that voice. . . .

Also by Michael Prescott

THE SHADOW HUNTER
STEALING FACES
COMES THE DARK

MICHAEL PRESCOTT

last breath

A SIGNET BOOK

SIGNET
Published by New American Library, a division of
Penguin Putnam Inc., 375 Hudson Street,
New York, New York 10014, U.S.A.
Penguin Books Ltd, 80 Strand,
London WC2R 0RL, England
Penguin Books Australia Ltd, Ringwood,
Victoria, Australia
Penguin Books Canada Ltd, 10 Alcorn Avenue,
Toronto, Ontario, Canada M4V 3B2
Penguin Books (N.Z.) Ltd, 182–190 Wairau Road,
Auckland 10, New Zealand

Penguin Books Ltd, Registered Offices:
Harmondsworth, Middlesex, England

Published by Signet, an imprint of New American Library,
a division of Penguin Putnam Inc.

First Printing, December 2001
10 9 8 7 6 5 4 3 2 1

PUBLISHER'S NOTE
This is a work of fiction. Names, characters, places, and incidents either are
the product of the author's imagination or are used fictitiously, and any
resemblance to actual persons, living or dead, business establishments,
events, or locales is entirely coincidental.

BOOKS ARE AVAILABLE AT QUANTITY DISCOUNTS WHEN USED TO PROMOTE PROD-
UCTS OR SERVICES. FOR INFORMATION PLEASE WRITE TO PREMIUM MARKETING DIVI-
SION, PENGUIN PUTNAM INC., 375 HUDSON STREET, NEW YORK, NEW YORK 10014.

I don't think any tragedy in literature that I have ever come across impressed me so much as the first one, that I spelled out slowly for myself in words of three letters: the bad fox has got the red hen. There was something so dramatically complete about it; the badness of the fox, added to all the traditional guile of his race, seemed to heighten the horror of the hen's fate, and there was such a suggestion of masterful malice about the word "got." One felt that a countryside in arms would not get that hen away from the bad fox.

—Saki (H. H. Munro),
The Unbearable Bassington

Prologue

C. J. Osborn was ten years old when the boogeyman came for her.

Some months earlier she had decided she was old enough to be left without a baby-sitter. A baby-sitter was for babies, by definition, and she was no baby. She rode horses—well, ponies—and climbed steep trails in the Big Maria Mountains and explored the shadowed canyons near her home. She shot rifles and pitched horseshoes. She was too much of a tomboy to be satisfied with her given name, Caitlin Jean, and so she had become C. J., a name that suited her better. Certainly at the advanced age of ten, she could be left alone for an evening, even if home was a ranch house in a remote outpost of the Mojave Desert, and the nearest neighbors were a half mile away.

"If there's any problem," C. J. explained to her mom and dad in her calmest, most adult tone of voice, "I can call you. Or the Gregsons. Or the police. I know what to do."

Despite her arguments, for the first half of 1985 her parents continued to hire Liddie Wilcox to sit for them when they went out, even though Liddie, presently sixteen, had begun baby-sitting at the age of twelve, only two years older than C. J. was now.

Finally, in August, after months of sustained prodding on C. J.'s part, her parents relented. They were attending a birthday party at a restaurant in Blythe, the nearest big town, twenty miles down Midland Road. They would not call Liddie. "You'll be on your own," C. J.'s dad warned. "You sure about this?"

"I'm sure," C. J. said with no trace of doubt. What was there to be worried about? What could possibly go wrong?

Before leaving, her parents gave her the phone number of the restaurant, and the numbers of the half-dozen neighbors within a two-mile radius, and the number of the Sheriff's Department, and a great deal of advice, which she only pretended to listen to.

Then they were gone, the old Chevy pickup rattling down the dirt road into the smoldering sunset. C. J. waved to them until they were out of sight. Then she was alone, really and truly alone, and she hugged herself for joy. She was a grown-up now.

Inside the house, she locked all the doors and windows, as her parents had instructed; the swamp cooler in the attic was sufficient to cool the place. She could hear it thrumming through the ceiling as she made dinner. Her mom had left a complete meal in the fridge—chicken, peas, and mashed potatoes, arranged in a tray like a TV dinner. All she had to do was heat it up. Not much of a challenge, but she felt a thrill of accomplishment when the meal was ready. "I did it myself," she said smugly, almost persuaded that she had prepared the dinner from scratch.

She carried her food into the den and watched TV while she ate, a custom ordinarily forbidden in the

Osborn household. But, as she reminded herself, she was the head of the household for the moment. She could do what she liked.

By nine o'clock she was beginning to get sleepy. Excitement had given way to drowsy boredom. She lazed in an armchair in front of the TV, congratulating herself on having taken her first step into adulthood.

That was when she saw the light.

A dim glow wavered outside the window of the den, not close, maybe twenty yards away or even farther, shimmering like a will-o'-the-wisp. She watched until it vanished beyond the window frame.

A first prickle of fear worked its way through her belly and up her spine. What she had seen was the beam of a flashlight. At least she was pretty sure it was.

There was no reason for anybody to be prowling the grounds of the ranch with a flashlight. And prowling was the right word.

Prowlers were burglars—or worse.

She almost ran to the nearest phone. But she couldn't be absolutely sure of what she'd seen. It might have been some trick of light—the high beams of a car on the power line road, maybe, or the reflection of a shooting star. Or maybe the product of her overworked imagination. People were always telling her that she fantasized too much.

Still, she took the precaution of rechecking every door and window to be certain every latch and dead bolt was secure. She turned on all the lights in the house. Darkness, she felt, was her enemy.

Finishing her rounds, she stopped in the kitchen to turn on the overhead light and to take a long, sharp knife out of the cutlery drawer.

The knife was not much protection, but if somebody was out there . . .

She turned off the TV and the swamp cooler. She wanted no extraneous sounds to distract her.

In perfect silence she sat on the sofa in the living room and listened.

Was someone out there? A drug addict or some other desperate person? She could picture him—him, yes, it had to be a man, women didn't prowl around in shadows and scare little girls. He would be shaggy-haired and beefy, and he would smell of stale sweat, and his eyes would glitter like small, polished stones.

There were vagrants in Blythe, panhandlers and shopping-cart people, who had that look. Maybe this man was one of them. If there was a man. If she hadn't imagined the whole thing.

She comforted herself with the thought that there was no way a prowler could enter the house without being heard. To get in, he would have to force a door or window. She would hear the splinter of wood or the shatter of glass.

Unless he could pick a lock. But she doubted he could defeat any of the dead bolts on the exterior doors.

She ought to be safe. Anyway, there might not be anyone outside at all. Already the glow she had seen through the window was beginning to seem like an image in a dream. Was it possible that she really had dreamed it—that she had dozed off and . . . ?

Wait.

A noise.

The creak of wood.

From the rear of the house, where the laundry room was.

There was a door back there, but it was dead-bolted like the others. He couldn't get in that way.

Could he?

Another creak. Closer than the last.

Footsteps.

That was what she was hearing—soft footsteps on the wooden floor of the hallway that led from the laundry room to the back bedrooms.

He was in the house.

It was impossible—there had been no sound—but somehow he had penetrated all her defenses, and now he was coming, closing in on her.

Suddenly the knife seemed like very poor protection, pitifully inadequate to the threat she faced. She needed help.

She left the living room, the hasp of the knife gripped in her shaking hand, and entered the kitchen. The phone sat on the counter, a black rotary-dial model. She lifted the handset from the cradle and dialed nine, then one—

She stopped.

New footsteps.

In the living room.

He had made it that far.

If she said anything into the phone, he would hear her, even if she whispered. He would hear her, and she would never finish what she had to say.

Carefully, making no noise, she hung up the phone.

He was searching the house room by room. He would look in the kitchen before long.

There was no way out of the kitchen except through the living room, and he was in there now.

Hide somewhere. Under the table? No good—he would see her easily. In the cabinet under the sink?

She looked inside, but the interior was crammed with dustpans and sponges and cleansers. She could never make enough room for herself.

She remembered the crawl space.

It ran underneath the house. Her dad had climbed down there more than once to fix the plumbing. The trapdoor that afforded access to it was in a corner of the kitchen, recessed in the hardwood floor.

She crept to the trapdoor and pulled on the metal ring embedded in the wood. The door was surprisingly heavy, but fear gave her strength. She lifted it, and miraculously the hinge, recently oiled, made no sound.

There was darkness below, and she had no flashlight or matches, and no time to find any. She lowered herself into the pit. Her Keds immediately touched bottom. She set down the knife on a bed of gravel, reached up, and eased the trapdoor shut.

Safe. Maybe.

She waited, huddling in the dark. Her fingers groped in the gravel until they found the wooden hasp of the knife. She drew it close to her.

Through the floor above her head, she could hear the vibrations of his footsteps. He was close—not in the kitchen but maybe in the den. He must have seen her through the window, and even if he hadn't, he would know someone was home. The TV must be still warm, and the remains of her dinner sat on a tray on the coffee table.

He must be a burglar, but she had never heard of any homes being burglarized here in Midland, a hardscrabble town at the eastern edge of California, near the Colorado River, a town of ranchers and miners and people who wanted to be left alone. Nobody out here was rich. There was nothing to steal.

Then why was he here? And why tonight of all

nights—the first night when she had ever been left alone?

Was he—the thought came to her like a sliver of a nightmare, intruding on rationality—was he *after* her?

Had he deliberately waited until she was alone? Waited for his chance to get her?

Crazy idea, but she couldn't shake free of it. Fears from earlier phases of her childhood returned to her. The monster in the closet. The bear under the bed. The boogeyman.

That was what he was. The boogeyman, the terror of all children.

And now he was in the kitchen.

She heard the tread of his steps moving closer to where she lay, diminishing, approaching again. He was circling the kitchen. He must suspect that she had gone in there. But how could he know?

Maybe he had searched every other room, and this was the last place left. Or maybe he could smell her, the way a bloodhound sniffs out its prey.

Stop it. Stop thinking like that.

She was safe. She had to be safe. He couldn't know about the crawl space. He couldn't possibly find her.

Nonetheless, she wriggled a few feet away from the trapdoor until she found a vertical plumbing pipe in the darkness. It was thin and provided little cover, but she dragged herself behind it anyway, the knife still clutched in her hand.

The footsteps drifted nearer.

Had he seen the trapdoor? Had he guessed?

She waited, breath suspended.

Then—light.

A faint but brightening fan of light from the kitchen as the trapdoor was raised.

It lifted noiselessly, as it had before. In the sudden spill of light she looked around the crawl space for another exit or a better hiding place. There was nothing—only the gray spread of gravel, confusions of plumbing pipes here and there, the cobwebby subfloor that made a low roof overhead, and patches of darkness in the far corners.

If she could reach one of those corners she might kick through the latticework and escape outside. It was worth a try.

She started to crawl, and abruptly the light from the open trapdoor dimmed as a human figure crouched over the entryway.

She froze. Any movement and she would be visible to him.

She couldn't see him, only his shadow on the gravel floor. He was squatting down, motionless.

Then the shadow disappeared in a new blaze of light. His flashlight had snapped on.

The long orange beam probed the crawl space, tracking over the dirt and the plumbing pipes and the whorls of spiderwebs. Dead insects littered the dirt—husks of beetles, dried remnants of houseflies. A few yards from her lay something small and skeletal, which might have been a long-dead mouse or pack rat.

The beam played over one side of the crawl space, then blurred in C. J.'s direction and finally settled on her. She looked into the bright cone of light with frightened, blinking eyes.

From behind the light came a voice—a male voice in a whispery falsetto, the most evil voice she had ever heard.

"I spy," he breathed, "with my little eye . . ."

Laughter, soft and mirthless, fading away.

The flashlight wavered. There was movement. He was shifting his position.

Climbing down.

Down into the crawl space with her, and when he did, there would be no place for her to go and no hope and no chance.

Blind terror drove her forward. She saw a slim, trouser-clad leg swinging down, and she lashed out at it with the knife.

He was quick, almost quick enough to anticipate the blow. The knife brushed his calf and tore the trouser leg, and then he was out of reach, squatting above her again.

She retreated a couple feet and waited, the knife held before her in both hands like a talisman.

Silence. Stillness.

Broken by his voice, breathless and mocking, still raised in a falsetto whisper. "You're a fighter, Caitlin."

He knew her name.

"Who are you?" she called out, fighting to keep her voice steady.

No answer.

"How do you know me?"

No answer.

"What do you want?"

This time, a reply. "I want you, Caitlin."

His voice was not what she had expected. She'd thought it would be husky, gravelly, a dark, croaking voice, but instead it was soft and almost soothing, seductive as a python's hiss.

"Want me for what?" she asked.

Laughter.

"Leave me alone!"

"Can't do that, Caitlin. I've waited too long."

She wanted to ask what he meant, but the words wouldn't come. He explained anyway.

"I've been watching you. Biding my time. And now . . . tonight . . . my long wait ends. Tonight, Caitlin. Tonight."

He had to be the boogeyman. Who else could he be?

The knife shook in her hands, but she did not loosen her grip.

In movies, she had seen how a panther or a tiger would coil up, then pounce. She knew he was doing the same thing. Tensing his body for a new attack.

It came. This time it was his arm that was thrust through the aperture, one gloved hand grabbing at her, nearly seizing her by the wrists. She twisted clear of his grasp and stabbed again, missing, and the arm retreated up the hole.

She edged sideways to a new position, then waited for the next assault.

She had seen little in the split second when he snatched at her, but enough to know that his arm was skinny and long. He wore a dark long-sleeved shirt and a black glove. He was not the raggedy man of her imagination. He was thin and sleek and quick.

How old was he? A teenager only a few years older than herself, or an adult? She couldn't tell. His whispery voice gave nothing away, and she couldn't see his face.

She hoped she never saw it. If she did, it would mean that she had lost the battle.

"Why me?" she called hoarsely.

"It has to be somebody, Caitlin."

"Why me?" she repeated.

"Because you're so very pretty. Do you know how pretty you are? Your hair is so smooth and shiny, chestnut brown streaked with sun. I'd like to run my fingers through your hair."

She shuddered.

"I've studied you," he went on. "In town . . . and here at the ranch. You fascinate me. You're a very special little girl."

"Just go away."

"I wish I could. But then I'd never learn the answer to the question that's been haunting me. What color are your eyes, Caitlin? Are they brown or blue? I've never gotten close enough to see."

Her eyes were green, but she didn't tell him. She didn't want him to know anything about her—even though he already seemed to know too much.

"I'll bet they're pretty eyes," he said, and then the gloved hand was upon her again, closing over her right wrist and jerking it back, and she dropped the knife. He grabbed for it, but she snatched it first with her left hand and slashed at him furiously, and she heard a hiss of pain.

He retreated again. In the glow of the flashlight she saw a thin red line painted on the knife blade. She had nicked him in the hand or the forearm. Hurt him.

She had never intentionally hurt any living thing before tonight, but now she wanted to maim and cripple and mutilate. He had called her a fighter. He was right.

"Bitch," the voice breathed.

Droplets of blood pattered on the gravel.

"Go away," C. J. whispered.

But she knew he wouldn't.

She steadied the knife. When he struck again, she would be ready. She would hold him off all night if she had to. She would never give up. Let him try again and again to invade her hiding place. She would inflict cut after cut until he either gave up or died.

"I'm going to kill you, Caitlin Jean Osborn," he said in a deadly monotone. "And I'll do it slowly. I'll make you pay—"

"Fuck you," she snapped. It was the first time she had ever said that word aloud.

She waited for the next onslaught. Strangely she wasn't scared anymore. Later there would be time for fear, but now there was only the beat of her heart and the feel of the knife and her total concentration on survival.

Come on, she thought. Try again. I'm not afraid of you. Try again . . .

The flashlight disappeared.

For a startled moment she thought he had switched it off. Then she heard the creak of floorboards in the kitchen, the tread of receding footsteps, and she knew he had left.

Had to be a trick. He was trying to fool her into coming out.

Or was he going to get a gun?

No, couldn't be. If he had a gun, why wouldn't he have brought it with him in the first place?

Well, because he was crazy, of course.

If he was planning to come back with a gun, then her only chance was to get out now, while the kitchen was clear. But suppose it was a trap, and she climbed out only to be attacked . . .

The fear was back. When things had been clear, when there had been only the simple job of fending him off, she had forgotten how to be afraid. Now that there was a decision to make, she was aware again of her terror and confusion, and aware also that she was only a ten-year-old girl, alone without a sitter for the first time ever, and this was all too much for her.

The house was silent. Had he gone? Really gone?

Maybe she could risk emerging. If she saw him waiting for her, she might have time to get back into the crawl space. She—

Footsteps again.

Returning.

Too late. He was back.

He must have brought a gun, *must* have.

No escape now. The knife was useless. She waited in terror until his silhouette appeared above her, his long, scrawny shadow stretched on the dirt floor, and she looked up into his face.

Her dad. Blinking down at her.

"C. J.? C. J., what the hell . . . ?"

"Daddy, is he gone, *is he gone*?"

"Is who gone? Get out of there, it's filthy down there!"

"Is he gone?"

"There's nobody here, C. J. Get out now."

By the time she climbed up, her mom was there as well, staring at her in bewildered concern. "What in the world?" her mom kept asking, over and over. "What in the world?"

C. J. told them what had happened. She told them about the man who had come for her, who had gotten into the house without making any noise, who had known her name, who had said he'd been watching her. "We have to call the sheriff," she said. "Please let's call now before he gets too far away!"

Her parents made no effort to pick up the phone. They merely traded a resigned glance.

"Come on," C. J. insisted, "we have to call!"

"C. J.," her dad said softly, "there was nobody here tonight."

She stood stunned, unable to register the fact that they didn't believe her.

"You got all worked up," her mom said in a gentle, soothing tone. "Maybe it was something you saw on TV. You know how that imagination of yours can get going sometimes."

"It wasn't imagination," C. J. whispered. "I cut him. Look."

She showed them the knife, but the blood on the blade had already dried to a thin dusky line like a gravy stain.

"C. J. . . ." her mom said, losing patience.

"There's some of his blood on the floor of the crawl space. You can see it!"

But no blood was visible on the gravel. She must have obliterated all traces when she climbed out.

Still, she wouldn't give up. She made her parents accompany her on a tour of the house. The man had broken in. There would be signs of it. A forced window, an open door . . .

There was nothing. Every door was locked, every window sealed.

"Are you willing to admit that it was your imagination now?" her dad asked sternly.

"He was real," C. J. said stubbornly. "He was the boogeyman." Even as she said it, she knew this was the wrong choice of words. Everyone knew there was no such thing as the boogeyman. Even she had known it until tonight.

Her parents wouldn't listen. When she pressed the point, they lost their patience. They sent her to bed, telling her that she would not be left without a sitter again.

The Sheriff's Department was never called. After a

while C. J. stopped talking about the intruder. Meekly she acknowledged that she must have imagined him. It was the safest thing to say. But it was a lie.

That man was real. And he might still be out there. Waiting, as he had said. Studying her. Biding his time.

How he had entered the house remained a mystery for a month or so, until she remembered the doggy door. The Osborns had no dog, but the ranch's previous owners had kept two schnauzers and had built a small swinging door at the rear of the house. It had not been used in years, but when she tested it, she found that the door still opened easily, and the hinges made only a faint squeal, inaudible at a distance.

The opening was small, and she herself could barely pass through it. But she recalled the man's long, skinny arm. He had been bony, almost skeletal, and somehow, by some incredible contortion of his shoulders and hips, he had crawled through the little door. And when he heard her parents returning, he'd crawled out again.

She knew this was so, because snagged on a splinter of wood in the doggy door's frame were a few black threads. She remembered the black trousers he'd worn.

Of course it proved nothing. There was no point in even raising the issue with her mom and dad. They would look at her strangely, and there might even be talk of consulting with a psychologist in Blythe, as there had been for a few days after the attack.

She didn't want to see a psychologist. She kept her thoughts to herself.

But from then on, whenever she played outdoors or rode a pony in the desert or climbed a trail to a high ridge, she kept watch for a tall, lean figure in black.

The boogeyman was out there.

And someday, she knew, he would return.

PART ONE

The Red Hen

NOON–8:00 P.M.
WEDNESDAY

1

Morrie Walsh hated autopsies.

He knew he was supposed to be accustomed to this part of the job after thirty years as a cop, but somehow it never failed to get to him—the unpacking of a human body, the utter violation of a person.

Of course, as he knew too well, Martha Eversol had already been violated far more profoundly. Nothing the pathologist could do to her really mattered. The true damage had been done by other hands.

Walsh stood beside the steel autopsy table, one of two tables in a specially ventilated room at the Los Angeles County Morgue, a room restricted to badly decomposed remains. Martha Eversol had been dumped in an abandoned minimall on Sepulveda Boulevard a month earlier, and the condition of her body was not good.

One saving grace was that there had been no rain. January, often the start of LA's rainy season, had been unusually dry this year, with some days approaching the windy dustiness of the Santa Ana season that normally developed in September. The dryness had helped to preserve the corpse. Instead of rotting, it had been mummified. The skin had a taut, leathery quality, and the other tissues had withered away, making the bones sharp and obvious beneath.

The body lay utterly limp. Rigor mortis had dissipated many days ago.

The medical examiner was a lean, ponytailed man named Sarandon who lacked most of the quirks associated with members of his profession. His only noticeable eccentricity was a habit of humming complicated melodies during an autopsy. He seemed partial to Bach.

Sarandon stood opposite Walsh, reviewing the tools in his kit: scalpel; surgical scissors; the wickedly sharp, long-bladed implement called a bread knife; and forceps, known as "pickups" by coroners everywhere. His assistant bustled about, making arcane preparations, while Sarandon turned on the microphone hanging over the table and dictated his opening remarks, beginning with today's date, January 31.

Walsh briefly shut his eyes. It was a date he'd been dreading since Martha Eversol's disappearance exactly one month ago.

Sarandon examined the body, finding ligature marks on the wrists and ankles—"antemortem," he noted, pointing to the swollen redness of the wounds. But of course they would be antemortem. There was no point in tying up the woman after she was dead. Martha Eversol had been bound while alive. She had been kept that way for precisely four hours. Walsh was sure of it.

Sarandon, humming a pleasant air that sounded suspiciously like a show tune, found bruises on Martha Eversol's neck. Antemortem or perimortem. Before death or at the moment of death.

"Consistent with manual strangulation?" Walsh asked, already knowing the answer.

Sarandon nodded curtly, not removing his gaze from the body. "Consistent, but we won't know for sure until we look at the trachea." He peeled back the corpse's eyelids and noted pinpoint hemorrhages on the insides of the lids and in the whites of the eyes. "Additional evidence of strangulation. Still not conclusive."

Walsh nodded. Manual strangulation closed off the arteries at the sides of the neck but left open the artery at the nape. Blood would continue pumping into the head but would be unable to leave. As blood pressure rose, capillaries burst, producing telltale petechial hemorrhages.

"How about the tattoo?" Walsh asked.

Sarandon interrupted his humming. "You haven't seen it?"

"The body was still clothed at the dump site. I heard SID found the tat when they undressed her." He pronounced it "sid," but he meant the Scientific Investigation Division—the crime-scene specialists.

"Yeah, they did. Just wait till we get a few pictures, and I'll show it to you."

Sarandon's assistant shot a roll of 35mm photos of the body. Then the ME and his helper eased Martha Eversol off the body block that supported her torso. The corpse slipped onto its side, exposing the left shoulder, and there on the shoulder blade was the tattoo.

"Postmortem," Sarandon said. "Like the other one." There was no reddening of the skin around the design, as there would have been if the ink had been applied during life.

More whirs and clicks from the snapshot camera. The exhaust fans incorporated into the table hummed busily, while the more powerful fans installed in the ceiling droned in counterpart. As yet there were no odors for the fans to draw off. But not for long.

Before the corpse was replaced on the body block, Walsh took a close look at the tat. It was a maroon hourglass, three inches long, rendered by hand.

He had known it would be somewhere on her body. On Nikki Carter it had been engraved in her right buttock. Evidently the Hourglass Killer didn't care where he made his mark.

"I've heard SID found a calling card," Sarandon said, shifting the body into a supine position.

Walsh stiffened. "Who told you that?"

"Little birdie."

"We don't want that information getting out. It's bad enough that the tattoo is public knowledge."

"Hey," Sarandon said, "you can tell me. I don't leak."

This was true, but Walsh cast a doubtful eye on Sarandon's assistant.

Sarandon noted the glance. "Raul's okay. Come on, Morris, you're among friends here."

Walsh thought of the bodies on gurneys and steel tables in every room and corridor in the morgue. Among friends? Among the dead, was more like it.

"Can you shut off the tape recorder for a minute?" Walsh asked.

Sarandon motioned to Raul, who killed the microphone.

"On both vics he left the same item," Walsh said. "A three-by-five index card. Both times, the same words, printed by hand in block letters: WELCOME TO THE FOUR-H CLUB."

Sarandon frowned. "Four-H Club?"

"Right."

"Could mean anything, I guess. The Four-Homicide Club, maybe. Or the Four-Hooker Club."

"Neither of the vics was a prostitute."

"To a guy like this, *all* women might be prostitutes."

"That's not what it means."

"No? Then you tell me."

"It's the Four-Hour Club," Walsh said.

"Four hours?" Sarandon lifted an eyebrow. "Because of the hourglass, you think?"

"Partly. And then there's the wristwatch."

"What about it?"

"The dial was frozen at two-seventeen. That's four hours to the minute after Nikki Carter's abduction."

"If the nightclub witnesses are reliable."

"I think they are. Carter went into the rest room at approximately ten-fifteen and never came out."

"Well, possibly. But there are a lot of ways for a Timex to get busted." The ME began snipping Martha Eversol's fingernails one at a time, placing each into a separate evidence envelope, which Raul neatly labeled. "Let's say the killer messed up the ligatures, didn't tie them tight enough. Carter gets free and struggles. He throws her to the floor, breaks her watch."

"You didn't find any defense wounds. Besides, letting her get loose would be a mistake on his part."

"So?"

"I don't think this guy makes mistakes."

Sarandon glanced at him dubiously, then returned to his work. "You're saying he smashed the watch on purpose, so the dial would freeze at exactly two-seventeen."

"Which is when he killed her. Which is why she's a member of the Four-Hour Club." Walsh shrugged. "The stomach contents support the same timeline."

"Come on, Morrie. Plenty of things can interfere with digestion. We can't say for sure how long Carter was kept alive."

"Your best estimate was six hours after her last meal, which would mean four hours after her abduction."

"Key word there is *estimate*. I didn't know you were going to take me so literally."

"It all hangs together—the hourglass, the wrist-watch, the Four-H reference."

"And you think this one followed the same pattern?"

Walsh nodded. "Martha Eversol was snatched from a side street around eight-thirty on New Year's Eve, on her way to a party. Someone rear-ended her, and she must've gotten out to exchange insurance info. I'm guessing she died at thirty minutes past midnight on the first day of the year."

"Probably didn't get a chance to keep her resolutions," Sarandon said blandly.

Walsh was tired of the conversation. "So are you going to look at her windpipe or not?"

"I aim to please."

The tape recorder was turned on again, and Sarandon resumed humming and set to work.

Walsh didn't care that the ME was skeptical. MEs were supposed to be skeptical. They were trained to look at an elderly woman who died of heart failure and think *cyanide*. They took nothing for granted.

Walsh was willing to operate a little more on instinct, and his instincts told him that time mattered to this man he and his task force were hunting, this man who carved an hourglass tattoo into the dead flesh of each victim before dumping her body in some remote location where it would lie hidden for days or weeks. First, Nikki Carter, found inside a jumbo garbage bag in an auto graveyard in East LA. Now the second victim, Martha Eversol, deposited in the shell of a failed minimall, where she had lain undisturbed throughout January.

Well, she would be undisturbed no longer. Walsh thought about that as Sarandon made the Y incision with his bread knife, opening up Martha Eversol from the shoulders to the stomach, then down in a direct line to the pubic bone.

Decomposition was advanced, and the smell was bad. Walsh tried to suppress his gag reflex as the gassy stench wafted up into the overhead fans.

Sarandon scalpeled the skin and muscle off Martha's chest wall, then bisected her ribs with a bone cutter. The chest plate came loose and was laid aside. He hummed something by Rachmaninoff—the Second Piano Concerto, Walsh thought. He knew these things. His mother had forced him to take piano lessons as a kid.

Body fluids began running in the gutters of the sloped table. Raul turned on a couple of spigots built into the table to wash the mess away. Sarandon switched to the theme from *Cabaret*. It sounded much too cheerful to be hummed as a dirge over Martha's mortal remains.

What came next in the procedure was known in the coroners' trade as the Rokitansky method. Another ME had once described it to Walsh as field-dressing a carcass. He had made it sound as if the deceased was just another trophy to be strapped to somebody's hood.

The Rokitansky method entailed dissecting the corpse from the neck downward. Walsh would have to witness the entire process in case anything unexpected came up, but it was the neck that interested him.

He already knew the Hourglass Killer had strangled Martha Eversol. He just needed physical confirmation.

Sarandon carefully separated the larynx and esophagus from the pharynx, then stopped humming and took a close look.

"Fractures of the cricoid cartilage," he reported.

"Strangled," Walsh said, not bothering to phrase it as a question.

Sarandon nodded. "Manual strangulation, consistent with the first victim."

Raul spoke up for the first time. "Was there ever any doubt?"

Walsh sighed. "Nope. No doubt at all."

Sarandon began humming again. He worked the bread knife south of the collarbone, beginning the process of unpacking Martha's vital organs, and Walsh stood silent, wishing he were somewhere else, far away from the autopsy and Sarandon's musical accompaniment. On Zuma Beach, maybe, with his surf-fishing gear. That would be nice.

Sarandon hummed, and in his mind Walsh cast his line into the tide and let the surf carry it far from shore.

2

The spider hung in her web, inches from her prey.

Gavin Treat leaned closer, watching. This was the good part. She would feed.

Yesterday evening he had released a cricket into the five-gallon terrarium that occupied a corner of his bedroom. Last night the cricket, hopping frantically, had become entangled in the funnel-shaped web. Though it had struggled, its efforts had only lashed it more tightly to the gluey strands.

Now it lay still. It had given up. It faced its own end with the equanimity born of unrewarded suffering.

The spider began to prowl.

Treat watched the eight legs navigate the mesh of quivering threads. The spider moved lightly, in a calm, unhurried gait.

She was a western black widow, *Latrodectus hesperus*, and Treat loved her as much as he could love anything. He had raised her from a spiderling after finding her and others of her brood scurrying amid a drift of timber in the mountains near Malibu. He remembered the thrill of the discovery and the care with which he had gathered up a dozen of the small darting shapes, loading them into a plastic sandwich bag and sealing the flaps.

Most of the spiderlings had died before maturity, but this one and a single male one-quarter her size had both survived. The male, of course, had perished after mating, devoured by the female. A papery egg sack now hung on the web. Soon it would open, releasing hundreds of babies.

He had never named the spider. He did not think of her as a pet. She was an avatar of darkness, a creeping symbol of predatory death. He admired her sleek beauty—the glossy black orb of her abdomen, the balletic precision of her gliding legs, and the jaws with their embedded fangs.

The cricket twitched. The spider moved faster, spurred by the shiver of the web.

Treat pressed his face to the terrarium's side panel. He had pulled down the shades of his bedroom windows to keep glare off the glass. The only light in the room was the glow of a forty-watt bulb in a gooseneck lamp overhanging the terrarium's screen cover.

The widow reached her prey. Treat knew the procedure she must follow, having witnessed it countless times. She would blanket the cricket in a silken attack wrap, and then her fangs would poison the prey, paralyzing it. Those same fangs would pump out digestive juices, and the cricket would soften, the enzymes doing their work outside the spider's body. Finally the victim's gelatinous form would be sucked into the widow's mouth.

He did not think it was an unpleasant death. Once immobilized by silk and venom, the cricket would know only the slow dissolution of its body in a bath of chemicals. It would simply fade away, its decomposition effected before death.

There were worse ways to die.

Treat knew all about that.

The spinning of the silk began. At some point during the ritual Treat remembered the sandwich in his hand. He had made it himself after coming home for his lunch hour. He had not guessed that it would be the widow's lunch hour as well.

He took small, distracted bites of the sandwich—tomato slices, feta cheese, and bean sprouts between two slabs of date-raisin bread—feeding along with the widow.

He watched her, rapt, until the cricket was entirely gone. Idly he wondered where the cricket's music went when it died. Perhaps the same place that women's screams went.

He finished his sandwich, swallowing a last wedge of bread and bean sprouts, with a soft, precise smack of his lips.

The spider lay on her web, digesting her food, sated. From this angle Treat could clearly see the distinctive mark common to all black widow females—the maroon hourglass on the underside of her belly.

The hourglass, symbol of time. Wasn't it Ovid who called time the devourer of all things?

They made an unholy trinity, Treat thought—time and the widow and himself.

3

Life was funny. She could go for weeks, months, believing she had put her past to rest and finally moved on. And then it would all come back in a hot rush, and she would be ten years old again, huddled in the crawl space with a kitchen knife in her hands.

C. J. pushed the memories away. She wasn't a little girl anymore; she was a woman of twenty-six, doing her job, and at the moment there was a crazy man with a gun to worry about.

The pathway at the rear of the house was narrow and bright under the midday sun. To her left was a chicken-wire fence protecting a vacant lot. To her right, the home's stucco wall and the large, overflowing Dumpster that abutted it. Above the Dumpster was a casement window, an inch ajar to let in any breeze that stirred on a January afternoon in LA.

No movement in the window. It seemed likely that the back room of the house was unoccupied.

C. J. muted the radio clipped to her Sam Browne utility belt, then lifted herself onto the lid of the trash bin and peered through the window. She saw a cot piled with disarranged sheets, a pair of threadbare oval throw rugs on a concrete floor, a crib, bare walls, and a doorway that glowed with the flickering light of a TV set in the front room.

That was where he was. In the front of the house. If it could be called a house when it was only a wood-frame garage partitioned into a bedroom, living room, lavatory, and kitchenette. The bedroom had a view of a trash bin, and the living room, windowless, had no view at all.

Crouching on the Dumpster by the window, C. J. listened. There was no sound from the television; the volume must have been turned down. Now and then rose the squall of a baby.

She wondered if she could open the window fully without making a noise that would alert Ramon Sanchez, the crazy man with the gun in the other room.

Never know unless you try, she thought gamely, and she gave the casement window a cautious pull, bracing herself for a squeal of hinges.

The window opened silently.

She knew she was limber enough to wriggle through, even when encumbered by her vest and her belt.

Question was, did she want to *do* this?

Ramon was out of his mind—his wife, Maria, had been very clear on that point, expressing herself vigorously in both English and Spanish. He was drunk and angry and out of work, and when he got that way, no one could reason with him. She'd called 911 from a neighbor's home, and the RTO had put it out over the air ten minutes ago.

"Any Newton Area unit, possible four-fifteen in progress at Fifty-fifth and Sloan."

C. J., riding shotgun in an A-car, had listened to the crackle of static over the cheap speaker. She and her partner, Walt Brasco, had been on duty since 6:15

A.M., chasing the radio for most of that time. Now it was one o'clock, and they'd been thinking about taking a Code 7 for lunch.

But Fifty-fifth and Sloan wasn't far from where they were cruising. C. J. looked at Brasco, who nodded and said, "Take it."

"Thirteen-A-forty-three," C. J. reported into the handheld microphone hooked to the dashboard. "We'll take the four-fifteen."

"Roger, forty-three. Monitor your screen. Incident three-seven-one-four, Code Two High."

Brasco flipped the toggle that activated the car's light bar and accelerated through a yellow traffic signal. Storefronts flashed past, bearing signs in Vietnamese and Korean and Spanish. A blind beggar held up a cardboard sign at a street corner, in front of a brick wall spray-painted with gang *placas*.

Welcome to Newton Area Division. Shootin' Newton, as it was known among Officer Caitlin Jean Osborn's colleagues in the LAPD. A few square miles of multiethnic slums bordered by five other high-crime divisions, a semicircle of blasted hopes: Hollenbeck, Central, Southwest, Seventy-seventh Street, and Southeast. The infamous Rampart Division, now synonymous with police corruption, was wedged between Central and Southwest, not quite touching Newton but close enough, perhaps, to spread its infection here. Crime rates might have dropped in both the city and county of LA, but no one could prove it in Newton.

C. J. kept her eye on the squad car's computer until it displayed the address of the crime scene. She read it to Brasco. He turned left at the next intersection and pulled to a stop alongside a curb littered with fragments of beer bottles.

A crowd of two dozen was waiting in front of a converted garage that served as somebody's home. Half the spectators were children with nowhere else to be on a school day.

Officers Osborn and Brasco got out, surveying the neighborhood. It was like so many in Newton, a barrio of one-story buildings that might have been nice once. Cars sat on blocks and faded in the sun. Graffiti webbed the walls and fences and even the tree trunks; there were gang names sprayed on and X'd out with what the gangbangers called "dis marks"; the number 187—the section of the California Penal Code that covered homicide—appeared prominently, a livid promise of death. Rap music blared from an open window down the street, and somewhere a dog wailed in counterpoint to the throbbing beat.

C. J. approached the crowd. The kids wore pants several sizes too big in the approved gangsta style, their sleeves rolled up to show off crude, malevolent tattoos. The adults glanced at her suspiciously and looked away.

"Who telephoned the police?" she asked in Spanish. Brasco was letting her handle it. He knew she was better at dealing with people.

A thin, frightened woman elbowed her way forward from the rear of the crowd, answering in uncertain English. "Me, it was me."

"Okay, senora. What's your name?"

"Maria Sanchez. It is my husband in there. My Ramon."

"You had a fight?" The dispatcher had called it a 415—domestic disturbance.

"No, no fight." Tears welled in the woman's large brown eyes. "He lose his job. He get drunk, try to shoot me. He has a gun, he is crazy!"

Drunk and crazy with a gun, C. J. thought. Terrific. "What kind of gun?"

"It is, how you say, six-shooter."

"A handgun? Like this?" C. J. tapped the Beretta 9mm holstered to her right hip.

Maria Sanchez nodded. "Like that, but old, an old gun he got from no-good friend."

"And he tried to shoot you with it?"

Frantic nodding. "Point it at me, and I run out the door. But he still in there. He got Emilio. I no have time to grab him."

"Emilio?" C. J. asked, hoping it was a dog.

"*Mi niño!*"

My boy. This was getting better and better.

"How old is Emilio?" C. J. asked.

"*Seis*—six months."

"We're gonna need backup," Brasco said abruptly. Tension had pulled his broad, pockmarked face into a stiff mask. "This isn't no goddamn four-fifteen. It's an ADW that's turned into a hostage-barricade."

"Let's see if we can talk to him first." C. J. didn't wait for Brasco's reply. She asked Mrs. Sanchez if her husband spoke English, and when the answer was yes, she rapped on the front door, raising her voice. "Mr. Sanchez, this is the police. Open up, please. We need to talk to you."

Silence from inside.

"Mr. Sanchez, we just want to talk."

Nothing.

"Open the door, Mr. Sanchez." She tested the knob and noted that it did not turn. Locked. "This is the police. Open up and let us talk to you, okay?"

Still no response.

"Fuck this," Brasco said. "I'm calling it in. We need SWAT down here with a CNT."

C. J. nodded, but she wasn't happy about it. She hadn't wanted to bring Metro SWAT into this. What had started as a drunken dispute could end up in a bloodbath.

She heard Brasco on the radio while she gathered additional information from Maria Sanchez. Layout of the house, possible exits, time elapsed since she fled the residence. Brasco came back and reported, "ETA ten minutes for another squad, thirty or more for SWAT and a negotiator."

C. J. pointed toward the back of the house. "There's a rear window. I'd better cover it. You watch the front door."

"Okay. Hey, C. J., you're just gonna *watch* the window, right?"

"Right," she said, though she wasn't at all certain what she would do.

And now it was decision time.

She could wait by the window until another A-car arrived, then wait much longer for the SWAT boys to get here with the negotiator. When Ramon Sanchez learned he was surrounded, he might surrender—or put the gun to Emilio's head and pull the trigger.

And if SWAT went in . . .

Five men with machine guns bursting into this tiny house, screaming orders, ready to fire at any shadow . . .

The baby shrieked louder.

C. J. made up her mind. She tried to ignore the trickle of sweat down her back as she drew her Beretta and climbed through the window.

4

When she dropped onto the cot, the springs creaked, but she was pretty sure the sound was inaudible in the front room, drowned out by the baby's cries.

C. J. shifted her service pistol into a two-handed combat stance. She didn't want to use the gun. Only once in her three years on the force had she shot anybody, and even then, the injury hadn't been fatal. She didn't deserve the damn nickname the other Newton cops had given her, and she didn't want to start living up to it now.

The baby began to sob.

She eased herself off the cot and planted both shoes on the floor. The bedroom was minuscule, and the front room couldn't be much larger. She estimated the home's total floor space at less than five hundred square feet. A few steps would carry her through the doorway, into the red zone.

The red zone. That was what Walt Brasco called it, Walt the football fan, in reference to the critical territory inside the twenty-yard line. As if going after the bad guys was no different from scoring a touchdown.

Shouldn't be doing this, C. J., a small voice warned. This is cowboy stuff.

She silenced the voice. It was wrong. This was not cowboy stuff. It was cop stuff. It was what she did, what any cop would do who wasn't a glorified paper pusher.

She advanced, treading silently, staying clear of the doorway. She reached the far wall and crept to the open door, the glow from the TV brightening as she approached.

The baby had quieted, its sobbing wails subsiding into hiccups. Hugging the doorframe, C. J. listened for any other sound. She heard an electric hum—a fan or a refrigerator motor—and softly, a man's voice.

"*Dios mio,*" Sanchez was murmuring, "*Dios mio, Dios mio . . .*"

The chant continued. The voice was low and close. Sanchez must be positioned near the bedroom. She couldn't tell if he was facing her way or not.

There was only one way to go in, and she did it, pivoting through the doorway, staying low to make herself a smaller target.

Sanchez hadn't seen her. He faced front, sitting in what looked like a rusty beach chair. No lights were on, and the only daylight came from the bedroom behind her. The room was illuminated solely by the shifting glow of a muted black-and-white TV resting on an apple crate. A car commercial flowed past in a ribbon of roadway vistas, and then a double-decker cheeseburger filled the screen.

The picture tube's bluish light flickered over the sweaty nape of Sanchez's neck, his loose shirt collar, and the curly-haired baby boy in diapers nestled in his lap.

C. J. took a quick survey of the living room. Mismatched odds and ends of furniture, an ironing table, a fake plant, a velvet painting of Jesus on the wall. No mirrors, no polished surfaces—nothing that might betray her by a reflection.

Her gaze circled back to Sanchez. With his left hand he stroked Emilio's belly, calming the child. In his right hand he held his gun, a long-barreled revolver, maybe an old Colt or Smith—a six-shooter anyway, like a relic of the Wild West.

"Dios mio . . . Dios mio . . ."

Emilio had ceased crying. It was Mr. Sanchez who was sobbing now.

C. J. almost called out to him, identifying herself again as the police, but if he panicked he might turn and fire, and she would be trapped in the doorway, unable to shoot back without endangering the baby.

She had to get the gun away from him.

The distance between herself and Sanchez was six feet. She could reach him in three short steps and snatch the gun.

Dangerous, but facing danger was what they paid her for, right?

C. J. moved forward, still bent low. She dragged her feet in a cautious slide-step, maintaining her balance, textbook high-risk-felony procedure.

One step. Two.

The revolver almost within reach.

Emilio screamed.

The baby had seen her coming, and his cry alerted Ramon Sanchez, who spun, rising, the revolver blurring toward her, and on pure instinct C. J. reached out with her free hand and grabbed it by the cylinder.

A revolver couldn't fire if the cylinder was prevented from turning.

That was the theory, at least. The reality was that some revolvers—the ones that were old, damaged, defective—might fire anyway.

Past the gray shape of the gun she saw Ramon's eyes, inflamed with weeping, big with rage.

"*Policia,*" C. J. snapped. "*Suelte la arma.*" Drop the weapon.

She could shoot him now. She could fire past Emilio, wrapped in Ramon's left arm like a small pink shield—fire into the man's abdomen or groin.

But if she did, he would try to fire back, if only in a reflex action. And his gun was pointed at her face from inches away, close enough for her to smell the lubricant on the muzzle.

An old gun, Maria Sanchez had said. A piece of junk, from the look of it. The kind that might fire even if the cylinder was immobilized.

She repeated the command taught to all recruits at the police academy. "*Suelte la arma.*" Even though Sanchez spoke English, it was a fair bet that he was more fluent in Spanish.

He must have understood her, but he still didn't comply.

She and Sanchez watched each other over the barrel of his gun. C. J. waited for him to pull the trigger. Waited to find out what kind of luck she had.

But he didn't try to shoot. Slowly he relaxed his grip on the revolver and let her take it from him.

"*Dios mio,*" he said again in a hoarse, defeated voice.

She snugged the gun inside her belt. "Put the baby down," she ordered. "Put him down. All right, raise

your hands. Now on your knees. Your knees! Lie on
your stomach. Hands out, away from your body. It's
okay, Mr. Sanchez. It's okay."

She had her knee planted in the small of his back,
and she was cuffing him while he lay in the felony-
prone position. She didn't relax until the second
handcuff clicked shut.

She searched him for other weapons, found none.
When she was certain he posed no threat, she holstered her Beretta. Outside, Brasco was yelling something through the door. He'd heard her shouting
inside.

"I'm all right," C. J. called back as she stood up.

Emilio was crying. She took a moment to comfort
the child and to stop herself from shaking.

Close call. For a moment there, staring into that
gun and those red eyes, she'd felt she was facing her
old enemy once more—facing him, maybe, for the
last time.

But she'd been wrong. Ramon Sanchez was not
the boogeyman.

The boogeyman, she knew, would have pulled
the trigger.

5

Noah Rawls liked his job, even if half the time he was filling out paperwork, and most of his remaining hours were spent manually reviewing log files provided by the owners of violated computer systems. He liked the thrill of the chase—not the Hollywood chase of screaming sirens and weaving traffic, but the subtler game of hunting crackers and phreakers and code-thieves, sniffing out IP addresses, defeating firewalls, beating on-line criminals at their own sport.

He was a hacker-tracker, or more accurately a member of the computer crime squad in the FBI's Baltimore field office. Some field offices had full-fledged Computer Intrusion teams of seven to ten agents, but here in Baltimore it was just Rawls and his partner, Ned Brand. They shared a small office with a view of an industrial park adjacent to Interstate 695, a view that rarely engaged their attention, since most of the time their windows were draped shut to prevent glare on the monitors. The monitors were, in fact, the only windows that mattered to either of them—the twenty-one-inch CRT screens that opened on another world.

"Hey, Ned," Rawls muttered. "Take a look at this."

Brand did not look up from his monitor. "I'm busy." His fingers clacked on his keyboard with the monotony of falling rain.

"Are you? Sorry. Say, you want me to get you that chamber pot? I think Baltimore PD's still got it in evidence."

This obtained the desired reaction—the squeal of the casters on Brand's office chair as he pushed away from his desk. "Okay, okay. Don't go comparing me to Tomlinson, damn it."

Rawls only smiled. Eddie Tomlinson was a phone-code thief who, in a remarkable feat of endurance captured by an FBI trap-and-trace, had remained on-line, typing continuously, for seventy-two hours straight. When his home was raided, he was found hunched over his keyboard, seated in a chair with a hole cut in the seat and an overflowing chamber pot underneath. Empty beverage bottles and discarded snack food wrappers littered the floor. Tomlinson put up no resistance to arrest, but it was observed that his fingers continued to go through the motions of typing even as he was led away in handcuffs.

Rawls had suggested the chamber pot option to Brand on several previous occasions, and it never failed to rouse him from his chair. There was something in Tomlinson's dogged determination to continue entering code string after code string, for days on end, that came a little too close to the reality of the agents' own lives.

"Whassup, bro?" Brand asked, leaning over Rawls's shoulder. Adopting an urban black patois was one of Brand's quirks, which he exercised even though he was not black and had been brought up as far from the mean streets as possible, in the very affluent, very white enclave of Stamford, Connecticut.

Rawls, on the other hand, was black, and moreover was a product of the urban hell of East St. Louis, rescued from a hopeless future by the nuns at the local parochial school, who had taught him self-discipline, the only lesson that really mattered. They had also taught him grammar. Rawls would never say *whassup.* Such an undignified expression was beneath him.

"This is what's up," Rawls said. He tapped his monitor, which displayed a dialogue box requesting authentication information—user name and password. The user name Rawls had typed was BLUE-BEARD. The password line was blank.

"Bluebeard?" Brand asked.

"I'm pretty sure that's the user ID, but I don't have the password."

"You lost me, buddy. Where'd the name Bluebeard come from?"

Rawls pulled a sheet of paper out of his printer and showed it to Brand. "This arrived in my Inbox a few minutes ago."

The printout was the text of an e-mail message.

Agent Rawlz,
   Something phunny going on. Do you like to watch? Say you're Bluebeard. You have to phind the key.

A Web site's URL had been listed below—a *www* prefix followed by several crude slang terms for the female genitalia, and ending in ".net."

"Huh." Brand's grunt, as always, signified new interest on his part. "Wish these hackers would learn how to spell."

This was a joke. Hackers had their own rules of spelling. *F* became *ph*. The plural *s* became *z*. The rules were elastic and meaningless, rebellion for its own sake.

Of course, a great many of the hackers really *couldn't* spell.

Anyway, it wasn't the spelling that had caught Brand's interest. Both he and Rawls had read hundreds of e-mailed tips. Hackers were not known for their loyalty to others who practiced their art. They frequently turned in rivals merely to settle a grudge. But when they sent these tips to the Baltimore field office, they used the general e-mail address listed on the office's Web site. They never sent e-mail directly to Agent Rawls or Agent Brand, for the simple reason that neither agent's personal e-mail address was public knowledge.

"This came right to you," Brand said, looking at the routing information on the printout.

"Yup."

"And it's anonymous, of course."

Rawls nodded. "Sent via a remailer. No log trail."

"Somebody went to a fair amount of trouble to get this to you without being traced. But they didn't give you the password."

"Guess they want me to show a little ingenuity."

"Could just be a prank."

"Yeah. But there's something about it I don't like. That name Bluebeard—it's got me worried. You know the story?"

"Vaguely. French guy, kills his wives. Right?"

"Right. I'm assuming the password has to be connected with the story somehow. Otherwise the tipster wouldn't have expected me to figure it out."

"We need more information."

"Way ahead of you." Rawls opened a new browser window and entered the address of an on-line encyclopedia, then searched for *Bluebeard* and found the article.

The story of Bluebeard, *Le Barbe Bleu*, was first published by a compiler of French folk tales named Charles Perrault. In Perrault's telling, Bluebeard was a handsome lord whose six wives had died of a variety of common diseases—or so Bluebeard claimed. But when his seventh wife opened a locked room in the castle, she stumbled on the six corpses of the women, victims of Bluebeard's psychopathy. He had strangled them, so the story went, "with his own hands." The seventh wife was saved from the same fate by the providential appearance of rescuers.

Brand, reading over his partner's shoulder, grunted again. "The message says you'll have to find the key. As in the key to a lock."

Rawls nodded. "And in the story, who opens the locked room? The seventh wife."

He entered various passwords that came to mind—wife7, wife#7, wifeseven, 7thwife, and others. All were rejected.

"No good," he said. "Unless it's her name."

"Which is?"

Rawls scanned the encyclopedia article again. "Not mentioned here." He guided the browser to a search engine and entered the terms *Bluebeard* and *wife*. The search results took him to an on-line glossary of folklore, where he found the relevant listing.

"Fatima," he said.

He returned to the original window and typed FAT-IMA into the password space. When he hit the Enter key, the screen reported AUTHORIZATION ACCEPTED.

"Bingo." That was Brand. He was always saying things like that, just like a TV cop.

The home page of the mystery site appeared. It consisted solely of text links against a white background, as plain-vanilla as any site could be. Rawls scanned the rows of print. "Chat room . . . bulletin boards . . . vidcaps . . . Here we go." Rawls guided his mouse pointer to a hypertext link that read, *Do you like to watch?* The words from the e-mail message.

He clicked the link, and a new page came up, empty except for the small, blurred image of a bedroom. There were no windows in view, only a pair of abstract paintings on the walls. An unmade bed, flanked by twin nightstands, took up one corner of the room. A doorway framed a bathroom with a stall shower.

The room was unoccupied, and only the flicker of sunlight on the walls from an unseen window indicated that the image was a moving picture and not a still. Bright sunlight, Rawls noted, yet at 4:30 it was already nearly dark on the East Coast.

"Webcam in a bedroom," Brand said, "oriented with a view of the bed and the shower."

"Probably a woman's bedroom." Rawls tapped the screen. "That bedspread has a floral pattern. Not the kind of thing most men would own."

"So she's a nice girl who just happens to enjoy sharing her bedroom activities with on-line voyeurs. Kinky but not criminal. Lots of weirdos put their private lives on the Web for bored lookie-loos to watch. There are a thousand sites like that."

"If this *is* a site like that."

"You think it's a little more serious? Maybe some-body's spying on this lady?"

Rawls nodded. "Like that creep who was running pee-cam sites in Virginia." He and Brand hadn't han-dled the case personally, but they'd heard about it—a perv who'd installed hidden cameras in ladies' toi-lets and uploaded the resulting footage to the Web.

"It's possible," Brand conceded. "But there's an equal chance that she set it up herself. She gets off on people watching her."

"Then why keep the site password-protected?"

"She might want to perform in front of a select audience. Or it could be a subscription-based service. Or maybe she and her boyfriend set this up so they can have a little cyber-nookie. They don't want strangers looking in."

"Could be."

"But you don't think so," Brand commented.

"No. I don't."

"Any particular reason?"

"Just one. That name—Bluebeard."

Brand had no answer to that.

6

At 3:30 P.M., in the women's locker room at Newton Station, C. J. changed out of her uniform. She stowed her boots, belt, gun, PR24 side-handle baton, and other accessories inside the locker, then donned civilian clothes—Nikes and a blue jumpsuit, along with a handbag that concealed her off-duty weapon, a J-frame Smith & Wesson .38.

She clanged shut the door of her locker, then leaned against the cold metal, her eyes closed. Again she saw it—the gun in her face, Ramon Sanchez's angry glare.

She hadn't told Walt Brasco or any other cop about that part of her adventure. The way she'd related the story, she had disarmed Sanchez without incident. Sanchez, of course, would say nothing to contradict her version of events. Pointing a gun at a police officer was a felony charge he could live without.

Her reason for hiding the truth was simple enough. She didn't want to be pushed into therapy for post-traumatic stress. Let a shrink get hold of a thing like that, and she would be on a couch for six months spilling her guts about every little thing . . . and eventually about things that were not so little.

Things like the boogeyman.

No one in the department knew about that. And no one would ever know.

Every cop had a private reason for wearing the uniform, she supposed. Hers was probably no weirder than anyone else's. Even so, she didn't intend to share it. Sharing would be too much like reliving the experience—not that she didn't relive it anyway, in bad dreams and memory flashes and every close call on the street.

She detoured into the bathroom and splashed cold water on her face. A shower would have been better, but she preferred to shower at home.

Drying her face with a paper towel, she looked at herself in the mirror. She wondered if anybody could see how scared she was. Not just today, but all the time. It was a fear that never left her, a fear that had dared her into defying it. She had challenged that fear by enrolling in the LAPD Academy, by earning a badge, by riding patrol in one of the city's roughest divisions.

People said that confronting your fears was the way to banish them. People were wrong.

She had been facing death and danger for the past three years, first as a rookie with a training officer, and now as a full-fledged patrolwoman with the rank of Police Officer-2 . . . and still the fear hadn't left her. She doubted that it ever would.

Was it fear that had goaded her into entering the Sanchez residence this afternoon? Was she still trying to prove something to herself, and if so, how long would she continue? Until she ended up getting killed?

She studied her reflection. Green eyes, pale skin, and a bob of brunette hair that could be tucked

neatly under her cap when she was on duty, or un-
clipped to fall loosely to her shoulders when she felt
free to relax. A woman's face, not a child's. So why
did she feel like a child so much of the time? She
was twenty-six years old. She had been working patrol since she was twenty-three. She had seen more,
faced more, than most men or women twice her age.
But she hadn't seen enough, apparently.

"Well, screw it," she said aloud.

This was a mood. It would pass.

She headed out through the station, swinging her
handbag over her shoulder. The place was busy in
midafternoon, but not as busy as it would be after
dark. Phones rang, voices shouted, and a news update droned on the TV in the patrol squad room.

She navigated the maze of hallways, past bulletin
boards cluttered with departmental memos and the
divisional softball team's scores. Some of the
nightwatch cops said hi, others said nothing. But
they all looked at her, following her with their gaze.

She was used to it. They never stopped watching,
just as they never stopped with the ribbing and the
moronic jokes and that stupid nickname that had
dogged her everywhere since her second month on
the job. Sometimes they smiled at her and sometimes
they didn't, but always they watched.

Their eyes studied her from every angle, memorizing the clean lines of her body, the suntanned curve
of her neck, the dusting of freckles on her sinewy
forearms. They watched her as she clipped back her
long hair to hide it under her cap, as she twisted in
the seat of her patrol car to grab the daily log, as she
jogged up to the first officer at the scene to get a
recap of what she'd missed.

She was crossing the squad room, wondering if

she ought to get a cup of coffee before heading out, when she noticed a blondish man in the uniform of a Sheriff's deputy standing by the coffee machine, filling a foam cup.

What was *he* doing here?

He saw her too. "Hey, Killer," he called, drawing a laugh from some of the night-watch guys who had come on duty at 2:15. "Waste anybody today?"

"That's funny, Tanner." She detoured across the room to face him, for no reason other than to prove she wasn't running from a fight. "Why're you crashing our turf?"

He held up his hands in mock surrender. As always, he was wearing shades. The thought crossed her mind that she had never seen him without sunglasses. He probably wore them at night.

"Hey," he said in a quieter voice, "chill, okay? We're all on the same team, Killer."

"I don't want you on my team, and stop calling me that."

"It's what everybody calls you."

"Doesn't mean I have to like it. You never answered my question."

"Why am I here? Well, it's real simple. First call on my watch, we get involved in a hot pursuit in Vernon. Suspect crosses Central." Central Avenue divided the Newton Area Division from Vernon, which was patrolled by the Sheriff's Department. "One of your squads joins up with us, and we corral the jerk a few blocks from here. I came in to expedite the booking, fill in a few details on the report. See, Sheriff's does all the work, and LAPD gets all the glory."

"And all the paperwork. What'd you book him on?"

"Grand theft auto."

"Nice car?"

Tanner shrugged disdainfully. "Minivan. Why the hell would somebody steal a set of wheels like that?"

"Maybe he's a family man." She started to move off. He stopped her with a question.

"How about you, C. J.? What've you been up to?"

"Nothing special," she said, not meeting the gaze behind the dark glasses.

"You look a little frazzled."

"Long day."

"Nights are longer in this part of town. Me, I'm working the late shift these days—and loving every minute of it."

"You were made for the nightlife, Tanner."

"You got that right. So you're really okay?"

He asked the question in a tone of genuine concern that startled her. "I'm fine," she answered.

"I don't think you're leveling with me."

"How would you know?"

"I can read minds. Well, a woman's mind anyway."

"Oh, jeez." Just when she began to think he was not a total creep, he proved her wrong.

"Seriously," Tanner persisted with a smile. "The female of the species holds no mysteries for me."

"What species would that be, exactly? Goats?"

"Now you're hitting below the belt."

"Not me. I need a bigger target."

"Ouch. You think I'm messing with you, but I'm not. I know all about you. I know things about you that you don't know yourself."

"Okay, impress me. Tell me something you know and I don't."

"Well, for one thing, your ex-hubby is waiting for

you in the lobby." He seemed to enjoy her expression of surprise. "Oh, yeah. He's out there."

"You're playing me."

"Scout's honor. I'll even describe him for you. He's about my height, I'd guess five-ten, five-eleven. But scrawnier than me. Early thirties. Blond hair, blue eyes. Currently wearing a lawyer suit. Smiles a lot. Has a certain rakish charm."

"Since when do you use words like *rakish*?"

"I read books."

"Larry Flynt's publications do not qualify as books."

"You underestimate me. You really do. So is it your ex or not?"

"It's him," she conceded. "How'd you know?"

"Heard somebody mention he was here. I sneaked a peek."

"What for?"

"Curiosity. I wanted to see what he's got that I don't."

"That's easy. A working brain."

Tanner took no offense. "My brain is functional. I just don't show it off. You have to get to know me. Which would be easy enough. Just let me take you out to dinner some night."

"Seventeen," C. J. said.

"What?"

"That's the number of times you've asked me out since I transferred here."

"At least you're keeping count. I take that as a positive sign. Besides, you know what they say. Seventeenth time's the charm."

"It's not going to happen, Tanner."

"Just tell me why not."

"We're not compatible. We're oil and water. We don't mix."

"See, that's where you're wrong. We're Scotch and soda. We mix great. Give me a shot. You'll see what I mean."

She was almost tempted to say yes, if only to get him off her back. And well, maybe for other reasons too. He really wasn't a bad guy.

But she knew she couldn't date him. It was too soon—or too late—or something. "I've got to get going," she said. "Better see what Adam wants."

"I can guess." Tanner took off the shades, and she saw his gray eyes narrowed in thought. "He wants you, Killer—I mean C. J. You dumped him, and he hasn't gotten over it."

"How do you know *he* didn't dump *me*?"

"No way." The glasses went back on, masking his eyes. "He wouldn't be that dumb. No one would."

She thought she might blush, which would be a disaster, so she rallied her reserves of cynicism. "Thanks for the compliment. But you're still not getting to first base."

"What've you really got against me, C. J.? I'm not as much of an asshole as I appear."

"I know that," she said softly.

"Do you?"

"Sure." She found a smile and beamed it into the black lenses of his sunglasses. "Nobody could be *that* much of an asshole. See you, Tanner."

She turned away, certain that the conversation was over, but Tanner surprised her.

"I have a first name," he said. "Better use it, unless you want me to go back to calling you Killer."

She looked at him. "See you . . . Rick. That better?"

"Sounded just fine."

7

Rawls knew he should resist the temptation to visit the site again. He had more pressing priorities. Anyway, he and Brand were nearly done for the day. The sun had long since set, and when he peered through a gap in the drapes, he saw a crescent moon, low over the horizon, gleaming on sooty piles of unmelted snow. Baltimore in January. He shook his head and tried not to think about the chill wind gusting outside, or about the Web site that was unlocked with Bluebeard's key.

But he couldn't help himself. His right hand, of its own accord, moved his mouse across the customized mouse pad displaying a family photo—himself, his wife Felicia, their son Philip—and guided the mouse pointer to the Internet browser icon on his screen.

Click, and the browser was active. There was no need to establish an Internet connection. He and Brand used a DSL hookup and were always on-line.

He logged onto the mystery site and returned to the page containing the video stream. He had hoped that by now the bedroom would be occupied; at least he would have a better idea of what was going on. But the room remained empty.

Still sunny too. The sunlight had a slightly orange quality that suggested late afternoon. He checked his wristwatch: 6:47. Must be two or three hours earlier in the location he was observing. If the woman worked from nine to five, it might be an hour or longer before she showed up.

Move along, folks, an inner voice chided. Everything's wrapped up here.

Even so, he lingered at the site, his hand moving the mouse idly, letting the pointer breeze around the screen.

In a corner of the screen the arrow icon changed to a pointing finger.

Hidden link. He had stumbled on it by accident. The hypertext string had been rendered in white, making it invisible against the white background of the page.

Rawls clicked the link, and a page opened in a new window, headlined VOTE TALLY.

Below the headline were columns of figures alongside three names.

MISS NOVEMBER 76
MISS DECEMBER 54
MISS JANUARY 109

At the bottom of the page were the words *Cast your ballot for the best babe of the bunch!*

"Three women," Rawls said quietly.

Brand looked up. "What's that?"

Rawls drummed his fingers on his desk. "The Bluebeard site. There have been three women under observation. The one whose bedroom is now on display is only the latest."

Brand got up and came around to look at his partner's computer. "She's Miss January, I take it."

"Must be."

"The most popular of them all. I'll bet she's a
looker. She home yet?"

"No."

"Shoot." Brand was disappointed. "So what do
you make of this?"

"I'm not sure." Rawls studied the screen. "Judging
by the number of votes tallied, I'd say the site's password has been restricted to a couple of hundred people. The site manager probably gives out the
password via e-mail after trolling for the right kind
of visitors in chat rooms or newsgroups."

"If they've spied on three women over a period of
three months, how do you think they managed it?
Peephole in the wall?"

"Could be. Or a boyfriend hides a surveillance
camera inside a gift that the victim keeps in the bedroom. Or it could even be some Back Orifice type of
program or some other Trojan horse on her PC."

Back Orifice was a program capable of taking over
a computer's microphone and video camera and
using them to spy on the unsuspecting user. Standard antivirus programs would detect it, but there
was always the possibility of a new, undetectable
variant.

"Let's take another look at that video," Brand said,
no doubt hoping Miss January had arrived.

Rawls pressed the Back button on his browser. The
bedroom was still empty, the sun on the walls still
bright.

"You think the feed is real time?" Brand asked,
probably thinking about the sunlight also.

"I'm betting it is. If it was a loop or a highlight reel, why show this part? An empty room?"

"Good point." Brand sighed. "Whatever's going on, it's something ugly. Too bad we can't chase it."

"Why can't we?"

"Hell, Noah, you know why. We got nothing here. We got a woman who may or may not be under clandestine surveillance. The only way we can know is to track her down and ask her, and how are we going to do that? I take it you already ran a route trace."

Rawls nodded. "The server's geographical location isn't in the database. But it's on a local net. Anyway, the server has to be in Baltimore."

"Why? If the video is real time, it would mean the victim is out west—either Mountain or Pacific time zone."

"The victim, yes. Not the site manager. He's here in town. Has to be." Rawls saw Brand's blank look and added in explanation, "The tipster contacted *me*. He went to some trouble to get hold of my personal e-mail address. He clearly wants Baltimore on the case."

"Which implies it's in our jurisdiction," Brand said. "I get it. Still, we can't follow up. Miller will never give us the green light." Frank Miller was the Baltimore field office's special agent in charge.

"Miller," Rawls said slowly, "can't control what we do in our spare time."

"Spare time? You mean tonight?"

"Why not?"

"No way, buddy. I put in enough hours as it is, and unpaid overtime ain't my idea of fun."

Rawls knew this was only bluster. "Come on, Ned,

you have anything better to do on a Wednesday night?"

"Sure I do."

"Like what?" Rawls knew Brand was divorced, not seeing anybody, and all he had to go home to was a microwavable dinner and CNN.

Brand hesitated, then confirmed the obvious with a weary nod. "Good grief, as Charlie Brown used to say. I guess you got me."

"I'm glad because I need you."

"Great. How's Felicia gonna feel about you missing another meal?"

"She'll be fine," Rawls said, hoping this was true.

"Well, damn it, if you're on the case, so am I. Have you e-mailed the sysadmin?"

"Yes, but he never returned the message. I'll have to call him." The phone number and e-mail address of the network system administrator were included in the data supplied by the trace route program.

"If he has any sense, he's probably gone home for the day."

Rawls picked up the phone. "Then I'll track him down at home."

"You really got a bug up your ass about this."

"Colorfully expressed." Rawls started dialing. "The sysadmin will give us the name and street address of the site manager. Then I say we drive over and pay the gentleman a visit."

"And shut him down."

Rawls nodded, thinking of Miss January and the two women before her—women whose lives, whose bodies, had been put on public display.

"Damn straight," he said. "We shut him down."

8

C. J. found Adam Nolan in the lobby, just as Tanner had said. He was deep in conversation with Delano, the desk officer, and C. J. glimpsed the easy smile that had first caught her attention across a Westside bar when she was new to the city, nearly four years ago.

"Hey, Adam," she said.

He looked up from the desk, and the smile flashed again, then faltered. "C. J."

There was an awkward moment when they didn't know how to greet each other—with a hug or a handshake. The hug won. They embraced briefly, and she had time to notice that he had lost some weight and gained some muscle. He wasn't quite as scrawny as Tanner thought.

"Working out?" she asked when they separated.

He shrugged. "Joined a gym. Nothing serious. You look good."

"Thanks. You too."

More awkwardness. She had no idea what he was doing here.

Glancing around the lobby, she saw Delano eyeing them with a smirk.

"Show's over, Fred," she said coolly. "Nothing more to see here."

Delano merely chuckled.

Yeah, it was definitely good for a laugh when Officer Osborn's ex-husband showed up unexpectedly at the end of her watch. Just another installment in the ongoing soap opera that was Newton Station.

"So," Adam said, shifting his weight self-consciously. He was outfitted entirely in blue—dark blue suit, tie and shirt of a lighter shade. A lawyer suit, as Tanner had observed. The tones brought out the blue in his eyes. "You taking care of yourself?"

"Always do." She didn't tell him she'd nearly gotten shot a couple of hours ago. "How's Brigham and Garner treating you?"

"Like the genius I am. I've brought in three new clients already."

"You're a rainmaker."

"Pulling my weight anyway. Not too shabby for a junior associate counsel."

"Speaking of which, shouldn't you be at work now?"

He shrugged. "I'm taking a late lunch."

She glanced at her watch. Nearly four o'clock. "Very late. I guess you just happened to find yourself in the neighborhood . . ."

"Not likely."

"I didn't think so. This isn't exactly your territory." Adam lived in Brentwood and worked out of law offices in Century City. Both districts were well to the west of Newton and considerably more affluent.

He gave in, admitting the obvious. "I came over to see you. Timed my break so I'd catch you when you were getting off work. Although as it turned out, I had to cool my heels awhile."

"Why?"

"You tell me. I assumed you were putting in a little overtime."

"No, I mean, why'd you come over?"

He swept a stray hair off his high, tanned forehead. His hair looked blonder than she remembered it. He must be spending time outdoors, maybe at the beach. "I thought maybe we could grab some coffee before you go home and I head back to be a lawyer."

"Coffee?"

"Is that so strange?"

"Frankly, yeah. I haven't seen you in what, two months?"

"I've been busy. They work you ragged when you first sign on. I've called you," he added defensively.

"True."

"I've tried to stay in touch."

She turned away briefly, thinking of what Tanner had said. *He wants you, Killer.* "I guess that's what I'm wondering about. Why you would do that." She looked at him. "We're not a couple anymore, Adam."

He straightened his shoulders. "I think I'm aware of that. The divorce proceedings made it reasonably obvious."

"Right. I know. I'm sorry." She asked herself why she was apologizing to him.

He reached out and touched her arm. "Just because it's over, does that mean we can't get together sometimes and, you know, talk?" He smiled, and once again she glimpsed his insouciant charm. "I mean, is that so nuts, to still want to be friends?"

"No," she said softly, "it's not so nuts." *You dumped him,* Tanner's voice reminded her, *and he hasn't gotten over it.* "Except I'm not sure where you think it might lead."

"It doesn't have to lead anywhere."

"As long as we're clear on that."

"We're clear. So . . . coffee?"

She had no desire for coffee. All she wanted was to go home and step into a hot shower. But she couldn't disappoint him when he'd come all the way over here.

"Coffee it is," C. J. said brightly.

9

"Man," Tanner said, "she is really a hard case."

Deputy Leonard Chang glanced at him from the passenger seat of the Chevrolet Caprice. The slums of Walnut Park blurred past in the slanting light of late afternoon. It was only four o'clock, but in January the days ended early.

"I take it," Chang said, "you're talking about Osborn again?"

Tanner saw the look on his partner's face—a blend of irritation and boredom. He tried to justify himself. "She gets to me," he managed.

"I noticed."

"Okay, so I'm hot for her. I mean, come on, she's got the whole package."

"With that kind of sweet talk, you can sweep her right off her feet."

"I didn't mean . . . When I say 'the whole package,' I'm talking brains, guts, attitude."

"And looks."

"Well, yeah. But not *just* looks. I'm not that shallow."

"You're not?"

"Well, I can be, but in this case there's more to it."

"Think she knows that?"

"Hell, sure she knows. I've told her how I feel."

"Have you?"

"What are you, my shrink? I've asked her out—seventeen times by her count. I turn on the charm every time I see her."

"Maybe you should turn off the charm and just be, you know, a regular guy."

Tanner reflected on this. "It's an idea."

"Hardly original, but I'll take the credit anyway."

"Thing is, I'm not sure I can be just, you know, regular. When I'm around a woman, it's like I've got to prove something. Like being just me isn't good enough. Shit." He chuckled. "You really *are* my shrink."

"I'm charging a hundred bucks an hour, partner. Pony up." Chang paused. "There might be another reason she's not going for you."

"What's that?"

"Maybe—well, maybe it's because you're SWAT."

Tanner glanced at him, incredulous. "You kidding? SWAT is an asset, man, as you ought to know." Chang was a member of Tanner's SWAT call-up team. "Haven't you ever used it for a pickup line?" Tanner dropped his voice an octave and intoned, "Yeah, baby, I'm a cop, all right—and I'm on the SWAT team. We go after the *real* bad guys."

Chang was laughing. "Hell, with a line like that, what do you need Osborn for?"

"Guess I don't," Tanner said.

"So forget her."

Tanner nodded. It was good advice, and he abided by it for all of thirty seconds before he turned to Chang. "Why'd you say that anyway? About SWAT?"

"I thought the plan was to forget her."

"I'm just curious. I mean, whoever heard of a cop who's got a problem with SWAT?"

"Some cops do."

Tanner steered the Chevy Caprice onto Wilmington Avenue. "What's that supposed to mean?"

"Never mind. It's not important."

"The hell it isn't." Tanner was getting ticked off now. He pulled up to a curb, parking the patrol car, and pivoted in his seat to face Chang. "What are you trying to tell me anyhow?"

Chang found a stick of gum in his pocket and took his time about unwrapping it and putting it into his mouth. Finally he answered, speaking around a wad of Bubblicious. "She came out of Harbor Division, didn't she?"

"So what?"

The radio crackled with a priority call, but it was nowhere near their location and another unit took it.

"Come on, Rick," Chang said. "Don't you remember what went down in Harbor two, three years ago? The warehouse thing?"

"Oh," Tanner said slowly. "Yeah."

"She might have been there. Might have seen it."

"I never thought of that."

"That's why I'm the brains here. Now let's cruise, okay?"

Tanner nodded and pulled away from the curb, thinking.

The warehouse thing had been one of the worst failures in the history of LAPD Metro's D Platoon— the SWAT team. Three bank robbers armed with automatic rifles had been pursued into an industrial district outside of Long Beach, at the western edge of Harbor Division. Trapped, they had taken refuge inside a warehouse. But they hadn't gone in alone.

En route from the bank they had carjacked a station wagon after crashing their van into an embankment. The four people in the wagon—father, mother, two kids—had become hostages. The family of four went into the warehouse too.

It was a standoff. Classic hostage-barricade situation. Negotiations failed. Shots were heard inside the warehouse. There was fear that the hostages were being killed. SWAT went in.

The robbers, still heavily armed, put up massive resistance. When the firefight ended, two SWAT officers lay wounded, and the three bad guys lay dead.

And the family . . .

Dead. All four.

They had died in the cross fire. Some nonlethal wounds had been inflicted by the robbers. But the fatal bullets had all been fired by D Platoon guns.

During the aftermath, almost every cop in Harbor Division had been at the scene. It was highly likely that C. J. Osborn had seen the damage, up close and personal. She would have been new to the force back then, still a "boot"—a rookie. Her training officer would have explained to her that the robbers had used the hostages as human shields, that it wasn't the cops' fault. But maybe she hadn't bought it. And why should she?

Tanner had heard all the same excuses back then, and he hadn't bought any of them either.

It was SWAT's job to keep people alive. But who could believe it, after the fiasco at the warehouse? Only the same people who thought the FBI's Hostage Rescue Team had done an A-1 job at Waco.

"You think that's it?" Tanner asked quietly, sobered by the thought.

"Man, I don't know." Chang smacked the gum. "It's a theory, that's all. If you really care, ask her."

"I just might."

"Good for you. And if it all works out, I want to be best man at the ceremony."

"Give me a break. I mean, I'm serious about her, but . . . not *that* serious." Tanner frowned. "Am I?"

Chang settled back in his seat. "You're pretty slow sometimes, you know that? You don't even know what's going on in your own mind."

"But you do, I guess? You can read me?"

"Like an open book, partner." Chang laced his fingers behind his head and grinned through the wad of gum. "Like an open book."

10

Down the street from Newton Station was a coffee shop run by Filipino immigrants. It was a hangout for cops, though it did less business than the local bars. Cops saw a lot of things that encouraged drinking. C. J. herself avoided alcohol, but she sometimes wondered how long her resolve could hold out against the daily assault of drive-bys and arson fires and craziness.

She led Adam to the coffee shop, past a legless beggar on the curb rattling a tin cup, an image out of Calcutta.

The shop was small and close and crowded. The air conditioner made a great deal of noise but produced little change in temperature. There were biscuit crumbs and horseflies on the Formica surface of the nearest available table. C. J. shooed the flies and sat down.

"Nice place," Adam said with a wince as he settled into a wobbly-legged chair. "Come here often?"

"Believe it or not, I do. Mr. and Mrs. Salazar are good people." She saw his questioning glance and added, "They run the place."

"Keep it nice and clean too." Adam swept some of the crumbs away with his sleeve.

"They don't have enough help. This is the busiest time of the day—right after shift change." She caught Mrs. Salazar's eye and held up two fingers. "Two lattes," she explained to Adam. "That okay?"

"Sure."

"It's the best thing they serve. Stay away from the frappuccino."

"I'll remember that if I ever bring a client here."

She indulged him with a laugh. "I guess it's not the greatest place in town, but you know, I'm used to it."

"How long has it been since you transferred to Newton?"

"A year. I moved over here just after—well, you know."

"After you filed for divorce."

"Right."

"You can say the words, C. J. I'm a big boy." He leaned back in his chair, which creaked ominously. "You know, I used to think you were nuts."

"Did you?" She felt a spasm of irritation at him and hid it behind a smile. "How so?"

"Doing this job. When I hear gunshots, I run the other way. You go *toward* them. There's a certain element of insanity in that behavior, don't you think?"

"We can't all be lawyers," she said peevishly.

"I'm not being confrontational. I just mean, what you do is so foreign to me. Always has been."

"Sometimes it feels foreign to me too. When I hear gunshots, I'd *like* to run the other way, just like you."

"But you don't. I admire that. I don't profess to understand it, necessarily—but I admire it anyway."

The compliment silenced her. She was not accustomed to kindness from him.

The caffe lattes arrived, carried by Mrs. Salazar. C. J. sipped the foam in silence and considered what Adam had said. Did he admire her? Had he ever? She suspected his actual feelings were closer to contempt—not for her alone, but for people in general, all those people who were not smart enough or flashy enough or suave enough to rise to the heights he was scaling. She might be wrong, though. She hoped so.

"C. J.?" Adam asked. "You still here?"

She looked up, remembering where she was. "Sorry. Guess you kind of startled me with that little testimonial."

"I'll take it all back if it makes you feel better."

She smiled. "No, I liked hearing it. Except, you know, there are times when I think you might be right about the insanity part. I wonder if maybe there's not a kind of death wish in what I do." The words came out before she had time to consider them.

Adam leaned forward, frowning. "Crisis of confidence? That's not like you."

She wished she hadn't said anything. But that was how it had always been with her and Adam—his simple presence seemed to bring out her innermost thoughts.

"It's nothing," she said. "I'm not myself today, that's all."

"Why not?"

"Well, there was this situation—" She stopped herself, thinking, There I go again.

"Situation?"

"We don't have to talk about this."

"It's okay," Adam said.

She wondered if it really was okay—to open up to this man who had betrayed her. It felt wrong, and yet he was here, and she needed to talk to someone.

His blue eyes watched her, patient, waiting.

"It was a hostage situation," she said slowly. "My partner had called for backup. We should've waited for SWAT."

"But you didn't?"

"No."

"You and your partner went into some kind of SWAT situation without backup?"

"Not my partner. Me."

"Alone?"

"Yup."

"Christ, when you said you had a death wish—" He cut himself off. "Sorry, that didn't come out too well."

"It came out fine. You're right. It was a stupid thing for me to do. Except, see, there was a child involved. And I thought he'd be safer if I went in alone."

"Isn't SWAT trained to handle these things?"

C. J. looked away. "Their training doesn't always work out so well in the real world. I didn't want a bloodbath in there."

"Bloodbath?"

"It happens." She had never told him what she'd seen at Harbor Division, and she wasn't going to share it with him now.

"I thought SWAT were the elite, the pros."

"They are. But . . . well, sometimes things go wrong. You know, everybody says this city is a war zone, and they're right. But maybe we shouldn't fight

on those terms—or at least we shouldn't be so gung
ho about it. These SWAT guys—you haven't seen
them. They get all dressed up in their paramilitary
duds, and they go in with their machine guns and
their flash grenades, and civilian casualties become
acceptable losses . . ."

She realized she was babbling and shut up.

"Is the kid okay?" Adam asked after a short
silence.

"He's fine."

"And you?"

"Didn't lose any fingers"—she waved her hands
at him to demonstrate—"or toes, or any other vital
parts."

"You shouldn't take risks like that, C. J."

Someone has to, she almost snapped at him, but
she knew her anger was inappropriate, an aftereffect
of stress. "Well," she said lightly, "it turned out all
right, anyhow. You know, I hate talking shop. Let's
change the subject."

"Fair enough." Adam finished his latte and set
down the mug. "How about Emmylou Harris?"

"Emmylou Harris?"

"You still like her?"

"Sure," she answered warily.

"Well, she's playing at a club in the Valley. Some
honky-tonk cowboy saloon, the kind we used to go
to. How about it?"

She was grateful to have an excuse. "Sorry, I can't.
Tonight's my volunteer work, remember? Every
Wednesday night, at the junior high, the at-risk kids'
program—"

"I'm not talking about tonight. I meant this
Friday."

"Oh." Her excuse evaporated.

"Come on, let's do it. You and me, sipping some brewskis, listening to some C and W from the pre-Shania era."

Her heart sped up a little, and she realized that what she felt was fear. "That sounds almost like a date."

He sensed her alarm and tried to wave it away. "No, not a date. A little reunion, that's all. You know, for old times' sake. Frankly, I wouldn't have brought it up, except there's nobody at the firm who goes in for country-western, and I hate going to a show alone."

Is that it? C. J. wondered. Or is it that you hate being alone, period?

"Maybe she'll play our song," she said quietly, watching Adam closely to gauge his reaction.

"As I recall"—his expression was bland—"our song was 'She's Always a Woman.' That's in Billy Joel's repertoire, not Emmylou's."

"I didn't mean our, uh, official song. I meant the other one. The one that was playing when—never mind."

Had he really forgotten? Or was his studied blankness only a mask to hide what he was feeling? There had been a time when she had thought he couldn't deceive her, but events had proven her wrong.

"So it's not a date?" she asked, returning to the main issue.

Adam lifted his shoulders a little too casually. "Just two pals out on the town."

"Two pals," she echoed.

"Right."

"Who used to be married to each other."

"There's no law that says you can't be friends with your ex. I'm an attorney, I ought to know." That smile again. What was Tanner's word? *Rakish.* "Anyway, I want to catch up on what's been happening in your life. And I, well, basically I want to brag some more about my career. So you want to do it?"

Some part of her wanted to say no, but she couldn't decide if it was her more sensible self or merely the dull, cruel side of her that nursed a grudge.

"Well," she said finally, "as long as you understand—"

He held up both hands in mock surrender. "I understand. Just friends."

"Okay, then."

He flashed another smile, his teeth very white against the tanned planes of his face. "I'll call you with the details later this week. It'll be fun, C. J."

"Fun," she repeated. She hoped so.

Adam insisted on paying for the lattes. Outside the coffee shop, she said good-bye to him.

There was no hug when they parted. He sketched a salute, a habit he'd picked up the first time he saw her wearing a uniform, and she returned it with a smile. Then he disappeared down the street, and she stared after him and wondered if she should have listened to the inner voice that had wanted to turn him down.

But he couldn't possibly think there was any chance of reconciliation . . . could he?

Well, one night with Adam wouldn't kill her. And she had always liked his company, even if, in the end, he'd shown himself to be someone other than the man she'd thought he was.

Her car was in the station house parking lot. She walked back to the station and entered through the lobby.

Delano was still at the desk. He smiled when she came in. "That's your ex, huh, Killer?"

"None of your business, but yeah."

"I was talking to him before. Seems like an okay guy."

"He *is* an okay guy. As long as you don't trust him too much."

11

Autopsies weren't the only things Walsh hated. Running a meeting was another. He sometimes wondered why he had ever accepted a promotion to the rank of Detective-3. What he loved was being out in the field, and now, in his supervisory capacity, he rarely had time to investigate a case personally. Then again, at fifty-two, he supposed he had better leave the legwork to the next generation.

At the moment he was surrounded by representatives of that generation, who crowded three desks pushed together to make a single long table in the Robbery-Homicide squad room at Parker Center, the LAPD's downtown headquarters. He had called a meeting of the Hourglass Killer task force, or at least its core members. Over the past two months, since the abduction of Nikki Carter, the task force had grown to include liaison personnel from the Homicide Bureau of the Los Angeles County Sheriff's Department—Carter's body had been dumped in an auto graveyard in East LA, territory that was under the Sheriff's jurisdiction—as well as miscellaneous bureaucrats from the County Probation Department and the State Department of Corrections. So far the

FBI had been kept out of it, except for the obligatory psychological profile of the killer supplied by the Behavioral Science Section at Quantico.

If everybody connected with the investigation had been assembled, the squad room would have been filled to capacity. Walsh restricted most meetings to the LAPD Robbery-Homicide detectives who did the heavy lifting on the case.

Today's meeting had been scheduled to start promptly at 4:00 P.M. Naturally it was almost four-thirty when the last stragglers wandered in. Walsh knew he ought to dress them down for their tardiness, but he had never been much good as a disciplinarian. He had reared three kids without once raising his voice, and he figured he could handle a half-dozen Metro detectives with equal self-restraint.

"Okay," he said, silencing the chatter around the table, "now that we're all here, we can get started." Crisply he summarized the autopsy of Martha Eversol. "Anything new on the tats?" he asked when he had finished, directing his inquiry at Detectives Stark and Merriwether, who were working that angle.

"Nothing much," Stark answered. "We've visited every tattoo parlor in town, and I mean *every* goddamn one. No hourglass patterns. A lot of snakes, flags, hearts with arrows through them."

"And the style isn't recognizable," Merriwether added. "Most of the pros say it's an amateur working with a homemade stencil, applying the ink by hand."

"Like jailhouse tats?" Len Sotheby wondered. "Could mean our guy has a rap sheet."

"No, not jailhouse. Those are almost always gray and black, 'cause the scratchers can't get hold of any colored pigments. It's what the experts call blackwork. What we're looking at here is bold color in a geometrical design. They tell me it's similar to the original tattoo technique used in the Pacific—the Philippines, Samoa, Tahiti, places like that. In Samoa it's still done."

"What is the technique exactly?" Walsh asked, jotting down notes.

"Traditionally, the artist takes a piece of bone and files one end to, like, a serrated edge—you know, like a comb. Then he attaches it to a wooden handle, dips the pointy end in pigment, and drives it into the skin with a mallet."

Expressions of dismay and a grunted "ouch" made their way around the table.

"They tattoo every part of the body that way," Merriwether went on imperturbably, "even the genitals. It's a test of manhood."

"Really?" Donna Cellini said with a smile. "That's a test none of you guys would pass."

Laughter broke through the temporary discomfort in the room.

"Anyway," Merriwether said, "instead of chiseled bone, our guy has needles, and instead of soot and water, which the Polynesians and the Samoans used, he buys ink. It would take him maybe half an hour to apply the tattoo postmortem. He uses a 0.3-inch diameter needle for line work, 0.36 for coloring. Standard sizes, don't lead us anywhere. The ink is standard too—couple hundred thousand bottles sold each year."

"How about the hourglass design?" Walsh asked.

"It could be a stencil, which would speed up the process, but if so, it's one he made himself, not a commercially available variety. The fact that it's a geometric pattern—two triangles—might or might not be significant. The Polynesians were really into geometrical designs. They had this pottery done in what's called the Lapita style, and they used the same designs when making tattoos. So our guy might be knowledgeable about ancient Polynesian culture, but it's just as likely to be a coincidence. Most of the Polynesian designs were a lot more complicated than an hourglass. It was a real art form, the way they did it."

"Sounds like you're really getting into this stuff," Ed Lopez remarked. "You sure you haven't got 'To Protect and Serve' tattooed on your butt?"

"Ask your wife," Merriwether responded placidly, to general amusement.

"Okay," Walsh said, "since the tats are a dead end, I want you two to go back to working the index cards."

"Shit," Stark groused, "that got us nowhere. They're ordinary three-by-five cards. You can buy 'em in any stationery store."

"Work them anyway." Walsh sank back in his seat. "Ed, Gary, you have any better luck with the victims' background checks?"

Ed Lopez fielded the question. "We haven't found anything that ties Nikki Carter to Martha Eversol." Eversol had been assumed to be the Hourglass Killer's second victim even before her body was found; the date of her disappearance had fit the pattern begun by Nikki Carter. "Checked out their doctors, dentists, employers and their colleagues at work, neighbors, landlords, boyfriends, ex-boyfriends, every damn thing we could think of. No links."

"There's supposed to be six degrees of separation between any two people on earth," Gary Boyle added, "but not here."

Walsh shook his head. "Donna and Len, give me some good news."

Len Sotheby simply threw up his hands and said, "Nada."

Donna Cellini was more forthcoming. "There are unsolved stranglings all over the map, obviously. But we didn't find any parallel with the tattoos anywhere. Either our guy is new at this, or the tats are a new twist. I'm guessing the latter."

Lopez asked why.

"Didn't you read the profile?" Cellini sounded irritated. "It said the unsub was experienced."

"Unsub," Stark echoed with a smirk. The term was FBI jargon for Unknown Suspect. "Maybe you'll be enrolling in Quantico before long, huh, Cellini?"

"At least I'd associate with a better class of people." She said it with a smile that took the edge off her words.

"Any of the unsolved cases look promising?" Walsh asked.

Cellini consulted her notes. "There's a bunch of stuff that has possibilities. Serial strangulations of prostitutes in Portland, Oregon, 1996 to 1998. A coyote—you know, a guy who smuggles illegals across the border—suspected of strangling female clients in the southern Arizona desert near Nogales, circa 1995. Never caught. Guy named Charles William Baron, real estate broker in Philadelphia, strangled his wife and his mistress in the same night and disappeared. Still at large. That happened in 1993."

"He's probably in South America by now," Sotheby interjected. "He had a passport and overseas bank accounts."

"Anything else?" Walsh pressed.

"Janitor who strangled three female students at a junior college in Nebraska, 1989 and 1990. Still on the loose. Strangler of children who roamed the Mojave Desert, 1985 and '86—never apprehended. In 1982—"

"Okay." Walsh raised his hand. "We don't have to go back that far. Bottom line is . . ."

"Nada," Sotheby said again with stubborn pessimism.

"Any clue how he got access to the strip mall so he could dump the body there?" Boyle asked Walsh.

"We're still working on that," Walsh said, aware that everyone present knew this answer meant no.

"Security guard check out okay?"

"He looks clean. West LA is handling that angle. Checking out the building's owners, the guard—anybody who had a key."

Merriwether asked if there was any hope on the hair-and-fiber front.

"Nothing new," Walsh said. "Martha Eversol was covered with some of the same gray rayon fibers we got off Nikki Carter, but they're too generic to help nab this guy. They'll help convict him when he's caught, at least."

"If he's caught," Sotheby said.

"When," Walsh repeated.

No one disputed him this time. But no one met his gaze either.

Time to wrap up. Walsh leaned forward.

"All right, everybody. We know what today's date is. We know what it means."

There were a few unnecessary glances at the calendar on the wall, where Wednesday, January 31, was circled in red.

Nikki Carter had been abducted on November 30.

Martha Eversol, on December 31. Always the last day of the month.

"Tonight's his night to howl," Walsh said. "We don't know where he'll strike, but we know it'll be within the next eight hours. There are extra squad cars on the streets, extra plainclothes officers working bars and nightclubs. Stark and Merriwether, I want you covering the club where Nikki Carter disappeared. Lopez and Boyle, you cruise the neighborhood where Martha Eversol was rear-ended."

"He won't return to the scene," Stark said. "He's too smart."

"You're probably right. But we'll do it anyway. Maybe we'll catch a break. Christ knows, we need one."

Nobody could argue with that.

12

C. J. noticed the white van on Western Avenue as she headed north into the mid-Wilshire district. It was two car lengths behind her, visible in her rearview mirror.

There was nothing unusual about the van, except that she recalled seeing a similar vehicle pull away from the curb outside the Newton Station parking lot when she'd left.

Probably a coincidence. No reason to think the van was following her or anything.

As she guided her Dodge Neon onto Pico Boulevard, she watched her rearview mirror to see if the van duplicated the maneuver. It did not.

"Getting paranoid, Killer," she admonished herself. In private she sometimes used the nickname her fellow cops had bestowed on her, even though she disliked it.

She cruised west on Pico, planning her evening. Quick shower, bite to eat, some reps on her exercise machine, then the twenty-minute drive to Foshay Junior High School at Exposition and Western, a bad neighborhood. She was always mildly amazed when she emerged from the school and found that her car had not been stolen. Of course, it was only a matter of time until the little Dodge became another Grand Theft Auto statistic.

Oh, well. The risk was worth it. She really believed she was making a difference in the kids' lives. Some of them anyway.

Take Andrew Washington, a small, wiry teen with smoldering eyes and fidgety hands. He had glared at her nonstop during her first few visits as she sat amid a circle of kids and talked about the dangers they faced every day—the drug dealers trying to get them hooked, the gangbangers urging them to wear the colors, the petty temptations of shoplifting and vandalism.

Most of these kids had yielded to such temptations and influences already. Some had done time in juvenile camps. But they weren't altogether lost. If they had been, they wouldn't have been showing up three nights a week, talking with C. J. on Wednesdays and with two other off-duty cops on Mondays and Fridays. The talks were the price they paid for use of the gym afterward—basketball games, played indoors, safely out of range of drive-by shootings and the other insanities of the city.

Andrew had looked too small to be good at hoops, but she learned later that he had a mean jump shot and quick hands. She had been sure she wasn't getting through to him. His angry stare seemed to say, *Talk all you want, you white bitch. It don't mean shit to me.* Then one night another kid had asked her what was the most scared she had ever been. Her audience had expected her to talk about some experience on patrol, but instead she'd told them about the boogeyman. They listened silently, and even Andrew's eyes had regarded her with a flicker of interest.

When they were leaving for the gym, Andrew stayed behind. "That shit you told us about when you was a kid—that for real?" She assured him it was. He looked away. "Something sorta like that happened to me," he said. "Came home from school one afternoon, and there was a guy in the house. Fucking psycho off the streets, busted in through a window, stealing our stuff. Could see he was crazy. Had that look, you know? His face was all one big beard and fuzzy hair with eyes stuck in it. I hid in the closet, curled up real small, but he hears a noise and comes looking. I throw some dirty clothes over me. He looks in, don't see me. Shit, if he'd done seen me, he woulda fucking wasted me. I know it."

"What happened?"

"Guess hearing the noise spooked him. He booked out of there. Didn't take nothing."

"What did your mom say?" She knew he lived alone with his mother.

"Never told her."

"You didn't want her to worry?"

"Nah, that ain't it. She wouldn't never have believed me, is the thing. Just like your folks didn't believe you."

"People don't take kids seriously," C. J. said in a low voice.

Andrew nodded gravely. "That's how it is."

He had not glared at her after that.

So yes, she was helping. She was reaching at least a few of them.

At La Brea she turned north, stopping a few blocks from her house to pick up a few items at a market run by a Korean man who had been a dentist in his own country. She moved quickly through the familiar aisles, dropping fresh vegetables into her basket, paying at the checkout stand.

She was putting her groceries into her car when a glint of reflected light from down the street caught her attention.

A white van was parked at the corner.

She studied it. The driver's window was rolled down. The light she'd seen must have come from inside the van.

Reflected light. Binoculars, maybe, or a camera's telephoto lens?

She steadied herself. There were a lot of white vans in the city. This might not be the one she'd seen behind her on Western.

The van bore no commercial markings, but it had the windowless rear compartment typical of commercial vehicles. The kind of van a delivery person might drive.

So why was it sitting there at 4:45 on a weekday afternoon, with the window open, and a lens—if it had been a lens—trained in her direction?

She decided to walk over and find out.

But before she could, the motor rumbled to life, and the van pulled into traffic.

She stared after it, hoping to catch the plate number. The plate was blue on white, a California tag, but she had no chance to read it. The van had already disappeared into a stream of vehicles.

If she were still in the midst of divorce proceedings, she might have thought that Adam had hired a private eye to follow her and dig up dirt. But the divorce had been finalized months ago. Anyway, there was no dirt, and Adam knew it.

She shrugged. "Maybe the paparazzi have finally gotten around to discovering me."

As jokes went, it wasn't much, but it allowed her to pretend she wasn't worried. She kept a smile on her face as she drove the rest of the way home.

Her house was a bungalow with a detached one-car garage, where she parked her Neon. She lugged her groceries to the front door, and after some fumbling with keys, got the door open and stepped inside.

In her cramped little kitchen she put away her purchases. She thought of the van again. Here in her home, she found it ridiculous to imagine that anyone could have been following her, spying on her. She must be still worked up from the Sanchez incident. A hot shower was what she needed.

Nevertheless, before heading into her bedroom, she checked and double-checked the locks on the front, rear, and side doors. A sensible precaution, she told herself, though ordinarily she was not so wary in daytime.

Finally she was satisfied that the house was secure.

"You're all alone, Killer," she said aloud, chiding herself. "Nobody is watching you? Got that? *Nobody.*"

13

Treat arrived home just in time for the 5:00 P.M. news. He had expected to be the top story, and he wasn't disappointed.

He stood in front of the Sony Trinitron in his bedroom, his windows shuttered, the lights off. The phosphorescence of the picture tube painted the room in bright colors at first, as the newscast began with its two comely anchorpersons at their desk.

Then the taped report began, and the screen dimmed with a shot of a strip mall in the predawn darkness.

The mall, closed pending renovation, was on Sepulveda Boulevard south of Pico. Every morning for the past month, Treat had driven past the mall on his way to work. Today he had seen a crowd of squad cars parked outside, and he had known that his latest work had been discovered at last.

LAPD cruisers, roof lights cycling, threw scintillant stripes of blue and red across the camera lens. In the background lay the sad little mall, where his most recent victim had lain undisturbed until today. Treat wondered who had found her. A night watchman alerted by the odor? The smell must be fairly noxious by now. Or perhaps some wandering street person seeking shelter—they were always finding their way into sealed buildings, as resourceful as Treat himself.

It hardly mattered. He had known that she would be found eventually. By now, enough time had passed to ensure that her remains would yield no clues to the task force hunting him.

Now the news camera was moving forward, drifting, restless as a shark, among the squad cars, its lens focused on the strip mall wrapped in crime-scene ribbon.

At the time of Treat's reconnaissance this morning, the authorities had not yet brought out the body. It would have taken a good long while, he knew, for the criminalistics team to take the photographs and make the measurements, collect the raw data that would be filed away in a report in the cold steel drawer of a file cabinet, just as the subject of that report would be filed away in another drawer in another cabinet, this one in the morgue.

The report cut to later footage, recorded after sunrise—the body's emergence from its tomb. It had been stuffed inside a bag, and he saw nothing but its outline. Still, he was glad the shot had been included in the report. Seeing it on TV made it more real.

Odd how nothing was real these days unless it was a picture on a screen, how life itself had become only a succession of pictures on a succession of screens, and relationships had become transmissions of electronic data, people reaching across a void. Sad, in a way.

The shape inside the bag seemed unaccountably small. Treat had not realized that Martha Eversol was so petite. It seemed wrong of him to pick on someone who was not his size. He wasn't playing fair.

The camera followed the body until it disappeared inside the coroner's van. When the van drove away, the newscast cut to a standup of a babbling reporter at the scene, and Treat lost interest. He clicked the TV off. He was in darkness again, alone in the silence and privacy of his bedroom.

He stood still, conscious of nothing but the expansion of his belly with each slow intake of air.

He was in a contemplative mood, as was often the case shortly before a kill. There was something about the taking of a life that made him philosophical. He supposed it was the awareness of being so near the great and final mystery of death.

In darkness he crossed the familiar space of his bedroom. His notebook computer rested in its docking station on the bureau. When he raised the lid, the machine flickered out of suspend mode, and the screen—another of the many screens in his life—lit up.

His fingers, long and supple like a pianist's, prowled over the keyboard and the touchpad, initiating an Internet connection, then navigating to a bookmarked Web page.

And there she was—his next chosen one, or her electronic simulacrum. Undressing in her bedroom. Entering the lavatory. Disappearing behind the translucent shower curtain.

Treat inhaled, exhaled. Watched.

He was glad she was taking a shower.

He liked his ladies to be clean.

14

It took Rawls more than an hour to track down the network's system administrator at home. When he finally had the man on the line, the sysadmin admitted having given the Web site only a cursory inspection. Yes, part of his job was to survey the block of IP addresses assigned by his network and ensure that no unacceptable content was being displayed, but he concerned himself mainly with content stored on the network's servers. The Web site in question was stored on a private server; its owner used the network simply to connect his computer with the rest of the Web.

"So what's his name?" Brand asked after Rawls had concluded the conversation.

"Mr. Steven Gader," Rawls said. "At least that's the name on the billing account."

"He's local?"

"Sure is. Got his address and his phone number. But I don't plan on making a phone call." Rawls smiled. "A face-to-face meeting is what I have in mind."

"Let's hope he's home." Brand shrugged on his

overcoat. "Still seems like a lot of trouble to go to for a video stream of an empty room—"

"Hold on." Rawls leaned closer to his monitor. "It's not empty anymore."

He had returned to the site for a last look before heading out, just in time to see a female figure enter the frame. Her image was small but reasonably sharp, her movements rendered fairly smooth by the video stream's fast refresh rate.

Brand circled behind him and looked over his shoulder. He whistled. "Miss January is a looker. No wonder she got the most votes."

The woman was slender and fit, her smooth brown hair falling across her shoulders. She wore a blue jumpsuit and carried a handbag, which she tossed on the nightstand. With her back to the camera she began to undress.

Rawls reached for the button that turned off his monitor. "Maybe I should—"

Brand stopped him. "Don't you dare. This is evidence of a possible felony we're looking at. Major privacy violation, and we are on the case."

Rawls sighed. He didn't want to participate in some Internet peep show, but if he put a stop to it, he would catch hell from Brand. And he needed Brand with him on this.

The woman unhooked her bra and dropped it on the bed. She sat down and kicked off her shoes, then stood and began wriggling out of the bottom half of the jumpsuit.

"Here comes the good part," Brand whispered.

"You're a pervert," Rawls observed dryly.

"Can I help it if I know how to have fun on the job?"

She discarded the slacks and then her underpants. She stood naked, stretching her legs. Lean, limber legs, the legs of a dancer, an athlete.

Brand let out another low whistle and tried out his streetwise patois. "Man, she do look *fine.*"

Rawls cast a cold stare over his shoulder. "Notice that? She just turned on the bedside lamp. That means it's getting dark out." He checked his watch: 8:15. "It's been dark here since shortly after five p.m. I'm betting there's a three-hour time difference."

"Pacific time zone. She's three thousand miles away." Brand smirked. "Think she's a California girl?"

"I couldn't say," Rawls answered tonelessly.

The woman stretched her arms over her head, her back still turned to the camera. Rawls could see the faint shadows of her trapezius muscles and latissimi dorsi. She was fit, strong.

"How old you think she is?" Brand asked a little too eagerly.

"Above the age of consent, if that's what you're worried about."

"I'm serious."

"Mid-twenties, I'd guess."

"Mid-twenties. That's a good age." Brand himself was pushing forty, and Rawls had hit the half-century mark, a fact advertised by the whorls of gray in his hair. "You figure she's flexing for us? For her audience, I mean?"

"No. If she knew the camera was there, don't you think she'd turn around to give us a better show?"

"Maybe she will. This could be part of the tease."

"I don't think this woman has the slightest idea she's being watched."

"We may find out. If she turns around and flashes

a big come-hither smile, then we know she's aware
of the Webcam and it's consensual, and we can both
go home."

Rawls shook his head. "She's not going to smile at
us. And we're not going home."

A moment later the woman, without turning,
walked into the bathroom, where she could be seen
turning on the shower.

"Guess you're right," Brand conceded.

She stepped inside the shower stall, pulling the
curtain shut, and then she was only a smeared silhouette against the translucent plastic.

Rawls stood up. "Well, let's pay Mr. Gader a
visit."

"You sure you don't want to, uh, monitor the site
a little longer? I mean, at least until she comes out
of the shower?"

"Come on, Ned." Rawls punctuated the request by
switching off his computer.

"You never let me have any fun," Brand groused.

Rawls ignored him. He pulled on his winter coat
and headed out of the office, on his way to see the
man whose Web site was a locked door that opened
with Bluebeard's key.

15

C. J. stood in the shower, her head thrown back, eyes shut, letting the cone of rushing water wash away the gritty feel of the streets. Letting it wash away, as well, the memory of the white van, of the sense of being hunted—and of the boogeyman, her old nemesis.

Stupid to be thinking of him. Irrational.

Whoever that man had been, he was long gone in the California night. A wandering psychopath, a drifter. Probably he had moved on to another part of the country years ago. By now, he was in prison or he was dead.

She shut off the shower and dried her hair with a towel, left the bathroom and wrapped herself in a robe. She wandered through the bungalow.

People who knew her only from work would have been surprised by her home. It reflected a different side of her, one she kept hidden from casual acquaintances—and most of her fellow cops fell into that category. She was a collector of items that could be described either as art objects or as knickknacks. In truth, C. J. didn't much care how they were described. She knew what she liked.

Small things mostly. Handmade, always. The older

the better. She liked the feel of living among other people's histories. She liked to run her hands over a carving board and imagine the family gatherings in which it had served as a centerpiece, or operate an antique sewing machine and think of the elegant dresses it had produced for debutante balls. She liked to hold a locket carrying the cameo of a woman she had never met, a woman long dead, and to study the frozen image of that woman's face and live for a minute in her long-ago world.

LA was a city of mass production and relentless improvement and noisy, roaring progress, but she had made her home a sanctuary from all that.

Most of these items had been inexpensive, a necessity imposed by her limited budget. She had started off haunting flea markets and swap meets, but when auction sites began appearing on the Internet, she had switched to that mode of buying. She could browse through the cast-off treasures of the whole continent, and via the miracle of e-mail, she could dicker with a lady in Vancouver over a hand mirror in an ivory frame, or haggle with a gentleman in Louisiana over a set of steak knives with hand-carved teakwood handles. She had been ripped off a few times, but most of her on-line transactions had gone smoothly, and in the past year she had filled her home with charming oddities that pleased her.

The past year. Yes, only that long. She had pursued her hobby in earnest only after her divorce.

She stopped circling the room long enough to peek through the front curtains for a look at the dimming sky. A breeze shivered the leaves of the eucalyptus tree in her yard, and from the branches came the pleasant noise of birds. The sun was nearly gone, the western horizon purple like a bruise.

People said there were no seasons in California, but they were wrong. The winters, though not harsh, had other qualities of winters elsewhere—the shortened days, the early dusk, the settled sense of bleakness.

Or maybe it was just her mood.

She moved away from the curtains and took another look at the collectibles around her. She knew that filling her home with the bric-a-brac of strangers was, in part, an attempt to fill the emptiness of her own life.

Her marriage had been far from perfect. But when it had ended, there had been nothing else for her, except her job. And the job alone wasn't enough.

Was it enough for Adam?

Seems like a nice guy, Delano had said.

As long as you don't trust him too much, she'd answered.

She had met Adam Nolan in a bar on Ventura Boulevard a month after her arrival in LA. At the time she'd had no intention of becoming a cop. Having spent four years at UC Riverside with nothing to show for it but a BA in educational psychology, she had come to the city with the vague hope of landing a teaching job at a private school.

It hadn't taken long for her to learn that such jobs were hard to come by, and most of the teachers filling those positions had master's degrees in their subjects. Her savings were running out, she'd made no friends in the city, she felt lost and directionless, and she didn't know what to do.

Then she and Adam made eye contact at Happy Hour in the Studio Tavern. He bought her a margarita and said he was starting law school at UCLA.

Law school didn't impress her, though clearly it was meant to. What impressed her was that he was polite and he didn't push. He seemed content to just have a conversation—an actual two-way dialogue—and when she talked, he listened attentively. Even after only a month in LA, she already knew how rare it was for anyone to listen.

They dated for two months before she slept with him. She remembered it vividly—better than he did, it seemed. They were in his Culver City apartment, and an Emmylou Harris CD was playing on his boombox, and as he took her into his bed, the song that came over the cheap speakers was "Save the Last Dance for Me."

She had always thought of it as their special song, but Adam, evidently, had forgotten. She wondered why it hurt her to acknowledge that.

He was only the second man she'd been with, the first having been a college boyfriend who drifted away in their senior year. Adam wasn't much more experienced, as he cheerfully admitted while fumbling with her bra strap. Their first time together went quickly—the song was hardly over before Adam was finished too. But, she had to admit, he had improved with practice.

Shortly after he began law school, she was accepted to the LAPD Academy. The idea, which horrified her parents and baffled Adam, had come to her one night as she lay awake. Why had she studied psychology? To understand fear—her own fear, the fear that had haunted her since that awful night in her childhood.

But it wasn't enough to understand fear intellectually. Fear had to be confronted, attacked. A teaching post at a private school would be only an escape from what still terrified her. She needed to stop running. She needed to fight back.

On the day before she enrolled in the Academy, she and Adam were married by a judge in a small, simple ceremony. There was no honeymoon. They'd meant to take one later but had never gotten around to it.

The Academy training lasted seven months. After graduation she was a P-1—a patrol officer with probationary status partnered with a training officer, whose job was to help her forget everything she'd learned in class. She was assigned to Harbor Division, where she became familiar with the Vietnamese and Cambodian gangs that fought vicious battles over drugs and turf. To call Harbor a war zone was no exaggeration; the Vietnam War had never ended there.

She spent two years in Harbor, rising to P-2 rank, while Adam completed law school. She paid the bills for both of them. "I'm a kept man," Adam would joke, but she knew it hurt his pride to take her money, just as it bothered him to know that his wife cruised the streets with a sidearm while he toted a backpack full of law books.

She worked a lot of night watches and graveyard shifts, and Adam was at school during the day and holed up in the law library most evenings. They saw too little of each other. When they were together, they seemed to have less and less to say.

C. J. blamed it on herself. Her job was exhausting and brutal, and it simultaneously wore her down and made her hard. Adam would talk about his day— classroom lectures, oral exams, mock trials. It felt like kid stuff to her after nine hours spent chasing the radio from one 911 call to the next, seeing the corpses of gang-war victims, comforting the bereaved, sneaking down alleys in response to a shots-fired report. It was real, it was electric, and Adam knew nothing about it. When she spoke of what she had seen and done, he didn't know how to respond. After a while she knew he wasn't listening anymore.

Then, just about a year ago, in the first week of February, she came home earlier than usual, punching out before the end of her watch because she had a fever and a queasy stomach. She entered the house—their house, *this* house, the little fixer-upper they'd bought with her salary—and walked into the bedroom, intending to lie down with a cold compress on her head.

And found Adam with a woman named Ashley, who was, as she later learned, one of his classmates.

The affair had been going on for months. Evidently Adam had found someone worth listening to, someone whose world was not so different from his own.

C. J. filed for divorce the next day. Adam fought it. He wanted them to stay together. He swore they could make the marriage work. He might even have believed it. She knew better. Yes, she could understand what he had done. At a certain intellectual distance she could even sympathize.

But she could never trust him again.

She resumed using her maiden name, a decision that seemed to upset him as much as the divorce itself. She kept the house, which she, after all, had paid for. Adam moved to a studio apartment in Venice and took a part-time job while finishing his studies.

She had kept in touch with him to some extent. She knew that Ashley had left him, that he'd plowed his energies into his schoolwork and had obtained his degree with honors.

Now it was January, the twelfth month since their breakup. She had redecorated the house and transferred to a new division, feeling obscurely that she had to make a fresh start. Adam had found work and moved to a two-bedroom condo in Brentwood.

New lives for them both.

Sure.

She knew that neither of them had gotten fully back on track since the divorce. That was why it was dangerous to get together. There was too great a temptation to revive the old relationship. It would be so easy. She had always loved him, even at the end. Loved him, hated him, distrusted him—all at the same time.

She sighed. "You're a piece of work, Killer," she murmured, "you know that?"

She went into the den and sat before her desktop computer, logging on to the Internet to check her e-mail. As usual, it was mostly spam—junk mail for the information age. She wondered why they called it spam, anyway. Perhaps because nobody liked it, but it never seemed to go away.

One message was different from the rest. It consisted of one sentence.

WELCOME TO THE 4-H CLUB.

She had heard of 4-H, of course. Some sort of club for people who raised livestock or something.

Whatever it was, she had never tried to join, and even if she had, this cryptic message was hardly the way to welcome a new member.

Must be a joke, she decided. Or maybe the rest of the message had been cut off.

She almost deleted the e-mail, but hesitated. The message disturbed her for some reason. She thought of the white van. Now this.

There couldn't be any connection. Of course not.

Even so, she saved the message on her hard drive, though she wasn't sure why.

She logged off and shut down her computer. Suddenly she was restless. Returning to her bedroom, she threw on some clothes, then dragged her collapsible home gym out from under the bed.

She set to work doing butterfly curls. Generally she did a minimum of fifty, with the resistance set at a moderate level. She had learned not to train too hard. A pulled muscle could hamper her activities in the field for days, even weeks. It was better to do more reps at a lower setting. Besides, she was mainly interested in toning her physique.

Finished with the curls, she readjusted her position and did leg lifts. It was more efficient to alternate upper and lower body exercises, allowing one set of muscles to recover while the other set was being worked.

She had never been a fitness maven until she had enrolled in the Academy. Then she had set to work on improving her physical conditioning even before the first day of class. Her greatest fear had been humiliation—she hadn't wanted to be a washout, hadn't wanted to find that she couldn't complete a set of push-ups or a jog around the track, while all the other recruits handled it easily. As it turned out, she had proven to be one of the fittest members of the class—a mixed blessing, since it meant that her

instructors often singled her out to lead the class in
an exercise routine.

Some cops gradually lost their conditioning once
they were in the field. She was determined not to
follow their example. In the Academy, slow reflexes
or poor coordination could have cost her a few points
with the instructors. On the street, the same failings
could get her killed.

Suppose she had been a fraction slower when she
grabbed Ramon Sanchez's revolver . . .

"Don't think about it," she gasped, flexing her
thigh muscles in another lift.

She was alive, she was healthy, she was safe. No
need to think about might-haves and what-ifs.

No need to worry about anything at all.

16

Treat enjoyed working out with Caitlin.

He lay on his bedroom floor, his laptop computer resting a few feet away on the smooth carpet, the video feed clearly visible. She exercised her abs and shoulders and back, and he practiced bending.

Bending—that was what he'd called it ever since childhood, when he discovered the remarkable suppleness of his limbs. In medical argot he was hypermobile; in common parlance, double-jointed—the word *double* being used in its less familiar sense of *fold* or *bend*. Some of his flexibility had diminished with age, but through daily exercise he remained limber enough to hyperextend each elbow by more than fifteen degrees, to bend his knees forward to the same extent, to touch his forearm with his thumb, and to perform other such carnival tricks.

He ran deftly through his series of stretches, working first the ankles, then knees, then hip joints, and so on, bending into pretzel shapes, tucking his legs behind his ears, enfolding himself in his thin, malleable limbs. He had to be careful not to dislocate a shoulder. As was typical of those who had inherited

Marfan syndrome, his joints could easily pop out of their sockets when subjected to unusual strain.

On the computer Caitlin continued her equally rigorous program of self-improvement. Of all the things she did, her exercise regimen was the one that pleased him most. And if he could judge by the comments dropped in certain chat rooms and newsgroups that he frequented, there were others who shared his tastes.

It was funny. The two previous women had been highly promiscuous, even oversexed. Miss November, especially. She had switched bed partners on a weekly, sometimes semiweekly, basis. She had invited all sorts of casual paramours into the sheets with her—overweight middle-aged men all too obviously picked up at singles bars, young studs with the hard, sculpted bodies of would-be actors who spent their lives at the gym, willowy artistic types who seemed, at times, more feminine than Miss November herself. In her bed, before the unseen camera's eye, she had performed magnificently with her various partners, executing every imaginable variation on the theme of heterosexual coupling.

Caitlin was not like that. In the month that Treat had watched her, she had slept with no one in her home, and she had never been out all night, except when she was working. Treat owned a police scanner and recognized her unit's call sign; he knew when she was on the street.

She had been celibate for this month—perhaps for much longer. And yet, to Treat, she was the most alluring one of all. And he was not the only one who felt that way. Miss January had garnered more votes than any other contestant.

He supposed it was the appeal of the unknown.

Miss November had left nothing to the imagination. She had depersonalized herself until she was merely a hunk of flesh, not only in the eyes of those who watched her, but in her own eyes as well. Treat was sure of that. He had looked long and hard into those eyes before he killed her, and he'd seen nothing there beyond dumb fear and an animal's helpless confusion.

Caitlin could not be objectified that way. She had maintained her dignity. Thus, paradoxically, she made a better victim. Killing animals was stupid, ugly work. Killing a genuine person, a person of self-respect and integrity, a person with an uncorrupted soul—well, that was ever so much more satisfying.

With a secret smile at this thought, Treat rose from the floor and began to pack, transferring tonight's necessities from his bureau to the tote bag on his bed, ticking off each item on his inventory.

Set of tattoo needles in different sizes.

Two bottles of ink—one maroon, the other black for line work.

Homemade stencil in an hourglass pattern.

Flashlight.

Knife—for self-defense only.

Bottle of chloroform and a rag.

Syringe filled with succinylcholine, a paralytic drug—in case the chloroform failed to subdue her.

Roll of tape to pinion her wrists and ankles.

Eyeless hood to cover her head during transit.

And gloves, of course—black leather gloves for his strangling hands.

Finished, he zipped up the tote bag. He checked the computer screen again. Caitlin was stowing the exercise rig under her bed. He watched as she took off her workout clothes and tossed them into a laundry basket, then toweled herself dry in the bathroom. She spent a few moments selecting an outfit to wear, and during that time she was naked on the screen of his computer—and, no doubt, on other screens as well. There were others who liked to watch.

But only one who was not content with mere watching.

She chose a yellow blouse and beige cargo shorts. Treat studied her as she dressed. He did not turn away even when she sat on the edge of her bed and laced up her sneakers. It gave him a peculiar feeling of intimacy with her to know that he was preparing for his evening just as she made preparations for hers. Almost like a real couple.

Soon they would share an intimacy purer and more intense than any lovers' tryst. They would know the closeness of predator and prey, of torturer and victim. They would share the wordless language of suffering, and together they would experience the final delicious frisson of death.

Treat shook his head, dispelling the vision his imagination had conjured. He looked around him. No more daylight filtered through his shuttered windows. Darkness had come.

He entered his walk-in closet and began to select his attire for the evening's entertainment. A formal affair, so he would wear black.

For Miss Osborn, on the other hand, the event was strictly come-as-you-are.

17

C. J. was making dinner when the phone rang. She glanced at the clock on the stove. Ten minutes to six. Salesperson, probably. She almost didn't answer, but on the third ring she picked up the cordless unit mounted by the fridge. "Hello?"

"It's me. Rick Tanner."

Tanner had never called her. "Hey, Rick. What's up?"

"I wanted to see how you were doing."

"How I'm doing?" Carrying the phone, she returned to the stove and used a wooden spoon to push around some stir-fry vegetables in her frying pan. "We just talked at the station a couple hours ago."

"Yeah, but at the time I didn't know what had gone down in that hostage situation. How you climbed in through the rear window and took away the guy's piece."

She turned down the flame under the saucepan. The broccoli was starting to scorch. "Where'd you hear that?"

"Pedro's. I'm finishing up a Code Seven right now." Completing his dinner break, he meant.

Pedro's was a Tex-Mex diner frequented by Newton cops and Sheriff's deputies who worked the Florence area. "Some guys from your division have been talking. I think you impressed them, Killer."

"You're not supposed to call me that, remember?"

"It was a slip."

"Anyway"—she ladled the cooked vegetables onto a plate—"I wasn't trying to impress anybody. I just didn't want . . . well, you know . . ."

"Another SWAT screwup? Like the warehouse in Long Beach?"

She took a long moment before answering. Sometimes Tanner really could surprise her. "How'd you know I was thinking of that?"

"I didn't. My partner did. He had to walk me through it real slow. I caught on eventually."

"I'll bet you caught on sooner than you'll admit. You're not so dumb, Tanner."

"That's what I keep telling everybody. But do they listen? Nah."

There was an uncomfortable pause when both of them realized they had temporarily run out of conversation.

"Look," Tanner said, "that's all I called to say. And, uh, I wanted to ask you a question."

"Ask away."

"Is it a problem for you—me being SWAT? I mean, is that why . . . well, you know?"

"Why I've been sort of unfriendly?"

"Right. Not that I don't deserve it. I probably do. I'm an asshole. Even my best friends tell me so."

"They might be underestimating you." She looked out the kitchen window, into the darkness. The sun was long gone. Again she found herself wishing night didn't come so early in the winter. "Look, you

SWAT guys have a job to do, and most of the time you do it well. Anyway, you had nothing to do with the warehouse. That was LAPD Metro's deal."

"Sure but, you know, once we put on our vests and goggles, we pretty much all look alike."

She laughed. "I don't have anything against you, Rick. I've just been . . . cautious since my divorce."

"Yeah, I can understand that. And, uh, I'm sorry if I've been, you know, coming on too strong."

She was touched. He had never apologized to her before, for anything. "Is this your sensitive side coming out?" she asked with a faint smile.

"Could be. I wouldn't know. I'm not too familiar with my sensitive side. But if I've been, well . . . acting like a jerk . . ."

"Maybe a little. But I goad you into it, I think."

"I guess I just need to, you know, chill out a little. Around you, I mean."

"Maybe we could both play it that way. You don't go for any three-point shots, and I won't try so hard to block."

"Basketball metaphors. I like that."

"First *rakish,* now *metaphors.* I'm starting to think there's more to you than you let on."

"That's what I've been trying to tell you. Uh, sorry—that was the old Rick Tanner."

"The old Rick Tanner's not all bad. Actually, I kind of like talking to him." This was true, though she hadn't realized it until right now.

"You'll like the new guy even better."

"I just might."

"So we're cool?"

She smiled. "We're cool." Absurdly she wondered if he was wearing his sunglasses right now, in the dark.

"Glad to hear it. Guess I'd better be going. Me and my partner are officially back on duty."

C. J. surprised herself by holding him on the phone a minute longer. "Can I ask *you* something?"

"Sure."

"You ever hear anything about the Four-H Club?"

"Bunch of farm kids trying to raise the world's biggest tomato?"

"No, I mean—well, it's sort of crazy, but I got this e-mail message welcoming me to the Four-H Club. Unsolicited and unsigned. I wondered if it meant anything."

"Like a threat?"

"It's probably nothing. But on my way home, I could've sworn there was somebody tailing me."

"Description?"

"White van, cargo-style, California plates. That's all I got."

"When did you receive the e-mail?"

"Today."

"So first you're followed, then you get this message?"

"It might not mean anything."

"I'll ask around. See if it rings any bells."

"No, don't bother." She was sorry she had mentioned it. "It's nothing. I'm being paranoid."

"In this city, with the work we do, paranoid is a good way to be."

"Don't go to any trouble. I'm sure it's a joke or something."

"I'll ask anyway. If I find out anything, I'll call."

"I think I'm just going crazy, that's all."

"I've been crazy for years. I can relate. Hey, Chang's telling me we're taking a one-eighty-seven in gangland. Gotta roll, Killer."

"Don't call me that," she said, smiling, but Tanner had already hung up.

She replaced the cordless handset in its charger, then carried her meal into the dining area. Picking at her veggies, sipping ice water, she thought about Rick Tanner. It seemed his playful come-ons weren't so playful, after all. He really did care about her. Underneath the macho facade, there could be a person worth getting to know.

Or maybe not. It could be just another act, a subtler come-on. She wasn't sure what to think. The divorce had left her wary, hypervigilant.

Still, calling had been a nice gesture on his part.

To be honest—she smiled sadly—it was more than Adam would have done.

18

Treat kept his white van in the underground parking garage of his apartment complex. The van, a Ford Econoline, was parked neatly between the stripes, flanked by a snazzy black Miata and a dented Honda Civic, a mix of vehicles that reflected the egalitarian mix of tenants in his building—rising corporate stars and showbiz types waiting for a break, recent college grads still living off their parents, and senior citizens surviving on fixed incomes.

When he signed his lease six months ago, the landlord had boasted that the building represented a rich diversity of people. Treat remembered thinking that his own particular skills would no doubt broaden the spectrum of this diversity by more than a few degrees.

He had moved often in his life—from one apartment to another, from one city to another, from one state to another. A man like him could not afford to stay rooted in one spot. Before long, no doubt, he would be on the move again. He had learned not to press his luck. One more killing after tonight—he had already selected a delectable Miss February, and a hidden camera was installed, the feed ready to be sent to the Web site whenever he wished.

After February, his contribution to the site would end, and the Hourglass Killer would be no more.

Another persona discarded. Another performance completed.

He boarded his van and switched on the engine and headlights. The vehicle rumbled under him as he guided it out of the garage, into the street.

Caitlin's home, which he had observed on many reconnaissance missions over the past month, was twenty miles from his apartment building. He put on a little speed, aware that he had to catch her before she left for her community-service program.

Oh, yes, he knew all about that. He had watched her closely, learned the ins and outs of her schedule. It had been the same with Nikki Carter and Martha Eversol. When the time had come for their abductions, he had known their weekly routines intimately.

This was the thing that people—average people, simpleminded people, the people who surrounded him every day, who had been part of his world for all the forty-one years of his life—this was the thing that such people never understood. Because his approach to murder was random, they assumed it must be impersonal, a faceless stranger killing an equally faceless victim.

But there was nothing impersonal about it. He knew his victims. He remembered each one in exquisite, sensual detail. He even cherished them, in his way. Not that he would ever be so stupidly sentimental as to visit their graves or mail a consoling note to their bereaved. Such gestures were pointless—worse, they were dangerous. He thought of himself as a professional, and as such, he maintained an appropriate distance from the subjects of his work.

Still, he did care for them. This was, in fact, the only way he had ever learned to care for anybody. He had never understood what movies and songs were all about when they addressed the topic of love. He could not imagine wanting to share his life with another human being or even with a pet, except perhaps for his arachnids, who required nothing from him save the occasional cricket to feed on. The idea of devoting himself to another person, diluting the purity of his self-contained consciousness in the tepid waters of another soul, was revolting to him.

And yet . . .

He did not seek to be entirely alone in the world. He sought a connection with others, a way to relate to fellow members of his species.

He had found that way, in the intimacy of homicide.

To select his victim . . . to learn her name, study her movements, observe her friends and family, live her life vicariously for days or weeks . . . then move in for the kill and *take* her, take her in the full meaning of the word, *possess* her more completely than any lover, force her submission to his will, his power, subjugate her utterly, then extinguish her life and leave only the rag doll of her body . . .

This was the only closeness he knew, and all he ever wanted to know.

Treat smiled, aware that he would know that intimacy with Caitlin very soon. He would enter her house via the back door, where he was least likely to be observed. Render her unconscious with a whiff of chloroform—marvelous stuff, delightfully aromatic, safe in moderate doses, even used as an anesthetic in an earlier century. Of course he would remove his Webcam and other incriminating gear before leaving with Caitlin in his van.

Then the ride to a condemned house in Silver Lake, a musty old place shrouded by trees, offering a fine basement, where he could hold her for the requisite four hours.

At the appointed time would come the strangulation, slow and sensual like lovemaking, and then the tattoo and his calling card, and the disposal of the body in a place where it was unlikely to be found for weeks.

Pulling onto the Pomona Freeway, speeding west, Treat breathed the heady wine of his intentions and found them sweet.

It was the last night of the month, the last night of Caitlin Jean Osborn's life.

19

Steven Gader's house lay on a tree-shaded street a few blocks from the University of Baltimore. Rawls guided his bureau-issue sedan to a stop at the curb.

"This is it," Brand said unnecessarily from the passenger seat.

They got out of the car, stepping over piles of slush, and walked up the slate path. Snow lay half-melted on a brown lawn. Lamplight glowed through windows protected by iron security bars. Rawls wondered fleetingly if the bars were hinged from the inside to allow escape in case of fire.

At the front door Rawls listened. He heard no sounds from inside. He rang the bell, holding his finger on the button for a long time. When there was no response, he rang again.

"Not home," Brand said, clapping his gloved hands against the cold.

Rawls tried once more, and this time he heard a clatter of footsteps and a muffled male voice saying, "Hold on. Christ, I'm coming."

Rawls saw Brand unbutton his overcoat for easier access to his Glock 10.

The door opened, and a man stood there in a terrycloth bathrobe, his hair uncombed and dripping wet. He was short and pale, mid- to late thirties, with a glaze of stubble on his cheeks and an earring in his left earlobe. He gazed at them with dark, suspicious eyes.

"What's this?" he snapped. "Jehovah's Witnesses?"

"No, Mr. Gader," Rawls said politely. "FBI. Agents Rawls and Brand." He allowed the man a glimpse of his FBI badge.

There were two things to watch now—his eyes and his hands. The eyes might betray guilt. The hands might pose a threat.

"FBI?" the man echoed. "Well . . . what do you want with me?"

"You are Mr. Steven Gader, correct?"

"Yeah, that's me."

"We'd like to speak with you, sir."

Gader realized he was being asked to invite the agents inside. "Can I have another look at that badge?"

Rawls held out the badge and allowed him time to scrutinize it thoroughly.

"I don't have to let you in," Gader said finally. "I don't have to talk to you at all."

"That's true, sir," Rawls acknowledged, the words coming out in a jet of frosted breath.

"I could say you have to talk to my lawyer. I'd be within my rights if I did that."

"Yes, you would. But we have only a few simple questions. Talking to us could help us out a lot."

"Help you out. Why should I help a couple of feds?" Gader ran a hand through his wet hair. "You got me out of the damn bathtub, you know."

"I'm sorry."

"Sure you are." His gaze flicked to Brand's face.

"What are you smiling at? So I was taking a bath. It doesn't make me some kind of faggot. My radiator's pumping out too much heat, and I can't fix the damn thermostat, so I figured I would cool off in the tub. Okay?"

Rawls let him ramble, then said quietly, "It's just a few questions. We'd like to clear things up tonight."

"Shit." Gader wavered in the doorway. "All right, I'm gonna catch goddamn pneumonia with the door open, so come the hell in. But I reserve the right to call a lawyer and order you out of my home at any time."

"Fair enough."

Gader led them into his living room, a small space with a low ceiling and dirty windows and a sooty fireplace that looked long unused. The carpet was worn, and there were soil marks on the sofa and armchairs. Gader hadn't lied about the thermostat. The place felt like an oven.

Gader plopped down in a chair and gestured to the sofa, where Rawls and Brand planted themselves, Brand positioning his body to have a view of the stairway in case there was anyone else in the house.

"So what's this all about?" Gader asked combatively.

"Can I ask what's your line of work?" Rawls began as he pulled off his gloves.

"I design Web sites."

"Well, that's what we're here to ask you about."

"Go ahead, ask. I've created sites for lots of local businesses, mostly mom-and-pop operations that want to go on-line, expand their market. I can give you my brochure—"

"We're more interested in a noncommercial site." Rawls recited the URL, pronouncing the string of slang terms with distaste. "What can you tell us about that one?"

Gader showed no expression, but Rawls could see his tongue moving around in the hollow of his cheek as he thought of a way to answer.

"You do maintain that site, don't you?"

"Yeah," Gader said slowly.

"A password-protected site. The password being Fatima, as in Bluebeard's seventh wife."

"How do you know that?"

Rawls smiled. "The password or the story?"

"The password."

"We guessed."

"You guessed." Gader looked from Rawls to Brand. "How about the name Bluebeard? You guess that too?"

"We got hold of it. Is Bluebeard one of your customers?"

"I don't have customers. It's a noncommercial site. You said so yourself."

"All right. One of your visitors then?"

"You could say that."

"Bluebeard—that's an odd name, isn't it? How do you suppose it was chosen?"

"You'd have to ask him."

"Ask Bluebeard? So who is he?"

"Beats me. I don't know."

Rawls let a beat of silence pass. Then he said, "You're Bluebeard, aren't you, Mr. Gader?"

"Me?" Gader laughed. "Shit, no."

His reaction seemed genuine. Even so, Rawls pursued the idea. "The password for the site is Fatima. You run the site. You selected the password. Isn't it logical to assume that you're Bluebeard?"

"No."

"Where did I go wrong, Mr. Gader? Are you claiming you don't run the site after all? Because if I had to guess, I would say that you run it off a personal computer, probably right here in this house."

"Are you going to search the house? Is that it? Because you can't search without a warrant. You can't do shit without a warrant."

"The man knows his rights," Brand said mildly. It was the first time he had spoken.

"I sure as hell do. And I don't appreciate two feds barging in here and, you know—"

"Getting you out of your bubble bath?" Brand smiled.

"It wasn't a *bubble* bath, and it's none of your goddamn business anyway. Get out of here."

"Mr. Gader," Rawls said, "you can make us leave, but we'll only come back with a warrant—the item you're so concerned about." He leaned forward, speaking slowly and reasonably, the way he used to speak to his son Philip when he was a toddler. Philip was a senior at U. Penn now. "Of course, you might think that if we go away for an hour or two, you'll have time to wipe the contents of your computer. Then you'll be home free, you might believe. But you'd be wrong. We've already downloaded your site onto a Zip disk. We have all the evidence we need. Besides, we can recover almost any data from a drive, no matter what you do to it. Any attempt at erasure would only make things worse for you in the long run."

"Bullshit."

"You don't think we know how to preserve and recover evidence?"

"I don't think you've got anything a judge would call evidence."

"We have a Web site that displays streaming video of a young woman in her home."

"So?"

"It looks like a serious privacy-rights violation."

"Not if, say, she's my girlfriend. In that case, well, she gets a kick out of letting me see her naked. The site's password-protected because we want visitors on an invitation-only basis. It's kinky, sure, but she's over the age of consent, and we get a kick out of it, so leave me alone."

"How about Miss December and Miss November? They your girlfriends too?"

"Maybe."

"Can you produce any of these women to back up your claims?"

Gader squirmed in his chair. "Let's say I can. But I won't. Not without a court order or whatever it takes."

"Then we'll get a court order—or whatever it takes."

"No, you won't. No way. A judge won't listen to you with what you've got now. What you need is my cooperation, and I'm not offering it. So get lost."

"What makes you think we would be deterred by your lack of cooperation, Mr. Gader?"

"Because this whole thing is too small-time and too much hassle." Gader seemed to gain confidence from his own words. "You've got too many other things to run down, higher priorities. You don't have time to screw around with this piece-of-shit case. Even if you want to, your higher-ups won't let you. They don't give a damn about some private Web site that might or might not be doing something skuzzy. They won't give you the go-ahead to waste the Bureau's resources."

He seemed cooler now. He had convinced himself.

Rawls glanced at Brand, who wore a tight, fixed expression on his face. Rawls knew that look. It meant *He's got us, Noah.*

"So that's how it is, Mr. Gader?" Rawls asked evenly.

"Yeah, that's how it is."

"Well, you're right." Rawls surprised both Brand and Gader by saying this. "Our superiors won't let us pursue this case on the clock. They want us handling other, higher-priority cases, just as you said."

"Great. I'm right. I win. You lose. Get lost."

"It's not quite that simple."

"Why not?"

"Because, Mr. Gader, we don't require any go-ahead from our supervisor if we choose to work this case on our own time. And that's what we're doing. We're not on the clock, are we, Agent Brand?"

"Wish we were," Brand said cheerfully.

"We're here, even though we're not getting paid. And we'll pursue this matter, whether or not our colleagues want us to do so. Isn't that right, Agent Brand?"

"Damn straight." Brand might or might not have believed this, but he was playing along.

"We'll pursue it as long as it takes. We're not going to drop this investigation. Not now, not tomorrow, not a week from now, not ever."

"We've signed on for the duration," Brand volunteered, getting into the flow. "We'll miss a lot of meals if we have to. But we're gonna get to the bottom of this mess."

Gader looked from one to the other. "You're shittin' me," he said.

Rawls steepled his hands in his lap. "Mr. Gader,

let me tell you a story. I have a daughter at Georgetown right now."

"I don't have to hear this—"

"Just listen," Rawls said patiently. "Last year,
when my daughter was a freshman, she found out
that somebody had installed a camcorder in the dormitory bathroom. The camera was shooting eight-
millimeter videotape of the women as they showered. This seems to have been going on for some
time—weeks, months. And it would still be going on
if my daughter hadn't dropped her shampoo bottle
and seen the camera inside a watertight bag under
the drain grate. See, it was pointed up, Mr. Gader.
You know the kind of footage it was taking.

"She called me, quite hysterical. I went up there
on my day off, and I interviewed the men in the
dorm—it's a coed dormitory hall. I talked to them
one at a time. Nobody confessed, but one young gentleman seemed nervous. I staked out his room. After
midnight he threw something away. I dug it out of
the trash. A bagful of videotapes. He'd gotten rattled,
and he was disposing of the evidence. That fine
young man isn't a student at Georgetown anymore.
Do you see the point of this story?"

Gader was trying hard not to look flustered. "I
think so."

"I'm a persistent man," Rawls said. "Especially
when it comes to privacy violations of this particular
kind. When I look at that woman undressing and
taking a shower on your Web site for the benefit of
masturbating voyeurs, it strikes home to me in a
rather personal way. It makes me think of my daughter. Now do you honestly believe I'm going to let
this case go?"

"Maybe not."

"Definitely not. So don't play games. Don't use delaying tactics. Don't be clever. Just tell us what we need to know."

Gader seemed very small inside his bathrobe. His chin was down, his eyes half-closed, his hands gripping the armrests, fingertips squeezed white with pressure. Down the street a dog started to bark. It was the only sound for a while.

"I'll cooperate," Gader said finally. "No problem."

Rawls smiled. "That's what we like to hear. Is the computer here in the house?"

"Yeah." Gader rose, tightening the belt of his robe. "It's upstairs."

He led them to the second floor. Climbing the staircase, Brand hung back a few steps with Rawls.

"Great story," Brand whispered.

"Thanks."

"Funny thing, though. I've met your family. And you haven't got a daughter."

Rawls smiled. "Well, let's keep that between ourselves."

20

C. J. was putting her dinner dishes in the sink when something drew her gaze to the kitchen window. She looked past her pale reflection in the glass, studying the darkness of her backyard.

Amid the shadows of the jacaranda trees, she saw a light.

For a moment she just stood there, transfixed by an emotion too deeply rooted to be immediately identified. Then she understood that what she felt was fear—not an adult's fear, but the stark, uncomplicated terror of a child.

It was him. The boogeyman.

She remembered how she had glimpsed his flashlight in the darkness outside her parents' house, and now he was back.

The light wavered, drifting like a will-o'-the-wisp, then winked out, and she returned to herself.

This was no monster from her childhood. It was a prowler, hardly unheard of in this neighborhood or in any part of this city. And she wasn't some terrorized schoolgirl, she was a cop. She could take care of herself. She could—

A noise.

Very soft, almost inaudible. Halfway between a creak and a squeal.

It might have been nothing, just the old house settling.

Or a door, opening. The back door.

Her gun. She needed her off-duty Smith. She looked around the kitchen before remembering that the gun was in her handbag, and her handbag, damn it, was in her bedroom at the rear of the bungalow.

The prudent course of action was to leave the house, drive to Wilshire Station, come back with a patrol unit.

But she wasn't going to do that. Wasn't going to be chased out of her home by a glimpse of light and a barely audible creak.

No gun? Then make do with another weapon.

She opened the cutlery drawer and pulled out a carving knife. Part of her recalled the knife she'd grabbed from another kitchen before descending into the crawl space. But she refused to think about that.

She studied the knife. It was long and wickedly sharp and felt heavy in her hand. She liked its weight, the gleam of its blade. But she would have liked her .38 Smith better.

Knife in hand, she advanced toward the rear of the house.

No lights burned in this part of the bungalow. She had turned off the light on her nightstand before leaving the bedroom. Now she wished she hadn't.

She reached the rear hall. It was empty.

Drawing back against the wall, she scanned the hallway. The back door appeared closed, but possibly the intruder had shut it behind him.

She looked for footprint impressions or tracks of dirt on the carpet. None were visible in the dim glow from the living room, but she could see only halfway down the hall.

The hallway opened onto three rooms. On the left were the guest lavatory and the laundry room. On the right, farthest down, was her bedroom.

If someone had gotten inside, he could have concealed himself in any one of those rooms. She would have to check each one in turn.

She advanced, the knife's wooden hasp cold against her palm.

The door to the guest lavatory stood open. She didn't think the intruder could have progressed that far without leaving some marks on the carpet. Even so, she took the precaution of pivoting into the bathroom doorway, knife raised.

No one there.

Emerging into the hall, she looked to her right, then left, then right again, like a child looking both ways before crossing the street.

The laundry room was next. That door was closed. She wasn't looking forward to opening it, so she did it fast, throwing the door wide and darting in.

This room, too, was unoccupied. Maybe there was no intruder. Maybe she had imagined the whole thing.

This thought, dangerously seductive, was instantly dismissed. With one room still to go, she couldn't afford to drop her guard.

She stepped to the laundry-room doorway, peering to her right, her left—

Sudden pressure on her face.

Gloved hand, wet cloth.

Couldn't see him in the darkness, could only lash out blindly with the knife.

Her thrust missed, and then his other hand clamped on her wrist, holding the knife at bay.

He pressed the cloth harder against her nose and mouth. Instinctively she knew she must not take a breath.

She flailed at him with her left hand. If she could find his throat, pinch the carotid artery—

He sensed her strategy and jammed himself closer to her, wedging her against the doorframe of the laundry room, restricting her range of movement.

She struggled against him. His face was masked, invisible. His body was pure darkness.

Her lungs demanded air. With a last effort she drew up one knee and pistoned out her leg, connecting with his gut. He loosened his grip on her face. The cloth came away. She sucked in a deep draft of oxygen, and then the cloth was over her nose again, and before she could stop herself she had breathed its fumes.

Cold.

A shiver of cold in her nasal passages, in her throat.

The fumes were sweet-smelling, intoxicating. They made her head spin. The world blurred, everything going double, no clarity anywhere, and she was tired, sleepy. Her fingers losing purchase on the knife, letting it fall, and though she knew that she was defenseless, she didn't care.

Far away, his chuckle of triumph. Then his words, low, spoken close to her ear.

"Got you now, C. J."

That voice.

She *knew* that voice.

Her last thought was a question, echoing unanswered.

. . . *Adam?*

21

Something nagged at Rawls. He knew there was more here than a voyeuristic Web site.

That name, Bluebeard . . . three women under surveillance . . . one for each month . . .

The connection was close but continued to elude him.

He and Brand followed Gader into the guest bedroom on the second floor. The room had been made into a work space cluttered with computers, printers, cables, surge suppressors, and battery backup units. The shades were down, the room lit only by a pair of gooseneck lamps, bulbs angled away from the equipment to minimize screen glare. The cold wind beat against the windowpanes.

It occurred to Rawls that computer people, himself and Brand included, spent far too much time behind closed windows in rooms like this.

The machine they wanted was easy to find. Rawls spotted it even before Gader led them to it. It was a Compaq Proliant server with a twenty-inch monitor and a standard keyboard. Superficially the setup resembled any other personal computer with a tower design, but because it was a server, it had capabilities that an ordinary PC did not.

"What OS are you running?" Brand asked.

"Windows 2000 Server edition."

"Log on. And, Mr. Gader, there better not be a format bomb or any other funny business." A format bomb would erase the contents of the drive when an incorrect log-on was attempted.

"There's no funny business." Gader sat at the computer and turned on the monitor, which had been powered down to save energy. The server itself had been left on. It would be active twenty-four hours a day, allowing visitors to access the site whenever they wished.

Rawls watched Gader type in the screen name NastyBoy and the Fatima password.

"NastyBoy," Rawls muttered. "Seems appropriate."

"Hey, get off my case, okay? You've got me all wrong."

Rawls ignored him. "How'd you pick the password anyway?"

"I didn't. *He* did."

"Bluebeard?"

"Yeah."

"You let a visitor pick the password to the whole site?"

"He's more than a visitor. He runs it with me. Well, the truth is, he pretty much runs it, period."

"From a remote location?"

"Yeah."

"You turned over your sysop duties to a remote administrator?"

"That's right. He wanted to do it, and I let him. I have other things to do. And he was contributing the most interesting content anyway."

"The content being the videos of these women?"

"Yeah," Gader said in a smaller voice.

"Once he took control, he changed the password to Fatima?"

"Right. That was his idea. Of course, you're supposed to change a site's password periodically. It's a standard security measure."

"Standard," Rawls echoed, but there was nothing standard about a name like Bluebeard. "Didn't you wonder why he chose that particular alias?"

"What, you're saying he's some kind of murderer or something?" Gader laughed. "I guess if he called himself Napoleon you'd figure he was a world conqueror. People pick crazy nicknames on-line. It doesn't mean anything."

"So it never worried you?"

"No."

"Well," Rawls said, "it worries me. What made you cede control of the site to a stranger?"

"He's not exactly a stranger."

"You've met him?"

"Not face-to-face, but we've corresponded—e-mail, I mean. We had similar interests. He liked my site, but he thought we could do more with it. Back then there was no video, just vidcaps from adult movies—stuff on Showtime at two a.m. I would pull some frames and put them on the site. Frontal nudity, bondage, babes in hot tubs—that kind of crap. It was nonprofit, just for kicks."

"Was the site kept secret?" Rawls asked.

"Pretty much. I had it password-protected, because I was a little worried about copyright-infringement issues. I'd heard of other sites being shut down for using pirated stills, so I kept a low profile. I gave out the site address and the password in e-mails to people I met in chat rooms. Bluebeard was one of them."

"And you two hit it off?"

"I guess you could say that. He checked out the site, then told me he had a way to spice it up. He sent me some footage as an e-mail attachment—an .avi file."

"A woman in her bedroom?"

"Right."

"And you had no qualms about putting that kind of material on your site?"

Gader swiveled his desk chair to face Rawls. "Look, he told me she knew about it. He *assured* me she knew."

"Knew what?"

"That she was on the Web. He said it was her idea."

"And when a second woman showed up on the site?" Brand asked. "Didn't that make you wonder?"

"Yeah, but again, he *assured* me. I mean, he gave me his assurance . . ."

He seemed to like that word *assure,* but Rawls was tired of hearing it. "Mr. Gader, stop trying to cover your ass and just tell us what happened."

"Okay, okay. Well, like I said, Bluebeard wanted to supply streaming video. I thought it was cool—way better than the stuff I was uploading. So I gave him my log-on info to let him access my site's file manager. That's when he started sending the video feed. Real-time video—at least I'm pretty sure it was. The first woman became Miss November. Next month, he sent video of Miss December, and now Miss January. I guess this is her last night—probably there'll be a Miss February tomorrow. And so on. It was Bluebeard's idea to have people vote for their favorites. Eventually he assumed so many responsibilities that I just let him administer the whole site.

It's still physically on my server, but he's controlling it through the network."

"So he could be anywhere?" Rawls asked.

"I guess."

"You don't know where he lives, or where these women live?"

"No. Well, I assume they live near him, wherever that is. He must have access to them."

"You can't tell me you were never curious as to this Bluebeard's identity."

"I was curious. Sure."

"Well, you're not exactly naive about computers. You know how to trace a visitor to your Web site."

Gader shook his head. "Tried that. No good. He sends the video feed through a proxy server. I can trace it back that far and no farther."

"With a court order," Brand said, "we could force the proxy's administrator to surrender their logs."

"If they keep the logs in the first place," Rawls mused. Some of those outfits routinely destroy all information to defeat any possible subpoenas. He looked at Gader. "How about the e-mails he sent you? Were those untraceable too?"

"Sent through a remailer. Scrubbed."

"You didn't find that suspicious?"

"Hell, a lot of people use anonymizer services on the Web. Big Brother's out there. As I guess you two ought to know, seeing as how you work for him."

Rawls brushed aside the jibe. "Bluebeard shut off the other video streams? He keeps only one going at a time?"

"That's right."

"Did you capture the other streams, or parts of them? You know, highlight reels?"

"No, never did."

Rawls leaned on Gader's desk and made eye contact. "Don't play games with me. You've got footage of naked women streaming into your computer, and you make no effort to save any of it for a rainy day?"

"Well . . . maybe some stills."

"Maybe?"

Gader shrugged. "Stills. A few."

"Where are they? On the site?"

"No, I posted a few of Miss November after she was off the site, but Bluebeard took 'em down. Guess he wanted to stay current. Funny, though. He seemed really upset about it—kind of flamed me. Said he wanted only that month's playmate on display."

"Playmate?" Brand asked with a smirk.

Gader was embarrassed. "That's what he calls them. You know, playmate of the month."

"He's a real charmer, this friend of yours," Brand said.

"Where are the stills?" Rawls asked.

"On the hard drive of my PC."

"Show us."

Gader kicked his swivel chair away from the server and rolled across the room to a Hewlett-Packard desktop system. He booted it up and activated a picture-editing program, then loaded three .jpeg stills.

"Here's a sample," he said, waving his hand over the tiled images. "Miss November, December, January."

The photos caught the women in medium shot or close-up. All were Caucasians, but otherwise they differed in appearance. Two were blondes, while Miss January, as Rawls had already noted, was a brunette. Their ages varied from early twenties to

perhaps late thirties. All of them had been video-
taped in their bedrooms.

"Are these the clearest facial shots you've got?"
Rawls asked.

"I guess so. I don't always concentrate on the faces,
if you know what I mean."

"Print them out. One photo per page, full sheet."

Gader obeyed. His inkjet printer buzzed and
whirred until all three sheets had been deposited in
the tray. Rawls picked them up and shared them
with Brand, fanning out the pages like a hand of
cards.

"What are we looking for, exactly?" Brand asked.

"I'm not sure. You know how something is on the
tip of your tongue and you can't quite remember?"

"You saying you may have seen these women
before?"

"The first two, yes."

"Where?"

"I'm not sure," Rawls said again. He stared at the
faces, ignoring Miss January, focusing on Miss November and Miss December. Two women with nothing obviously in common except the color of their
hair.

They had been spied on, each for a separate month.
When the month was over, the spying had stopped,
and they had not been seen on the site again. Bluebeard had been very vocal about keeping them off
the site. Why?

Because someone would recognize them? Someone
who might have seen them?

Seen them where?

On TV. In the newspapers.

Crime stories.

Victims.

"Damn," Rawls breathed, his voice so low and hoarse that both Gader and Brand turned to stare at him.

"Noah, you got something?" Brand asked.

"I've got *him*." Rawls didn't know if he was speaking to Brand or to himself. "I've got Bluebeard. That's who he is, all right, Bluebeard—and this site is his locked room."

22

It was odd. She was far away and yet very close. She was floating, weightless, yet she felt the limp heaviness of her body and the cold rigidity of the floor. She was not herself, but who else could she be?

There was no way of making sense of this. She concentrated on little things, single moments that were at least roughly comprehensible.

The hands moving over her. Gloved hands, she thought. Hands of leather.

They turned her on her stomach, pulled her arms behind her. She felt the brief, distant protest of the muscles in her shoulders—pops of pain that flared and vanished, unimportant.

Her wrists were pressed together in the small of her back, and something was wound around them. Rope, she thought, until she sensed its stickiness pulling at the soft down of her arms. Then she knew it was adhesive tape, thick and strong. Duct tape, probably.

For a moment she was a child again, laughing as her dad mended a sofa cushion with tape. She thought he called it "duck" tape, and the idea of duck tape was funny to her. She was five years old.

It was long before the boogeyman had come into her life, long before she had learned to be afraid.

The boogeyman—why think of him now? There seemed to be some relevance to the thought, some connection she could not grasp between the leather hands binding her wrists and the skinny, shadowy figure that had groped for her in the crawl space.

Her wrists were immobilized now. They twisted helplessly behind her back.

"No use, C. J.," his voice breathed.

Whose voice? She ought to know it. She had recognized it before.

Next the leather hands moved to her ankles, applying tape to the bare skin above her sneakers.

He's got me trussed like a turkey, she thought.

First ducks, now turkeys. Her mind was filled with birds. She liked birds, except for the mockingbirds that lived in the trees outside her bedroom window and kept her awake at night with their variety of songs.

Birds . . . She wondered if she could fly out of her body and be a bird in the sky, or a birdlike spirit, a thing no tape could bind, no leather hands could hold.

"This is the way I always wanted you," he whispered. "Did you know that? Did you ever suspect?"

She didn't understand, couldn't think straight. He was talking as if he knew her, as if they had a history.

Well, of course they did. He was the boogeyman, wasn't he? The terror of her childhood, come back to haunt her again . . .

His hands were on her mouth now, opening her lips, her jaws. She was in a dentist's chair and he was saying, "Wider, wider." No, she wasn't. She was on the floor in the hallway of her house, and the man with leather gloves was putting something into her mouth. It tasted like rubber. It was spongy yet hard, like a tennis ball—firm but hollow, squeezable. It filled her mouth and cut off her breath.

He's suffocating me, she thought, but then she drew air through her nostrils, and felt her lungs expand. She could breathe. Only her mouth was blocked.

"I got so sick of your yackety-yak," he said. "Should've done this years ago."

Now there was pressure on her cheeks and against the back of her head. The pressure increased as a strap was drawn taut and secured with a buckle or a Velcro fastener.

She knew what this was. She had seen it used on mentally ill arrestees who tried to bite the cops who restrained them. It was called a throttle. In plainer language, a gag.

He's got me bound and gagged, she realized, and those words—*bound and gagged*—registered with her in a way that her previous thoughts had not.

She was helpless. Couldn't fight, couldn't move, couldn't speak. He could do whatever he liked with her. Could kill her in her own house, and she couldn't scream for help.

Fear flashed through her, and she flopped on the floor, arching her back, fighting against the tape and the gag, and trying to see what she was up against, but she couldn't see, there was only darkness.

Open your eyes! she yelled inwardly, and then with a worse shock of fear she understood that they were open and had been open all along.

Blind? Was she blind? Or—

He slapped her. She felt the hard sting of his hand on her cheek.

"Why are you fighting me, you stupid bitch? This is only what you agreed to. You took a vow, remember? I guess it didn't mean anything to you, but it meant something to me. Remember, C. J.?"

She didn't remember. She didn't know who he was or what he was talking about.

"Till death do us part," he whispered. "That's what you swore. *Remember?*"

He was laughing, and the laughter, even more than his words, brought the memories back. The judge, the ceremony, the small handful of guests, the party afterward at a restaurant in Westwood. No honeymoon— they'd both been too busy for that.

Adam.

It was Adam.

His voice, his hands, his body next to hers.

Adam, not the boogeyman. Adam, not a random stranger.

A scream of anguished confusion welled in her throat and tried to force its way past the throttle in her mouth, but only a muffled squeal came out, overridden by his laughter, then silenced by his gloved hand on her face.

"Want another whiff, you bitch?"

The damp cloth, pushed into her face. She refused to inhale.

"Go on, breathe it in, C. J. We've got places to go."

Past his voice, past the hammering of her heart, a new sound.

Her phone was ringing.

For some insane reason she caught herself thinking that calls always came at the most inconvenient times.

23

Tanner and Chang were the first officers on the scene of the 187—California Penal Code parlance for homicide. There were three victims, only one of whom was deceased. The other two lay on the sidewalk, bleeding out, while a pair of paramedics waited at a cautious distance. They wouldn't move in until cops secured the scene.

"Come on, tube these guys. Give 'em plasma or something," Tanner yelled.

While the EMTs did their work, Tanner and Chang cordoned off the dead body with a length of crime-scene ribbon strung from a utility pole to a fire hydrant.

"Another lovely evening in the City of Angels," Chang observed.

Tanner just shook his head. Working this part of town had made him something of an expert in the unending rivalry between the Crips and the Bloods—or more precisely, between the ever-proliferating gang cliques, called "sets," that allied themselves loosely with one gang or another.

This stretch of turf was controlled by a set named the Neighborhood Crips. The three gunshot victims were part of that set, an allegiance they advertised by wearing the Crips' color—blue baseball caps, blue nylon jackets, blue T-shirts underneath. One of them, the dead one, even had blue socks and sneakers.

Tanner knew the dead kid's name, or at least his gang alias—Peep. He wasn't sure how the boy had gotten stuck with that nickname. Now he supposed he would never know.

The other two, the survivors, were unknown to him. Chang thought one guy, who looked like the oldest of the three, might have been a banger called Jarhead, but he wasn't sure. The guy hadn't been carrying any ID, and his face had been messed up so badly that his own mother would have had trouble identifying him.

There were plenty of witnesses, at least. While Chang guarded Peep's body, Tanner got busy interviewing them. Mainly he just needed their names, phone numbers, and addresses; the homicide detectives could follow up. But he asked enough ancillary questions to get the picture.

The three vics had been walking out of a video store with a couple of rented tapes, which turned out, unsurprisingly, to be pornographic movies of no evident socially redeeming value. They were strolling south on Hooper Avenue and had almost reached the corner when the gunshots started. It was a drive-by, but descriptions of the shooters' vehicle varied widely. All anyone could agree on was that it was dark in color.

Multiple rounds were fired at the three teenagers, who went down without returning fire. The shooters flashed gang signs identifying themselves as members of the Shotgun Pirus, a local Blood set. Then their car veered around the corner and disappeared. Somebody called 911, and that was that.

As Chang had said, it was just another evening in LA.

Homicide detectives normally took their time about getting to a crime scene, but tonight the wait wasn't long. It was 6:30 when an unmarked Chevy Caprice wheeled up to the cordon and two plain-clothes officers got out. Tanner knew them. Their names were Hyannis and James, and they worked Homicide out of the East LA Sheriff's Station.

Hyannis was the friendlier of the two, and the better cop, as well. Tanner gave him the rundown on what had happened, which was hardly necessary, since Hyannis's pale olive eyes had seen it all before.

"No tag number on the shooters' vehicle?" the detective asked.

"Not even a definite make and model. One guy thought it might be a jacked-up Monte Carlo, but someone else said an El Camino."

"Okay, Tanner. Thanks for holding down the fort. We can take it from here." Hyannis looked at the body on the sidewalk. "You know this asshole?"

"Yeah. Peep, they called him. I don't know his real name."

"Randall Washington." Hyannis sighed. "I ran him in a few times. Sent him to Kilpatrick once." Camp Kilpatrick was a county juvenile facility in Calabasas. "Know how old he was?"

"No driver's license in his wallet. I'm guessing fifteen."

"Fourteen," Hyannis said.

Tanner looked away. "Shit."

"That's one way to put it." Hyannis shook his head wearily, having long ago resigned himself to the city's ugliness. "Have a nice night."

"Thanks. Hey, Frank?" Distantly it occurred to Tanner that he had never used the detective's first name before.

Hyannis turned. "Yeah?"

"Got a question for you. Out of left field, kind of. It's got nothing to do with this."

"Okay."

"You ever hear of anything called the Four-H Club? I mean, not the actual club, but . . ." Tanner let his words trail off. He could see from Hyannis's face that the man had heard of it, and what he'd heard, he didn't like.

"Walk with me," Hyannis said. Without waiting for a reply, he stepped away from the cordon, putting distance between himself and the small crowd of spectators.

Hyannis stopped near Tanner's squad car. The light bar threw flashes of red and blue on the detective's gaunt face.

"Where'd you pick up that expression?" Hyannis asked.

"Friend of mine."

"Another cop?"

"Well, yeah. Not Sheriff's. LAPD."

"Your friend is in trouble," Hyannis said. "He's not supposed to be mouthing off about that. We're trying to keep it contained within the task force. Tell him to shut the hell up."

"It's not a him, and she wasn't mouthing off about any task force. She got an e-mail."

"What?"

"She got an e-mail message that said something

like, 'Welcome to the Four-H Club.' She thought it was weird—"

"Oh, Jesus Christ. She on duty now?"

"No, she's home, I think—"

"You know her home number?"

"Sure, I called her twenty minutes ago."

"Call her again. Right now. Tell her to wait in her home. Don't let her go outside. Then call *him*."

Hyannis thrust a business card into Tanner's hand. In the pulsing light Tanner read "MORRIS WALSH, DETECTIVE III, LOS ANGELES POLICE DEPARTMENT." Below it was a phone number with a Parker Center prefix.

"Tell Walsh what you told me," Hyannis said. "But call the woman first. Go on, do it."

"All right, but what's going on, anyway?"

"Maybe nothing—a prank. I hope so. Call."

Tanner had a cell phone in his car. He was digging it out of the glove compartment when Chang asked him what Hyannis was so worked up about.

"The Four-H Club," Tanner said. "Mean anything sinister to you?"

"Nope."

"Me neither. But I have a feeling it should."

He dialed C. J. Osborn's number, praying she was home.

24

Adam stopped fighting her when the phone rang. C. J. felt him stiffen, listening. For a moment the chloroform-soaked rag was taken away from her face, and she could breathe again without inhaling the soporific fumes.

On the fourth ring, her answering machine in the living room picked up. She heard her voice come over the speaker, saying, "Hi, this is C. J. I'm either out somewhere or soaking in the tub. Leave a message and make my day."

The cheery voice seemed unreal to her, like the voice of a ghost—her own ghost.

Or am *I* the ghost? she wondered blearily.

A beep, followed by Rick Tanner's baritone, urgent and breathless. "C. J.? If you're there, pick up. This is important. You may be in danger. No joke. I talked to a detective—"

"Shit," Adam hissed, springing to his feet and pulling C. J. upright. "Come on."

Her ankles were taped together. She couldn't walk, couldn't see. But now she knew she hadn't been blinded, only blindfolded with more of that damn duct tape. A strip of the stuff had been plastered across her eyes, the adhesive snagging her eyebrows and eyelashes. To blink was painful; she felt her lashes being plucked by the tape each time they pulled free.

Adam hauled her forward, while with one hand he fumbled at the clasp securing the mouth throttle. He pulled the gag away, and she could talk again.

"What the hell . . . ?" she gasped. Her mind was still blurry and slow. "Adam, what the hell . . . ?" It was all she could think of to say.

"You have to talk to him, tell him everything's okay." On the answering machine Tanner's voice continued, saying something about the e-mail message she'd received. "He's a cop, isn't he?"

She didn't respond, not out of stubbornness but simply because she couldn't get her brain to work.

Adam shook her. *"Isn't he?"*

"Yes," she managed to say.

"Damn it. I don't want him coming over. Not this soon. You tell him you're all right. Whatever he's worried about, it's a false alarm."

Tanner's voice was close now. Adam must have hustled her to the end table beside her sofa, where the phone and the answering machine rested. He knew where the phone was, of course. This had been his house too.

"You try anything clever," Adam said, "and I'll kill you right now, C. J., I fucking swear I will."

Her head cleared a little. "What are you gonna do, chloroform me to death?"

A press of cold metal against her chin. "This is what I'll do."

It was the muzzle of a gun.

For a moment she was back in Ramon Sanchez's converted garage, facing his ancient revolver. But this gun wasn't ancient. She knew it wasn't, though she couldn't see it. Adam would never buy anything cheap and old. He liked shiny new things. He paid top dollar. And he kept his toys in good working order—she smelled lubricant on the gun barrel and knew it had been recently oiled.

"Now I'm going to pick up the phone," Adam said, "and you'll talk to this asshole. I'll hear every word the two of you say. Got it?"

"Got it," she whispered.

Tanner was saying that he and his partner would be right over, and then his voice was cut off as Adam lifted the telephone handset from its cradle. An instant later C. J. felt it at the side of her face, the handset tilted so Adam could listen in.

"C. J.?" Tanner was saying. "Did you pick up? Are you there?"

"I'm here, Rick." She was surprised at how normal she sounded. "I'm, uh, I'm glad you called."

"Did you hear any of what I just said?"

"Not really. I was in the, um, the other room. Sorry."

"It's about that e-mail message—"

"E-mail?"

"The message you got. The Four-H Club."

"Oh. Right. The e-mail."

"Are you okay?"

"Fine. I'm fine. Look, I feel kind of, you know, silly about that whole thing. I mean, I don't know why some stupid message would, um, would get me all worked up—"

"I don't know why it would get Detective Hyannis worked up either, but it did." Tanner's voice crackled over the receiver, taut with tension. "He turned a lighter shade of pale when I told him about it. In-

sisted I call you ASAP. Then I'm supposed to call a
Detective Walsh, who works Robbery-Homicide in
Metro. Name mean anything to you?"

"Uh, not really. I mean, well, he's a D-three. Handles all the hottest cases." C. J. felt the handgun's
muzzle press harder against her skin. She forced a
laugh and hoped it didn't sound hysterical. "Sounds
like Detective Hyannis picked up on my paranoia.
Maybe it's contagious."

"I don't think so. Hyannis isn't the type to over-
react. If he says there's a problem, I'm inclined to
believe him. You planning on going out tonight?"

Adam whispered in her ear, "Say yes."

"Well, yes, actually, I am."

"Might be better if you stayed put. My partner and
I will come over."

"I'm way out of your jurisdiction."

"Don't worry about it. Just give me your address."

Adam's voice again, so low and close it might have
come from inside her own head: "Tell him you have
to go to the junior high."

She had forgotten all about that. "You know, I
really can't hang around. I've got this, you know,
community-service program to go to. I help run it
every Wednesday night. I need to be there." She
was babbling.

"This is more important," Tanner said impatiently.

"What is? An e-mail message? You haven't told
me anything."

"That's because I don't know anything. But Hyannis gave off some bad vibes. I think you'd better
stay in your home and arm yourself."

"No," Adam breathed.

"Sorry, Rick. I can't do it. Those kids are counting
on me. Look, I'll be fine, okay?"

"We're coming over. We'll be there in ten minutes—"

"I'll be gone by then."

"Damn it, C. J., this isn't some game. You could be in real trouble."

Tell me about it, she thought. "I'll be fine, Rick. Don't worry about me. Go out, fight crime. We'll talk tomorrow."

"C. J.—"

"Tomorrow. Sorry. Gotta run."

She heard Adam hang up the phone.

"You did good, C. J.," he said. "You're a pro."

"He may come anyway."

"Yeah, I know. He sounds like a stubborn bastard."

"He's worried about me. I guess he's right to be." She remembered Tanner's mention of Morris Walsh, no lightweight in the department. "Why would Detective Walsh be involved in this?"

"How should I know?"

"He's a big wheel at Metro. Doesn't get mixed up in anything less serious than . . ."

"Than what?" Adam's voice was subtly mocking.

"Multiple homicide," she whispered.

"Well, what do you know?"

"What exactly are you going to do with me?"

"Get you out of here, for starters. And then—well, let's just say I've got quite an evening planned."

"Adam, this doesn't make sense . . ."

"It makes perfect sense."

"Not to me."

"You never did understand me, C. J. If you had, you wouldn't have messed up my fucking life the way you did. You would have known you couldn't get away with it."

She wanted to reply in astonished indignation, *I messed up your life?*

He was the one who'd been unfaithful. He was the one who'd ruined their marriage. And she would have told him so, except the chloroformed rag was in her face again, another dose to put her under once more.

She struggled to break away. Adam held her.

"Can't hold your breath forever, C. J."

He was right. She felt her lungs crying out for oxygen, and finally she yielded, inhaling the dizzying fumes, and then it all fell away—her body and Adam's hands and the fear and everything—all gone, and she was gone too.

25

Walsh had remained at Parker Center after the meeting ended, reviewing the facts about the latest victim with Donna Cellini. Of all the task-force members, Cellini was the one he liked best. Some old cops like himself complained about the rising number of women in the department, but Walsh thought the gals were usually sharper than the men, and they had some extra quality—intuition or something—that sometimes afforded them insights the men overlooked. Besides, Martha Eversol and Nikki Carter had been young Caucasian females, so who better than another young Caucasian female to understand them?

Cellini was talking about Martha's refrigerator and what its contents implied about her lifestyle when the phone on Walsh's desk started to ring.

A sick feeling twisted his gut, and he thought, This is it.

He crossed the room and picked up the phone, praying not to hear news of a third abduction. His mouth was dry. "Walsh," he rasped into the mouthpiece.

"Detective Morris Walsh, Robbery-Homicide?" asked a man's voice—a middle-aged man like him.

"Speaking."

"Detective, this is FBI Special Agent Noah Rawls in Baltimore. I'm informed that you head up the task force for a serial murderer known as the Hourglass Killer?"

Walsh blinked. "That's right."

"My partner and I work the computer crime squad. We've come across something that's relevant to your case."

It occurred to Walsh that it must be ten o'clock in Baltimore. Whatever the two feds were up to, they were working overtime. "I'm listening," he said.

"We received an anonymous e-mail message tipping us off to a Web site. I'd like to direct you to the following URL—"

"The following what?" Walsh knew nothing about computers.

"To the Web site address. Can you do that?"

There was a hint of condescension in Rawls's voice that irritated Walsh. "I can manage," he said, gesturing to Cellini. "Just give me a minute."

Muffling the phone, he told Cellini to get on-line and go to a Web address he would dictate to her. Cellini, unlike him, knew all about high-tech gear. She had the Web browser up and running in a few seconds.

"Okay," Walsh said, "give me the address."

Rawls recited the *www* prefix and a short string of dirty words referring to the most interesting part of the female anatomy. Walsh repeated the words. For once he wished Cellini were a man. He felt like some dirty old coot talking to a woman this way.

Cellini entered the address. Rawls talked Walsh through the procedure necessary to log on to the site, and Cellini executed the user name and password entries.

"It's a porn site," Walsh muttered when the home page came up.

"Yes, sir," Rawls said, "but it's more than that. Click on the link that reads *Do you like to watch?*"

Walsh tapped a stubby finger at the link, and Cellini clicked it. The page that appeared was empty except for the dim, static image of a bedroom.

"What are we looking at?" Walsh asked.

"Live video feed of a woman's bedroom. The lights are off, but the Webcam's lens is sensitive enough to produce a readable image even in darkness."

"Whose bedroom is it?"

"We don't know. But we have still images of the woman—and of two other women whose bedrooms were similarly wired over the past three months."

"Two others?"

"Yes, sir. The first two victims of the Hourglass Killer."

Walsh caught his breath. "You're sure?"

"Absolutely. I read the memos and bulletins as they came in, so I was aware of the case. But to be certain, I went on-line and matched the photos to images of the victims from the FBI database. They're Nikki Carter and Martha Eversol."

"Christ. You said the tip-off message was anonymous?"

"Yes. Scrubbed, so we can't trace it. Probably a visitor to the site got suspicious and decided to let us know."

"Why you in particular?"

"The Web site's server is in Baltimore. But the camera must be in LA."

"Christ." Walsh took another look at the image on the computer. "Wait. You're saying this bedroom belongs to a *third* woman?"

Cellini was staring at him. Having heard only his end of the dialogue, she had no idea what the excitement was about.

"Right," Rawls said. "We have images of her but no name or address. She was in the bedroom earlier tonight."

"Damn. She's the next one. The next victim. This son of a bitch has been putting them on the Net before he kills them."

"That's the same conclusion we've reached," Rawls said. "He strikes on the last day of the month, I understand."

"Yeah." Walsh licked his lips. "He'll try to take her tonight. Agent Rawls, we've got to identify this woman immediately."

"I understand, Detective, but it may not be possible."

"You can't trace the video feed?"

"Unfortunately, no. It's being sent through a proxy."

Walsh didn't know what this meant, but he let it slide. "All right, look. Can you send me the images you've got? Of all three women, but especially the latest one?"

"I'll e-mail them to you. Just give me your address."

"Actually, I, uh . . ." Walsh was feeling more and more like a dinosaur as this conversation continued. "I don't have an e-mail account, but hold on." He asked Cellini for her e-mail address and recited it to Rawls. "Send the pics there."

"We're doing it now."

"Should we, uh, get off-line so the computer's not busy? You know, so the message can get through?"

Walsh thought he heard Rawls chuckle. "You're not really an Information Age type of guy, are you, Detective?"

"How'd you guess?" Walsh said sourly.

"The message will go through whether you're on-line or not. Let me give you my cell-phone number." He recited a number with a Baltimore area code, and Walsh scribbled it on his desk blotter. "Once you've received the images, call me back and we'll discuss our options."

"Right. Thanks, Agent Rawls. This is a break. This is our *only* break."

Walsh hung up, then briefed Cellini on the news. "You think this is legit?" she asked.

"We'll know when we see the pictures."

Cellini logged on to her e-mail account and found a message from Rawls. She opened the attached files and tiled them across the screen. Nikki Carter, Martha Eversol, and a third woman stared at them.

"It's him," Walsh said. "It's our guy."

"No doubt. Victims one and two."

Walsh tapped the last picture. "And three. Unless we find her right away."

"Any ideas?" Cellini asked.

"We print out her picture, photocopy it, distribute it throughout the divisions. Maybe we'll get lucky and someone will know her."

"What if we put her on TV?" Cellini was already sending the image to the printer, which went to work churning out pages. "Get her picture on KTLA, KCAL, KTTV, and KCOP at ten o'clock, follow up with the eleven p.m. broadcasts on channels Two, Four, and Seven. If enough people see it, someone will recognize her. She may even watch the news herself."

"Could work," Walsh said slowly. He was think-ing of the panic that would ensue if people knew that a serial killer was not only stalking his victims but putting them on public display over the Internet. "Or we could try to track her down ourselves. Is there anything in her bedroom that might give us a clue to where she lives?"

Cellini guided the Web browser back to the video feed. "Nothing I can see. No windows, so we can't look at any outdoor landmarks. No indication of whether it's an apartment or a house."

Walsh saw an unmade bed. Beyond it, the door to a bathroom. That was all.

"Could be anyplace," he muttered.

"God, this is sick. Guys have been watching this woman. She's been on the Web all month."

"Looks that way."

"Her bedroom on public display." Cellini shivered.

"He exhibits them before an audience and then moves in for the kill."

"Some of the visitors to the site must have recog-nized the victims once the reports showed up in the papers."

"At least one of them did. That's how the FBI guys got on to this. An anonymous tip-off, presumably from a visitor who caught on."

Cellini looked away. "Well, thank God for that much anyway. It may have saved this one's life."

Walsh wasn't prepared to be so optimistic. "Only if we get to her before *he* does."

He had rarely felt so frustrated—to have the next victim almost within reach and to be unable to pro-tect her, warn her, even know her name.

26

"Still busy," Chang said, clicking off the cell phone.

"Don't worry about it." Tanner spun the steering wheel, guiding the cruiser north on La Brea Avenue. "We'll call him later."

After talking to C. J., Tanner had instructed Chang to dial the number on Detective Walsh's card. Walsh's line had been tied up for the past few minutes, while the squad car sped from the Harbor Freeway to the Santa Monica Freeway, and now along the surface streets of the mid-Wilshire district.

"How far is it now?" Chang asked.

"Another six blocks. We're almost there."

"I thought she told you she wouldn't be home."

"Maybe I can catch her on her way out."

"But why? What's the emergency?"

"I don't know. It's just . . . She sounded funny."

Chang frowned. "What do you mean, funny?"

"Not herself. Just . . . off. You know?"

"Could be your imagination, man."

"I don't have that much imagination."

Chang considered this, then nodded soberly. "That's true."

"I'm just worried, is all."

"Because she sounded funny."

"It's a feeling I've got."

"A feeling that originates in the general vicinity of your crotch. You're hung up on this girl, Rick. You're reading too much into every little thing."

"Maybe. But Hyannis isn't hung up on her, and he was worried too. Anyway, we're almost there. In fact"—another spin of the wheel—"here's her street. Look for number eight-twenty-four."

Tanner slowed the squad car as Chang studied the rows of Craftsman-style bungalows drifting past on the right.

"That one." He pointed.

Tanner pulled into the driveway in front of the detached garage. He and his partner got out.

"See if her car's there," Tanner said in a low voice.

Chang approached the garage and shone his flashlight through a side window, then returned to Tanner's side. "White Dodge Neon."

"That's her vehicle." Tanner had seen it in Newton Station's parking lot. "She must still be home. Come on."

He and Chang circled around to the front door. Tanner rang the bell, then rapped hard. "C. J.? You in there? It's Rick Tanner."

No answer.

"C. J.? Hey, C. J.?"

Still nothing. Tanner and Chang exchanged a glance.

"It's the police," Tanner added for the benefit of anyone else who might be inside. He tested the door. Locked.

"Now what, boss?" Chang inquired. He called Tanner *boss* only when he was feeling a little stressed.

"We go in," Tanner said calmly, unholstering his 9mm.

"We've got no jurisdiction here."

"Screw jurisdiction."

"We've got no grounds to enter."

"We have exigent circumstances."

"Like hell we do. She told you she was going out."

"Her car's still here."

"Maybe somebody picked her up."

"Or maybe she's in trouble. You didn't see Hyannis's face when I mentioned the Four-H Club."

"We can't go busting in there. It could cost us big-time."

Tanner hesitated. He needed Chang with him if he was going to search the house. On SWAT call-ups Tanner was the team leader and Chang was the scout.

"How about a compromise?" Tanner said. "We check out the doors and windows, look for signs of intrusion."

Chang drew his service pistol. "What the hell? I never figured on making pension anyway."

Together they moved around the house, labeling the different sides SWAT-style—side one for the front, side two for the wall facing the garage.

On side three, the rear of the bungalow, they found the back door standing open.

"Still no exigent circumstances?" Tanner asked.

Chang merely frowned.

They kept their distance from the open door. There was only dim light beyond.

"Stealth entry," Tanner whispered. "I'm gonna slice the pie. If it's clear, we roll out."

He moved past the doorway in a wide arc, focusing on each section of the interior hallway as it came into view. By the time he had passed from the right side of the doorway to the left, he had scanned as much of the interior as it was possible to see.

There was no suspect in sight, but the hall was dark, illuminated only by the glow from the front of the house and by faint ambient light from outside.

Tanner hugged the left doorframe while Chang took up position on the right. Chang looked for the "clear" sign. Tanner gave him a thumbs-up.

On a silent count of three, they entered the hall, Tanner first, Chang directly behind him. Tanner crossed instantly to the opposite side of the corridor, the last safely cleared position, and put his back against the wall. Chang joined him shoulder to shoulder a moment later.

Hallways were dangerous. Slots, they were called in tactical training maneuvers. An officer didn't want to get caught in a slot, without cover or concealment.

Three doors lined the hall. Three rooms, any of which could be unfriendly.

Tanner pointed to the nearest room, the door ajar. Then he sliced the pie again, his quick footsteps tracing an arc before the doorway as he scanned the interior.

Bedroom. Mirror on the far wall. No movement reflected in the glass.

When Tanner had positioned himself to the right of the door, Chang moved to the left side.

They had gone into a hundred empty rooms and had survived every time.

Tanner hoped their luck would hold on the hundred and first.

27

"Maybe we could go at this from the other direction," Cellini said as Walsh paced the squad room. "Whoever's doing this has to be a computer guy, right? We can check the billing records of the two previous vics and see if they had a computer repairman come to their home."

Walsh looked at her. "Do they do that? Make house calls?"

"It's called on-site service. You can sign up for it when you buy the computer."

"Could we have missed something like that? The same repairman visits the two women and we don't flag it?"

Cellini glanced away. "I'd like to say no, but we weren't focused on their residences. Neither victim was snatched from home."

"But SID would have found cameras if they were planted in the bedrooms."

"Not if the killer removed the gear first. We have to figure he went in, either before or after the abductions, and took the cameras and whatever else he installed."

"Okay, we'll review all repairs and maintenance

work in the victims' homes for at least two months prior to their abduction. And not just computer repair. For all we know, this guy could be a goddamned plumber who's picked up some high-tech smarts—hey. What the hell's that?"

Walsh was looking at the computer, where the grainy video feed of the unknown woman's bedroom was suddenly shivering with movement.

Cellini spun her chair around. Walsh leaned over her shoulder.

Dim, indistinct shapes played across the screen.

"Someone's in there," Cellini whispered. "The killer maybe."

"If so," Walsh said, "there's more than one."

Tanner was primary through the bedroom door. Just across the threshold, he and Chang came together, back to back, and surveyed the darkness, then advanced with shoulders touching, pistols lowered in the search position.

They checked out the blind spot behind the bed and the dangerous unknown of the walk-in closet, then the bathroom with its stall shower.

Nothing.

"Clear," Tanner breathed.

He flicked on his flashlight to be sure.

The video image flared briefly as a bright light came on inside the room. Then the camera lens adjusted to the new conditions, and the two figures in the bedroom were clearly visible.

"Cops," Cellini said.

Walsh nodded. "Sheriff's deputies."

"Hold on." Cellini leaned close to the screen, her nose nearly touching the glass, and stared at the officer whose flashlight had lit up the room. "I know him."

"Who is he?"

"Let me think. Works out of East LA. Met him at a couple of crime scenes. Kind of a jerk. Thinks he's God's gift. Name is Donner . . . no, Danner . . . Tanner, that's him. Deputy Tanner."

Walsh grabbed a phone from the nearest desk and dialed the Sheriff's Department.

The bedroom was clean, but the rest of the house remained unknown territory.

Tanner switched off his flash, and then it was back into the slot, down the hallway, hugging one wall to minimize exposure in the kill zone.

His gaze was focused far ahead, and he missed the object Chang indicated with a snap of his fingers.

On the floor lay a kitchen knife, dropped by someone in the hall.

There had been a struggle here.

Tanner had been trained to take nothing for granted, and he stuck with his training now. He and Chang methodically explored the rest of the house, using covert entry techniques for every room and closet and corner.

But it was a waste of time. Tanner knew it with a sick certainty deep in his gut.

C. J. was gone.

When the house had been thoroughly cleared, he dialed up the volume on his radio and heard the dispatcher repeating his call number with a note of urgency. He answered.

"Someone's waiting for you on tac one," the dispatcher said, meaning tactical frequency one, a radio channel used for semiprivate conversations.

"Who?"

"Detective Morris Walsh, LAPD."

Tanner traded a glance with Chang. "I'll meet him on tac one."

He switched over to the specified frequency and heard a gruff voice demanding, "Deputy Tanner, are you there?"

"Yes, sir."

"Give me your exact location."

"Sir?"

"Do it!"

Tanner recited the street address.

"That's well within city limits, Deputy. What are you doing there?"

"I was concerned for the safety of a, uh, friend."

"So you broke into her house and searched her bedroom?"

Tanner blinked. "How the hell . . . ?" He remembered courtesy. "I mean, what makes you think we're inside the house?"

"Because I saw you and your partner. You're on the Internet."

"We're what?"

"I'll explain later. I assume you didn't find the lady?"

"No, but the rear door was open, and there was a kitchen knife discarded on the hall floor."

Silence for a moment, and then Walsh said in a softer voice, "You think there was an abduction?"

"Yes, sir."

A sigh fluttered over the cheap speaker. "So do I. Goddamn it, I knew we'd be too late."

"Sir, can I ask—"

"Not until I get there. I'll be at your location in ten minutes. Meantime, don't touch anything. One more thing, Deputy. What's the woman's name?"

"C. J. Osborn. You know her?"

"Why in Christ's name should I know her?"

"Because she's one of yours, Detective. She's LAPD. She works patrol out of Newton."

Another silence, longer this time.

"No, Deputy," Walsh said, "I don't think I've met her. I hope I get the chance."

28

This time there was no confusion. C. J. swam out of unconsciousness into waking reality, and instantly she remembered the surprise attack in the hallway, the phone call from Tanner, and above all Adam's voice.

She was still blindfolded, and he had gagged her again with the rubber throttle. He had propped her in a sitting position, her back against something hard and straight. A wall? No, a post.

The floor was stiff and cold. Concrete. Not part of her bungalow. Not Adam's condo. Someplace else.

She had been relocated while she slept. She might be anywhere now. A basement, maybe. No, she felt cold air—fresh air, outdoors air—moving across her face. There must be windows or other openings. She listened for sounds of traffic from outside, music, jet planes, but heard nothing.

Carefully, afraid to move too much and betray the fact that she was awake, she tested her wrists and found that they were still bound behind her back. Her ankles too—taped together, her legs curled under her. Her head had slumped forward while unconscious, and she did not raise it, not yet.

She wondered why she had not fallen prone on the floor. When she drew in a deep abdominal breath, swelling her belly, she had her answer. A cord had been tied around her waist, securing her to the post.

Footsteps on the concrete floor.

He was close, perhaps six feet away. Moving toward her, then away.

She prayed he didn't know she had revived. Every minute that she maintained the pretense of unconsciousness was a reprieve from whatever fate he had in mind for her.

Not that there was much mystery about it. He'd told her himself, hadn't he?

Till death do us part.

The footsteps continued circling, now joined by a new sound, hard and regular. It took her a moment to understand that what she heard was the beat of her heart in her ears.

The sound of her own pulse frightened her. Each beat was like the tick of a clock, announcing that her time was limited and fast running out. She almost wished he would just go ahead and do it—whatever it was he meant to do—do it and get it over with and spare her the ordeal of waiting.

But that thought flared and died, replaced by another. She had not lived long enough. She had not done enough.

What did she have to show for her life? A bungalow with a mortgage, a uniform in a locker? Not much for twenty-six years on this earth.

And now he would take even that away from her. But why? How was it even possible? The man she'd married was capable of lying, cheating on her, but he couldn't do something like this, something insane . . .

Involuntarily a groan escaped her, so low and muffled that she wasn't sure Adam heard.

But he did. His circling footsteps stopped abruptly.

She froze, hating herself for the weakness that had voiced itself in that groan. She had shortened her remaining time, and she couldn't afford to lose any of it, not when every minute was precious now.

He came toward her. She heard the sharp claps of his footfalls on the concrete. He was wearing hard-soled shoes—his dress shoes from work? No, he wouldn't be that stupid. He would know that shoe prints could be identified by forensics experts. He would not make such an obvious mistake.

A stir of air, and she sensed that he was kneeling by her. Rustle of clothing, caress of leather on her cheek.

His gloved hand. Touching her.

She struggled not to react. He did not necessarily know she was awake. People groaned in their sleep, after all. As long as she stayed absolutely still, he might not be sure if she remained unconscious or was merely playing possum.

It was all about buying time, more time. Time seemed suddenly the most important thing in the world, or maybe it always had been, and these circumstances were required to bring home this truth that she always should have known.

His gloved finger slipped under her chin and stroked her. Tickled her.

"Hey, C. J. Wake up, sleepyhead."

Words he used to say to her on lazy weekend mornings. Then as now, he had tickled her gently. Then as now, he had eased his hand under her chin, fingering the sensitive hollow of her jaw . . .

Abruptly his grip tightened. His hand clutched her throat.

She jerked her head back with a gasp.

He withdrew.

"Thought that would get your attention," he said.

No purpose was served in pretending to be unconscious any longer. She tried to pose a question to him: "Where am I?" The hollow rubber ball clamped between her teeth distorted her words and made them almost unintelligible. She tried again. "Where . . . am . . . I?"

"I heard you the first time, C. J. Where are you? You're in the same place you put me for the last year. You're in hell."

29

Walsh called the other members of the task force on his cell phone while Cellini drove him from Parker Center to the Wilshire Division address. If they had been TV cops, they would have used a dashboard flasher to clear away the traffic, but in reality few unmarked cars carried one. Cellini made good time anyway, guiding the Caprice west on freeways and surface streets. Walsh, in the passenger seat, filled in Stark, Merriwether, Boyle, and Lopez with the bare details.

"Sounds like the real thing," Ed Lopez said, his voice crackly and faint on the cell phone's cheap receiver.

"It is," Walsh affirmed. "And the worst part is, this woman he's got—she's one of our own."

Walsh finished the last call, leaving a message on Len Sotheby's answering machine, just as Cellini pulled into the driveway of C. J. Osborn's bungalow. He was glad to be done with the calls. Ordinarily he would have used a landline to convey sensitive information, but tonight there wasn't time. He had to hope these digital phones were as resistant to eavesdropping as the manufacturers claimed.

Tanner and his partner, whose nameplate read "CHANG," were waiting at the back door. The two deputies led Walsh and Cellini inside the house, pointing out the knife that lay untouched on the hall floor.

"What's this about you seeing us on the Internet?" Tanner asked while Cellini first photographed the knife, then sealed it in an evidence bag.

"There's a camera in her bedroom," Walsh explained. "It's a, uh, whatchamacallit."

"Webcam," Cellini said without looking up.

"Right. Live TV feed from the bedroom to the Internet."

Tanner frowned. "C. J. wouldn't be into anything like that."

"No, but the guy who kidnapped her is."

"So you know who we're dealing with?"

"Not by name—but I've seen his work," Walsh said, thinking of Martha Eversol on the autopsy table.

"Well, whoever he is, he must have been following her. C. J. told me she was tailed earlier today by a white van."

"Make, model?"

"She didn't know."

"Damn. She tell you anything else?"

"She got an e-mail that spooked her. Spooked Detective Hyannis too, when I told him about it."

"What e-mail?"

"It said, 'Welcome to the Four-H Club.'"

Walsh looked at Cellini. "Oh, Jesus," Cellini said.

"That's pretty much the way Hyannis reacted." Tanner was losing patience, which Walsh figured was understandable, especially if C. J. Osborn was his girlfriend or something. "What is all this shit about the Four-H Club anyway?"

"I'll explain later," Walsh said. "Show us the rest of the house."

Tanner and Chang led the two detectives through the living room and into the kitchen. Walsh spent some time looking at the dinner dishes in the sink.

"We'll have to call her husband," Tanner said.

Cellini glanced at him. "She's married?"

"Ex-husband. Adam somebody. He needs to know."

"They still close?" Walsh asked.

"I don't think so, but I saw him with her today."

"He came by the station to see her," Chang added.

"Huh." Cellini pursed her lips. "Under other circumstances he'd be a prime suspect."

"Maybe he is anyway," Walsh said. "Maybe he's our guy."

"And the other women?"

"Diversions. He killed them just to throw us off the trail."

"Weak," Cellini said.

"Very," Walsh conceded. "I need to interview him anyway. His phone number must be in Osborn's file."

"Excuse me," Tanner cut in, "but what other women?"

Walsh patted the deputy's arm, a fatherly gesture rare for him. "She's the third one taken this way. The third one who was spied on over the Web."

"The third?" Then Tanner understood. He took a step backward, as if to put distance between himself and Walsh's reassuring touch. "The Hourglass Killer. You're heading up the task force. And Hyannis—"

"Detective Hyannis is the LASD liaison. You see . . . Hell, Donna, you tell him."

"The two previous victims were both found with

index cards that said 'Welcome to the Four-H Club,' " Cellini said. "We think the term stands for Four-Hour Club and that the victims . . . well, that they're kept alive for exactly four hours."

"How come this four-hour angle hasn't made the papers?" Chang asked. "They're covering the Hourglass Killer like crazy."

"We kept a lid on it," Walsh said. "It almost got into the *LA Times*. They were set to run with it, but we prevailed upon the Metro editor to kill the story. It never ran in print, but somehow it turned up as a rumor on the Internet. Probably some copy editor at the *Times* blabbed in a, uh, what are those things called?"

"Chat room," Cellini suggested.

Walsh shook his head. "God, I hate this Internet stuff."

"But maybe now it can help us," Cellini said. "We may be able to trace the e-mail if it's been saved on her computer."

"Worth a shot," Walsh agreed. "Unless it's like the video feed—sent through a proxy. Can you do that with e-mail?"

"Sure. And probably that's exactly how it was sent. Whatever else you can say about this guy, he's not stupid."

Tanner had been listening to all this with a blank expression. Now he said simply, "Four hours?"

Walsh nodded.

"When I talked to her on the phone, she sounded funny."

"Speaking under duress?"

"Could have been."

"What time was this?"

Tanner looked at Chang, who checked his watch. "Forty-five minutes ago."

"So," Tanner said, "if your theory is right . . ."

"She has three hours and fifteen minutes left," Walsh said.

The room was silent after that.

30

It was hard to talk with the throttle in place, but not impossible. She struggled to force out each word.

"Please, Adam. You don't . . . want to . . . do this."

"If that's what you think," he answered, "then you really don't know me at all."

"*Adam*," she moaned, the gag blurring the word.

No response.

She had to think of something to do. There must be a course of action she could follow, a miraculous way out. She was the good guy in the story, and the good guy didn't die like this, trussed and humiliated and cut off from help.

She had always believed that life, for all its apparent senselessness, had a purpose behind it. But where was the purpose in dying like this? Was everything just a sick joke, and would Adam get the last laugh?

"Why?" she mumbled.

He withdrew a little—she could feel the movement of the air displaced by his body—and she thought he wasn't going to answer. Then he said, "Well, that's the big question, isn't it? I'm not sure I can explain the why. It requires a logical justification that may be lacking in this case."

She waited, knowing he would say more if he chose to.

"Why," he said again, as if testing the word. "That's what journalists are taught to ask. Who, what, why, where, when? But they leave out the most important one. How? That's the real question. If you know how a thing happened, you don't need to know the why. Prove exactly how a man killed his wife—just as an example—and his motivation can be filled in by the jury. They've all seen enough episodes of *Murder, She Wrote*. They'll give you the why. You have to give them the how."

So tell me how, she thought. Tell me anything, Adam, talk to me.

"Of course I'm just a corporate lawyer. Not an expert in this sordid criminal stuff. I may be getting it all wrong. Still it seems to me that if you knew how, then the *why* would present itself to you. Do you want to know the how of it, C. J.? Would that please you, satisfy your restless curiosity?"

She made no response, not even a nod of her head. She knew he would tell her what he wanted her to hear. He enjoyed toying with her. And hearing himself talk had always been one of his chief pleasures.

"Okay, picture this. You dump me, right? You walk out of my life. You say, 'Fuck you,' and you go. Now I'm sure you felt you were justified. I had, after all, been balling Ashley behind your back, but you know what? It wasn't anything you didn't deserve. You're the one who broke our vows, not me. You swore to be there for me, to have and to hold, all that crap. And were you? Were you there for me, C. J.? Were you there for me at night? No, you were riding around in a cop car, cuffing bad guys. Were you there for me on the weekends? No, you had to work extra shifts. Were you ever there? To have and to hold—shit, I would've settled for a little quickie squeezed into your busy schedule. But you didn't have time for that. You were into your own thing. You walked out on me a long time before Ashley came into the picture."

There were so many answers she could give, and none of them would help her. She was almost glad he had gagged her, glad the conversation had to be one-sided. An argument would be worse than pointless now.

"So you catch me with Ashley, and you get all aggrieved, like I'm the one who's done something wrong. Okay, you're gone, and I'm alone. I move into that shit-hole apartment in Venice. You were there. You saw it. Living the high life, right? Ashley leaves me—I think you scared her off when you confronted her on campus. You even had to take that away from me. Nice, C. J. Hell hath no fury, and all that jazz. Well, you got what you wanted. I was alone. Every night. Stuck in that two-by-four apartment with no air-conditioning and next-door neighbors who played Eminem at top volume all night long. It was like being in jail, except in jail I would've had more company."

She realized he expected her to feel sorry for him.

"So I do what a lot of lonely guys do. I start spending too much time on my computer. I surf the Web. I look for women on-line. I try chat rooms, but it's just a lot of garbage. Nobody knows how to have a conversation in those forums. Have you ever tried one? PrettyGirl says, 'What's the weather like where you are?' And Man-at-Work says, 'Overcast, might rain.' And Lilypad says, 'I like the rain.' Blah, blah, blah. And the dirty ones are worse. Maybe some

guys can get their rocks off, looking at a bunch of
sexual fantasies typed on a computer screen, but it
doesn't do squat for me. So that's out. I start looking
for other kinds of relief on-line. Porno, the raunchier
the better. I download some of these pictures, and
let me tell you, C. J., I imagined your face on every
body. If I'd had one of those picture-editing programs, maybe I would have actually put your face
in there. Picture it. C. J. in chains, tickled by a cat-
o'-nine-tails . . ."

She swallowed, hearing not only his words but the
growly ugliness of his voice.

"Yeah, I got into the S-and-M stuff before long.
There's a lot of it on the Web. You can find anything
if you look hard enough and if you've got time. I
had plenty of time. You know there are sites where
they take celebrities' faces and paste them into bondage shots? A lot of supermodels are going under the
knife, and not for a breast implant. They've even got
fucking cartoon characters in bondage. You want to
see Wonder Woman all tied up with nowhere to go?
She's on there somewhere. It's a whole subculture,
every fetish you can think of. And message boards,
chat rooms, instant messaging to go along with all
of it. It's a substitute life for people who don't have
any real life. I guess you'd picture virgins in dorm
rooms doing most of this stuff, and here I was, a
divorced guy, thirty years old, going for a law degree, and I was one of them. Do you know how
humiliating it was for me to be reduced to that level?
I'd never been lonely and desperate in college, not
even in high school, but now I was. You did that to
me, C. J. I couldn't get over you, couldn't get past
what had happened to my life when you kissed me
off. So if you're wondering whose fault it is that

you're here tonight, well, it's your goddamned fault. Think about that. Your fault, C. J., not mine. Keep that in mind while I'm killing you."

Killing you.

There. He had said it outright. He had expressed his final intention, and what was so frightening was that there had been no hesitation in his voice, only cold certainty.

"They say you can't pull off the perfect crime." He was still talking somewhere in the darkness around her. "I'm proving them wrong. I've worked it all out. It's a thing of beauty, really, though I'm not surprised if you fail to appreciate its aesthetic merits."

She had wanted him to explain things, but suddenly his voice was intolerable to her, and she just wished he would shut up.

"The key to any successful deceit is misdirection. Magicians know that. Well, I've found a way to misdirect the police—and the best part is that I didn't have to create some elaborate ruse. I merely had to take advantage of an existing situation."

He was so pleased with himself, and so confident. The confidence scared her most of all. Adam was an intelligent man, and if he felt sure of himself, he had a good reason.

"I told you I was spending hours on-line every night. My life was school and the computer, nothing else. One night I was scrolling through an 'alt.sex' message board, trying to find out about sites I'd overlooked, and I read about a secret site, password-protected. At first it didn't sound like anything special. It had the kind of name all these sites have—you know. Well, no, I guess you don't. You use your computer to buy curiosities at auction sites, don't you? Tame, C. J.,

very tame. The Web has a lot more to offer, if you
know where to look."

She was glad she hadn't known where to look. She
wasn't in the market for what the dark side of the
Web seemed to be selling.

"These sites have names like sexpussy.com or lick-
me.com, anything that's dirty and enticing. This
one—I don't even remember the damn name now. I
bookmarked it so I didn't have to keep typing the
address. Anyway, I was just bored enough to ask for
the password via e-mail. I received it and logged on,
and that site led me to something I never expected
to find, C. J. It led me to you."

There was silence in the room. She sat very still,
trying to understand what he could possibly mean.

"That's right. You, my ex-wife, focus of my obses-
sion. You were there. I could watch you. I could
study you whenever you were home. It was like living with you again. I'd come home from UCLA and
there you were, waiting for me. Sometimes getting
dressed for a night watch, or going out with friends,
or doing reps on your home gym. Never any sex,
though. Guess you knew that anybody after me
would be a disappointment. That was a joke, by the
way. I'm not that vain."

No, she thought, you're just out of your freakin'
mind.

It seemed clear what had happened. After his
hours of living vicariously through the Internet, he
had lost contact with reality. He had imagined seeing
her on the computer, the way schizophrenics imagined that the news anchor on their TV was talking
directly to them. It was the only explanation.

"I watched you, but not only you. There were

other women who'd been featured on the site. I knew that, because there were references to previous contestants. That's what you were, C. J.—a contestant. Well, I wanted to see those other women, but their images had been taken down. I figured I might find them on the server if I could hack into it. Never knew I was a hacker, did you? Well, it's amazing what a little determination can do. I read some stuff on-line about how to enter a site through what they call a back door—never mind the details. It was easy enough. I got in, found the pics, saw the other women. And that's when I realized I'd stumbled onto a bigger secret than a hidden Web site. And I knew what I had to do."

He had lost her completely. She had no idea what he was talking about.

"So I worked it all out, down to the last detail. When it's over, you'll be dead, and even though I ought to be the first guy in the lineup, nobody will ever suspect me. There'll be another suspect, a much more plausible one. He calls himself Bluebeard, by the way. That's another thing I discovered after I got in through the back door and started snooping. Bluebeard's his name—very appropriate—and his password's Fatima, and right now he's about to get nailed for a whole bunch of crimes he committed and for one, just one, that he never got around to. But who'll believe his denials? Who'll listen to him at all? See how beautiful it is, C. J.? Like a fine work of art!"

She wouldn't have answered even if she could. There was nothing beautiful about any of this. There was only the disjointed rambling of a crazed mind.

"From this point on, it's all about timing. In case you're interested, you're going to die at exactly ten forty-five p.m. No earlier, no later. It's seven forty-five now, so you've got three hours to go. I hope you use the time well. Maybe you can think about all the things you could have done to make our marriage work. Maybe you can see for yourself why you're ultimately to blame—"

A shrill cry from across the room cut him off. It took her a moment to recognize it as the ring of a cell phone.

"What the hell?" The interruption had rattled him. She could tell he hadn't been expecting this call.

There were two more rings before he answered.

"Hello? . . . Yes, this is Adam Nolan."

Once again he sounded calm, in control, but now she knew it was an act.

"Yes, Officer, how can I help you? . . . What? Did something happen to her? Was she in an accident?"

Goddamn him. He was a better liar than she'd ever realized.

"We were divorced a year ago," he was saying in a well-modulated tone of dread. "Sure, we keep in touch. I saw her today at the station—she said she had some volunteer work to do tonight . . . Is that it? Did something happen at the junior high?"

So convincing. Every nuance, every choice of words, every stammer and hesitation. She almost believed him herself, just as she had believed he was faithful to her, just as she'd thought he was sincere about wanting to be friends, to go out on Friday for an evening of music and conversation.

He had deceived her completely, and he would deceive the police too.

"If you won't give me the details over the phone, at least tell me if C. J.'s okay . . ."

She could not let him get away with this. She struggled to force a scream past the throttle in her mouth, but the loudest sound she could produce was a strangled moan.

His footsteps eased farther away, putting distance between himself and any noise she made. He kept talking.

"Of course I'll come in. But I wish you could reassure me—all right, all right, I understand."

She couldn't scream. Impotently she kicked her sneakers against the concrete floor. No use. The noise was probably inaudible over the phone, and even if it did get through, it would mean nothing to anyone who heard it.

"Wilshire Community Police Station on Venice Boulevard, just west of San Vicente. Got it. I'll be there as soon as I can."

Another click as the phone was flipped shut. The call was over.

She could hear his quick breathing, a release of tension after his performance. Then a muttered curse. "God*damn* it."

Why was he upset? He must have anticipated that the police would call him. Then she remembered what he'd said at the house when he heard Tanner on the answering machine—"I don't want him coming over. Not this soon."

And a few minutes ago—"It's all about timing."

He'd said she would die at 10:45. "No earlier, no later."

It wasn't the phone call itself that had rattled him. It was the fact that it had come too soon.

As if in confirmation, she heard him whisper, "Fuck," in that petulant tone he always used when he didn't get his way.

If his plan's timing had been disrupted, did that

mean he wouldn't wait three hours for the kill? Would he end things now?

Footsteps. He approached her. She waited, thinking of the gun that had nuzzled her chin. Was the gun in his hand? Was he about to pull the trigger?

She wished the son of a bitch hadn't taped over her eyes.

Then with a chuckle, he said, "Not yet, C. J."

The words ought to have come as a relief, but hearing him address her in that fraudulently affectionate tone only shot another surge of fury through her. She twisted her wrists behind her back.

"Your friends at the LAPD are moving faster than I thought," he went on. "But it doesn't matter. Doesn't matter at all."

She caught the quaver in his voice and knew he was working hard to convince himself that things would still be okay. He hated surprises, hated to improvise. He was a control freak—always had been. A place for everything, everything in its place.

"Anyway, I have to go away for a while and talk to a detective about you. Should be a very interesting conversation. But don't worry. I'll be back. I guarantee it. In the meantime, you just sit tight. Think good thoughts."

He walked off, his footsteps receding. From what seemed like far away he spoke again, his voice raised to cover distance.

"By the way, I lied about not remembering that song. And, darling—I've saved the last dance for you."

PART TWO

A Countryside in Arms

8:00 P.M.–MIDNIGHT
WEDNESDAY

31

Treat paced his bedroom, clenching and unclenching his fists, lifting his hands to run his long fingers through his hair. He almost believed that he was agitated, but he was never agitated. He prided himself on his self-control. The world could not touch him. He had risen above it. He had mastered death and life.

Even so, he could not stop pacing. He traced a series of irregular ellipses over the bedroom carpet.

By now he should have had her. Should have already begun the night's entertainment. And it would have been such a special night, because *she* was special.

Instead she had been removed from his reach, and why? Because the police were on to him.

It was the only explanation for the insane vision that had greeted him when he drove down her street at 6:45, only an hour ago. He had expected to see lights burning in the windows of her bungalow, the yard dark. Perhaps there would be the soft chatter of television voices from inside. That was how it had been on other nights, when he had reconnoitered the house.

Instead he had seen a police car—a Sheriff's Department patrol unit—parked in her driveway. At her front door, two deputies.

He had cruised past without slowing. Whatever was happening, he could not afford to be seen there.

For fifteen minutes he had driven aimlessly, trying to decide what to make of this unwelcome development. Deputies at her house? It made no sense. The mid-Wilshire area was not even under the Sheriff's jurisdiction. There was no reason for any deputies to be there.

Perhaps they were friends stopping by to say hello. If so, they might already have left.

Once this cheering prospect occurred to him, he had returned to her neighborhood for a second look.

This time things had been worse.

The deputies' car was still there, but joining it were three unmarked sedans, obviously official vehicles, and a pair of LAPD squad cars. The bungalow blazed with light. Uniformed and plainclothes cops were visible inside.

Again he had driven past without reducing speed. Then he had headed home.

He had not permitted himself to formulate any opinions until he had more information. Hasty, unwarranted speculation was anathema to him, the bane of methodical reasoning.

Once home, he had switched on his laptop and checked the Web site's video feed. It was still running. The lights in her bedroom were on, and cops wandered in and out. Nobody was looking at the camera or seemed to suspect its existence. That was one good thing, at least.

He owned a police scanner, which he tuned to the frequencies used by the LAPD's Wilshire Division.

He monitored the cross talk as the scanner hopped from band to band.

Finally he turned on his TV and clicked through the channels in search of a news bulletin. He saw nothing but entertainment programs, each more witless than the last.

His gaze had kept returning to the computer screen. Once, he saw an older, rumpled man in a wrinkled suit walk slowly through the bedroom. He knew that man's name. Morris Walsh, head of the task force hunting the Hourglass Killer.

Now what the hell was *he* doing there?

There could be only one answer. The police must have discovered that Caitlin was his next target. He had pressed his luck too far, following her after she left work. She had seen the van—he'd caught her looking at him outside the Korean market. No doubt she'd reported the incident to her fellow cops. Somehow a white van had been linked to one or more of the previous Hourglass Killer slayings—perhaps somebody had spotted it near one of the abduction sites or the dump sites of the bodies. Walsh had moved Caitlin to a safe house and was now inspecting her home for clues. Nor had they discovered the Web site itself. If they had, they surely would have taken it down by now.

What to do, what to do?

He didn't know, and he hated not knowing.

Uncertainty was rare for him. Ambiguity was not a daily feature of his life. He felt lost, and this was a feeling both new and disagreeable.

He stopped in the middle of his bedroom, worn out by worry. For a few moments he just stood there. The TV flickered in a corner; the computer, resting in its docking station, displayed the video feed; the scanner hissed and crackled with snippets of radio code.

Treat ignored it. He looked at himself in the mirror over the bureau, a tall man with thinning hair and sharp features and a spindly, angular body. For a moment he saw the teenager he had been, the lonely, remote, pale thirteen-year-old dubbed Spider-Man by his peers—not from any similarity to the comic-book crime-fighter, but because he had reminded them of a spider with his double-jointed appendages branching out in weird directions.

He hadn't minded the name. He liked spiders. He admired their patience, their craft, and their cold ruthlessness. Even as a child, he had known that these were the special qualities he wished to nurture in himself. He had taken to raising spiders in the cellar. His parents hadn't objected. They had heard that it was advisable to encourage a gifted boy in his hobbies and interests. Besides, they were afraid of their son.

He had learned much from spiders, so much that he supposed he had become something of a spider himself. Certainly he was a creature who spun elaborate webs and even lived, in a sense, on the great Web of the Internet.

But now he felt entangled in a web not of his own making—and he didn't like the feeling, didn't like it at all.

Perhaps he should flee. He had done it before, in other circumstances, when he had begun to feel that his luck had run its course.

Oh, but he hated to leave when Caitlin's fate was still unknown. When there was still a chance he might have her.

Besides, he was safe in his apartment. His shock

troops would protect him against all intruders. In the event that the barbarians stormed his castle, he could count on holding them off long enough to flee.

He decided to risk staying a little longer. Had the victim been anyone else, he would have yielded to prudence and made his escape. But Caitlin was indeed special.

He had wanted her for so long.

32

Walsh was in C. J. Osborn's living room, conferring with members of the Scientific Investigation Division, when his cell phone buzzed.

"Detective, it's Noah Rawls in Baltimore. I see your men have found the house."

Walsh almost asked how Rawls could know this, but the answer was obvious. He was still monitoring the video feed.

"We're here, all right," Walsh said, "trying to figure out our next move."

"Maybe I can be of help."

"I hope so."

"Have you tried looking for the Webcam accessories he installed?"

"What accessories?" Walsh covered one ear to muffle the noise of conversation and police radios crackling everywhere. "And remember, you're talking to a computer illiterate."

"Then I'll keep it simple. We already know he's been shooting real-time video of this woman in her bedroom. But it's not enough just to record the images. He has to get them onto the Web."

"Right," Walsh said, following so far.

"The camera presumably is equipped with a transmitter that sends the signal to a receiver. Since the transmitter's range is probably quite limited, the receiver must be hidden either inside the house or near it."

"So we look for a receiver? Like a TV set?"

"No, Detective, a computer. Most likely a portable computer, one with the necessary hardware and software to pick up a TV signal and convert it to digital form."

"How is this computer connected to the Web?"

"Via a phone line, probably—although he could be using a wireless modem. Either way, he's sending the video feed from the computer to the proxy server on the Web, which then sends it to the Web server here in Maryland."

"Okay, we look for a computer, right? A laptop model?"

"That's correct."

"And it could be in the house or nearby?"

"Yes."

"I'm betting it's someplace on the grounds. It would be easier for him to obtain access to the yard than to the house."

"But he had to be inside the house to plant the Webcam."

"I'm going on the assumption that he obtained access to the place on some pretext. Repairman, say. He planted the camera while the victim wasn't looking. Installing this other gear would have required a separate visit."

"Possibly," Rawls conceded. "If that's so, where would he hide it?"

"Could be in the garden. Or along the fence. Or in the garage."

"Is there a light in the garage?"

"I think so, yeah."

"Then that's your best bet."

"Mind telling me why?"

"Because a light means electrical wiring—and he would want to wire the computer into the main current. Laptop batteries don't last very long."

"Good point. We'll check the garage first. Can you stay on the line?"

"I'm not going anywhere."

"Great. Hold on."

Walsh pulled Cellini away from a conversation with Boyle and said he required her assistance in a search.

Together they crossed the yard. Beyond the picket fence, clusters of neighbors and other spectators stood watching, their faces garish in the flickering glare of the patrol cars' light bars. What they didn't know was that Detective Lopez, inside the house, was taking their photos with a long-lens camera. There was an outside chance the killer was among the gawkers at the scene.

"Should've thought of that myself," Cellini said when Walsh summarized Rawls's suggestion. "Thing is, I can't figure out why he would leave *any* of his equipment in place."

"Maybe he planned to return later and retrieve it."

"Too big a risk of the evidence collectors coming across the stuff."

"Well, in this case he might've left in a hurry. Let's say he's still in the house when the deputies arrive. He hears them banging on the door, and he gets spooked. Flees out the back way before the deputies can reach it. While they're searching the interior, he's making his getaway."

They reached the garage, where C. J. Osborn's Dodge was parked. Shelves lined three walls. Walsh took the right side, Cellini the left. They both pulled on rubber gloves to avoid contaminating the scene. The SID forensics experts hadn't checked out the garage yet.

As he searched through racks of hardware supplies, Walsh crooked his cell phone under his chin and asked Rawls if he was still there.

"Sure am," Rawls said, sounding much nearer than three thousand miles away.

"We're looking through the garage now. Is there any progress on your end in tracking this guy down?"

"We're pursuing a couple of angles. For one thing, he corresponded via e-mail with the subject here in Baltimore. We're reviewing the e-mails now. They were scrubbed—sent anonymously—but there may be some clue in the actual content of the messages."

"Don't you have document analysis experts for that?"

"Yeah, we've sent copies of the e-mails to one of our documents guys. His initial reaction was that there wasn't much to work with, so don't get your hopes up."

"Okay, what's the other angle?"

"Do you recall how I told you that he's been routing the video feed through a proxy?"

"Yeah."

"We've obtained a subpoena to see the information in that client's account."

"So soon? Fast work."

"The Bureau never sleeps, Detective," Rawls intoned sententiously, then laughed. "Unfortunately it may take time for the proxy to comply with the order. You ought to see the delaying tactics these outfits will use."

"Why would they delay in a case like this? They're protecting a serial killer."

"It's a privacy issue," Rawls said mildly.

"Tell them about C. J. Osborn's privacy. Tell them— hey, wait a minute. I found something." Walsh motioned to Cellini, who joined him at the rear of the garage.

Behind a row of paint cans rested a small black computer, its green LED dimly glowing, and duct-taped to it, a cell phone. Neither detective touched the equipment. There was a small chance the killer had left prints, fibers, or other evidence on the gear.

"Jackpot," Cellini said. "We can track him down through his cell-phone account. If that fails, we'll get the serial number of the computer. He might have registered it with the manufacturer. If so, he's in their database."

Walsh told Rawls what they'd found. "In the garage, just like you thought."

"He must have wired the phone into the main current also," Rawls said. "Otherwise it would have gone dead weeks ago."

"So," Walsh said slowly, "if I wanted to shut down the video feed, all I'd have to do is unplug the phone?"

"Or shut down the computer. If that's what you want to do."

"It isn't."

"I didn't think so. I've been watching from here, remember. I've seen the police going in and out of her bedroom. None of you has even glanced at the camera, though you must know it's there."

"We can guess its approximate location . . . Probably hidden inside the curtain rod of the window facing the bed. But everybody's under orders to play dumb. And we're going to continue the moron act for a while."

"You don't want him to know you've figured out the Internet angle."

"Exactly."

"Why?"

"Because he's one step ahead of us in every other way. This is the one area where we may—*may*—have an edge on him. And right now, we need any edge we can get if we want to save C. J. Osborn's life."

There was silence for a moment, and then Rawls said very softly, "Detective, are you telling me he's abducted that woman?"

Walsh closed his eyes. "Oh, shit. I've just been assuming you knew."

"I only know what I see on the monitor. Police in the house. I thought you had tracked her down and taken her into protective custody."

"He beat us to her. Not by much."

"Is she . . . Do you think she's already . . . ?"

"Probably not yet. He, uh, takes his time with them, I think."

Another silence on the Maryland end of the call. Walsh wished he hadn't broken the news that way.

Finally there was a sigh from Rawls. "This is some job we've got, isn't it, Detective?"

Walsh found a smile. "It has its ups and downs. How long you been with the feds, Special Agent?"

"Twenty-six years."

"Thirty for me. You think we're both getting too old for this work?"

"I think, Detective, these young guys need old farts like us to keep their butts in line."

Walsh laughed. He felt the same way. "Call me Morrie, okay?"

"Okay, Morrie. I'm Noah. We dinosaurs ought to be on a first-name basis. You get to work on the electronic gear, and I'll see if we can put a little more pressure on this proxy outfit. Maybe we can make faster progress."

"I just hope it's fast enough," Walsh said.

"He takes his time with them," Rawls reminded him.

"Yeah. But not *much* time."

He ended the call and checked his watch. 8:15. She had been abducted at approximately 6:45.

If C. J. Osborn truly was a member of the Four-Hour Club, her time was quickly running out.

33

Couldn't see. Couldn't move. Could hardly even breathe with the damn rubber ball wedged in her mouth.

C. J. had one advantage. Adam had left her alone—and while alone, she could try to find a way to free her hands. If she could loosen the duct tape around her wrists or cut it somehow . . .

Then she could remove the gag, the blindfold, the tape on her ankles, even the cord that lashed her to the pillar.

With her hands free, she could do anything.

There had to be some way to get the tape off. She fingered the post behind her. The surface was concrete—most likely reinforcing a substructure of steel. Were there cracks in the surface, rough spots where she could abrade the tape?

No such luck. The concrete was as smooth as if it had been freshly poured.

What she needed was a tool. Some sort of debris—a shard of glass, a sharp piece of metal.

Wherever she was, the place had a concrete floor and concrete posts. It might be a work space of some kind, a place where she just might find a discarded screw or a rusty nail lying around.

She extended her legs and reached out, feeling the concrete floor with the tips of her sneakers.

She wished he hadn't blindfolded her. Wished she could see what she was doing.

Damn Adam anyway. Damn him to hell.

He'd said that if she knew the how of it, the why would explain itself. But the question *why*? still rang unanswered in her mind.

There seemed to be nothing directly in front of her. The floor felt smooth and clean.

She extended her legs to her left, exploring the floor on that side of her body.

Still nothing.

She turned in the opposite direction and again made a sweep of the area near her.

This time her sneakers snagged a large object, flat on the side facing her.

She tapped it with her feet and heard a hollow thump. She kicked it, felt it shiver.

A box? A crate?

She kicked it again and heard a glassy rattle.

Were there tools in the box? Or on top of it?

Goddamn it, if only she could *see*.

Frustration made her reckless. She launched another kick at the box, slamming the soles of both sneakers into its flat face, and she heard the box creak and tip over with a thud.

Then there was the tinkle of small objects, either glass or metal, hitting the floor. One of them shattered. Another rolled toward her. She heard it turning over and over on the smooth concrete like a pencil on a tabletop.

Twisting at the hips, she lowered her body nearly

to the floor and groped with her bound hands, praying she could intercept the thing, whatever the hell
it was.

It stopped rolling.

Still out of reach. But close. She was sure of that.

She bent her legs at the knees. Her sneakers made
contact with the thing. It was small and lightweight
and felt fragile. She eased it toward her, tucking her
legs under her lap.

Finally her hands closed over their prize.

She wasn't certain what she held. Lightly she ran
her fingers over the thing. It was a few inches long,
with rounded sides, and it tapered to a narrow tip . . .

A sharp tip.

Needle sharp.

That was what she had. A needle of some kind.

Not a hypodermic needle—she detected no
plunger at the other end—but some needle-tipped
tool anyway. What it was used for, why it was here—
she had no idea, and she didn't care.

It was sharp. It was the tool that could set her free.

Now came the tricky part. She had to point the
needle upward and press the tip against the tape
binding her wrists.

She gripped the needle in both hands, aiming the
sharp point upward, trying to maneuver it so she
could spear the coil of tape around her wrists. The
job was hard. Her wrists weren't made to work
that way.

A wash of perspiration spread over her face. Her
breathing came fast and shallow through her nostrils;
her mouth was blocked by the gag.

Finally she maneuvered the needle into position.
She felt the needle dimpling the tape. She pushed
upward, and the needle punched through.

A minuscule hole. Hardly big enough to matter. But if she could punch another hole and another and another, eventually the tape would give way. It wasn't going to be easy, and it wasn't going to be fast.

She worked the needle up and down, shoulders and arms trembling with strain. Her thoughts returned to Adam.

What was his motive? Simple anger? Was that all? Was it enough?

Maybe it was. Just look at the people she arrested every day—gangbangers, drunken brawlers, angry husbands like Ramon Sanchez.

Angry husbands . . .

How much did Adam hate her? How deeply had the divorce wounded his masculine pride, his sense of self?

Yes, he had precipitated the divorce by cheating on her. But he had never intended to get caught. Even after she had filed the papers, he'd done his best to talk her out of it.

She remembered their last argument, in the apartment he'd rented in Venice after moving out of the bungalow. It was a sad little studio apartment with thin walls and noisy neighbors and cheap, rented furniture. She knew he hated the place and hated what had happened to his life.

"I don't want to lose you," he kept saying in a desperate, pleading voice she didn't want to hear.

"You already did," she replied, fighting off any surrender to sympathy.

"C. J."—his arms outstretched, hands open—"you don't understand. I need you. I'll fall apart without you."

He looked so wan and forlorn in the dim lamplight. She turned away, refusing to meet his gaze.

"You won't fall apart, Adam. You always manage to keep it together so you can look after your number-one priority—yourself."

"That's not fair."

She looked at him then, and whatever was in her eyes made him shrink from her. "Now *I'm* the one not being fair? Funny, I thought that would be you. Was it *fair* to take Ashley to bed behind my back?"

"It only happened once."

He said it with complete sincerity, but she knew it was untrue. She had already tracked down Ashley on the UCLA campus and asked her how long the affair had lasted. The girl had been too startled and intimidated to lie. "Four months," she had blurted.

"Only once," she echoed, watching Adam's face for any trace of shame. She saw nothing but guileless candor, and the thought flashed in her mind that her husband—soon to be ex-husband—was an awfully skilled liar, better than she'd ever known.

She didn't speak again, merely turned away from him in disgust and walked out the door. His plaintive voice had pursued her down the hallway of the apartment building, then down the graffiti-scarred stairwell to the lobby.

"Don't do this, C. J. Please, you *can't* do this to me."

She noticed the irony of his utter self-absorption. He thought *she* had wronged *him*.

And of course he still thought so. She had walked out of his life. She had reduced him to the humiliating posture of a beggar—and worse, she had not even listened to his pleas. She was the villain. She had taken his manhood, his dignity.

So now he intended to get even—by taking her life.

She had succeeded in puncturing the tape three or

four more times. But when she tested it, it felt as strong as ever.

How much time had passed? A half hour already?

Adam might be talking with a detective even now. If he wasn't a suspect, the interview would be brief.

Then he would be back for that last dance.

Not gonna happen, she promised herself. You'll get out of this, Killer.

Bet your life you will.

34

"Dead end."

Cellini shook her head slowly as she switched off her cell phone. Walsh, standing in C. J. Osborn's kitchen, lifted a quizzical eyebrow.

"The stuff in the garage," she explained, sounding weary. "I thought for sure it would be a breakthrough. But this is one clever son of a bitch we're up against."

"The computer couldn't be traced?"

"He filed off the serial number."

"How about the cell phone? Couldn't you track down the account?"

"Oh, I tracked it down, all right." She gave a bitter laugh. "It's registered to Pacific Bell. They're paying the bills."

Walsh looked at her blankly.

"Don't you get it, Morrie? It's a hacker's joke. He tapped into the PacBell system and put the account in their name. He's got the phone company paying his phone bill for him."

"So," Walsh said, "we're no closer to ID'ing him than we were before."

"That's what 'dead end' means," Cellini snapped,

then apologized. "I'm sort of wrung out. I really thought we had him."

"Maybe Sotheby's gotten somewhere with the receipts."

But he hadn't, as he explained when Walsh and Cellini joined him in the laundry room, where C. J. Osborn kept her bank books, canceled checks, and receipts. "I've looked through everything," he said. "She hasn't had any work done on her house in the past six months—or if she has, she paid cash for it. No plumbers, no electricians. And no computer-repair guys. Nothing."

Gary Boyle stuck his head in the doorway. "I'm skeptical about the computer-repair angle anyway."

"Why?" Cellini asked. It had been her idea. "It makes sense. He's obviously into computers."

"Yeah, but Nikki Carter didn't own one. I just checked the inventory of her possessions to be sure. No computer on the list."

"How about Martha Eversol?" Walsh asked.

"She owned a PC."

"See if there's any record of her getting it serviced— especially at-home service. What's it called again?"

"On-site," Cellini answered.

"Right. Check that out."

Boyle disappeared from the doorway. Sotheby stared after him. "Even if she did get her computer repaired," Sotheby said, "it won't prove much."

"Think positive," Walsh told him, though his own thinking was pretty negative at the moment.

He left the laundry room and returned to the front of the house, where Boyle was flipping through the case file. Walsh saw his lips moving as he scanned the pages. A mouth reader.

"Okay, here's something," Boyle said.

Walsh looked over his shoulder. Boyle stabbed at an entry with a ragged fingernail.

"Eversol got a house call from an on-site computer-repair service on November twenty-second, about five weeks before her abduction, and about one week before her image went on-line. The guy could've planted the camera when he fixed her PC."

"We must have checked out the repairman," Walsh said.

"We did. He's William Bowden. Married, two kids. Lives in Reseda. West Valley interviewed him, said he seemed okay."

"But that was before we knew about the Webcam," Cellini pointed out.

Walsh nodded. "Donna, I want *you* to talk to Bowden. Call him, see if he's home. Don't identify yourself as a cop. Act like you're selling something or soliciting for charity. Don't spook him. If he's there, you and Sotheby go see him with at least two West Valley patrol cops as backup. Ride him hard. I don't know why, but I've got a feeling about this guy. I don't trust these computer people."

Cellini smiled. "You don't trust any technology invented after the Eisenhower administration."

"Just do it."

"Shit, Morrie, you're starting to sound like a TV commercial." She jotted down Bowden's phone number, listed in the case file, then pulled out her cell phone again.

Walsh told Boyle to search the LAPD's database for other homicides and abductions with an Internet connection. "Get Lopez to help."

"Local crimes only?" Boyle asked.

"No, statewide. Within the past five years. And—"

"Detective?" a voice interrupted.

Walsh glanced behind him and saw a uniformed cop standing there. "Yeah?"

"Watch commander at Wilshire says there's a guy waiting for you at the station."

"Name?" For a crazy moment Walsh imagined the patrol cop saying, *William Bowden—he's waiting to make a full confession.*

But he answered, "Adam Nolan. I think he's the victim's ex-husband."

"Hell." Walsh had forgotten all about the man. "All right, I'll head on over."

He sketched a wave to Cellini, who was on the phone and barely acknowledged him.

The drive to Wilshire Station was short, but it gave Walsh sufficient time to consider his plan of attack. When interrogating a suspect, there must always be a plan of attack.

He decided to do his Peter Falk impression. That usually got results.

Most cops didn't watch police shows, but Walsh liked them, and his favorite of all time was *Columbo*. Oh, sure, the show was totally unrealistic, but Walsh didn't care about technical accuracy. He loved the show because Columbo was middle-aged and rumpled and eccentric, not unlike Walsh himself. Neither of them would ever be mistaken for Clint Eastwood. They both owned clunky old cars, although Columbo drove his when on duty in contravention of LAPD policy, which required the use of a department-issued Caprice or Crown Victoria. They both came across as relics of an earlier, pretechnological age. They both loved their work and had little else in their lives.

At night Columbo went home to his invisible and

presumably dowdy wife, and Walsh went home to a house that had been empty since his wife left him, to a phone that never rang because his three grown kids were always too busy to call, to bowls of microwaved chili and reruns of *Columbo* on cable TV.

He parked behind the Wilshire divisional station on Venice Boulevard and entered through the rear door, then quickly made his way through to the reception area in front, where he asked the desk officer for Adam Nolan. He was directed to an unused office on a side corridor. Good thing the watch commander had been smart enough not to put Nolan in an interrogation room. He didn't want the man thinking of himself as a suspect.

He pushed open the office door and saw a man of about thirty seated in a metal chair, wearing dark chinos and a tan, zippered windbreaker.

"Mr. Nolan? I'm Detective Walsh, Robbery-Homicide."

Walsh regretted the introduction as soon as he saw the look of cold dread pass over Nolan's face at the mention of the word *homicide*. He held up a reassuring hand. "Your wife isn't dead. That is, we believe she isn't."

"Ex-wife," Nolan mumbled, rising from his chair.

"Sorry."

"C. J.'s alive?"

"We think so, yes."

"But you're not sure?"

"She's missing, Mr. Nolan." Walsh closed the door, then took his time moving around the desk and seating himself behind it. "She's been kidnapped."

"Kidnapped?" Nolan echoed. He sat down, facing the desk. "Who the hell would *kidnap* her? She hasn't

got any money. She's not involved in anything politi-
cal." He blinked. "Is it—could it be somebody she
arrested? A revenge thing?"

"Anything's possible at this stage. The person re-
sponsible could be anyone." Including you, Walsh
added silently.

He didn't think Adam Nolan was implicated in
this crime, but until he had more facts, he wasn't
making any assumptions.

"When did this happen?" Nolan asked.

"We're not sure." Walsh leaned forward, asserting
himself. "Mr. Nolan, I'm afraid you'll have to let me
ask the questions."

"Right," Nolan said. "Of course." He ran a hand
over his blond hair, mussing it distractedly. He was
a good-looking guy, Walsh noted, with crisp, regular
features, a light suntan, and smoky eyes tinged with
blue. Women would go for him.

"When did you and C. J. get divorced?" Walsh
asked.

"A year ago, approximately. Why is that relevant?"

"I'm just getting some background information,"
Walsh answered vaguely. "Have you kept in touch
with her?"

"As I said over the phone, I saw her just a few
hours ago."

"It wasn't me you talked to on the phone. It was
Detective Boyle." Walsh spread his hands apologeti-
cally and cocked his head in ingenuous humility.
"Sorry if I'm covering some of the same ground."

Nolan seemed disarmed by these overtures. "It's
all right. Ask whatever you want."

Walsh nodded. Thank you, Lieutenant Columbo.
"You saw your ex-wife today?"

Nolan said yes. "At Newton Station. She was coming off duty. We went for coffee down the street."

"Where?"

"I don't remember the name of the place. It was run by a Filipino couple—she told me that."

"Why did you see her?"

"To invite her out."

"Tonight?"

"No, she does volunteer work tonight. I mean, normally she does. I mean—"

"I understand. Go on."

"It was for Friday. I thought we might go to a club, hear some music."

"You do that often? Get together with her?" He was fully absorbed in his Columbo persona now—polite, apologetic, gently probing.

"No, not really. We try to keep in touch. But it's a strain, you know. The divorce wasn't entirely amicable."

"I guess they never are," Walsh said, thinking of his own divorce ten years ago. "Can I ask why you split up?"

"We were just going in different directions. She became a cop. I became a lawyer."

"Criminal law?"

"Corporate."

"Good money in that."

"So they tell me." A brief, forced laugh.

"Did C. J. express any concerns about her safety?"

"Today?"

"Ever."

Nolan thought about it. "No, I'm sure I'd remember if she had."

"Did she mention an e-mail she'd received?"

"E-mail?"

Walsh waved off the issue. "Never mind."

"Did someone send her—"

"I can't go into it." Another Columbo moment. "I'm sorry. Really." He let his sympathy mollify Nolan, then continued. "Did you leave the coffee shop together?"

"We parted outside. She walked back to the station for her car."

"What did you do?"

"Drove to the office. It's Brigham and Garner in Century City."

"What time did you leave her?"

"Four-fifteen, four-thirty."

"Did she say where she was going?"

"Home, I assumed. She'd worked a full shift, or watch—whatever you call it. She'd nearly gotten herself killed. I think she was ready to chill out."

"What do you mean, nearly got killed?"

"She told me she handled a hostage situation all by herself. Resolved it successfully. I have a feeling she was breaking a few rules—not to mention risking her neck."

Walsh hadn't heard about this. "You don't seem too surprised by her heroics."

"Why would I be? That's C. J. I guess that's why they gave her that nickname."

"What nickname?"

"You don't know? Killer. That's what the other cops call her."

"Killer? Why? Any special reason?"

"Oh, it's quite a story." Walsh heard a note of pride in Nolan's voice. "Happened when she was new to the street—back when she was a rookie working Harbor Division. One night, on only her third week on the job, she and her training officer get a report of loud music coming from an apartment. Doesn't seem like anything serious, so the training officer lets C. J. handle it. They go up to the apartment, and there's rap music blasting from inside. C. J. bangs on the door, yells, 'Police!' And guess what happens?"

"Tell me."

"The guy inside the apartment starts firing through the door. If he'd been using a shotgun, C. J. and her partner would've been killed. But it's a handgun, and the shots miss."

"Christ," Walsh said. It was rare for any cop to be fired on, and rarer still for a boot fresh out of the Academy.

"The training officer pulls C. J. to cover and calls for backup, but then they hear somebody screaming for help. C. J. says they've got to go in. Her partner doesn't want to. She goes in anyway—and he follows. She shamed him into it, I guess.

"They kick down the door and enter, and the guy with the gun starts firing from the bedroom, and they're returning fire. It's a real shootout. C. J. told me she emptied one clip and put in another. Her partner did the same. That's, what, thirty rounds?"

"Something like that."

"Finally the guy stops shooting. They got him. He's been hit twice in the abdomen, and he's lost consciousness. C. J. goes past him into the bedroom and finds another guy in there, next to the stereo, which is still booming out the rap music. This guy is tied to a chair. He was being tortured—tortured to death. The music was turned up loud to cover his screams."

Walsh shook his head. "Why was the victim being tortured?"

"Drug dealer thing. The one guy decided to eliminate his competition."

"Did the gunman die?"

"No, he pulled through. So C. J.'s not really a killer. But they started calling her by that name anyway. Because she had the killer instinct."

Walsh took this in. "What's it like, being married to a woman with a killer instinct?"

"She didn't display it with me. I think the other cops misinterpreted it anyway. It's not that she wants to be Dirty Harry. It's just—well, something happened to her when she was a kid."

"What?"

"I don't know, exactly. She never talks about it much. But *something* scared her. I think she became a cop to deal with that fear. I think she went into that apartment for the same reason. She's lived with fear for a long time, and I think this is her way of dealing with it." Nolan shifted in his chair. "I'm not sure how helpful any of this is."

"Let me just clear up a few more little things. You said you left C. J. between four-fifteen and four-thirty this afternoon?"

"Yes."

"And went back to your office?"

"Yes."

"When did you get there?"

"Maybe quarter of five."

"People saw you return?"

"Sure. The receptionist, Anna. Some of my colleagues. A client . . ." His words trailed off. He seemed bewildered by this line of questioning.

Walsh pressed on, aware that his Columbo act was about to run out of steam. "What kind of vehicle do you drive?"

"BMW 325 coupe."

"Is that it? No other car?" Or a white van, he added wordlessly.

"I'm one person. How many cars do I need?"

"Did you have any further contact with C. J. today?"

"No."

"Didn't call her this evening?"

"No. I worked at the office until six, then went home."

"Home is where?"

"Brentwood."

"Anyone see you arrive home?"

Nolan stiffened. "What's this about?"

"I'm just asking—"

"You're trying to verify my movements—is that it?"

"I'm sorry, Mr. Nolan," Walsh said in his best Peter Falk voice. "It's routine, that's all."

"Routine. Right." Nolan seethed for a moment, then said reluctantly, "Hell, I don't know if any of my neighbors saw me get in. Probably not. I didn't see any of them."

"And then?"

"Made dinner, turned on the TV—want to know what I watched?" he asked with sarcasm.

"Okay," Walsh said.

"The news. The local news. Channel Four. Then a movie on HBO. *Field of Dreams*, the baseball thing. Around eight o'clock I got a phone call from Detective Boyle. Now I'm here." He lifted his arms and let them fall limply in his lap. "That's it."

"All right, Mr. Nolan."

"You through asking questions? Can I talk now?"

"Go ahead."

"Good. Because I've got something to say." There was no expression on his face, only a deadly stillness. "This is bullshit. You start this interview by telling me you need some background information, and you end up treating me like a goddamned suspect."

"I'm sorry," Walsh began, but Nolan wouldn't let him be Columbo anymore.

"I don't want to hear it. You drag me in here and waste my time, and what's more important, you waste *your* time. Are you running this investigation?"

"As a matter of fact, I am."

"Then what the hell are you doing here with me? How does this help you to get C. J. back?"

"It's impossible at this stage of the investigation to say what will be helpful—"

"Cut the crap. You're here so you can say you followed procedure, so you can make a check-off mark in your notebook. 'Talked to ex-husband,' check. And meanwhile somebody's got C. J., and for all we know she could be dying *right now*."

"Mr. Nolan—"

"Quit talking to me, and get off your ass and find her, Goddamn it! Just *find* her . . . find . . ." Abruptly he slumped forward in his chair, all the anger hissing out of him. "Oh, shit."

He cradled his head in his hands, rocking back and forth.

"We're doing everything we can," Walsh said.

Nolan just shook his head.

Walsh was almost sure this wasn't the guy. But he reminded himself that Adam Nolan was a lawyer, and every lawyer he'd ever met had been skilled at deception. He'd better ask for the names of those witnesses who saw Nolan return to work. Then maybe send someone from West LA Division to talk to Nolan's neighbors—

His desk phone rang. He picked it up. "Walsh."

"Morrie?" It was Donna Cellini, breathless and tense. "We've got a suspect."

He sat up straight. "You serious?"

"No, I'm joking around. Of course I'm serious. Look, I can't go into it now. We're setting up a command post in Hacienda Heights. Corner of Hacienda Boulevard and Newton Street."

He'd expected her to say Reseda, where William Bowden lived. Hacienda Heights was in the opposite direction, an unincorporated district in the southeast corner of LA County. "That's Sheriff's jurisdiction," Walsh said.

"Right. They're handling it, and we're along for the ride. Get over here fast."

"I'm on my way."

Walsh hung up and glanced at Adam Nolan across the desk. "Sorry, Mr. Nolan. I need to get moving."

"What is it? Did something happen?"

"I can't talk about it now."

"Do you know where C. J. is?"

"I'm not sure what we know. We have your phone number. Go home and wait. When there's news, you'll be the first to hear it."

"Tell me what's going on."

"I can't tell you anything. Look, you said you wanted us to make progress. So don't stand in our way. Let us do our jobs."

Nolan hesitated, then stood up. "Just get her back, all right?"

Walsh wanted to say something reassuring, but there was no time. "We'll do everything we can."

35

The interview had gone as well as could have been expected. Even so, Adam was troubled.

He gripped the steering wheel of his BMW and sped east on the San Bernardino Freeway, cruising past the barrio neighborhoods of City Terrace and Monterey Park. He had to remind himself to stay within the speed limit; he couldn't afford to be pulled over by a highway patrol car. It was difficult to keep his speed under sixty-five when every instinct demanded that he race back to C. J., take care of things, do it, do it *now*.

Damn. He really was rattled, wasn't he?

It wasn't Detective Walsh's line of questioning that had him on edge. He had prepared himself for the predictable inquiries about his relationship with his ex-wife, his feelings toward her, his whereabouts throughout the afternoon and evening. He had gone to considerable pains to ensure that his answers would be satisfactory.

Take his meeting with C. J. this afternoon. He had wanted to be seen with her, seen by her fellow officers in the Newton police station, so that when her disappearance was discovered some of them would be quick to think of him. He had wanted to be called in and interrogated. What better way to establish an alibi during the crucial hours of her absence than to let the police do it for him?

They had dialed his home telephone number and he had answered. Ergo, he must have been at home. It was the simple, natural assumption to make. It was also false—hadn't these people heard of call forwarding? A readily available, very convenient service, one that more criminals ought to take advantage of.

Criminals. Yes, that was what he was now. Breaking and entering, kidnapping, and soon . . . homicide. A hell of a change of pace for a guy whose worst crime prior to tonight had been running the occasional stop sign.

Well, too late for doubts now. He was in this thing, and he had to see it through.

Anyway, Walsh and his pals would never realize that the call had been forwarded to Adam's cell phone, that he hadn't been home when he answered. They would never even look in that direction, not when they already had a much more plausible suspect in their sights.

There had been a second purpose behind his visit to the police station. If anyone inquired further, the desk officer at Newton Station and the waitress at the coffee shop would both report that he and C. J. had smiled together, laughed a little, and seemed comfortable with each other. He doubted the investigation would ever get that far, but if it did, he wanted their testimony in the record.

Besides, it had been a kick to play with C. J.'s head.

He wondered what she was thinking right now. He didn't know—one of the things that had always irked him about their marriage was that he'd never been quite sure what she was thinking. She had a mind of her own, did C. J.

But one thing was certain. Tonight he figured in her thoughts. She might have pushed him out of her mind and out of her life, but he had come back, all right. Back with a vengeance.

"Nobody fucks with me," he muttered, repeating the words that had become his credo, his mantra. "Nobody makes me their bitch."

He caught himself pressing down on the accelerator and lifted his foot to reduce his speed. Outside his windows, the city of El Monte flashed past in a blur of lights under a moonless sky.

So, yes, he'd been prepared for that part of the interview. Walsh's other questions had posed no difficulties either. After leaving C. J. at the coffee shop, he really had driven back to the office, working until six.

After that, however, his narrative had parted company with the truth. He had not driven to Brentwood, had not fixed a meal and watched *Field of Dreams*—although he had been careful to check the TV listings to see what was on.

No one could prove he hadn't been home. His condo building featured individual enclosed garages; it was impossible for a neighbor to know whether or not a tenant's car was parked inside. The units were soundproofed, and the rules of the condo board regarding noise were strict. No one ever heard anyone else's TV or stereo.

Instead of heading to Brentwood, he had driven east, into C. J.'s neighborhood, parking in the alley behind her house—the house they had once shared— shortly after six. In the early January darkness he had changed out of his suit into chinos and a windbreaker, donning gloves and rubber boots that fitted easily over his shoes. The boots were two sizes too large—deliberately so. If he left any shoe prints, he wanted them to be different from his own.

He had stowed his provisions in the windbreaker's copious zippered pockets. A vial of chloroform he'd ordered from a chemical supplies firm, using a phony name and a post office box, and paying with a money order made out to cash. A ski mask, which he had slipped over his head before entering the house—he knew that the bedroom was under constant surveillance, and he didn't want his face to be caught on video. A Walther 9mm, which he had bought at a gun show in San Diego County, a private transaction conducted with the utmost discretion and without the use of any names.

He'd never had any intention of using the gun. Even so, he'd felt it necessary to carry one. C. J. kept an off-duty firearm in her purse. He couldn't afford to be at a disadvantage.

Entering the house had been simplicity itself. He still owned a spare set of keys, and C. J., trusting soul, had not changed the locks.

Somehow she must have heard him anyway, or maybe she'd seen his flashlight when he entered her backyard. He took cover inside the bedroom, crouching low and hoping he was out of camera range, as she came down the hall. When she checked out the laundry room, he left the bedroom and positioned himself outside the doorway, squatting low, invisible in the dark.

The phone call from her cop friend—boyfriend? Did it matter?—had taken him by surprise, but he had handled the situation well enough. Once she was fully unconscious, gagged and taped and blindfolded, he'd carried her into the alley and put her in the trunk of his car, wrapping her in a blanket to prevent the transfer of hairs or fibers.

Of course, he'd known she would be missed before long. When she didn't show up for her community-service program, inquiries would be made. A patrol unit would visit her house, where the cops would find obvious evidence of her abduction—the knife she had dropped, the back door unlocked and ajar.

He had left those clues intentionally. He wanted the police to know it had been a kidnapping. He wanted them to search the house—something they might not have done if he had snatched her from another location.

They had to find the Webcam.

The Webcam was the key to everything. When the police found it, they would know that she had been spied on by her abductor. They would track down the Web site. They would discover that the two other women featured on the site had fallen prey to the Hourglass Killer.

To ensure that they made all the necessary connections, he had taken two additional precautions. He had sent an anonymous e-mail to the FBI's Baltimore office, alerting them to the existence of the site. And he had e-mailed C. J. herself.

He had worked it out perfectly. Nothing could go wrong. By roughly ten o'clock, he had expected to hear from the police. He would kill C. J., matching the four-hour MO of the serial killer, then speed back to LA and put on a performance for the cops.

But it hadn't worked out that way. Things were happening too fast.

The call had come at eight—too early. Worse still,

the interview at Wilshire Station had been conducted by Detective Walsh, the man in charge of the Hourglass Killer task force.

Adam knew there was no reason for Walsh to be assigned this case unless the connection to the serial killer had already been made.

His surprise must have shown on his face when Walsh introduced himself, though fortunately the detective had interpreted it as concern for C. J.'s wellbeing.

Then at the close of the interview, Walsh had taken a brief, urgent phone call that seemed to imply a breakthrough in the case.

Had they put the pieces together so fast? Were they already closing in on the Hourglass Killer?

It wasn't supposed to happen that soon. He'd expected the authorities to take hours, even a day or two, to add it all up. Instead, they might have the serial killer in custody before long.

Adam wished he could call the crazy son of a bitch and warn him that the police were hard on his trail. But he didn't know the killer's identity. Though he had hacked into the man's Web site, he didn't know his name.

So there was only one thing to do. Get back to C. J. as fast as possible. Kill her, and dump her body where it was sure to be found.

He checked the dashboard clock: 9:40. He could finish the job by ten. That was a little shy of the four-hour mark, but autopsies weren't that accurate in determining the time of death. Besides, the four-hour thing was only a theory—a rumor circulating on the Internet, which he'd picked up on a message board devoted to LA crime while researching the case.

Ten o'clock, ten forty-five—it made no difference. His plan could still work. He could kill her and never be suspected.

But only if he did it soon enough to be available when the police decided to talk with him again, either to question him or to update him on the case. By then, he had to be snug in his living room, awaiting their phone call or their visit, like any other perfectly innocent man.

Kill her by ten o'clock.

Twenty minutes to apply the tattoo.

Ten minutes to ditch the body.

Half hour to drive home.

Eleven o'clock by then. Dicey. The Hourglass Killer might be in custody by eleven, if this break in the case panned out. And once the killer was caught, Walsh or his associates would want to see C. J.'s ex-husband a second time.

He accelerated to seventy, risking a traffic ticket. His timetable was tight. No margin for error. Even so, he would make the plan work. He would get away with it. Justice and righteousness were on his side.

"Nobody makes me their bitch," he whispered, drawing strength from the words. "Nobody."

36

The tape was starting to split. C. J. could feel her wrists begin to separate as a gap opened in the lower half of the binding.

She would get herself out of this jam. And she would put Adam in a nice maximum-security state prison—New Folsom up in Sacramento, say, or maybe Pelican Bay. No, better, how about Corcoran, home to Sirhan Sirhan and Charlie Manson? A swell place for her ex-husband to hang out.

What the hell, the bastard deserved it—and not just for kidnapping her.

He had thought he *owned* her. There was no way she would let him get away with that.

Had he ever really loved her? Maybe what he'd loved was only the image she first presented—the naive young woman on her own in the city. Was it a coincidence that he had drifted away soon after she entered the LAPD Academy? Or that his substitute for her had been a skittish young graduate student, easily cowed?

On patrol, she had handled many domestic disputes. In a high percentage of cases, the root of the marital problem was simple—the husband regarded his wife not as a person but as property.

She had never imagined that Adam could see her that way. But he had. Then she had gone and challenged his assumptions by building a life for herself—and walking out on him. He could not forgive her for being an autonomous human being. To him, she was only his toy.

Had there been red flags she should have seen? Hints of the volcanic craziness below his bland exterior?

She remembered the time they played doubles tennis with another graduate student and his wife on the UCLA courts. She had missed a backhand, sending it wide, costing them the first set, and Adam had screamed at her, actually screamed. She could still see the wildness in his eyes, the twisted shape of his open mouth. Could still hear his echoing shout— "God*damn* it, keep your eye on the fucking *ball*!"— and the embarrassed silence from their friends on the other side of the net.

A moment later he had apologized, joking that he'd always been overly competitive, but the episode had lingered in her thoughts, a small piece of a puzzle she had not tried too hard to solve. Maybe she had not wanted to solve it, had not wanted to face the dark side of their marriage.

The dark side . . .

A memory returned to her of the morning when she emerged from the bathroom and found Adam hunched over her purse. She crept close enough to see that he had taken out her off-duty gun and was handling it with a slow, loving caress, almost fondling the stubby, oiled barrel. Then he realized she was watching him. "Fuck, don't sneak up on me like that!" Anger again, as if she had done something wrong. When she asked why he'd been holding her gun, he said something about an interest in firearms. But he had never exhibited any such interest before, and even then she knew his answer was less than the truth.

Had he been wondering how it would feel to shoot her with her own gun? To take control—ultimate control—of this woman who was slipping from his grasp? To turn the emblem of her own independence against her?

The idea had not occurred to her at the time. Or maybe it had, but only in flashes of awareness that faded, like lightning strokes, before they could be fully perceived. At times when he made love to her, she would open her eyes and glimpse his face in the split second before orgasm, and what she would see was not love but resentment and rage. Then with his shudder of release, his features would slacken, and whatever expression she had read in his face would be gone.

Small things. Moments. Fragments. Nothing she could put together or make sense of. Only the uneasy intimation that there was another person behind the man she knew, a person who was cruel and cold and controlling.

Most of the time that side of Adam was entirely hidden. Though often distant, he was charming, considerate, kind. Or so he seemed. It had been an act, and she had bought it. She had underestimated his skill at deception. He wore his mask effortlessly. He was a world-class prevaricator and manipulator. If lying were an Olympic event, he would get the gold.

Their marriage had been only lies and sick games. And she hadn't known, hadn't allowed herself to know. Bad enough to be blind. Worse to blind yourself, to keep your eyes shut because you're afraid of what you might see.

Anger at herself spurred a new surge of adrenaline. She punctured the last stubborn segment of the tape and pulled her wrists apart.

Free. Almost.

Putting down the needle, she undid the clasp that secured the throttle and spit out the rubber ball. A wave of nausea shuddered through her, but she suppressed the impulse to retch. She could not afford any weakness, not now.

She peeled off the tape blindfolding her. The adhesive plucked hairs from her eyebrows in a series of quick, painful pops, but she didn't care.

She could see again. Blinking, she raised her head and took a look around.

She was in a large room colonnaded with posts that supported a flat, featureless ceiling. The floor was utterly flat also, a spread of poured concrete, and where walls should have been, there were long open spaces that let in moonlight and starlight, but no artificial illumination.

For a baffled moment she was too disoriented to grasp what she was seeing. Then she realized it was a parking garage.

The pylons were evenly spaced between open areas large enough to accommodate several vehicles parked diagonally. Squinting, she could even make out stripes painted on the concrete to mark off the spaces. But no lights overhead, only meshworks of electrical wiring that led nowhere.

A half-finished structure. Abandoned, deserted—a concrete tomb.

Tomb. Wrong word to choose. She was a long way from being dead tonight.

Adam took the Garey Avenue exit ramp from the San Bernardino Freeway and headed north through Pomona and Claremont. North of Claremont lay unincorporated county land, desolate and dark. He followed Live Oak Canyon Road to a newly paved turnoff that wound through hilly land. Above him rose the tree-studded crests of the Angeles National Forest, good hiking country offering scenic vistas. But he wasn't going that far.

Half a mile down the side road he switched his headlights off. The moon was bright enough to guide him the remaining few hundred yards to his destination.

He opened the padlocked gate, then drove through and secured the lock behind him. He wanted no visitors.

Keeping his headlights off, he drove down the main boulevard of the complex. Blocky buildings of no particular style eased past on both sides. Toward the rear of the property lay the parking garage, three stories high. It was a grim concrete structure, ugly and severely functional, and Adam had chosen it as the place where his ex-wife would die.

The garage was largely finished, except for the fluorescent lighting fixtures that had never been installed in the ceilings. The concrete entry ramp was blocked by a heap of lumber, but that was all right. He wouldn't have driven inside anyway. To navigate the curving entryway and avoid the rows of pylons, he would need his headlights, and he was reluctant to turn them on and reveal any sign of activity in the complex.

As he had before, he parked alongside the garage, killing the BMW's engine. Last time he'd arrived here, he'd faced the exhausting chore of lugging C. J. inside. This time there was nothing for him to carry—except his handgun, retrieved from the glove compartment where he had stowed it before entering the police station. There had been a metal detector in the doorway of the station house, and it wouldn't have been smart to be caught with a gun in his windbreaker.

He checked his side pocket for his cell phone and glanced at it to be sure it was on. If Detective Walsh or any other cop called his home number, the call would again be forwarded to the cell phone. He would have to answer and, if necessary, make tracks back to LA.

A quick kill, then. Not exactly what he'd hoped for, but life required certain compromises.

As did death, he added with a smile.

He left his car in a rush, not even bothering to slam the door, and sidestepped the lumber, hurrying up the entry ramp into the garage.

The tape binding C. J.'s ankles came off easily. In less than a minute she had unwound the wrapping and freed her legs.

Now for the rope lashing her to the post. It coiled around her belly like a belt, fastened with a large, complicated knot at her midsection. She fumbled at it but found without surprise that it was a good, strong knot, difficult to unravel.

Adam must have enjoyed tying the knot tight. She could picture his gloved hands working on the rope, drawing it taut, while he thought about the deterioration of their love life, the gradual process by which

she had become the dominant partner, the breadwin-
ner, the street cop, while he remained a student, a
perpetual adolescent. She could see his red face, his
narrowed eyes, the twist and jerk of his wrists with
each angry thought.

This is for wearing a uniform.

This is for carrying a gun.

This is for being more of a man than I was.

She tugged at the knot. It didn't loosen.

Could she wriggle free of the rope? Not likely. The
rope was tight, constricting her abdomen, offering
little room to maneuver.

She inhaled deeply and tried to squirm free, but
although she prided herself on narrow hips, they
weren't quite narrow enough.

Wouldn't work. She had to cut the rope. What she
needed was a knife or . . .

Glass.

On the floor near her was a glass vial, one of the
items dislodged from the crate she'd overturned.
Blindfolded, she'd had no idea it was there. Now she
snatched it up easily. It contained some sort of dark
liquid, which splashed over her hand when she broke
the vial on the floor.

Ink. That was what it was. Dark red ink, she
thought, although in the dim light it was hard to
distinguish color.

She wiped her hand on her cargo shorts, indiffer-
ent to the stain, then selected the longest shard from
the litter of glass.

The edge was sharp. She sawed the rope, cutting
through the entwined fibers one by one. Not long
now. When Adam returned, she would be gone.

She could visualize the exact expression on his
face—she had seen it when she caught him under

the sheets with Ashley. It was a look of utter defeat—
not guilt, but simple astonishment at having lost
the game.

Now he would lose a second time.

Finally the rope came apart, sagging to the floor.

"Did it," she breathed, and then she lifted her head
and there was Adam, limned in the ambient light,
standing at the far end of the garage.

He was watching her, leaning against one of the
pylons, hands in the pockets of his chinos.

And smiling.

She knew it, though his face was lost in shadow.

She could feel the cold energy of his smile.

"You're so resourceful, C. J.," he said, his voice
echoing off the concrete floor and ceiling. "It's admi-
rable, really. You've always been a survivor—until
tonight."

37

Walsh reached Hacienda Heights at 9:45 and parked across the street from a thirty-foot motor home customized as a mobile command post for the Sheriff's Department. Law enforcement agencies outside crowded metropolitan areas often used even larger vehicles, but thirty feet was the maximum length suitable for maneuvering in the narrow streets of LA's older districts.

It was not an undercover vehicle. The LASD logo was stamped on the side panels. The staging area must be far enough from the suspect's residence to make subterfuge unnecessary.

He crossed Hacienda Boulevard and rapped on the vehicle's back door, which swung open to admit him. The rear compartment of the motor home had been converted into a communications room. The civilian who welcomed him aboard after checking his badge was a radio operator who probably worked out of the Sheriff's dispatch center in East LA. Walsh glanced around and saw multiple Zetron radio consoles as well as high-frequency and military-band radio gear. The equipment hummed, powered by an onboard generator.

A second radio operator was talking into a microphone, asking for an ETA.

"Six minutes," a voice crackled over the speakers. "Roger that."

"Someone else invited to this party?" Walsh asked the two technicians.

The one who'd let him in nodded. "SWAT."

Walsh felt a stab of hope. A SWAT raid wouldn't be ordered unless the suspect was believed to be at home.

Had he taken C. J. Osborn to his residence? Was that where he killed his victims? It seemed impossible. How could he get the women inside without being seen? For that matter, how could he get the bodies out?

Then again, when dealing with nutcases of this type, anything was conceivable. Look at Jeffrey Dahmer, who'd committed multiple murders in his apartment, even dismembered the bodies with power tools, and had never raised the suspicions of his neighbors. Hell, the Milwaukee police had paid him a visit and hadn't noticed anything awry.

The Hourglass Killer could be home right now—with C. J.

And four hours hadn't passed yet.

There might still be a chance to save her.

Walsh hurried into the middle compartment of the motor home, which was used as a command area. Whiteboards had been tacked to the walls, some bearing arcane marker scribbles from a previous operation. More radio equipment crowded the shelves, along with a fax/photocopy machine, several phones, and two notebook computers that shared an inkjet printer. There was also a closed-circuit TV that could receive live video from the Ikegami color camera on the roof. The camera, operated by remote control, could scan in a full circle, but it wasn't running now.

A small galley and a lavatory were among the amenities; a closed door hid a cache of weapons. Most of the room was taken up by the conference center—a shaky metal table flanked by several equally shaky metal chairs. Despite the chairs, everyone was standing. Walsh saw Donna Cellini, the two deputies from C. J. Osborn's house, and Captain Hector Garcia, who ran the Sheriff's station in nearby City of Industry.

"Hec," Walsh said with a handshake as the door rumbled shut behind him.

"Morrie. Good to see you. Too bad about the circumstances."

"Maybe we can improve the circumstances. What've we got?"

Cellini answered. "I called the computer repairman, Bowden. He was home. Sotheby and I went over and talked to him. It was obvious he was holding back, so finally we told him a woman's life was at stake. Then he opened up. Said he didn't do the service call at Martha Eversol's apartment. He was supposed to, but it was his kid's birthday, and he wanted to take him to Disneyland, so he let another guy cover for him."

"What other guy?"

"Mr. Gavin Treat, of Hacienda Heights. He lives two blocks from here, in a third-floor apartment. Treat used to work for Bowden's company. Then he went freelance. He's an independent contractor, gets called out when the full-time employees are booked up. Hires out his services to any company that needs him on any given day. That particular day, he took over Bowden's assignments and let Bowden sign the paperwork."

"And Bowden never said anything—"

"Because he could lose his job. He's not supposed to hand off his day's work to somebody else."

"He should've called in sick."

"He had a bad case of the flu last summer. His sick days were maxed out."

"Anything to link Treat to Nikki Carter or C. J. Osborn?"

"Carter, yes. We checked Treat's DL." Driver's license. "He changed his address six months ago. Previously he resided at the Westside Palms."

"Shit." That was Nikki Carter's apartment building.

"He was two floors down from her. They might've met in the laundry room or the elevator—whatever. It's a security building, but when he moved out, he probably held on to a duplicate key to the main entrance. Then he could pick the lock on her apartment, install the Webcam while she was out."

Walsh grunted. "How about Osborn?"

"That, we can't figure. Since there's no record of her PC being serviced, Treat must have singled her out some other way."

"The ex-husband suggested it might be a revenge thing—somebody C. J. arrested. Does Treat have a record?"

"No, he's clean. Not even a parking ticket."

"There goes that theory."

"Well, hell, we don't need to know *everything*. We've nailed the guy, Morrie. Be happy."

"I'll be happy when he's in custody and Osborn's safe and sound. I take it we're operating on the assumption Treat is home."

"His vehicle is parked in the apartment building's underground garage."

"What kind of vehicle?"

"White 1999 Ford Econoline E-150, commercial model."

Deputy Tanner spoke up. "Like the one C. J. saw following her this afternoon."

Walsh nodded. "Additional confirmation—as if any was needed. So we don't *know* he's home?"

Cellini said no. "He might have taken a second vehicle, although his DMV records list only one. We can't probe his apartment with infrared sensors or long-distance microphones—too much ambient heat and noise from other units in the building. We could call him and see if he answers—"

"But we don't want to spook him," Deputy Chang said.

"Even if we pretend it's a sales call," Tanner added, "he might get suspicious. Then we've got a barricade situation."

"With a possible hostage," Chang said.

Captain Garcia nodded. "So we're going in hard. Deputies Tanner and Chang are members of a SWAT element. Tanner's the team leader. Chang's the scout. We've called out the rest of the team."

"Lucky break, having you here," Walsh said.

"Lucky for us," Tanner said coolly. "Unlucky for Treat—if he's home."

One of the radio operators leaned into the doorway. "Raid van's here." He meant the SWAT van loaded with the gear necessary to carry out an armed assault—flak vests, assault weapons, tear gas, flash-bang grenades, night-vision goggles, Nomex fire-resistant hoods, the works.

Tanner and Chang moved toward the rear of the command post. "Time to suit up," Tanner said.

Walsh almost told them to be careful, but he knew it would just sound stupid. SWAT team members were trained to be careful.

He hoped Tanner's team lived up to SWAT's reputation—because he had a feeling that where the Hourglass Killer was concerned, they could not afford mistakes.

38

"When . . ." C. J. heard the hoarseness in her voice and had to start over. "When did you get back?"

"Just now." Adam stood there, watching her. "Glad to see me?"

She got to her feet, kicking away the rope. In her right hand she still held the glass shard, her only weapon.

"You shouldn't have taken off the blindfold," Adam said. "It's easier to die when you can't see what's coming. That's why they blindfold the victim of a firing squad. Act of mercy."

"I didn't expect mercy from you."

"That's good. Because you won't be getting any."

She watched him across the dim, cavernous space. He wore slacks and a windbreaker with bulky pockets. When he moved toward her, she raised the shard, letting it catch the moonlight. "Don't come any closer."

"I've got a gun, remember?"

"So use it."

He removed a gloved hand from the side pocket of his windbreaker, taking out the gun. Even at a distance, she could see that it was a pistol, probably a 9mm. The gun flashed toward her, and for an instant she was back inside Ramon Sanchez's converted garage, facing his ancient revolver.

But he didn't fire. "Put down the piece of glass, C. J."

"Make me."

"You're a stubborn bitch—you know that?"

"And you're a fucking psycho."

He still didn't fire, and she began to think he wouldn't. But why not?

"I can take that weapon away from you anytime I want," he said.

"Go ahead."

"It'll be no problem—just like jumping you in the hallway. You didn't put up much of a fight, you know."

"An ambush is one thing. Taking me here and now is another."

"I'll risk it."

"You'll get stuck." She displayed the shard. "How'd you like it in your neck? Your eye?"

He studied her. She knew he was asking himself whether or not he could wrest control of the weapon without getting sliced.

"You can't," she told him, letting him know she could read his thoughts. "I'm too quick for you. I know too many moves."

His reaction surprised her. He laughed. "Good old C. J. A fighter to the end." His gaze shifted to the upended crate. "I shouldn't have left my gear with you. I thought it was out of reach."

His gear, he'd said. She saw other needles scattered on the floor, as well as more vials of ink. She wondered—

"It won't save you, C. J.," he said, cutting off her thoughts. "We're still going to share that last dance."

"I'm not much in the mood for dancing. You know what I was thinking about the whole time you were gone?"

"How to get free and save your ass?"

"Besides that."

"What?"

"You. How you could do something this sick, this crazy."

"It's not crazy. Sick—yes. I plead guilty to that charge. But I'm perfectly sane. I'm just doing what any normal spurned spouse would do, given half a chance."

"I hope you don't believe that."

"But I do." His hard-soled shoes clicked on the floor as he began to circle a few yards from her, and she moved, as well, keeping her distance from him. "People aren't nearly as civilized as they like to pretend. I'll bet there isn't anybody who hasn't fantasized at one time or another about subjecting an enemy to a painful, violent death. Every kid who gets slammed around by the school bully, every teenager who's grounded by his parents, every office drone whose boss is on his case—they've all thought about it." A knowing smile came to his face. "After you found me in bed with Ashley, didn't you think about it?"

The truth came out reluctantly. "I guess."

He spread his arms. "Well, there you are."

It occurred to her that he was arguing a case. Like one of those mock trials in law school. Showing how clever he was, how he could twist logic and facts to prove anything.

"Thinking is one thing," she said, still sidestepping to match every step he took, the two of them circling each other like knife fighters. "This is reality, Adam. You're really doing this. Do you understand? *This is for real.*"

"Of course it's for real. It's life and death. My life. Your death."

"Because I left you?"

"Well, yes, that—and because I was handed the golden opportunity." A disarming smile. "Pure serendipity. It would have been ungrateful of me to turn it down. Think about it. The chance to kill my ex-wife and escape all suspicions. To use a serial killer as my fall guy. The perfect crime."

Serial killer?

She almost asked him what he was talking about, and then she understood.

The stuff on the floor. Needles, ink.

Tattoo equipment.

The Hourglass Killer.

She'd had nothing to do with the investigation, but it had been in the papers. Everybody knew about it.

So that was his plan. To playact as the Hourglass Killer. To pass her off as the latest victim.

Some of her fear left her. "It won't work," she said.

Her tone of voice—unnaturally calm—caught his attention. He stopped circling. "Sure it will."

"No. You can't imitate a serial killer that easily. The police are always alert for copycats. They'll find some details of the crime that don't match the MO, and they'll know it's not the same guy."

"Oh, really? I never thought of that."

He came a little closer, and she let him, standing her ground. She could see his smile now, his white teeth against his tan face.

"Joke about it all you want," she said. "What I'm telling you is true."

"Ordinarily, yes. But not in this case."

"Why not?"

"Because"—he leaned toward her, and involuntarily she stepped back—"he really *had* targeted you, C. J."

"What?"

"If he continued his usual pattern, he would have struck tonight. I beat him to it, that's all."

"What are you—"

"He'll be royally pissed off when he figures out what happened, don't you think?"

She struggled to register the words. The Hourglass Killer after her? It was impossible. She hadn't been stalked or followed or—

Followed.

"The white van," she whispered.

"What's that? A little louder, please."

"A van tailed me home today. Was that you?"

"Nope. Must've been him. I told you he was getting ready to go for it. It's the last day of the month, after all."

Her head spun. Absurdly all she could think of was the one question that haunted her, always, though it was utterly irrelevant now.

Was it him?

The boogeyman?

She blinked the thought away.

"You know," Adam was saying in a pleasant conversational tone, "in a way, it's almost a public service I'm performing."

She gasped out a laugh. "Is it?"

He started circling again, and so did she, and distantly it occurred to her that they *were* dancing, after all—a slow waltz of death.

"I'm removing a vicious multiple murderer from the streets," Adam said. "I'm saving lives. Who knows how many more victims there might have been if this guy had remained on the loose? In the larger scheme of things, your life is an insignificant price to pay for bringing him to justice."

He was being a lawyer again, arguing before an invisible jury. She turned his own logic against him. "If he was going to kill me anyway, why didn't you let him? Then I'd be dead, and there'd be no risk to you."

"I thought about it." His voice changed, the jury disappearing from his imagination. "I really did, C. J. But I couldn't let it happen that way."

"Why not?"

"Because he doesn't deserve you. Who are you to him? Nobody. A random target. Somebody he spotted at a shopping mall and followed home—or maybe he saw you on patrol, or he delivers your mail. Whoever he is, he's not part of your life in any meaningful way. So why should he be part of your death?"

She was silent. She didn't know what to say.

"*I* do the killing, C. J. *Me.* Because I earned it. I put up with you for three years—"

"Put up with me?"

"—and I get to finish you now. To do it myself, with my own hands. That's how he kills them, you know. How I'll do it too. Strangulation. You'll look at me as you take your last breath."

"You really are goddamned insane."

"I thought that's what you always loved about me." He shrugged. "Hell, C. J., you would've been dead one way or the other. At least this way we keep it between friends."

39

Tanner didn't say anything to his team during the elevator ride to the third floor. There was nothing to say. The instructions had been given, the plan of attack laid out. It would be a dynamic entry—break down the door of Apartment 310 and flood the interior. Use caution when engaging the target; possible hostage situation. Clear your background. Take no chances.

As the arrow above the elevator doors climbed to number two, Tanner inventoried his gear. Colt .45 1911 semiauto pistol in a strongside thigh holster. A backup Colt in the pocket of his tactical vest. Flashbangs, smoke grenades, and other diversionary devices clipped to his utility belt. On his head, a ballistic helmet and a LASH two-way radio headset with a throat microphone on a breakaway strap.

The four men with him in the elevator were similarly attired in full BDU—battle dress uniform. McMath and DiMaria were the two assaulters; in addition to their Colts, they carried Heckler & Koch MP-5 9mm submachine guns, each capable of firing eight hundred rounds per minute on full automatic. Weldham was the rear guard, armed with a Benelli

Super90 M1 twelve-gauge shotgun. Automatic rifles like the MP-5s got all the press, but Tanner knew that a twelve-gauge was the deadliest gun on earth.

Finally there was Chang, the scout, wearing his earphone and stalk microphone, carrying the 180-degree mirror he'd made himself—an eighth of an inch of mirrored plastic affixed to a telescoping handle. Using it, he could peer around corners without exposing himself to a head shot.

The elevator reached the third floor, and the doors opened. Everyone tensed, but the hallway was clear.

"Last door on the right," Tanner reminded them. "Switch your flashlights on."

The flashlights were mounted to the barrels of the MP-5s. In the bright corridor they were unnecessary, but there was no telling what would happen once the shooting team got inside Treat's apartment.

Tanner led his men down the hall to the door marked 310. There was no legal problem about entering; a judge had already given telephonic approval to a search warrant and an arrest warrant. Even without the warrants, exigent circumstances would have justified the search-and-seizure operation. Treat was no longer protected by anonymity, and he was no longer protected by law.

His apartment was next to the rear stairwell. Just in case Treat managed to get past the tactical team, a pair of deputies from the City of Industry Station had been deployed in the lobby to watch the stairs. Another two deputies in an unmarked car watched Treat's windows from the street. If he tried to climb out, he would be spotted.

No escape.

Unless he was already gone. This was the thought that nagged at Tanner as he prepared to break down the apartment door. Sure, Treat's van was in the garage, but he might use a different vehicle when committing his crimes. He might be miles away, the apartment empty.

Now that they knew his identity, they would catch him eventually. But not in time to save C. J. . . .

He cleared his mind of those fears and motioned to the first assaulter, who launched the hand-carried battering ram at the door, striking it directly beside the lock. Wood splintered, the door yielded, and then Tanner and Chang were inside, the two assaulters rushing after them, Weldham bringing up the rear.

As always in a raid, he found reality instantly reduced to a series of impressions—stray facts noted almost at random, without evaluation or context.

Living room. Brightly lit by a halogen floor lamp. Unoccupied. To his right, a kitchenette with a wet bar. To the left, an interior hall lit by a low-wattage overhead bulb—

Movement in the hall.

"Stop, police!" he yelled.

The figure vanished into a room at the far end of the hall, slamming the door.

Tanner's instinct was to run for the door and force it open, but his training told him to always cover his back. "Check the kitchen," he said to DiMaria. It was possible for someone to hide behind the counter.

DiMaria looked. "Clear."

"Roger." Tanner crossed the living room and opened the linen closet. Empty. Then he was in the hall, pivoting into a guest bathroom. No one there. Halfway down the hall now, his men behind him, Tanner acutely aware that slots were danger areas and he was the first target Treat would hit if he opened fire through the door. He was grateful for the heavy flak jacket, the aramid fibers that would stop most calibers of ammunition.

Another closet to examine—empty also—and finally he was at the door Treat had slammed. It was locked. No surprise.

The overhead light switched off. Now the hall was lit only by the flashlight beams that swept up and down like crisscrossing searchlights.

Tanner kicked the door. It didn't yield. Not wood. Metal. A steel door, hardly standard issue for a residential apartment. Treat must have installed it himself. It was the door to his inner sanctum—a soundproofed room, maybe, where he brought his victims. Where C. J. might be held prisoner right now.

"Blow it open," he told Weldham, whose twelve-gauge was best suited for the job.

Weldham took a step forward, feeding a Magnum slug into the tube, and then the screaming started.

It was McMath who screamed first, a high, feminine shriek like no sound any SWAT commando ever wanted to make, followed by a flurry of gibbering profanities and the words, "They're all over me!"

Tanner swung his flash in McMath's direction, but he had no time to see what was happening because suddenly DiMaria was screaming too. It had to be screams he was hearing, though at first they sounded like raucous, hysterical laughter. "Get 'em off, *get 'em off*!"

Now Chang was slapping at the back of his neck, and Weldham was stomping his boots in manic desperation.

Tanner didn't understand until he looked up, his flashlight beam following his gaze.

Spiders were dropping from the ceiling.

They fell in clouds, like confetti. He knew they

were spiders because even in the chancy, flickering light he could see the black bulbs of their abdomens and the stringy strands of webbing that floated down with them, wisps of cotton candy, unreal in the semidarkness.

It was a trap. He'd been trained that hallways were the ideal place for an ambush, but in all his training he'd never heard of an ambush by spiders.

"*Retreat!*" he yelled, pushing Chang toward the front of the hall, but Chang merely fell, eight-legged shapes whispering across his face. In his flashlight's glow Tanner saw one of the shapes scuttle inside Chang's collar and vanish beneath his clothes.

Instinctively he checked his arms, the front of his flak jacket. He saw one spider clinging to his utility belt and flicked it away. Another one, larger—a tarantula?—had landed on his trouser leg and was curling up in a defensive posture, threatening no harm, but Tanner kicked it loose anyway, not wanting the goddamned thing on his person.

He couldn't force a retreat—his men, who had been bunched up at the midpoint of the hall and had received the brunt of the downpour, were incapable of withdrawing, incapable of anything except slapping at the spiders that plastered them in quivering bunches.

All right, go forward.

He grabbed the shotgun out of Weldham's hands, jammed it into the door beside the dead bolt, and fired point-blank, the Magnum slug cratering the metal. Still the door didn't give. He fired twice more—the Benelli's standard load this time, 00 buckshot shells—the reports thunderous in the confined space.

One side of the door was a scorched, smoking ruin.

The lock had been torn apart. Tanner gave the door his shoulder, and Chang, recovering sufficiently to assist, rammed it at the same time. The door heaved open, tilting on its hinges.

Tanner rushed through—he had no time to slice the pie, and no patience for it either. Dimly he knew that Treat would be counting on him to make the kind of stupid mistake he'd just made.

Well, come on, asshole, Tanner thought. Give me your best shot.

His flashlight swept a large bedroom. Table lamps on nightstands flanking a neatly made bed. Some kind of aquarium in the corner—no, a terrarium, housing another spider, this one behind glass. TV against one wall. A few other items of furniture, none big enough to hide behind.

No C. J.

No Gavin Treat.

Where was he? Bathroom?

Tanner ducked inside. No one there.

The closet, then.

He kicked open the closet door and stepped back, expecting a volley of shots. Nothing happened. He risked a look inside and saw shirts and trousers meticulously arrayed on wooden hangers, several pairs of shoes, a tie rack—and a hole in the wall.

It was a neat rectangular hole, obviously cut with care some time ago. The panel of cutout drywall leaned beside it.

Tanner reviewed the apartment's layout in his mind and saw that this closet was adjacent to the stairwell.

"Fuck." Into his radio mike: "He's taking the stairs, repeat, taking the stairs. Could be going up or down. Watch the lobby and the roof. Control the perimeter. And we've got officers down—send an RA." Rescue ambulance.

He turned to look at Chang and found him leaning on the bed, a sick look on his face. "Itches," he managed to say.

"Where'd it bite you?"

Chang touched his breastbone. "Here."

Tanner remembered the spider that had skittered under Chang's collar. He tried to remember if any spiders injected enough venom to prove fatal to a healthy adult. The black widow, maybe. And the brown recluse? He wasn't sure. "You're not gonna die on me, are you?" he asked with a strained smile.

"I'm okay. Just get that cocksucker."

Chang rarely swore. Tanner liked hearing it. It showed he had some fight left.

"Count on it," he promised, and he went into the closet again.

The crawlway in the wall was narrow. This Treat must be as thin-shouldered as a girl. With an effort Tanner forced his way through. Then he was on the stairwell landing.

Treat could have gone up or down. The lobby ought to be secured by the unit on the ground.

Tanner went up, wishing they had a helicopter to cover the roof. Treat couldn't get anywhere if he was pinned in a chopper's searchlight. But Captain Garcia hadn't wanted to call in an air unit—afraid the beat of the rotors would tip off the suspect.

He ascended the metal staircase at a run, pausing on the fourth-floor landing to visually clear the hallway. No sign of Treat, so he pounded up the last flight of stairs to the roof access door. Opened it and retreated a step, scanning the roof by degrees, then emerged into the open air and turned instantly to put his back against the stairwell door.

He had an unobstructed view of the entire roof— yards of black tar under the moon and stars.

On the north side, five yards away, lay a dark, prone shape.

Treat? Lying on his belly, armed, sighting his quarry?

Tanner knelt, making a smaller target, then unhooked a smoke grenade from his utility belt. Pulled the pin, lobbed the weapon. It traveled in a high arc and dropped near the shape, releasing a cloud of gray smoke.

The shape didn't move.

Tanner waited for the smoke to clear, then cautiously approached the shape. As he drew near, he saw that it wasn't a man. It was a ladder.

"Shit."

The ladder had been fully extended and stretched horizontally between the roof of this building and the one behind it—another apartment complex, as Tanner recalled from his briefing.

Treat must have scrambled across like a monkey on a branch. The other roof was empty. He was already gone.

Tanner used his radio again, telling the deputies on the ground that Treat had escaped via the building to the rear. Garcia's voice came back to him over his earphone. "We're sending two units to reconnoiter. He won't get away that easily."

He already has, Tanner thought.

Then another voice, which Tanner didn't recognize, said, "Jesus, what the hell happened in here?"

Backup had reached the apartment, found the four

SWAT commandos. Even over his headset Tanner could hear moans of pain. He pictured his men writhing.

"They need antivenin," Tanner said. "They've been bitten by spiders."

"What kind of spiders?" Garcia snapped.

"All kinds."

It was true. They had come in every shape and size, even in different hues—some lithe and small like puffballs with threadlike legs, others large and hairy, some jet-black, others brown or reddish.

Tanner took a moment to inspect himself. He found a spider entangled in the laces of his boot and smashed it with his fist. Another one was making its way slowly up his sleeve like a determined climber attacking Everest. He wiped off that one on the stairwell door, leaving a brown smudge.

No others. And none—he patted himself, front and back—none under his clothes, against his skin.

He'd been lucky. As team leader he was supposed to be in front of his men, in a position of maximum exposure, but in this case it had been the safest position to occupy. The rain of spiders had been concentrated in the middle of the hall.

Another minute passed while the units on the ground reconnoitered the second building. Then Garcia reported, "There's a fire escape from the roof to the ground. Grass near the fire escape has been trampled."

Tanner sighed. "He's booked."

"Roger that. We're calling in other units to sweep the streets."

"They won't find him."

Garcia's voice was a dry crackle. "I know."

"Any sign of the victim?"

"No. Maybe he never had her."

"Of course he had her," Tanner snapped.

Walsh had said she had four hours to live. He'd been wrong. It was only 10:15, and she was dead already. Had to be.

C. J. was dead.

40

"We aren't friends," C. J. said softly. "We never were."

"Ouch." Adam grimaced. "That stings."

"Quit grandstanding. This cold-blooded killer act isn't working. I can see right through it."

"Can you?"

"You're more scared than I am right now." Which is saying something, she added silently. "You know you won't get away with it."

"I know I will. It's all set up, right down to the e-mail I sent you."

"The Four-H Club—I still don't get it."

"Private joke. But Detective Walsh will figure it out when he checks the contents of your computer."

"I deleted the message." This was a lie. She remembered saving it, but she wanted to rattle him.

She failed. "No problem," he said nonchalantly. "It'll still be in the Web cache. Probably still on the ISP's server, as well. Someone will find it."

"And trace it to you."

"It was scrubbed. Sent through a mixmaster—that's tech talk for a service that renders e-mail anonymous. It can't be traced. I've been very careful, C. J. I just spent a half hour with the great Detective Walsh himself, and by the end of the interview he was ready to hold my hand and comfort me in my distress. That's how convincing I was."

"You're not that good an actor."

"I fooled you, didn't I? All those months when I was banging Ashley, you never suspected a thing. She was a lot better than you, by the way. Fucking you was more like a domestic chore than an erotic adventure."

This was so transparent, she actually laughed. "You're pathetic. God, how did I ever fall for a loser like you?"

She saw his mouth twist in anger, then smooth into a smile. "A loser who's holding all the cards in this particular game."

"You're not holding any cards. You can't shoot me. It's not the right MO. The method of murder is the most distinctive thing about a serial killer. You fire a gun at me, and you might as well turn yourself in to Walsh right now."

"That's bullshit."

"To kill me, you've got to disarm me. Want to try? Come within reach, and I'll slice your carotid artery. Severing that artery causes death within seconds. No blood to the brain."

He looked uneasily at the shard. "You can't hold me off all night."

"You can't afford to be here all night. Walsh will want to talk to you again. You know he will. Even if you're not a suspect, you're still my ex-husband. And if you gave as good a performance as you claim, he'll be sure to keep you posted on developments in the case—just for your own peace of mind."

"You going somewhere with this?" He sounded

irritated, and she knew she was finally breaking down his facade of composure.

"No, I'm not, Adam. That's the point. Neither of us is going anywhere with this. It's a stalemate. You've played this game to a draw."

"Maybe so, C. J. Maybe this particular strategy is a dead end." He pocketed the gun. "But you know what that means? It means I have to improvise a new approach."

He bent and picked up the overturned crate. With one downward swing he battered it to pieces against the floor. What was left in his hands was a single plank, ragged at one end, with two or three nails still imbedded in the wood.

"See that, C. J.? See how well I can think on my feet?"

He whipped the plank back and forth like a batter warming up at the plate. C. J. retreated, feeling the breeze on her face.

"The Hourglass Killer doesn't club his victims either," she said.

"First time for everything. They say these guys get more savage as time goes on. Just killing doesn't get it up for them anymore, so they start getting . . . creative. Maybe I'll get creative with you, babe."

The plank flashed at her, cutting an arc through the air, and she withdrew another step.

"No," he said. "On second thought, I really don't have time. Got to do this quick and dirty. So here's the plan. I'll whack you good, you'll go down, and I'll get you all duct-taped again. Then slap you awake so you can be there when you die."

He swung the plank at her head. She ducked, narrowly avoiding the blow, and backed up still farther.

"Wouldn't want you to miss the grand finale, after all. That's when I wrap my hands—my gloved hands, naturally—around your throat and squeeze, squeeze, squeeze, all the time looking into your wide-open green eyes."

She didn't dare glance behind her, couldn't risk taking her gaze off the plank in Adam's hands, but she knew—sensed—that she was running out of room. He was backing her into a tight spot where she would be unable to maneuver, and there was nothing she could do about it. The glass shard was useless now. She couldn't slash at him without bringing herself within range of the plank.

"The tattoo," he went on, his voice toneless and almost calm, "will be applied postmortem. I understand that's how *he* does it. Which is a shame, really—I'd like to carve it into your flesh while you're still around to feel the pain."

"You really need to get out more," she said.

"I intend to. I'll have a lot of celebrating to do. It's not everyone who can pull off the perfect murder. Of course a large part of it is selectivity. You have to choose the perfect victim. That's you, C. J."

He feinted with the plank, and she drew back, her shoulder blades thumping against concrete.

A wall.

But there are no walls in here, she wanted to protest. After she removed the blindfold, she'd looked around and seen only open space at the perimeter of the garage.

Hadn't looked behind her, though, had she? The rear of the garage did have a wall, and she was up against it now—up against it in more ways than one.

"Gotta tell you, C. J., I am thoroughly enjoying this."

The plank again, circling toward her face. She dropped to one knee and sliced at his leg with the shard, hoping to cut the hamstring, cripple him, but he sidestepped the attack and brought the plank down.

She flung herself clear, scrambling along the wall into a doorway that opened on a new space—a stairwell, heading up—but before she could take the stairs, Adam was there, his foot on the first step, cutting off her exit.

"No way, babe. This is as far as you go."

She was trapped on the landing, and all she could do was retreat on hands and knees into the far corner while Adam advanced.

Deep darkness here. The light from outside barely penetrated this niche. She could see Adam only as a vague silhouette against the dim glow in the doorway.

She was stuck in the corner now. Nowhere to go. The shard was her only weapon, and it was no good to her.

She groped for some new tool to use against him, and behind her, in a recess in the wall, her fingers touched a tangle of wires.

Electrical wires, rubber-insulated. The plate that would cover them had not yet been installed.

Live wires? Was the power on?

Could be. The workmen needed power tools.

And she was due for a little luck.

Adam had paused a few feet away. Couldn't see her in the dimness. Knew she was close by, so he was waiting for his vision to adjust to the minimal light.

It wouldn't take long. She had seconds, no more.

She pocketed the shard and reached into the nest of wires. She knew that wires came in three varieties—

hot, neutral, and ground. The hot wire and either of the other two would complete a circuit.

Adam took the final steps, closing on his prey.

She grabbed two of the wires, holding them by their rubber sheaths, praying that one of them was the hot wire and that the current was on.

Without sight, somehow she knew that Adam had raised the plank for the knockout blow. Lunging forward, she jammed the wires against his body.

And there was light.

A sudden spark, dazzling in the gloom—there *was* current in the wires, 120 volts that had raced from the hot wire to the other one via the intermediary of Adam's body—and with a howl of pain, he staggered backward, falling, the plank gone from his grasp as he clutched himself and rolled.

Without meaning to, she had zapped him in his most vulnerable spot. She'd gotten him in the balls.

"Well, fuck you, mister," she breathed. He deserved it.

He had been saved from unconsciousness or worse only by his reflexive retreat from the shock. He'd broken the circuit before it could seriously fry him.

If she could shock him again, she would put him down for the count. But he was too far away for the wires to reach.

She dropped the wires and darted around the spot where he lay. Even stunned, he wasn't helpless. His hand caught her by the ankle. She stumbled, kicking free, but already he was struggling to rise.

The plank.

She grabbed it and batted him, deliberately aiming for his crotch this time, but he drew up a knee to ward off the strike and she heard the crack of the plank against the side of his thigh.

"God*damn* it," Adam gasped, jerking the plank away from her before she could use it again.

She couldn't get past him, out the doorway, not when he had the plank in his hands, so she took the stairs, heading up to the second level of the garage.

Already he was following. Whatever damage she'd inflicted had barely slowed him down. Adrenaline could do miraculous things for the human body, enabling a person to absorb punishment and summon reserves of stamina unknown in ordinary circumstances.

"You can't get away from me, you bitch!" His shout echoed up the stairwell.

We'll see, she thought.

The stairs were barricaded after the second landing. She couldn't go all the way to the roof. Just as well—the roof would be a dead end anyway.

She ran onto the second level, identical to the first except that no stripes had been painted on the floor.

Adam burst out of the doorway, limping on his injured knee, but seemingly oblivious to the pain.

At the far end of the garage was a concrete ramp that must lead to the ground floor, but she didn't think she could reach it in time.

Instead she veered to her right, toward a low guardrail. Got there, looked down. A twenty-foot drop onto asphalt. Not good.

Adam was closing in. She ran along the guardrail. For a crazy moment the image entered her mind of a mechanical rabbit at a dog track, speeding along an electrified rail while the hounds pursued.

Still no place to jump. And he was nearly on top of her now.

Again she glanced down. This time she saw something other than black asphalt below.

Dirt. A huge pile of excavated dirt.

Her best chance.

Adam reached for her—she felt the plank whisper an inch above her head—as she vaulted the rail and plummeted into space.

A cry escaped her, a long involuntary shriek, and then she landed atop the hill of dirt, all the breath shocked out of her by the impact.

She looked up. Adam had discarded the plank. He was drawing his gun.

Shit.

She dived down the slope, rolling onto the asphalt, then sprinted for the nearest cover, a trash bin ten feet away. Reached it and hunkered down, her breath explosive, heart hammering.

Adam hadn't fired. Either he still didn't want to alter the MO, or he simply hadn't had a decent shot.

One thing was certain. He hadn't given up. He would be after her.

She had to get the hell out of this place, wherever it was, and she had to do it fast.

41

Rawls had his hands full dealing with Steven Gader, whose mindset in the past two hours had changed from reluctant cooperation to indignant defensiveness and finally to outright hysteria. "I didn't know about the women," he kept saying. "Jesus, I didn't *know!*"

"Of course you didn't, Mr. Gader," Rawls said evenly. As Gader's tone had risen in pitch and intensity, Rawls's own voice had dropped half an octave and slowed down, as if to compensate. "You didn't know anything. I hear you."

"Well, all right. All right. I knew there might be some . . . funny business. You know, maybe the women weren't aware, *fully* aware, that they were being taped. I mean, that was a possibility. A remote possibility."

"Remote," Rawls echoed, his voice deepening still further, entering the James Earl Jones range.

"But the other stuff, these killings, it's news to me. I mean, a complete shock. I never had the slightest . . . Look, if I had even suspected . . ."

Rawls said nothing. He believed Gader, actually. But he wasn't about to let him off the hook so easily. The man was scum. Let him sweat.

"Maybe I'd better call a lawyer," Gader finished.

"That's your right."

Gader trudged out of the room. Rawls stared after him, then glanced at Brand.

"What a prick," Brand commented without looking up from Gader's computer.

Rawls laughed, his first laugh in quite a long while. "Ned, you always know the right thing to say."

His cell phone chirped. He took the call, and his smile vanished when he heard Morris Walsh's first words.

"Got good news and bad news." There was no life in his voice, and no hope. "Which do you want to hear first?"

"Just tell it all."

"We identified Bluebeard. SWAT just raided his apartment. He was there, but he got away."

"He's at large?"

"Afraid so."

"And the victim?"

"No sign of her."

"You think he already did her?" Rawls hated that ugly euphemism, *did*, which stood for everything from consensual sex to rape to homicide, but he couldn't bring himself to say *killed*.

On the other end of the line, Walsh sighed. "We don't know. I had this theory that he holds them for four hours, but . . . Well, it looks like I was wrong."

He sounded tired. More than tired. Defeated. As if he had given up. Not a good sign—for him, for the case, or for C. J. Osborn, if she was still alive.

"Possibly not," Rawls said, trying to give Walsh some encouragement. "He may have stashed her somewhere."

"And gone home? Maybe. I don't think so. You know, the four-hour thing was based mainly on the tattoos."

"The hourglass," Rawls said.

"But I guess they had a different significance. Our guy is into spiders."

This was such a non sequitur that Rawls could only echo, "Spiders?"

A grunt from Walsh. "He laid a trap for our SWAT team . . . or for anybody else who tried to corner him in his lair. Installed the cover of a fluorescent lighting panel on the ceiling of the hallway inside his apartment. But there's no light fixture behind it. Instead, there's spiders."

"How many?" Rawls asked softly.

"A million of the goddamned things, for all I know. The asshole locks himself in his bedroom behind a steel door, then kills the hallway light—he rewired the switch so he could operate it from inside his room—then activates a hydraulic cable that runs through the ceiling. Simple principle—the Plexiglas cover of the lighting panel is spring-loaded, and the cable releases the spring. Cover slides back, spiders fall out."

"A million of them."

"Give or take."

"Venomous spiders?"

"Oh, sure. Probably not normally aggressive, but when they've been dumped out of their cage like that . . ."

"They bite. How bad is it?"

"We've got four SWAT members in the hospital, plus another Sheriff's deputy who got bitten when he reached the scene. Fumigators are spraying the apartment now. Probably have to evacuate the building . . .

It's got central air, and some of the spiders may have gotten into the ducts."

"Nightmare," Rawls breathed. No wonder the detective sounded beaten.

"Hasn't been my best day. Or anybody else's either. Except for the suspect. He got away clean through a secret exit."

"Take anything?"

"His computer, it looks like. A laptop, obviously. He must own one. There's a, whatchamacallit, docking station in his bedroom."

"If he has a mobile connection or he can get access to a phone jack, he can monitor the Web site."

"And the video feed. I know. I kept it up and running. He knows we're on to him, but he doesn't necessarily know we're aware of the site."

"Does that help us?"

"Who knows?" Walsh sighed again. "Can't hurt. Frankly, I'll take any advantage I can get over this creep. Hold on a sec."

Rawls heard Walsh talking to somebody in the background, relaying orders in an exhausted voice. He glanced at Brand. "It's a mess in LA."

"So I gathered. Hey, this guy always strikes on the last night of the month, right?"

"So?"

"Just strikes me as funny, that's all. The coincidence, I mean."

"Coincidence?"

"You getting the tip-off e-mail on the same day when this dude is getting set to knock off victim number three."

Rawls stared at him, thinking. "Now that you mention it," he said finally, "it is kind of funny."

Then Walsh was back on the line. "Sorry about the

interruption. Things are pretty hairy here. I've got to go."

"Just one thing, Morrie. You never explained about the tattoos. When I asked, you started talking about spiders. What's the connection?"

"Black widows. They have that same hourglass mark."

"I see."

"That's what the tats were all about. Goddamned spiders—not time." Walsh was beating himself up, taking the blame for having made the wrong deduction. Rawls heard the harsh self-accusation in his voice.

"It could be both," Rawls said gently. "A symbol for both things."

"Could be, but evidently it isn't. Christ, did I ever fuck this up."

"Morrie—"

Walsh kept talking, unwilling to be consoled. "He never had a four-hour timetable. Even the name we had for him was wrong. He's not the Hourglass Killer. He has another name for himself. A better name."

"What name?"

"It's right here in his journal. Yeah, we found that, or at least the Sheriff's crime-scene people did. He tells us who he really is on the very first line."

Rawls waited.

" 'I am the Webmaster,' " Walsh recited. "Kind of says it all, doesn't it?"

42

I am the Webmaster.

Treat repeated the words to himself, driving through a village of names.

His car was a secondhand Buick, which he had kept in a parking space six blocks from his apartment specifically for emergencies like this. After his escape from the local gendarmes, he had roved through alleys and side streets until he reached the Buick. The key, as always, was hidden in a magnetic case under the chassis. The car was registered under an alias and could not be readily connected to him. Stowed in the trunk were a set of false IDs, wads of cash, a passport, a disguise kit, and an overnight bag containing a change of clothes and a toothbrush. He believed in being prepared.

At first he considered driving out of state, beginning a new life somewhere else. Or ditching the car at LAX and taking a flight to the Midwest—someplace safely banal, like Omaha. But there was a chance the police would be looking for him at the airports. Even the roads might be blocked, though he doubted it.

Besides, he wanted to hang around. There was

Caitlin to think of. He still wanted his chance
with her.

In the meantime, he had to go someplace. One possibility was the house in Silver Lake where he had committed his crimes. He could hole up in the basement,
perhaps. But the defects in this plan were obvious. The
authorities had already identified him and tracked him
to his home. They might just as easily have discovered
his killing ground. He had to steer clear of Silver Lake.

Good thinking, but it had left him with nowhere
to go. Aimlessly he'd headed north from Hacienda
Heights until he entered the sprawling community
of West Covina. Then he had known where his instincts were carrying him, and he'd bowed to their
wisdom, driving east on Amar Road and turning
south into a sizable tract housing development. He
had driven here on other nights. For him, it was a
relaxing place to be, a place to decompress.

There was a fashion among housing developers of
choosing a theme for street names. Often the streets
were named in honor of the wildlife species they had
displaced—Spotted Owl Circle, say. Other times a
western motif was selected—Stagecoach Lane, Corral
Avenue, Saddleback Court. He had seen communi-
ties that reached for a regal air with streets like King
Henry Drive and Prince Edward Way. But the build-
ers of this particular development had opted for a
theme more congenial to Treat's tastes. Nearly every
one of the twisting, winding avenues and byways
bore a woman's name.

He motored slowly through the complex, past neat
little houses, windows aglow with reading lights and
television sets, and he scanned each signpost as it
moved past the Buick's windshield.

Kimberly Drive.

Then a series of courts—Joan Court, Kate Court, Kerry, Kathleen, June, Jessica, Justine.

Jacqueline Drive. Helen Lane. April Way. Sarah and Sonya and Stacey and Stephanie. Regina and Rebecca and Ruth and Ruby.

So many memories. And the promises of new memories to come.

There had been a Kimberly for him in Utah. She was a waitress in a roadside diner, and he killed her with a garrote at the end of her shift. Her hair was red, and her waitress uniform was red, and her blood was red as it trickled down her neck from the line incised across her throat by the taut piano wire.

And there had been a Kate, as well. Schoolteacher in Boulder, Colorado. He had been repairing telephone lines back then. He fixed the static on her line, then returned a few weeks later and fixed her. He had always disliked educators, and it had given him special pleasure to teach her this final lesson, a lesson in pain.

Oddly, he'd had no J's. No Joan, June, Jessica, Justine, Jacqueline. He could have—should have—had a Caitlin Jean tonight. But he preferred not to think about that. No point dwelling on a rare failure, when he had enjoyed so many successes.

The S's had been particularly productive for him. Never a Sarah, but there'd been a Sonya in Austin and a Stacey in Wyoming and two Stephanies. The first had been a nine-year-old girl in the Mojave— this was during his desert wanderings. The second, more recent—a nurse in Salem, Oregon. He didn't think her body had ever been found. There was a lot of wilderness in that part of the country, and carrion flesh didn't last long.

He drove farther along the curving avenues. Patty

and Petra and Priscilla passed him by without elic-
iting any nostalgic recollections. But Paula Street
brought a smile to his face. Paula had been a memorable one. Barmaid, Houston, 1991. Hot summer
night, with that insufferable Texas humidity choking
the air. She went home with another man. Treat followed. The man didn't stay the night. When he left,
Treat broke in and smothered Paula under a pillow.
The pillowcase had been a daffodil print—funny how
he remembered that. Later he read that the unlucky
bar patron who'd picked her up had been arrested
and charged with the homicide. Treat had never followed up on the case to learn if the man had been
convicted.

Yes, Paula. A good one.

Serial killers were said to take souvenirs, memen-
tos of their kills. No doubt most did, but Treat had
never been much of a collector. He saw no point in
weighing himself down with a lot of bric-a-brac
when he was so often on the move. And why give
the police any help in apprehending him, or in making a conviction stick? A room full of incriminating
evidence was just the break they needed.

So he had not followed the example of other killers
like himself. He took nothing from his victims except
their breath, their lives, and their names. This was
the secret hoard stashed in the treasure chest of his
soul. He remembered their names, always.

Amanda Street. Bernadette Court. Cynthia Court.

He'd had his share of A's, B's, and C's, but not
those particular ones. He headed toward the other
end of the community, past more sleepy homes, more
droning TV sets, more affectionate couples and
cranky kids, more of the normality that surrounded
him but never touched him, was never fully real.

Into the G's now. Gabriella, Gina, Gloria, Gail. He'd had a Gina in West Palm Beach. Left her dead in her condo with the air-conditioning turned up high to keep the body cold. He hadn't wanted the smell of decomposition to alert the neighbors until he was far away.

Faith, Frieda, Flora, Felicia. He recalled a Faith in the Mojave, eleven years old. A Felicia, too, though she had been one of his less satisfying kills—a patrol car had nearly spotted him as he was dragging her into an arroyo, and he'd had to quickly cut her throat and flee in case the cops doubled back to investigate. A waste. Treat sighed sadly. He hated waste.

Erica, Erin, Evangelina, Evelyn, Elena . . .

So many names. And he'd had no small number of them. Erica in Las Cruces, killed in an alley during a street festival, left on the pavement with cotton candy sticking to her face. Erin, another child of the Mojave. Evelyn—she'd been a driving instructor in San Francisco, whom he'd met during a stroll in Golden Gate Park. She had rebuffed his advances, but she hadn't noticed him follow her home. San Francisco was a fun town. All those people living atop an earthquake fault line that could rupture at any moment. Crowded life and mass death so closely intertwined. He would like to return there someday.

More streets, more names. He paid less attention. Occasionally a sign would catch his eye—Christie Lane; he'd known a Christie in New Orleans, pretty girl, slightly plump, squealed like a stuck pig when he put the ice pick in her skull—but mostly he just drove and let his thoughts wander.

After a traumatic experience, such as his run-in with officers of the law in their stormtrooper regalia, it was best to relax and reorient oneself. Nervous exhaustion would lead to panic, and panic produced stupidity, and stupidity was the single vice he could not abide.

Had he been stupid, he would not have lasted this long.

He'd been at the game for twenty years now. His first kill had been claimed at the tender age of twenty-one. He had preyed on children in the early years. In retrospect, he could see that his choice of victim had been dictated by his youthful insecurities. He had not felt competent to go after adults.

There had been children in Montana and Nebraska and the Mojave Desert. One of those children—a rare failure—had been Caitlin Osborn, age ten. He had seen her in the shopping district of her small hard-scrabble town and had been instantly captivated. Such a pretty little thing. He'd known he must have her. He had followed her home and watched her parents' house on and off for days, until the opportunity offered itself.

She would have been a memorable kill. He had planned to strangle her with his gloved hands. Strangulation had been one method he employed during his early wanderings, but not the only one.

Even in those formative years, he had begun to perfect his craft, testing new techniques, seeking variety. His inspiration was the famed Zodiac killer of California, who had never been caught. The Zodiac was unusual among predators of his kind because of his willingness to alter his modus operandi. Other killers repeated the same shopworn MO, invariably relying on the knife or the garrote or the gun, but the Zodiac had been more clever, more creative than that. He had tried different methods of execution, while varying the locale of his crimes.

More important, the Zodiac had resisted the temptation to advertise. There was a fetishistic impulse among serial killers to identify themselves with a "signature"—a term of art used by psychological profilers and other overpaid savants to designate a nonessential, highly personal feature of the crime. To kill with a knife was an MO. To mutilate the corpse in a distinctive fashion was a signature.

Because the Zodiac varied his MO and left no signature, for a long time his homicides, occurring in different jurisdictions, perpetrated by different means, had not even been connected. There was still some debate as to whether certain crimes were his work or someone else's.

At first Treat, emulating his hero, had left no signatures. Later he devised a variation on this approach. He concocted a specific persona, complete with MO, victim profile, and signature, for a brief stint of killing. Then he relocated, adopted a new MO and a fresh signature. He was the man of a thousand faces, protean in his ability to reinvent himself, prolific in his output.

He did not fool himself that he had mastered every nuance of his work. What was it old Chaucer had said, in a rather different context? "The life so short, the craft so long to learn." Yes, that stated it exactly. He could never be the complete master of such a complex art. Still, he had progressed. And he'd had his fun.

Having read the literature on serial murder, he knew that it was the fashion among investigators to classify a killer as organized or disorganized, social or asocial, according to the condition of the victim's body and the crime scene. He played games with the small minds that would pigeonhole him so neatly.

He matched the profile of a disorganized asocial killer on some of his outings, then switched to the organized social type, then mixed and matched, all the time moving from state to state, until the authorities in their blessed confusion must have thought they were dealing with three, six, a dozen separate maniacs.

As his confidence grew, he expanded his menu of victims. He put the lie to any accusation of gender bias by selecting the occasional boy, though the females always pleased him best. He overcame his insecurities by graduating to teenagers, then young adults, and finally to anyone who struck his fancy.

He had been the Bay Area Doctor, dispensing lethal injections to red-haired housewives; the Seattle Bedroom Invader, who killed couples—the husband executed with a silenced pistol shot, the wife asphyxiated with a plastic bag; the Twin Cities Arsonist, who burned his victims in their mobile homes; and others.

Now he was—or had been—the Hourglass Killer of Los Angeles. He'd preyed on single women in their twenties and thirties, leaving his signature tattoo, his coy calling card. He kept his victims alive for four hours. Why four? Well—why not? The time period had no significance to him. Neither did the hourglass tattoo, except as a private joke relating to his passion for black widows. Such details were merely part of his latest act, virtuoso flourishes in the new role he had written for himself, a magician's sleight of hand. While the police were writing their profiles and studying the pattern of his crimes, he would simply vanish, then reappear in a new guise, with new ground rules, in a new locale. And nobody would make the connection. Nobody would link the

Hourglass Killer in LA with, say, the Mesa Campus Stalker or the Boise Bride Snatcher or whatever new identity he crafted for himself.

By this means, he stayed always one step ahead of the authorities. Tonight, admittedly, had been a close call, and in retrospect he should have left town immediately upon noting the police presence in Caitlin's house. Still, his precautions, a product of experience and long habit, had served him well. He was free, sufficiently far from his home territory to make his arrest unlikely, and he could start over somewhere else, under a new name, in a new occupation.

In his dash for escape, he had left behind his van, most of his clothes and all of his furnishings, not to mention his arachnid menagerie. All he had was the old Buick—and his laptop computer, which he'd grabbed as he fled, and which now rested on the passenger seat. He was glad not to have lost it. Of course, the hardware could be replaced easily enough—in addition to the cash in the trunk, he had money banked in untraceable accounts, readily available, and he was quite an accomplished burglar as well. But there was a great deal of private information on the computer, including his bookmarked Web pages, one of which was the video display of Caitlin Osborn's bedroom.

As far as he could tell, the police remained unaware of the Web site. They had exhibited no knowledge of the secret surveillance and had neither disconnected the camera nor pulled the plug on the site. Conceivably he could continue to use it.

To watch Caitlin, if and when she returned home.

To watch . . . and perhaps to strike.

He shook his head. Smarter to forget her. Smarter

to move on, reinvent himself once more, start the games anew.

But she had eluded him once before. It galled him to have been cheated of her not once, but twice. To leave their relationship unconsummated.

Well, perhaps all was not yet lost. Anything was possible. And he was patient. He could wait for her.

He had already waited so long.

43

No way out.

C. J. had sprinted past blocks of lightless buildings, across swards of brown grass, until she reached the chain-link fence at the edge of the complex. From a distance it hadn't looked like an insuperable barrier. Only when she'd drawn close had she seen the coils of razor wire cresting the fence like spiked, unruly hair.

The wire would cut her to pieces if she tried to climb over.

Next she had skirted the perimeter in search of a gap in the fence or an open gate. She found no gaps, and the gate, when she came to it, was padlocked.

Pick the lock? She didn't have any tools. Cut the chain or the hasp? Not without a hacksaw.

Craning her neck, she peered up at a sign over the gate, which read "COMING SOON—MIDVALE OFFICE PARK."

Below the words was an artist's rendering of an immaculately landscaped commercial development on narrow, winding streets. The colors were bright and clear, and the picture had the wholesome appeal of a storybook illustration. But it was streaked with

dirt and rain, and she guessed that construction on
the project had halted some time ago.

She looked through the steel mesh of the gate
at the surrounding darkness. There had to be a
road or a home nearby, some sign of habitation
or activity.

There was nothing. The office park lay in an un-
populated wasteland of sere desert hills, an environ-
ment that reminded her a little of the Mojave Desert
where she had grown up. In the congested sprawl of
the LA basin, Adam had managed to find that ultimate rarity—a secluded place.

She leaned against the gate, fighting for breath, trying to decide what to do.

Well, there was one option. She could bust her
way out.

Adam must have parked his car near the garage,
although she hadn't seen it during her escape. If she
could find it . . .

Maybe she could hot-wire the engine. All she
needed was a tool to pry off the ignition cylinder—
any bit of scrap metal would do. Then ram the gate
and blow it off its hinges.

The difficulty lay in defeating the BMW's antitheft
system. But maybe she would get lucky. Maybe
Adam had left the car unlocked. Even if he had, the
system might automatically lock the doors and arm
itself after a set period of time. Well, she would face
that problem when she came to it. For all she knew,
Adam had left the doors open and the key in the
ignition. She could dream, couldn't she?

At least it was a chance. A plan.

Carrying it out meant returning to the vicinity of
the garage. If Adam had anticipated her strategy, he
might still be there, lying in wait.

No, that was crazy. He couldn't read her mind, for God's sake. Anyway, she had to risk it.

She headed back toward the garage, hoping Adam wasn't smart enough to set an ambush there.

44

Adam had hated his ex-wife for a long time, but until tonight that hatred had been impersonal, driven by the conviction that she had wronged him, that justice demanded retribution.

Now he knew what real hatred was. He knew it with the agonized throbbing of his genitals, where she had shocked him—Jesus, shocked him like some prisoner in a Third World jail with his nuts hooked up to a car battery. He knew it with the complaint of his left knee, already stiffening up. She'd struck him with the flat of the plank, hard against his lower thigh, close to the knee, and though he didn't think there was any permanent damage, he could feel the swelling of a nasty bruise.

She had hurt him.

He repeated the thought in his mind, trying out different emphases—*she* had hurt him, she had *hurt* him, she had hurt *him*.

No matter how it came out, it sounded equally incredible.

For her to hurt him had never been part of the plan. He was the one who was supposed to inflict pain and punishment. Hell, he was *entitled* to.

Now here he was, limping through the dark streets

of Midvale Office Park, his balls aching, his knee on
fire, and she was out there somewhere, uninjured as
far as he knew, having equalized the contest.

He was pretty sure she couldn't escape. That was
one reassuring thought. He knew the complex well,
and with the gate locked, it was a giant cage.

A cage. That was the first thought to strike him
on the night when Roger Eastman had shown him
this place.

Eastman was another attorney at Brigham & Garner,
but unlike Adam he was no newcomer to the firm.
He'd been there fifteen years, developing a healthy ros-
ter of clients and an even healthier paunch, which
hours on the golf course did nothing to reduce. For
some reason he had taken Adam under his wing.

One day three weeks earlier, Eastman had asked
if Adam had plans for the evening. "Nothing important," Adam had said, aware that the only item on
his personal agenda was a visit to the Web site he
had discovered, the one showing C. J.'s bedroom.

"Great." Eastman smiled. "I want to show you
something."

He had been very mysterious during the drive out
of town. He refused to answer any questions. "You'll
see" was all he would say as he steered his Lexus
away from the last remnants of the January sunset.

It was fully dark by the time they reached his secret
spot. Adam remembered the moment when the Lexus
turned onto the unlighted asphalt road that seemed to
lead nowhere—and then Eastman had flicked on his
high beams to illuminate a construction-site sign.

"Midvale Office Park?" Adam asked. "This is
where you wanted to take me?"

"That's right, kid." Eastman often called him kid.
Adam hated it. "And you know why?"

"I can't imagine."

"Because it's mine."

From his coat pocket Eastman produced a ring of keys—not his regular keys, but the kind of heavy chain a night watchman would carry. He unlocked the gate, pushing it open, then returned to the Lexus and drove into the complex, past shells of three-story buildings, lightless, bare of trees or other foliage. The artist's rendering on the sign over the gate showed a Tudor architectural motif, but the facades had not been put up, leaving only featureless wood-frame walls with dark, glassless windows.

"Mine," he said again. "Well, partly mine anyway. I've got this client, Tommy Binswanger—I've mentioned him."

"Sure."

"Tommy's a broker. Handles commercial real estate. He tipped me off about this place. Prime investment opportunity. The original developers hit a financial snag, had to shut down construction, declare bankruptcy, unload all their assets. Tommy put together a group of investors, and we snatched this place for a song. To ante up my share, I had to burn through my portfolio, take out a second mortgage, pay IRA penalties for early withdrawal. The wife didn't like it, let me tell you. Well, fuck her. She never approves of anything I do. This deal's gonna make me rich."

You already are rich, Adam thought. But he merely said, "Wow."

"Wow is right. The developers were so desperate for ready cash, they were in no position to bargain. Tommy estimates this facility will be worth a minimum of twenty million when completed. We paid a fraction of that."

"Has construction resumed?" Adam asked, looking at the dark avenues gliding past, the empty windows, the excavations and dead ends.

"Not till next year. March is the tentative start date. We need to work out a few details first. Legal matters, tax issues, all that crap. Tommy's handling it." He waved his hand vaguely.

It was clear to Adam that Eastman had no idea what the details were or how long they might take to work out. He had put his faith in the infallible Tommy. Adam hoped his trust was misplaced. It would be amusing to see Roger humbled by financial ruin. He could imagine the fat blowhard crying over his martini—he still drank those—and cursing Tommy Binswanger and the injustice of the world.

"Looks like you lucked into something big," Adam said. "Wish I'd known about it."

Eastman laughed. "You? On your salary, you couldn't get on board a deal like this, kid."

Kid again. "Guess you're right."

"But I'll tell you what. When we have our grand opening, you're invited."

Eastman completed his tour of the office park. He drove through the gate, then got out and padlocked it again.

"Gotta protect my investment," he said as he drove away. "Not that there's any risk of vandalism. Got no neighbors except a few horse ranches a mile away or more. Anyway, the place is sealed up tight. Ten-foot perimeter fence topped with razor wire. Nobody can get in."

"Or out," Adam muttered, thinking of the complex for the first time not as an office park but as a huge steel cage.

"What's that?"

"Nothing. Say, Roger, I'm developing a thirst.

What do you say we stop off for adult beverages on our way home?"

"The wife'll kill me. I'm late enough as it is." Eastman shrugged. "What the hell. I feel like celebrating. Every time I visit that place, I see dollar signs, kid."

Adam didn't even mind being called kid now. He laughed along with Eastman, laughed at his locker-room jokes and his anecdotes about golf and the firm and "the wife," who evidently had no actual name. He laughed when they shared a table at a tavern on Melrose, and he laughed when after several drinks Eastman fumbled with his coat.

"Let me help you with that, Rog," Adam offered, still laughing as his fingers slipped into the coat pocket and closed over the ring of keys.

He found the key ring now, in his pants pocket, and fingered it for reassurance. As long as the place was locked up, C. J. was trapped. He could hunt her down. She couldn't fight him.

Or could she? Already she'd proven more dangerous than he had expected. He'd thought it would be so easy. He'd rehearsed her death for days. He'd killed her a thousand times in his thoughts.

And always his mantra played in counterpoint to the stream of images, the mantra he recited now, through gritted teeth.

"Nobody fucks with me. Nobody makes me their bitch. Nobody—"

Another stab of pain in his knee. Damn. He wouldn't be able to walk much farther.

To track her down, he would have to use his car.

45

Gader had made good on his threat to call an attorney. Around 1:30 A.M., a grim, bearded, bespectacled young man had arrived at the house and ordered Rawls and Brand to leave. His client did not wish to extend further cooperation to the federal authorities until they returned with a search warrant.

"It could be an arrest warrant," Rawls had said, getting in a parting shot. Gader had paled, but the attorney had been unmoved.

So now, at twenty minutes before two in the morning, Rawls and Brand were speeding back to the FBI field office. Rawls was at the wheel of the sedan, Brand in the passenger seat with his notebook computer on his lap. He had pulled up a copy of the tip-off e-mail message, which he had stored on a floppy disk.

Agent Rawlz,
  Something phunny going on. Do you like to watch? Say you're Bluebeard. You have to phind the key.

"Any ideas?" Rawls asked as they pulled onto I-695.

"Maybe. I don't see any clues to who he is. But there may be a clue to who he isn't."

"Translation?"

"This hackerspeak he uses—it seems kind of phony, like it's a persona he's putting on."

"He isn't a real hacker?"

"Well, he found a way inside Gader's server. Got Bluebeard's user name and password. He must have some skills. But it's not who he *is*, if you get my drift. It's not what he's all about."

"You're saying he probably isn't a teenage kid hanging out in chat rooms, bragging about his latest hack."

"Right. He just wants to be seen that way."

"How does that help us?"

"I wonder." Rawls lapsed into silence as the car sped through the frigid night.

It was Brand's comment about coincidence that had turned their attention to the anonymous e-mail message. If a visitor to the Web site had figured out what was going on, why wait until the day of the next abduction before alerting the authorities? It was almost as if the e-mail was part of a game someone was playing. But who? The killer himself? Or somebody close to him?

No way to know. But Rawls and Brand were now convinced that the tipster must not be allowed to remain anonymous.

Rawls thought about what Brand had said. The informer wasn't a true hacker. He was only masquerading as one. Yet he'd known enough to send the e-mail through a remailing service that had scrubbed off all routing information and made a trace

impossible. And he'd known enough to bypass the
field office's e-mail address in favor of Rawls's personal account—

His personal account.

"We've been going at this backward," Rawls said.

"How so?"

"It's not the message that matters. It's how he got
it to me."

"Sure, but we can't trace—"

"We don't have to. He obtained my e-mail address.
Now, how would he do that? How would *you* do it?"

Brand considered the problem. "First I'd have to get
your name. It's not listed on the field office's Web site,
so I'd probably have to look in archived newspaper
stories. The *Baltimore Sun* ran a story on the Myers
case a few months ago. You were mentioned."

Rawls nodded. "And identified as part of the computer crime squad."

"He could have found that article in a database
search. Okay, so he's got the name of an agent in
Baltimore who knows computers. Now he needs the
e-mail account to go with it. So he searches e-mail
directories—"

"Right. That's how he got to me. And that's how
we'll get to him."

"Will we?"

"Those directories keep logs of searches and hits.
We can find out who's searched for my name—"

"And with any luck, the search will be linked to
the searcher's IP address. But maybe he thought of
that. He might have used a public terminal or routed
his search request through an anonymizer."

"I don't think so. If he's just playacting as a hacker,
he won't know all the ins and outs. He'll think he's
more anonymous on the Web than he really is."

"Worth a shot, anyway." Brand was already using the laptop's wireless modem to get on-line.

By the time the sedan pulled into the parking lot of the field office, Brand had searched for his partner's name on the half-dozen largest e-mail directories. Only two listed a Noah Rawls.

In the office, Rawls got on the phone to the first directory's technical assistance number, identifying himself as a federal agent, while Brand used his own phone line to contact the other service.

Strictly speaking, a warrant was required to force the system operator to relinquish private information to law enforcement agents. But the directory services were mainstream, commercial operations, and unlike remailers and anonymizers, they were not eager to force a confrontation with the FBI. The sysop at the first service checked his logs immediately, no questions asked.

"Sorry, sir," he reported. "I see zero hits on the name Noah Rawls during the past three weeks. We don't keep records longer than that."

"Thanks anyway." Rawls hung up, wondering if they'd reached another dead end.

Then he saw Brand scribbling on his desk blotter, and he knew they had something from the second service.

"The FBI appreciates your cooperation," Brand said into the phone, then cradled the handset. "One hit, ten days ago. We got the IP address."

"Trace it."

"Will do." Brand searched a CD-ROM containing millions of known Internet Protocol addresses. He reported that it was a dynamic IP address assigned by a major Internet service provider.

Most providers maintained huge blocks of IP addresses and assigned a new address to the user whenever he dialed in. The addresses were doled out at random, and the same user would have a different address every time he established a new connection.

Even so, the specific user could be traced, if the date and time of the connection were known.

"We've got the date stamp and the time stamp on the e-mail directory search," Brand said in response to Rawls's unvoiced question. "If the ISP will open up their logs, we're golden."

Brand phoned the provider and got through to the sysop. Rawls waited, wondering if they would encounter resistance. The big providers were sensitive to protecting customer privacy. Sometimes they demanded a warrant.

Then Brand covered the phone's mouthpiece and said, "They're cooperating."

"Hallelujah," Rawls breathed, and for a moment he was back inside the hot, overcrowded church in East St. Louis where his mother had dragged him every Sunday, wearing his only suit, a threadbare hand-me-down from his cousin Theo.

Praise be to God, the congregation would announce. *Hallelujah, oh, hallelujah!*

He asked himself if God was watching over him now—and over C. J. Osborn.

46

C. J. found Adam's black BMW a few yards from the parking garage, near a pile of lumber blocking the entry ramp. For the first time that night, she actually felt lucky—because the door on the driver's side had been left open. It hung ajar a few inches, inviting her inside.

A trap? More likely, Adam had been in too much of a hurry to close the door. That meant the antitheft system had never been activated.

If the key was in the ignition, she might start to believe in miracles. She slipped inside and checked.

No key. Well, she could get the car started anyway. She'd picked up a long steel screw from the roadside while doubling back to the garage. It would make an adequate prying tool. She set to work digging the screw into the ignition cylinder, trying to find purchase on the slippery metal ring.

The thought occurred to her that Adam would kill her if he knew she was scratching up his car.

Ha-ha, very funny.

He really was embarrassingly proud of this set of wheels, his first tangible proof of success. She remembered how he'd dropped by her house, shortly after signing on with Brigham & Garner, just to say hello, of course. And he'd been driving his shiny new Bimmer—the 325 coupe, he'd informed her—184 horsepower, audio console upgrade, sand leather interior. She had wondered why he still wanted to impress her, why it mattered to him.

She still hadn't pried loose the cylinder. If she had a knife or a screwdriver—

Wait.

Footsteps on asphalt.

Adam was coming.

No time to get the car started. She had to take cover, hope he didn't notice the scratch marks on the steering column.

She slipped out of the car, easing the door almost shut without making a sound, and scrambled behind the pile of lumber. Huddled there, breathing hard, as Adam came into view.

He was limping badly now. She'd struck him pretty hard with the plank. The muscles of his leg must have stiffened up. She hoped it hurt like hell.

He stopped by the black coupe and opened the door, sliding in. The dome light illuminated the car's interior. She could see him clearly. His face was drawn and pale, his pretense of composure long gone.

Was he leaving? No chance. He couldn't run away now—unless he meant to run all the way to Mexico.

Go, Adam, she urged voicelessly. You can cross the border before I find a way out of here.

She didn't even care if he was caught. She just wanted him gone, out of her life forever.

The BMW's engine turned over with a dull grumble.

Adam started to close the driver's door, then hesitated, looking down at something in the car.

The scratches she'd made? No, his gaze seemed fixed on the seat. Adam ran a hand over the seat cushion, then raised his hand to the glow of the dome light.

There was something dark on his fingers.

She looked down at her own hand, invisible in the shadows, and remembered smashing the vial of tattoo ink. Her hand had been stained a bloody maroon hue. Though she'd wiped off the worst of the spill, her fingers and palm remained dark with ink.

She'd left a handprint on the BMW's seat—a print that would show up plainly against the sand leather.

Glare.

The coupe's headlights came on, then the high beams, flooding the whole area with light.

She scrunched down lower, hoping the lumber would hide her from the halogen beams.

The car began to turn in a slow semicircle, high beams sweeping over the lumber pile.

The fans of light swept past the spot where she lay prone in the weeds . . . stopped . . . then swung back.

She was pinned in the glare.

He'd seen her.

The car's motor revved.

Run.

The BMW screamed forward, plowing into the lumber, scattering it like kindling, but she was already up and sprinting along the side of the garage.

The coupe reversed, then swerved toward her in pursuit. She picked up her speed. Brightness flared behind her.

She reached the corner of the garage. Looking back,

she flung the screw at his windshield. It cracked the glass, leaving a starburst of fractures.

Running again, legs pumping hard. Childishly she felt better. He was so proud of that stupid car.

She ran faster, and behind her the coupe turned the corner, its high beams closing in.

47

"Get a load of this," Cellini said. She'd been thumbing through Gavin Treat's journal with gloved hands while she and Walsh sat together in the mobile command post.

"A lead?" Walsh asked. He'd told her to skim the book in the hope that Treat had jotted down a reference to a hideout. So far the patrol units combing the neighborhood had found no sign of him.

"No. It's just . . . weird. His connection with C. J. Osborn. Remember how we couldn't account for it in terms of the computer-repair scenario? Well, it turns out he didn't make contact with her that way. He tracked her down."

"Why? They have a prior relationship?"

"You could say that. Take a look."

She held the journal open before Walsh. His hands weren't gloved, and no prints had yet been lifted from the book. Ninhydrin would be used to pull any recoverable latents off the pages. Cellini, knowing this, was careful to handle the journal only by the edges.

Gavin Treat's handwriting, every *t* crossed and

every *i* dotted, slanted in graceful cursive down the
page.

December 21.

*Today I found her, she who had been lost, the prod-
igal. She thought she could hide from me, did Caitlin,
or perhaps she thought I had forgotten her after all
these years. Or is it that she assumed my tastes ran
exclusively to children? But we who are connoisseurs
and esthetes in matters of Thanatos must continue
to mature and to acquire more sophisticated tastes.
Stagnation is the death of soul. As for me, I have put
away childish things.*

*Still, it is true that I had forgotten her, or to put
it more precisely, I had not made her the focus of my
thoughts for a considerable time. I have been otherwise engaged. One must not dwell on the past.*

*It was by mere chance that I rediscovered her. Today
there was a television report on a local shooting, and
one of the patrol officers interviewed was a young
brunette who looked so hauntingly familiar. Only
after the newscast had ended did I make the connection to my past. Still, I wasn't sure. I waited for the
replay of the report on the late local news, and this
time I video-recorded it. Though the officer was un-
identified on-screen, when I freeze-framed the tape I
could read the nametag on her uniform.*

OSBORN.

Now there is no doubt.

*Naturally, work remains to be done. I must learn
her home address—unlisted, of course, like any police
officer's. But I anticipate no insuperable difficulty
about that. The shooting took place in Newton Division, logically implying that she works out of the
Newton station house. Were an inconspicuous indi-*

vidual to watch the station's parking lot for a day or two, said individual would be sure to see Officer Osborn enter or leave. Then it would be only a question of following her, or of tracing her license plate.

After so many years, to be reunited with Caitlin! I'm all a-quiver. I believe I'll make her Miss January—she's certainly attractive enough. She'll be such a lovely specimen on display. Yes, give her another month or so to breathe the air. Come late January, she'll breathe no more.

P.S. Today is the winter solstice, turning point of the year. How apropos. Happy Saturnalia to me! Here's to a rich harvest of a fine young crop.

"Christ," Walsh said, looking up from the journal. "What the hell do you make of that?"

"It sounds like this creep has been active for a long time," Cellini said. "And he used to be into kids."

"And one of those kids was Osborn." Walsh frowned. "Her ex said she'd been through some painful childhood experience. He didn't know the details."

"And now her past has caught up with her. Damn it." Cellini closed the journal. "The son of a bitch wasn't even looking for her. It was just a fluke. A sound bite on the news."

"And now she's dead," Walsh whispered.

"We don't know that for sure."

"Don't bullshit me, Donna. Or yourself. Treat snatched her and killed her, and we let him get away so he can keep on doing it . . . again and again and again . . ."

His cell phone chirped. Walsh pulled it from his pocket and stared at it, thinking emptily that this had better be good news.

"You gonna answer that?" Cellini asked.

He clicked the keypad. "Walsh."

"Morrie, we've got something here." It was Rawls, his voice crackling over a long-distance connection.

Walsh couldn't imagine what Rawls could have come up with in Baltimore that would be relevant now. "Give it to me," he said curtly, in no mood to be affable.

"We got to thinking about whoever sent us the e-mail that tipped us off to the Bluebeard site. Decided to trace it. Linked it to an ISP—that's an Internet service provider—and obtained the identity of the person who owns the account. He lives in LA. He's somebody you'd better talk to."

"What's his name?" Walsh asked, and then suddenly he knew. He knew even before Rawls answered the question. He knew, and he could have killed himself for not seeing it sooner.

"Adam Nolan," Rawls was saying. "Spelled N-O-L—"

"*God*damn it."

Walsh uttered the profanity so loudly that one of the radio technicians from the communications room leaned into the command center to see if things were okay.

"I gather you don't need me to spell it," Rawls said dryly.

"No." Walsh swallowed hard, ignoring the stares of both Cellini and the technician. "No, I don't need you to spell it. I've met with him. Damn it to hell, I was in the same room with him three hours ago. He's her ex-husband, damn it. He set this whole thing up"—he was speaking half into the phone and half to Cellini—"played with us, used Treat for cover. Used a goddamned serial killer as a diversion.

That's why Treat was home tonight, why he didn't have her. He *never* had her. Nolan did—and still does, if she's alive."

Cellini took out her cell phone and speed-dialed.

"Any idea where Nolan is now?" Rawls asked.

"No, but we'll find him. We'll find the son of a bitch."

"You sound like yourself again, Morrie."

"Who'd I sound like before?"

"Somebody who'd given up."

"Fuck no. Not me. I'm on the case, Noah. And if it's humanly possible, I swear to God I'll save that woman's life."

48

C. J. lay in a shallow ditch, flat against the ground, while headlights swept over her head.

The ditch had been excavated for the purpose of planting hedges. Heaps of dirt rose up on both sides. She had seen the depression in the ground and taken cover there, and now she waited, praying the car would pass by.

The car. Absurd to think of it that way, but on some level she saw the car itself as her enemy, the demon car with its shining halogen eyes and its engine's guttural purr. Its tires were paws that meant to maul and savage her. Its exhaust was an animal's panting breath. Its stops and starts, its pivots and reverses, were the maneuvers of a predator on the prowl.

More than once it had come close to grinding her under its wheels. But in the chase she'd had certain advantages over her pursuer. She could take short-cuts a car couldn't use. She could cut down narrow alleyways, climb over piles of debris, dive into foliage and lose herself in shadows.

Growing up, she had seen hounds chase desert cot-

tontails. Now she was the rabbit and the car was the
hunter, sniffing out her trail, relentlessly closing in.

She pressed her face to the dirt and waited. Above,
near the edge of the ditch, the BMW had slowed as
if debating where she could have gone.

There were several possible hiding places within
view. An unfinished fountain lay across the road in
the center of an artificial pond, bone dry. She could
have concealed herself there, or behind one of the
concrete benches that ringed the pond, or in the ra-
mada on the opposite side. Farther away stood a line
of fig trees, newly planted, spindly, bare of leaves
but still offering shelter. Behind her lay the start of
what appeared to be a bike path or a hiking trail,
winding between shelved hillsides landscaped with
rocks and wildflowers.

Many places she could have gone. So why had the
car stopped alongside the ravine, its engine idling
dangerously?

She groped in the dirt and found a rock. A pitiful
weapon, but she would use it if she had to. She
would not go without a fight.

The car hesitated a moment longer—then backed
up with a squeal of tires and shot across an open
courtyard, past the pond, into the night.

Gone.

She'd done it. She'd gotten away.

She rose to one knee, then hung her head in exhaustion. She was dirty and bruised; her clothes
stuck to her in patches of sweat; her sneakers were
thick with clotted mud.

The mud would leave a trail. She kicked her sneakers against the ground until most of the dirt had been
knocked loose.

Then she considered what to do.

The car, of course, was not her real adversary. Still, if she could conceal herself someplace where the car couldn't find her, she was likely to be safe.

All she had to do was enter an office building, leaving no sign of trespassing, and then Adam could circle and recircle the complex for hours without success. Even if he did surmise that she was hidden in one of the buildings, he wouldn't be able to search them all.

She nodded in approval of her plan and stood up, her legs shaky after the long helter-skelter run. Slowly she climbed out of the ditch, then broke into a weary jog trot, heading down an avenue lined with dark streetlights.

The nearest building was a three-story structure with tiers of windows checkerboarding the unpainted wooden walls. There were panes in the windows, crisscrossed with tape. She pushed upward on one window, but it was locked. To get in, she would have to break the glass.

Adam might notice a broken window. She wondered if she should find another hiding place—

No time.

The car was coming back. She heard the warning growl of its engine, louder than before.

He must have realized he'd lost her. He was retracing his route.

C. J. ran to the farthest window, partially screened by a sapling held upright by two taut ropes. She snapped off one of its branches and used it to punch through the glass, then brushed shards away from the frame to clear a larger entryway.

It was big enough now. Go.

She hoisted herself through the window as a memory of entering Ramon Sanchez's converted garage flashed in her mind. How long ago was that? Ten hours? It seemed as if weeks had passed, and the scared man with the baby in one hand and the gun in the other was only a half-forgotten dream.

She dropped into a dark space—a room or stairwell or hallway—then risked a glance outside.

Headlights. The car was approaching.

If Adam saw the litter of glass, he would know where she was. She had to go deeper into the building, find a hiding place near an exit. If he searched the place, she would hunker down as long as possible, reserving the option to escape if necessary.

She turned and took a step forward into the darkness, and then somebody was screaming.

No. Not a scream. An alarm. Shrill and piercing, a hundred-decibel siren inside the building.

The place had been equipped with a security system, and she had triggered it—not by breaking the window but by moving forward.

Motion sensor, probably mounted on the wall or ceiling, with at least a twenty-foot range . . .

Wasn't important. What mattered was that the siren could be heard from outside. Through the window the glare of Adam's headlights brightened.

She took off down a stretch of blackness that revealed itself as a corridor, then stumbled against a wall and groped her way to a doorway and went through into a large open space that would be a work area when it was finished. Now it was only bare walls and empty floor. The building was a shell. There was no place to hide. And still the alarm was reverberating throughout the hollow interior.

It occurred to her that now she knew why the power had been left on. The whole complex must be protected by a security system, which had been installed early in construction, so the wires could run inside the walls.

If the system was monitored by an outside agency, then a patrol unit would be dispatched to investigate the ringing alarm.

She could hope so. But no patrol unit's response time would be fast enough to save her if she didn't find a way out.

She crossed yards of emptiness and blundered into another wall, then crabbed along it, seeking a doorway. Her hip smacked against something that rattled—a worktable. She groped among a selection of tools and closed her hand over a large claw hammer. A weapon.

Finally she discovered a doorway and scrambled into a hallway that glowed with ambient light at its far end. She ran for the light and found herself in what must be the lobby. Windows flanked a central door. She got the door open and burst outside, shutting it behind her, muffling the alarm.

Let Adam waste time searching the building. Meanwhile she would find another, safer place to hide.

She was sprinting across the street when the BMW rounded the corner at full speed.

He hadn't pursued her into the building. He had known she would escape out the front.

She flung herself sideways even as the car veered to mow her down.

A patch of scraggly weeds flew up into her face, and then she was rolling down a short incline while the car overshot its mark, screamed to a halt, and reversed.

At the bottom of the slope lay another office build-

ing, outwardly identical to the one she had just left.
She tumbled up against the foundation as the car
plowed down the slope. In the headlights' dazzle she
saw an opening between the foundation and the
first floor.

Crawl space.

A shiver of fear eddied through her, but she fought
it off and bellied inside. Fans of bright light wavered
past her to illumine a low, claustrophobic passageway interspersed with lumber posts and knots of
copper plumbing pipes.

She wriggled into the center of the crawl space and
peered around in the glare of the headlights, looking
for another way out.

There wasn't any. The building, erected on uneven
ground, allowed access to the crawl space only from
one side. The other walls were flush against the foundation blocks.

The car eased to a stop. The headlights snapped off.

She was in total darkness now. Huddled, waiting,
a hammer in her hand.

A child again.

Only back then she'd had a knife—a better weapon.

Maybe I was meant to die this way, C. J. thought.
In a crawl space, in the dark.

She waited for whatever Adam would do next.

49

Adam Nolan resided in a two-bedroom condo in Brentwood, not far from the infamous spot where two of the most famous homicides in LA history had occurred a few years earlier. As the whole world knew, it was a neighborhood where, even after dark, people liked to go out for a stroll or walk their dogs.

Tonight, however, Brentwood seemed empty. There were no pedestrians on Nolan's side street. No dogs barked. No traffic passed by.

Walsh found the stillness spooky. He glanced at Donna Cellini, riding beside him in his department-issue sedan, and wondered if she felt the same way.

Probably not. Cellini was remarkably levelheaded about most things. More levelheaded than Walsh himself. But then, she was young. She hadn't seen as much.

He parked at the curb, making no effort to conceal the car, even though it screamed *police* with its boxy contours, its DARE bumper sticker, its outsized antenna protruding from the trunk.

There was no need for stealth. Nolan wasn't home. The garage reserved for his unit had already been checked by two West LA cops, who'd found it empty. The same cops had then buzzed Nolan's condo for five minutes, getting no reply.

He was someplace else. And so, no doubt, was C. J. Osborn.

Another woman as the victim of an obsessed ex-husband. What the hell was it about this part of town?

"So how'd Nolan strike you in the interview?" Cellini asked as they got out.

"Very fucking sincere."

"Good liar, then."

"The best."

"You do your Columbo impression?" Cellini knew his methods.

"Yeah." Walsh grunted. "Thought I was so slick, and all the time he was playing me. The bastard."

"He's a lawyer," Cellini said, as if that explained something—his slickness or his being a bastard. Maybe both.

Another unmarked car pulled up, and Boyle and Lopez got out. "This the place?" Boyle asked unnecessarily. Nobody answered.

A minute later a patrol car parked behind the two unmarked vehicles, and a pair of West LA officers emerged. Walsh asked if they were the ones who'd checked out the garage and buzzed the intercom.

"Yes, sir," answered one cop, whose nametag read "JOHNSON."

"Where the hell did you go? Doughnut run?" Sarcasm was unusual for Walsh, but he was peeved at having to wait.

Johnson was unruffled. "No, sir. Saw a BMW cruise past and thought it might be the suspect's car. Followed it up to San Vicente and got a look at the tag. False alarm."

"Lotta BMWs in this neighborhood," his partner added pointlessly.

Walsh accepted the explanation. He wasn't really angry at the patrol cops anyway, or even at Adam Nolan. He was angry at himself. He'd been in the same room with the son of a bitch and, good liar or not, the guy should not have been able to fool him.

"Okay," he said, "let's go in."

"Wait." Cellini held up her hand. "There's one more in our party."

Another sedan, clearly official, pulled up behind the patrol car. Its markings were obscured behind the glare of its headlights.

"I didn't contact anybody else," Walsh said.

Cellini looked away. "I did."

The headlights switched off, and Walsh saw that the car was a Sheriff's cruiser, and the man stepping out was Deputy Tanner.

"I called him at the hospital," Cellini said. "He was looking after his men. I told him we had a lead. A chance to save her."

Walsh didn't like it. "This is LAPD jurisdiction."

"He's her friend, Morrie. He deserves to be part of this."

"You should've cleared it with me."

"You were busy. Besides, I knew you'd say yes."

She was right, but Walsh didn't say so. He glanced at Tanner, jogging up to the group, and snapped, "Fall in, Deputy. We're entering unit four-nineteen."

The two local cops had a master key to the building, which got them through the security gate and the lobby door. In the elevator Lopez asked about a warrant.

"Telephonic approval from Judge Lederer," Walsh said. Lederer was known to be a soft touch for warrants,

and once or twice Walsh had actually gone bowling—
bowling!—with the man to cement their friendship.

Tanner spoke up. "You seem pretty sure Nolan is
our guy."

Walsh remembered the distraught young man cra-
dling his head while he fretted about his ex-wife.
"We're sure," he said curtly. "How's your SWAT
team doing?"

"Multiple bites, a lot of venom in their systems.
Pain, swelling, fever—but they'll live."

"You okay?" Cellini asked.

"Not a scratch. Any word on Treat?"

"He's disappeared," Walsh said. "Like smoke."

Then they were on the fourth floor and there was
no more conversation, only a quick march down the
hall to the door marked 419.

Officer Johnson and his partner paused outside the
door, listening. "Don't hear anything," Johnson said
after a moment.

Walsh rang the bell, then rapped on the door and
yelled, *"Police!"* When there was no response, he
looked at the patrol cops. "Open it."

Johnson used the master key. The door to 419
swung wide.

The patrolmen entered first, followed by Tanner.
Walsh and the other task-force members took up the
rear.

The living room lights had been left on. Adam Nolan's condo was small but neatly kept, with a view
of the Indian laurel trees lining the sidewalk below.
Abstract paintings hung on the walls. Chrome appli-
ances were arrayed in a tidy kitchen—toaster, waffle
iron, electric grill, coffeemaker—looking like a line of
demo models in a store display. Only the coffeemaker appeared to have been used.

"Hard to believe anybody lives here," Cellini said.

Walsh had been thinking the same thing. The place had the blandness, the absence of personality, that he associated with motel rooms and other way stations.

Tanner and the other two uniformed cops had already checked out the rest of the condo. "All clear," Tanner reported.

"We'll have to call in SID," Cellini said. "Maybe they can find some clue to where he took her."

"Maybe." Walsh was thinking hard. "Get Boyle in here."

The detective entered the kitchen a moment later, hands spread in mock apology. "What'd I do now?"

"You called Nolan to set up the interview, right?"

"Sure."

"Called his home number?"

"Only number I had."

"But he couldn't have been here. Not if he was with *her*."

Cellini saw where Walsh was going. "You think he had the call forwarded?"

"That's possible, right?"

"Absolutely. The phone company offers residential call forwarding for a monthly fee. Once you've signed up for the service, you can activate it anytime by entering a two-digit code on the keypad."

"Let's find his phone bills," Tanner said.

Adam Nolan was as meticulous in his record keeping as in the other aspects of his domestic life. The bills were in a folder labeled "TELEPHONE" in a file cabinet in the den.

"Last month he paid three dollars and twenty-three cents for call forwarding," Tanner said.

Walsh studied the bill. "No way to know the number he's forwarding the calls to?"

"Probably his cell phone," Cellini said. "That's how it usually works. You want your calls forwarded to your mobile number."

Tanner leafed through the folder and found Nolan's cellular phone bills. "Here's his account number. We can find out if there was any activity on his cell account when Detective Boyle made the call."

"If there was," Cellini said, "it'll give us the cell-phone tower that transmitted the signal. The tower closest to Nolan's location at the time."

Tanner nodded. "And if he was with C. J. when he took the call—"

"Then we'll have some idea where he's hidden her," Cellini finished. "Trouble is, the cell site will narrow down the search area only so much. We could still be looking at an area anywhere from a couple square blocks to several square miles."

"There's another problem," Walsh said. "We'll need a court order to pull Nolan's records. It's not as straightforward as getting permission to enter his residence. It takes time."

Cellini frowned. "There might be a better way. Those Baltimore feds we've been working with— they're in the computer crime squad, right?"

"I think so, yeah. So what?"

"You know how they say it takes a thief to catch one? That's true of cybercrime too. To catch a hacker, you've got to *be* a hacker."

Walsh took this in.

"Rawls isn't going to like it," he said softly. "He won't like it at all."

50

"You want to know why I married you, C. J.?"

The question, bizarrely irrelevant, echoed through the crawl space. She didn't answer.

"Want to hear what really turned me on about you? It was the fear in you. The fear you're always fighting, always denying, always overcompensating for. I could sense it. And I liked it."

I was never afraid of *you*, she thought fiercely. And I'm still not.

She expected him to say more, but instead she heard the BMW's engine rev up, then a crunch of tires on gravel.

What was the plan? Did he intend to ram through the crawl space? It made no sense.

She tightened her grip on the hammer and waited.

The car pulled away, then maneuvered briefly before easing toward the crawl space again. This time the motor noise sounded different, and she caught a glimmer of red light from outside.

The engine resumed idling as the car shifted into park.

"I told you why I married you." Adam's voice was

startling like a slap. "Now you want to know a bigger secret? Why do you suppose *you* married *me*?"

I thought it was love, she answered inwardly.

He surprised her by responding as if she'd spoken aloud. "It wasn't love, not really. It was need." He made a sound somewhere between a grunt and a chuckle. "You need protection. You thought if you could just feel safe enough, the fear would go away."

She wanted to deny this, at least to herself, but she knew it was true.

"You weren't aware of that, were you?" Adam taunted.

Yes, she had been—but she'd never known that he'd been aware of it also. She had thought better of him than that. Now she saw that he'd been on the prowl right from the start. Like a predatory animal he had sniffed out her fear and vulnerability, tasting the scent and relishing it.

"You didn't feel strong enough to face your fears alone," he was saying. "And when you arrived in LA, you were alone—all alone—for the first time in your life."

No, not quite the first time. She remembered that other night when she had huddled in a dark crawl space.

"You were alone and scared," he went on, "and you latched on to the first nice guy you met, the first guy who treated you with respect."

It was true—even if the respect had been an illusion, even if the nice guy had turned out to be a control freak and a cheat and, now, a psychopath. She shut her eyes, wishing he would stop talking and just go away.

"You think you're so independent, so self-reliant.

It's all bullshit. You're weak, too weak to face the future by yourself. I'm the only one who sees it. That nickname your cop friends gave you—what a joke. You're no killer, C. J." Another grunt of laughter. "But I am."

She opened her mouth to tell him she was glad not to be a killer and she hated that damn nickname—but what came out was a cough, hoarse and racking.

It was hard to breathe. The air in here . . . the air . . .

Then she knew what he'd been doing with the car. He had turned it around—the red light had been the glow of brake lights—and backed it up against the crawl space. Now, as the engine idled, the tailpipes were pumping fumes into this narrow, airless place.

He meant to asphyxiate her. Or more likely, drive her out into the open where he could finish her with his own hands.

She shrank away, retreating into the deeper recesses where the fumes had not yet penetrated.

A stopgap measure only. Before long, carbon monoxide would fill the entire passageway.

I have the hammer, she thought desperately. I can crawl out, take him by surprise . . .

It was hopeless. Half-asphyxiated, she would be unable even to defend herself, much less to attack.

He had outplayed her. He had won. Unless the security system really was monitored by an outside agency. If it was, the police might be on their way, or if not the police, then a private security patrol— the rent-a-cops she and her colleagues in uniform always looked down on. She wouldn't cast aspersions on them now, if they came. If anybody came.

But no one would. The truth hit her hard, robbing

her of strength. She coughed again, doubling over,
as the air thickened around her.

Adam would know if the alarm system was monitored. It was exactly the kind of detail he would
check—Adam, with his lawyer's mind, his eye for
detail, his careful planning.

Had help been on the way, he would have fled
already. But he hadn't fled. He knew there was no
danger.

"Getting a little woozy in there, C. J.?" he called.
"This LA smog is getting worse all the time."

God, she hated him. She ran her fingers over the
steel hammerhead, the large striking surface and
twin-pronged claw. She wished she could bury it in
his skull. She wished—

The hammer.

She glanced upward, touching the low ceiling that
was actually the floor of the building above.

A plywood subfloor, not a concrete slab. Three-
quarters of an inch of plywood, if standard specifica-
tions had been met.

She knew all about this stuff. She remembered
shadowing the building inspector as he checked out
the bungalow she and Adam had purchased. The
bungalow, too, had a crawl space under a plywood
subfloor. She had forced herself to belly in there with
the inspector, overcoming her fear of the confined
area and the memories it roused. To distract herself,
she had asked many questions, and he'd answered
patiently, perhaps intrigued to find himself in the
presence of a young, pretty woman with an interest
in plywood underlayment.

Above the subfloor, there would be a second
floor—hardwood, nailed or glued down. Another
three-quarters of an inch. One and a half inches in all.

Could she batter her way through one and a half inches of wood before the fumes finished her off?

She could try.

With new determination she retreated to the farthest corner of the crawl space, navigating around lumber posts and plumbing pipes. She flipped on her back and groped upward, touching thick lumber girders that traversed the subfloor and provided additional support. Perpendicular to the girders ran the thinner floor joists, and in the spaces between the joists she felt the plywood sheets of the subflooring itself. She searched for a wood seam between the sheets—the weakest spot, or so she hoped.

Finally she found a seam and attacked it in a flurry of hammer blows.

Behind her, a burst of light. Something small and tubular rolled on the gravel in the center of the crawl space, sputtering brightly.

A flare, one of those roadside emergency things. Adam must have taken it out of the BMW's trunk. He'd heard the pounding and wanted to see what was going on.

The flare came to rest a few yards away. Its light barely reached her. She didn't think Adam could see her yet.

She kept on swinging the hammer. Wood splinters rained on her face.

More light. A second flare.

This one rolled nearer. It stopped just out of her reach, close enough to cast its light on her. Its glare reflected off the interwoven plumbing pipes at her back and threw crazy shadows on the subfloor, illuminating plastic strips of vapor barrier stapled to the joists.

Her hammer swung again, and this time it

punched through the wood and was momentarily imbedded in the gap until she wrenched it free.

She'd made a hole. Only a couple of inches in diameter, but it could be widened.

She attacked the hole with the hammer's claw, peeling off chips of wood. Six inches wide now.

Gunshot.

It thundered in the crawl space, the blast of a pistol.

Adam had fired at her.

And missed. He was still outside, far away, and she was dimly illuminated and half-hidden by the plumbing.

Still, he might not miss again.

She gave up using the claw and pounded the edges of the hole, breaking off chunks of plywood that pattered on the gravel where she lay.

Twelve inches wide now.

Adam fired again. She heard the pistol's report and the bullet's ricochet in the same instant.

The shot had struck the plumbing pipes behind her.

She was pushing her luck. Needed to get out of here right now.

Another swing of the hammer, and something snapped.

The hammer. Its head had broken off.

And the hole was still too narrow.

A third shot. Gravel sprayed her face. The round had landed close.

And the fumes were reaching her now. She started coughing again. Her eyes watered.

"You're not getting out, C. J.!" Adam screamed.

She wanted to tell him to fuck himself, but she didn't have any air in her lungs, only sawdust and toxins.

Had to widen the hole, or she was dead. No hammer. Okay, improvise.

She braced herself against the copper pipes, then pistoned her legs upward, slamming her sneakers into the subfloor.

Loose wood at the rim of the hole broke away. She kicked again. More debris.

The hole was wide enough now. She twisted into a crouch and grabbed the edges of the hole, ignoring the bite of splinters in her palms. She pulled herself up.

Gunshots behind her. She didn't think she'd been hit. Couldn't be sure. Veteran cops had told her that sometimes you took a bullet and didn't feel it till you saw the blood, touched the wound.

She hoisted herself all the way out, into a corner room with two windows letting in the moonlight.

Knelt for a moment, wheezing, fighting for air until her lungs were clear and she could raise her head and see where she was.

It was a kitchen. A break room, more accurately, for the benefit of the office workers who would inhabit this building. Sink, dishwasher, counter space. The floor was parquet, lustrous in the moonlight, a small touch of elegance that explained the plywood subfloor. Parquet flooring on a concrete base would absorb moisture from the stone, then buckle and fail. Another thing the building inspector had told her.

She struggled to her feet, unlocked a window and raised it. An alarm went off. Every building in the complex must be wired. It was okay. Adam already knew she was inside.

She glanced again at the floor—so shiny—then at two cans with hinged metal handles resting in a corner. She sniffed them both, then picked up the second one and hauled it through the window as she climbed out.

Adam was coming. She could see the brightening glow of the BMW's headlights.

She ran, lugging the can. It was heavy, gallon-sized, and it slowed her down, but she would not abandon it.

It might be just what she needed to turn this battle in her favor—and give her ex-husband a very nasty surprise.

51

"So how do we get in?" Brand asked, pacing the office while a cold wind howled and bleated outside. "We don't have time for a low-and-slow, and if we bombard them, they'll get their guard up right away."

"I know," Rawls said, staring at the home page of the cellular phone company whose server he had to break into.

There were two obvious methods of testing a company's perimeter defenses. Low-and-slow port scanning was one way. Data packets, small enough to be missed by most intrusion-detection software, were sent to the corporate network over a period of days. Entry was accomplished by flying under the radar and taking a long time—low and slow. Eventually all open ports would be identified, and a skilled hacker could map the network.

The alternative was to bombard the target with data packets—an NMap FIN scan, in hacker argot. There was nothing slow about this approach, but unfortunately it wasn't clandestine either. An all-out scanning attack would trigger an immediate security alert.

Rawls needed to get in fast but surreptitiously. Tall order, but there was always a way.

His fingers moved across his keyboard and pulled up a program that allowed him to launch a null session—a NetBIOS connection established with a blank user name and password. A null session could get him into any vulnerable server and allow him to read some of its contents.

"You can't get to Nolan's account that way," Brand said, watching over his shoulder.

"I'm aware of that, Ned." Rawls heard testiness in his own voice. Well, it was after 2:00 A.M. He had a right to be testy.

The null session got him into the corporate server and gave him read-only access to the registry. "They're running NT 4.0," he said, "service pack five, option pack four."

"Outdated," Brand observed.

"That's what I was hoping for. You remember the problem with this build of NT?"

"There were lots of problems."

"The big one."

"You mean the iishack thing?"

"You got it."

"There's been a patch for that since last year."

"But if the sysadmin hasn't upgraded his OS, he may not have kept current on the patches either." Rawls was already searching his hard drive for a file named "ncx.exe." He uploaded it to the Baltimore field office's Web site, then typed a telnet command, sending a 500-byte file—a small program called "iishack"—to port 80 of the cell-phone company's Web server. The port was open, as it had to be in order to receive Internet traffic. The question was: Would it run the program, or had the server been upgraded with a security patch that would reject the file?

"No way they didn't patch it," Brand said.

"There are hundreds of holes in NT," Rawls countered. "No one can patch them all."

"Don't even need a patch, really. Sysadmin just has to disable script mapping for .htr files."

"Well, let's hope he didn't."

They waited. The "iishack" program would instruct the server to find the *ncx.exe* file at the Baltimore field office's URL. It would take a couple of minutes for the file to be downloaded and run. Or the request might already have been denied.

When two and a half minutes had passed according to Rawls's wristwatch, he entered a new telnet command and reconnected with port 80 of the victim server.

"Moment of truth," Brand said, leaning closer to the screen.

The corporate home page vanished, replaced by a black screen with the copyright notice for Windows NT. Below it flashed a DOS prompt.

"We're in," Rawls breathed. The flickering C:\ looked beautiful to him.

He was past the firewall. He had access to the corporate server.

Quickly he scrolled through the directory, then went to ACCOUNTS, entering the Read command followed by Adam Nolan's account number, which was probably the filename.

A request for log-on identification came up.

"Shit." Brand sighed. "I guess their security's not as lame as I thought."

"We can crack it." Rawls returned to the directory and located a list of user names. No passwords were shown, but he didn't think he'd need one. He scanned the list until he found the user name BACKUP. He tapped it with his fingertip. "Sounds like a back door."

Brand agreed. "Give it a shot."

Back doors were simple means of access left in place by maintenance and diagnostic personnel who didn't want to be bothered with memorizing complicated user IDs and passwords. Often they left the manufacturer's default settings intact. Even when they modified the settings, the changes were usually easy to guess.

Rawls went back into Accounts and typed the user name BACKUP. A password request came up. He retyped BACKUP. He knew how a lazy person's mind worked. It was easier to remember one word than two.

A moment later the screen filled with lines of text. Adam Nolan's account in detail.

"Man, you are on a roll," Brand exulted.

The most recent cell-phone activity came at the end of the list. Nolan's last call began at 19:54 Pacific Standard Time and continued for three minutes twenty-three seconds. The terminal cell site was given as a string of figures—the cell tower's geographical coordinates.

Rawls wrote down the numbers, then stood and pulled out his cell phone. "I'm calling LA. Can you clean up?"

"No prob," Brand said, settling into Rawls's seat.

Rawls pressed redial and heard the long-distance call go through. Behind him, Brand went about the business of covering their tracks. He would schedule the deletion of the ncx.exe file from the phone company's server, and for good measure he would go into the server's log file and erase all references to the intrusion. He would delete *ncx.exe* from the field office's Web site, as well. It wouldn't be a good idea for anyone to find it, since what Rawls and Brand had just done was highly illegal.

"Walsh." The familiar voice from three thousand miles away.

"We've got the cell site."

"This fast?"

"What can I tell you, Morrie? We're bona fide federal agents. We're the best of the best."

52

In the farthest corner of the office park, C. J. found the warehouse.

It was a large metal shell of a building with hangar doors and two smaller doors, all padlocked. Cut into the side wall was a casement window four feet square—intended, presumably, for ventilation.

She peered at the window, looking for evidence of security wiring—a magnetic contact sensor or a sound-activated glass-break detector. In the dim light, with the moon hidden behind the roof of the warehouse, she found it hard to be sure.

There.

Strands of wire, barely wider than individual hairs, ran up the sides of the glass and connected to small black nodules.

Pressure sensors.

Break the glass, and the alarm would go off, even before she had a chance to reach inside.

Well, that was all right. Might even be helpful, in fact. The noise of the alarm would add to the confusion and urgency she was counting on.

The window faced an alley that ran between the warehouse and the complex's perimeter fence. Fig trees grew outside the fence, and their leaves, shed in winter, had blown over the loops of razor wire to lie in dry drifts along the alley. C. J. knelt and touched them, heard them crackle under her fingers.

Perfect.

Elsewhere in the complex, the two alarms—one from each building she had violated—must still be ringing, though she couldn't hear them from this distance. Couldn't hear the BMW's engine either, but she knew the car was out there, circling like a shark, trolling for its prey.

Adam would find her before long.

She kicked the leaves into a thicker pile not far from the window, making a nice firm bed. It was all part of her plan—a dangerous plan, but she would risk it. She was through hiding. She had wriggled into her last crawl space. She had played the victim long enough. Now it was time to go on offense.

Adam thought she was weak. Well, let him find out how weak she was.

She expelled a breath of pure rage and saw it turn to frost in the night air, chillier than before.

He had tried to *fumigate* her, for God's sake. Like a *cockroach*.

Even now he must think he had her trapped. She couldn't escape the office park, couldn't enter any buildings without setting off an alarm, couldn't hide outside because there was too little cover.

Couldn't run. Couldn't hide.

But she could fight. That was the one thing he hadn't counted on.

She knelt and pried off the lid of the one-gallon

can she'd swiped, using a sharp stick for leverage. Slowly she swirled the can's contents.

"I'm going to win this game, Adam," she whispered. "And you—you son of a bitch—you're going down."

53

The distance from Brentwood to the Santa Monica Municipal Airport was two miles, a trip that normally took about fifteen minutes in the congested streets. The police convoy made it in five, with Tanner in the lead, flashing the light bar of his squad car and blaring the siren.

He pulled into the airport parking lot just as the big Sikorsky helicopter was setting down on the helipad. The Sikorsky was one of four U.S. Navy SH-3H Sea Kings recently purchased by the Sheriff's Department, three of which had been adapted for search and rescue operations. Most of the time, this meant carrying paramedics to remote locations, but occasionally it was a Sheriff's SWAT team that took the ride.

Tonight was one of those times. A SWAT squad led by Deputy Garrett Pardon was already forming up. The Sikorsky, which had flown north from the department's Aero Bureau Station in Long Beach, would head to a county airfield east of downtown LA, which would serve as the rendezvous point.

Tanner wasn't part of Pardon's squad, but he figured Pardon wouldn't object to another man on the job. And if he did, to hell with him. Tanner had come this far, and he wasn't bugging out now.

He waved the LAPD detectives—Walsh and Cellini, and the two others whose names he hadn't caught—out of their unmarked cars and led them across the asphalt to the chopper. The air crew hailed him when he climbed aboard.

"Hear we're lookin' for a bad guy," the pilot yelled over the thrum of the motor.

Tanner nodded. "Near San Dimas. Got a cell site and that's all."

"Cell tower in that part of the county could cover a lot of territory."

"That's why we need to be airborne. For the bird's-eye view." And for speed, Tanner added silently. There was no faster way to cover the thirty-seven miles from the Westside to San Dimas than by air.

The chopper's interior had been stripped down for medevac use, and the only seats were benches along the walls. Walsh and the others took their seats, and instantly the Sikorsky was under way, floating upward as the land diminished to a checkerboard of lights. Tanner saw that the Sea King was equipped with a video display screen that showed its current location, tracked via GPS, superimposed over a moving topological map. Heading and distance were displayed on the screen in digital readouts. There would be a FLIR display as well—Forward Looking Infrared, which picked up the heat signatures of vehicles and even persons, showing them on the video screen.

If Adam Nolan was there, they would spot him. And C. J. too—if she was alive.

Tanner shifted restlessly. The Sikorsky was flying fast, but maybe not fast enough.

He thought of the slick blond man in the lobby of

the Newton station house, the guy who dressed like a young lawyer and conveyed a lawyer's phony charm, and he wondered if the fucker was murdering C. J. right now, at this minute.

"Hang on, Killer," he breathed, talking to her across the miles. "Cavalry's coming."

54

Adam had to admit that he was now seriously ticked off.

He'd thought for sure the exhaust fumes would get her. Instead she was still on the loose, and time was passing. It was already 11:35—much too late. His only consolation was that his cell phone hadn't buzzed. The police hadn't tried calling him yet.

His luck couldn't hold much longer. He had to find her, kill her. Had to win.

"Nobody fucks with me. Nobody makes me their bitch . . ."

He steered the BMW past the padlocked gate, circling the front of the complex. His car windows were down to let in the cool night air and the sound of a new alarm, if one should ring. When the office park was finished, the security system would be linked to a monitoring station in San Dimas, but either the telephone hookup had never been established or it had been disconnected when the project fell into limbo. Roger Eastman hadn't been clear on the details when Adam quizzed him over drinks, but he had been lucid enough on the one point that mattered—the alarm would not draw a crowd.

At the time Adam had been worried that he himself might inadvertently trip the system. It hadn't even occurred to him that C. J. could get loose.

The BMW motored along the south side of the office complex, its high beams searching the night. He stared through the web of fractures in his windshield, looking for any hint of a human figure.

He had underestimated her, he supposed. Probably he should have killed her right away, while she was chloroformed and unconscious. Would have been simpler that way. Nothing would have gone wrong.

But he'd wanted to let the full four hours pass. Wanted to match the Hourglass Killer's MO.

And there had been more to it, hadn't there?

He reached the rear of the office park and guided the coupe among a checkerboard of poured foundations. The only building back here was a warehouse occupying the northeast corner.

Yes, there had been more than simple practicality. Even leaving aside the serial killer's MO, he'd wanted to see her squirm and sweat as long as possible, wanted her to feel the bottomless fear of true helplessness, and most of all, he'd wanted her to be awake and alert when he caressed her neck and the caress became a strangling squeeze . . .

He still wanted it, all of it. Still wanted to choke off her last breath while staring into her frightened green eyes.

Except somehow that no longer seemed good enough, satisfying enough, did it? She had injured him, humiliated him, outmaneuvered him. She had put him through hell, and now he wanted her to find out what hell felt like.

He cruised past the big front doors and the alley on the side, still looking into every shadow.

The Hourglass Killer didn't torture his victims. But maybe it was time to risk playing a little fast and loose with the MO. Make her suffer a little more . . .

He'd picked up some ideas from those S & M Web sites he'd visited. He might put some of them into practice—

There.

In the alley. Movement.

He spun the wheel, the BMW's high beams cutting through the shadows, and yes, there she was, retreating at a run down the strip of grass between the warehouse and the fence.

She'd taken cover there. Wrong move, C. J.

He gunned the motor. The tires kicked up a spray of dirt as the coupe accelerated, barreling into the alley, closing in on his prey. C. J.'s lithe figure came into focus in the halogen glare, brown hair bobbing on her shoulders, arms and legs pumping. She still had a nice tight ass, he noticed, with a distant memory of cupping his hands over her buttocks and feeling their lean muscular strength.

He stamped harder on the gas pedal, and then C. J. sprinted to her right and picked up something that looked like a paint can, flinging it with both hands.

He hit the brakes, expecting the can to shatter the windshield.

But it wasn't aimed at the car. It flew through the side window of the warehouse, setting off a new alarm. C. J. scrambled through the window frame and disappeared into the darkness within.

Adam parked the BMW near the window. He left the lights on, engine idling, as he prepared for the endgame.

She was finished now. The warehouse, as he'd noted on his reconnaissance missions to the office park, had only this one window. Its remaining means of access were two huge doors and two smaller ones, all securely padlocked.

C. J. was cornered. He could track her down and then do whatever he liked with her and make it last a good long time.

With a smile he removed a flashlight from the glove compartment, then pushed open the car door and limped down the alley, his shoes crunching on dry leaves.

With the flashlight to guide him, finding her shouldn't be hard. The warehouse was big—sixty thousand square feet, by his estimate—but it would be empty. No hiding places, no crawl space, only an open floor penned in by metal walls under a high metal roof.

As a kid, he used to pick up bugs and put them in a tin can for safekeeping, and that was what C. J. was now—a bug in a tin can.

He reached the window and drew his gun. He would go in cautiously. It was possible she'd be crouching just inside, wielding a makeshift weapon. He would take no chances now, not with the contest nearly won . . .

Wait.

He smelled something acrid, tangy.

Smoke.

He glanced around the alley, and in the glare of the high beams he saw a dim mist, which was not mist, rising from beneath his car.

The engine was still idling. And the leaves, the dry leaves—the heat of the catalytic converter must have set them smoldering.

No big deal, but he'd better shut off the engine.

He was limping back to the car when a new scent reached him, unfamiliar and vaguely threatening.

For the first time he considered his situation. Narrow alleyway, fence on one side, metal wall on the other, little room to maneuver.

C. J. wasn't stupid. She wouldn't allow herself to be trapped so easily.

Unless it was a way of trapping *him*.

The leaves, smoldering . . .

That other smell.

Oil.

Goddamn it. It was *oil*.

Adam knew what was going to happen, and his body reacted with an instinctive pivot and then a desperate leap toward the window, and behind him—

A whoosh of combustion. A rush of heat.

"What the fuck is *that*?"

The shout came from the Sikorsky's copilot, who'd been watching the FLIR data on the video display screen and had seen the screen nearly white out with a bloom of incandescence.

But it didn't take an infrared sensor to detect the red splash of light wavering northeast of the chopper, in the desolate hills.

Tanner glanced at Walsh, peering over his shoulder. "It's gotta be her," Tanner said.

Walsh turned to the pilot. "Set us down over there!"

Behind them, there was movement—Deputy Pardon, his scout, his two assaulters, his rear guard, and an attached sniper team of shooter and spotter, all checking their utility belts, goggles, and firearms.

They'd sat stiffly patient since boarding the chopper in downtown LA, but now they were coming to life.

Tanner knew the feeling.

Showtime.

55

Brightness at his back. White heat in a solid wall.

It singed Adam Nolan's neck, his ears, and for a split second he thought he was on fire, actually ablaze like a corpse on a funeral pyre, and then the momentum of his leap carried him through the broken window and he landed on a concrete floor, his injured knee crying out.

While the alarm shrieked around him, he rolled over and over, trying frantically to smother any flames on his clothes or his hair, but there were no flames. The heat had reached him, seared him, but that was all.

He remembered C. J.

Up in a crouch, the gun still in his hand. He snapped off two rounds into the dark. The shots echoed above the alarm's ululant siren.

He hadn't hit her, but he must have convinced her to keep her distance.

Now just switch on the flashlight, hunt her down . . .

No flashlight. He had lost it in his dive through the window. The only light in the warehouse was the fireglow from outside, and it did not extend more than a few yards into the interior.

He would have to track her in darkness, with the alarm wailing and his knee pulsing with pain.

Goddamn, he hated that whore.

In the flickering firelight he saw the can she'd flung inside. The label read "WOOD STAIN."

Oil-based. Inflammable.

She must have poured the can's contents over the leaves, where she had known he would stop. She had counted on him to leave his motor running, counted on the heat of the catalytic converter to ignite the fuel. She'd meant to roast him alive.

"You cunt," he breathed, then raised his voice to be heard over the alarm. "You fucking *cunt*, C. J.!"

He glimpsed her white sneakers blurring into the darker recesses of the warehouse, and he fired again. Missed her, damn it, and already the light from the window was dimming as the fire died down. The inflammable liquids had vaporized, and there was nothing left to burn but dry grass and leaves.

At least the BMW's fuel tank hadn't ruptured; there had been no explosion. Car must be ruined, though. Undrivable. How the hell was he supposed to get home? And even if he did, how would he explain the missing car, the injuries he'd suffered?

Everything was fucked up. His perfect crime, his cover story—all shot to hell.

He forced himself to calm down. Hard to think with that alarm clanging in his skull. And he was tired, worn-out. But he had to keep it together. He almost had her. And once she was dead . . .

He would steal a car for the drive home. Clean himself up in his shower, and with fresh clothes and a false smile, he wouldn't look much worse for wear.

As for the BMW—why would the cops even ask to see it if he wasn't a suspect? He was the grief-stricken ex-husband, remember? He had fooled Detective Walsh before. He could do it again.

Things would still work out. There were complications, sure. Well, when life gives you lemons . . .

"Make lemonade," he said with an odd, lopsided grin that felt strange on his face. He thought he might be laughing. It seemed strange to laugh at a time like this. He might be cracking up.

If he was, it was C. J.'s fault. This whole mess, from start to finish, was her doing. She had walked out on him, ended their marriage. She had wormed her way inside his brain until he could think of no other woman. She had fought him and hurt him and cost him time and pain.

She had done her best to fuck him up.

Now it was time to return the favor.

56

C. J. reached the wall at the far end of the warehouse and groped for an exit, any kind of exit, a door or a window or a hole to crawl through. There was nothing, just smooth metal that stretched in all directions like a sheet of solid darkness.

Stop. Think.

There was no exit. The window was the only way in or out. The doors were padlocked from the outside. She had seen the heavy locks and chains.

She was stuck in here, and Adam was with her.

She'd been waiting for a flashlight to come on, but he must not have a flash. He would find her anyway. He had all the time he needed, and she had no place to hide.

The worst thing was that she couldn't tell if he was right behind her or fifty yards away. The screaming alarm covered any sound of footsteps.

Covered her own footsteps too. She ought to be grateful for that, but she was past being grateful for anything.

Her ambush had failed. She had worked it out so carefully, and in the end all she'd accomplished was to get herself trapped in a steel cage with a madman.

Nice going, Killer. Real slick.

She didn't think he'd even been hurt. When he'd called out to her, she had heard no weakness in his voice, only rage—and an edge of hysteria.

He was out of control. There was no telling what he would do to her, how bad it might be . . .

That line of thought would get her nowhere. She needed a strategy.

The window was her only way out. If she could slip past Adam in the dark, then climb through the window unobserved . . .

She took a step toward the fireglow dimly visible in the window on the opposite side of the warehouse, and then there was silence, slamming down like a hammer.

The alarm had shut off.

She stopped, aware that Adam could hear her footsteps if she moved.

The glow in the window died away. The last light in the room vanished.

No sound. No light. Utter stillness.

She waited, suspended in an ocean of darkness, with only the contact between her sneakers and the floor to convince her that she was still part of physical reality.

Then Adam's voice, echoing around her. "You can't hide, C. J. I can hear you breathing. I can hear the pounding of your goddamned heart."

He was trying to goad her into answering or running. Either way she would reveal her position.

But she couldn't just stand here.

She still had to get to the window—if she could find it with no light to guide her.

She crouched, untied her sneakers, pulled them off, and tied them by the laces to a belt loop on her cargo shorts. Her socks came off next; they were slippery, and she needed traction on the smooth floor. She wadded them up, stuffed them in her pocket. Then stood.

The floor was cold against the soles of her feet. She took an experimental step, then another.

He couldn't hear her. Couldn't see her.

She froze. Heard something.

Footsteps. The click of hard soles on stone.

Unlike her, he hadn't taken off his shoes.

How close was he?

Couldn't tell. But she could judge the direction. He was on her left.

Click. Click.

Coming closer.

Did he know where she was? Could he really hear her breathing, her heartbeat, as he'd claimed?

She untied one of the sneakers from her belt. Waited, standing with shoulders hunched, eyes darting uselessly.

Another footstep. Very close.

She threw the sneaker behind her. It hit the floor with a soft thud.

Laughter. "Think I'm stupid, C. J.?"

He hadn't been fooled. Was still coming.

Her only hope was an all-out sprint to the window.

She ran—

And there was a shock of impact, a body heavier than hers flung against her, driving her down, and Adam saying, "Game's over, bitch."

57

She landed hard on the floor with Adam on top of her. His thighs clamped on her hips as he straddled her, and crazily she thought of the first time they'd made love.

"God, I've wanted this," he breathed. The same words, then and now—spoken then with passion, now in hate.

She thrashed and flailed at him, and his hand closed over her right wrist, squeezing hard. "Fuck you, C. J."

He twisted her wrist. She jerked sideways and rammed her elbow into his face. A shout of pain, a crunch of bone, but his grip on her wrist didn't loosen.

"Broke my nose," he muttered. "Goddamn it, you broke my fucking *nose*."

She'd ruined more than that. "Guess what, Adam? You can't get away with it anymore."

"Shut the fuck up."

"Busted nose. Very visible. No way to hide it." She panted out the words, her whole body shaking with raw triumph and raw fury. "How will you explain *that* to the police, asshole?"

Silence from Adam as he took this in. Then a croak of rage. "I'll kill you."

I sort of thought that was the idea, C. J. almost said, then felt cold metal against her cheek.

The gun drifted lower, its muzzle kissing her lips.

"Open your mouth," Adam said.

She wouldn't.

"Come on, C. J. You used to like it when I put it in your mouth."

The noise that escaped him was less a laugh than a high, hysterical shudder.

"Open up. And don't tell me how it doesn't match the MO. You're right. I can't face the cops, so it doesn't matter anymore. Come on, Officer Osborn. I want you to go out with a bang."

She clamped her jaws. She would not yield to him in this last contest of wills.

"What's the matter? You won't open up for me? You won't put out? Nothing new about that. You were always too goddamned busy. Why do you think I took up with Ashley? She knew how to have fun. I'll bet you haven't been fucked since you walked out on me." He laughed again. "Well, you're fucked now, C. J. *You're fucked now!*"

Ringing in the darkness.

The alarm again? No, the sound was too soft.

His cell phone. That was what it was.

It seemed to take Adam a moment to remember the phone. Then he swore, and she heard a rustle of clothing as he removed it from his jacket. It rang again, but he still didn't answer.

The gun shifted position, and now the muzzle was under her chin, in the hollow of her jaw.

"Make one sound, I blow you away," he whispered.

Click, and the phone's keypad light came on, illuminating Adam's face. She stared up at him. His eyes seemed to have sunk into deep hollows. His mouth was a ragged line.

But when he spoke into the phone, his voice was calm, almost normal. "Adam Nolan."

He was close enough to hear the reply over the phone's small speaker. "Mr. Nolan, this is Detective Walsh."

Adam closed his eyes briefly, as if a headache was coming on. "Oh. Yes, Detective. I—I've been waiting for your call. How is she? Did you find her? Is she okay?"

C. J. wanted to scream. Wanted more than anything to incriminate him. But she couldn't. She had fought so hard to live, and she still wanted to extend her life, even if for only another minute. A minute was a long time. Anything could happen in a minute. Anything.

"We're not sure, Mr. Nolan," Walsh was saying.

"What do you mean you're not sure?" A good imitation of concern. It was all in his voice. His face remained blank, a mask. "Did you find her or not?"

"Oh, we've found her, all right. But as for her condition, I'm afraid you'll have to fill us in on that."

A beat of silence, Adam's eyes shiny and faraway, and then she saw the heavy swallowing motion of his throat.

"Mr. Nolan?" Walsh asked, a tinny voice, like a buzzing insect.

"What is this," Adam said finally, "some kind of sick joke?"

"No joke, sir. Your ex-wife is with you, in a warehouse in an unfinished business complex called, uh, Midvale Office Park, I believe. And I'm right outside—me, and some friends of mine."

"You . . ." Adam's face had gone slack. The light in his eyes was dead. "You couldn't . . . you can't . . ."

"We did. Come out, Mr. Nolan. Come out right now."

Hesitation, and then she saw a new coldness in his eyes, a sudden resolve. "No way."

"Be reasonable, Mr. Nolan."

"Fuck reasonable. You want to know C. J.'s condition? She's alive, with a gun to her head. I've got a hostage—you hear that? Anyone comes in here, and she fucking dies."

Click, and Walsh's voice was gone, and so was the light.

They were in darkness again, the two of them.

"You're not going to survive, C. J.," Adam whispered. "That's a promise. Till death do us part, remember?"

58

"You can get out of this, Adam."

"Sure I can."

Her words and his, two voices floating in the dark.

"They'll negotiate," she said. "That's why Walsh called you. They want to talk."

"Talk me into surrendering—so I can spend the rest of my life in jail."

"They can work something out. A deal."

"Bullshit. He said he and his friends were outside. Tell me what that means, C. J. You're a cop. What's standard procedure here?"

"Standard procedure is to negotiate—"

"And if I won't cooperate?"

"They'll be patient. They won't force anything."

"Suppose *I* force something."

"What do you mean?"

"A gunshot—that would get their attention, wouldn't it?"

"Yes."

"They hear a shot fired, they come in, right?"

"Yes."

"How? Who are they?"

She swallowed. "SWAT, probably."

She was thinking of another warehouse, another hostage situation. Harbor Division. Long Beach. Family killed in the cross fire. Mother, father, two kids, all dead. Casualties of urban war. The first civilian deaths she'd seen on the job. Now she might die the same way, killed by friendly fire.

"SWAT team's outside?" Adam said, his voice ragged.

"I think so."

His phone buzzed again. He ignored it. "How many cops would that be?"

"Five or seven, depending."

"Depending on what?"

"Whether a sniper team's attached."

"Sniper team. Jesus. How will they get in? The window?"

"Or the doors."

"Doors are padlocked."

"They can breach the doors with Magnum slugs."

"And they come in wearing body armor, helmets, all that crap?"

"All that crap. Yes."

"Submachine guns?"

"Yes."

"Grenades?"

"Flashbangs. Diversion devices. Tear gas."

"Fuck."

The phone was still ringing. "You *have* to negotiate, Adam."

"I don't have to do any goddamned thing. Shut up."

She could smell the reek of his sweat.

"So there's no way I can outgun them," he said finally.

It was not a question, but she answered it anyway. "No."

"It's surrender or die."

"I guess it is."

"Christ." His voice broke, and she heard a stifled sob. "It was supposed to work out better than this."

"Things don't always work out the way we want."

"You're telling me, bitch. Our marriage is exhibit number one in that department."

"It's not worth dying for," she said quietly, unsure whether she meant the marriage or its failure or the rage he carried with him.

"I don't know." Another sob, then a noise like laughter. "I thought it was worth killing for, didn't I? Kill and die, two sides of the coin. Kill and die . . ."

The phone had stopped ringing.

"Sounds like they're not as patient as you thought," Adam said.

"They'll try again. Or they'll use a bullhorn. They won't do anything rash."

"No? You told me at the coffee shop that a SWAT raid can turn into a bloodbath. That's your word, C. J. *Bloodbath.* That's why you went in to save that kid all alone. Didn't want a bloodbath, you said."

"I was just . . . talking."

"Sure you were. So how about it, darling? How about a bloodbath right now?"

"Adam, no—"

She tasted metal.

The gun barrel, in her mouth.

"Suck hard, bitch. You're good at that. I remember."

She grabbed his arm, trying to push him away, but he only forced the gun in deeper.

"Don't fight it. It's over—for both of us. You go bang. Then your friends swarm in and take me out. Suicide by cop—isn't that what it's called? Appropriate, huh?"

She held on to his arm, waiting for the shot she would never feel.

"It's come full circle. You wearing a uniform is what killed our marriage. Now some other uniforms get to kill me."

She felt the muscles of his forearm tighten, knew he was applying pressure to the trigger.

"Good-bye, C. J.," Adam whispered.

Gunshot.

Her head snapped back, thumping on the concrete floor.

Blood in her mouth. Bitter taste. Copper pennies.

He'd shot her—blown off the back of her skull—so why was she alive?

More blood. On her face, in her eyes. Blood everywhere, and the alarm again, shrieking—

Not the alarm.

Adam.

She was still holding his arm, and she felt wetness coating her hands and realized the gun was not in her mouth any longer, and not in his hand either.

His hand, which flapped limply on a stalk of pulverized bone. His hand shattered at the wrist and spurting blood.

From across the room, a booming fusillade. Parts of the walls fell away as dark figures streamed through.

Adam screaming.

Blood.

Hands on her face, her throat—

"No!" she shouted, sure the hands were Adam's. "Get off me, *get off*!"

"It's okay, Killer." A familiar voice in her ear. "You're okay."

Lights came on. The drifting beams of flashlights. Men in flak jackets toting rifles. They seized Adam and wrestled him away as his screams subsided into hiccuping sobs.

Beside her, kneeling, Rick Tanner. Touching her face.

"His blood or yours?" Tanner asked.

She read concern in his eyes as he peered down at her, lit by his own flashlight. Concern and something more. Tenderness.

"C. J.—is it his blood or yours?"

The question got through this time. "His. I think."

The SWAT team members were bandaging Adam's wrist, ordering him to hold still, while he whimpered in pain.

"What happened?" C. J. asked, sitting up slowly.

"I had to take the shot. Wasn't supposed to, but he didn't leave me any choice."

"Talk slower. Explain."

"We landed a chopper right outside—the alarm covered the sound of our arrival. Once we were on the ground, we killed the power to the alarm so we could negotiate. We were ready to talk all night. But when I took up my position in the alley, I heard him threatening you. Got to the window in time to see him put the gun in your mouth."

"Saw him how? It's pitch-dark."

He pulled down goggles, covering his eyes. "Night vision. Swiped it out of the SWAT squad's gear when we deplaned."

She saw herself reflected in the lenses. "It looks good on you. Better than those sunglasses of yours."

He raised the goggles. "Shades are more my style. Anyway, I didn't want to risk the shot from that distance, so I came inside and got close."

"Contrary to procedure . . ."

"Yeah, well, I got news for you, Killer. You're not the only one who can climb through a window in a hostage-barricade situation to face a crazy man with a gun."

She had to smile. "Never said I was."

"Anyhow, I was only five feet away when I unloaded. Blew the gun out of his hand. Was afraid if I went for a head shot, he might squeeze the trigger in a death spasm."

"You could have called for an invasive entry."

"Then he would have killed you for sure. Besides, you know what they say about those SWAT raids. They have a way of going wrong sometimes."

"So I've heard," C. J. said, and she squeezed his hand.

"Now come on. Let's get you to a hospital."

"I'm okay."

"Like hell you are. You're getting a complete physical, Killer."

"I told you not to call me that."

"Tonight it seems appropriate." He glanced at Adam and smiled. "You took Mr. Nolan for an E-ticket ride."

She couldn't argue.

Adam had been subdued now. He lay on his back, hands cuffed over his stomach, a wad of bandages on his wrist. The bandages were already soaking through with blood.

"We need to evac this asshole right now," one of

the SWAT guys was saying. "He's got a spurting wound. We wait too long, he'll bleed out."

"Load him up," another man ordered.

Tanner led her past Adam, who gazed up at her from the floor. She expected to see hatred in his gaze, but there was only exhaustion.

"You've got to admit," he whispered, "it was one hell of a last dance."

She just looked at him. "Try not to die, Adam."

"Why? You thinking we could get back together?" At least he said it with a smile.

"I'm thinking," she answered, "how much I'll enjoy testifying against you."

He laughed. A bubble of blood leaked out of his broken nose.

"You really are a bitch, C. J." He shut his eyes, still laughing silently. "Goddamn, I wish I'd killed you."

"Better luck next time," she said, walking away.

Tanner whistled. "That's what I call a love-hate relationship."

"Heavy on the hate."

"But it was love once?"

"I don't know what it was."

"What'd he mean by that crack about the dance?"

"Nothing. Never mind." She glanced at Tanner. "You happen to like Emmylou Harris?"

Tanner took a moment to reply. "I can pretend to."

"Good enough. Friday night, a club in the Valley? Chicken wings and beer?"

"Sounds good, Killer." He held up a hand before she could protest. "C. J., I mean. See how fast I learn?"

She thought about Adam, her three years wasted with him, and the year of loneliness since. "Faster than I do, I hope."

Then they were outside, under the bright stars and the setting moon, and a rumpled man in a rumpled jacket was reaching out to take her arm. "Officer Osborn, I'm Detective Walsh."

She recognized his voice. "You interviewed Adam."

"Not my finest hour. He snowed me."

"He's good at that. Got me to marry him."

"At least I didn't go that far."

The SWAT team moved past, carrying Adam on a gurney. They put him aboard the big chopper that sat not far from the warehouse, its rotor blades glinting like the wings of some fantastic insect.

"How'd you find me?" C. J. asked. "Where is this place?"

"Foothills near San Dimas. As for how we got here—you know the old joke that goes, 'We're from the federal government, and we're here to help you'?"

"Yes?"

"This time it was no joke." Walsh turned serious. "Listen, I hate to tell you this, but your problems aren't over. There's someone else who may be after you."

"The Hourglass Killer," C. J. said.

"You know?"

"I know. God, I have the worst luck with men."

Walsh smiled, but there was no humor in his voice. "This wasn't luck. He selected you deliberately. There seems to be a history."

C. J. stopped.

"What?" she breathed.

"Did something happen to you as a child? Were you ever threatened, menaced? Because this man . . ." Walsh let his words trail off, and C. J. knew he could read the answer in her face.

"The boogeyman," she whispered so softly that only Tanner, standing beside her, could hear.

"What was that?" Walsh asked.

She shook her head. "How close are you to nabbing him?"

"We *were* close," Walsh began, "but—"

"He outmaneuvered us." Tanner picked up the thought. "It was my operation, C. J. I let him slip away. I'm sorry."

She was barely listening. Part of her was in the crawl space of her parents' ranch house, gripping a kitchen knife while a stranger's tread vibrated through the floorboards.

"This isn't the time for pointing fingers," Walsh said. "Bottom line is, he's been killing for years— decades. He has some kind of fixation on you. And as Deputy Tanner indicated, he's still at large."

C. J. hugged herself against a chill, but when she spoke, there was no tremor in her voice.

"Not for long."

PART THREE

The Bad Fox

MIDNIGHT–2:00 A.M.
THURSDAY

59

Gavin Treat, the Webmaster. Bluebeard. The Hourglass Killer.

These were some of his names, but of course he'd had so many others through the years. The San Bernardino Stalker, the Pied Piper of Taos, the Mojave Strangler. In Dallas he had been the Night Shadow, and in the high country of Colorado he had been the Forest Trail Murderer. An incident in New Orleans had given him a sobriquet he especially liked—the Angel of Death.

These were names bestowed on him by himself or by the media. Then there were other names given to him by his victims in their last minutes or hours. Freak, psycho, piece of shit—the words people used when pain and terror had driven them past all calculation into the realm of pure emotion.

He cherished those names most of all. They were badges he wore with pride. Medals of honor, ribbons bedecking his chest, notches in his gun.

He wondered what name Caitlin Jean Osborn had for him. There must be one. He had traumatized her as a child. Such experiences, even if repressed, were never wholly forgotten.

He would like to ask her what she called him in her private thoughts. Perhaps he would. Soon.

His laptop computer—wired into the AC power to save the battery, connected to the Web via a wireless modem that used an ISP shell account—displayed the video image of Caitlin's bedroom. The clock on the computer screen read 12:01 A.M. The Webcam was still running. The bedroom was visible in real time.

It was empty, as it had been all night. But Caitlin would have to return home sometime.

And he was patient, as patient as a trapdoor spider lying in wait for its prey.

He had waited sixteen years for his second chance at her. He would not give up now.

"You sure you want to do this?"

C. J. shut her eyes briefly, fighting off a wave of fatigue. "I'm sure."

"You don't have to. We'll catch him eventually. It's not necessary for you to put yourself in jeopardy."

Her eyes opened, and she faced Morris Walsh. Because she knew he was only trying to be kind, she kept her voice level. "First of all, I won't be in jeopardy. I'll be safer than I've ever been. Isn't that right, Rick?"

Tanner, seated at the far end of the table in the Parker Center conference room, hesitated only a moment before answering. "The way we'll be covering your house, there's no way he can get past us. He'll be spotted no matter what he tries." He swiveled toward Walsh. "We'll have infrared sensors, long-distance mikes, telescopic lenses trained on every door and window."

"Plus they'll be watching the live feed on the

Web," C. J. said. "They can see me in my bedroom even with the curtains closed."

"Maybe," Walsh persisted, "but it's still unnecessary."

"Wrong. It's very necessary. We have to stop this guy." C. J. glanced at Detective Cellini, seated next to her. "You've read parts of his journal?"

Cellini nodded. "And the forensics crew found news clippings in his bureau. Some of them were taken from newspapers that aren't even in business anymore. He's been doing this for a long time— twenty years, we're guessing. The body count by now . . ." She let the statement trail off unfinished.

"He can't get away this time," Walsh said.

C. J. refused to accept that argument. "Why not? He's been getting away with it for two decades."

"But now we know who he is. We know his name. We have his driver's license photo, his social security number."

"Until he changes his name, gets fake ID, a new birth certificate, a new SSN. Come on, Detective. This man is smart. He'll know how to lose himself. He's probably got it all planned out. He might be on his way out of state right now, with a new identity, a new face."

Walsh spread his hands. "Well, if he's left town, your plan won't work anyway."

"It might."

"If he's not watching your house . . ."

"He'll be watching, even if he's fifty miles away. Look, you told me he took his computer with him when he fled. He can hook into the Internet from any phone line."

"He doesn't even need a phone line," Cellini said. "His phone bill gives no indication that he was using a dial-up modem. Most likely he's gone wireless. Or he uses a modem linked to a cell phone, with the cell account under another name."

"Any way you look at it"—C. J. plowed ahead—"he can monitor the Web site. That's how he'll watch the house even if he's nowhere near. And when he sees me in the bedroom . . ."

"He'll come after you," Walsh said. "If he's as obsessed as you think."

"Detective, I haven't been able to get him out of my mind for sixteen years. I'm betting he feels the same way about me. If he sees an opportunity to get me, he'll take it."

Walsh lowered his head in resignation. "You're determined to go through with this?"

"Of course I am."

"Then let's get it done." He looked at Tanner. "How many officers will be undercover at the scene?"

"Twenty LAPD, including Metro's D Platoon. Fifteen Sheriff's, including Pardon's SWAT squad and yours truly. Plus technicians to set up the surveillance, and EMTs on standby."

"EMTs," Cellini said with a glance at C. J.

"For Treat," Tanner added hastily. "Or for our guys, if Treat resists." He looked at C. J. "He won't get near you. There's no way he can penetrate the perimeter and get inside the house. Simply not possible."

"So everything's copacetic," C. J. said with her best imitation of a smile. "How soon can we start?"

Tanner checked the clock on the wall, which read 12:45. "One-thirty," he said. "With luck, we'll have Treat in custody before dawn."

60

"There she is."

Rawls nodded at the screen of his desktop computer, where the live video image on Steven Gader's Web site showed C. J. Osborn entering her bedroom, wearing an LAPD jacket that looked too large for her.

The lamp on the nightstand had been turned on by the police when they inspected the house hours earlier, and it remained lit, casting a dim glow over the room. Low illumination, but sufficient for the Webcam's sensitive lens.

C. J. circled the room, pausing at the nightstand to handle a shapeless blob of blue, unidentifiable in the low-resolution image. She left it where it lay and entered the bathroom to get a drink of water.

"She's checking out the place," Rawls said. "Wants to make sure she's alone."

"Of course she's alone. That's the whole point—to lure him to her."

"I guess she's not taking any chances. Can you blame her?"

"No, but I'm betting she's got nothing to worry about. He's had three hours to make tracks. I say he's nowhere near her house. This whole thing is an exercise in futility."

Rawls smiled. "You can go home if you like."

"Hell, no. I'm staying put, even if we have to pull an all-nighter."

"You mean, in case you're wrong?"

"It could happen." Brand shrugged. "There's a first time for everything."

C. J. took some comfort from the sight of her purse on the nightstand, and more important, from the feel of the handgun inside. Nice to know it was still there. The off-duty gun was an old friend, and she liked having it close.

She considered removing it from the purse and putting it inside her jacket but decided against it. If Treat was watching, he would wonder why she had moved her purse out of camera range. And if he so much as suspected a trap, he would not come.

Besides, she didn't need the gun. She already had one, a 9mm Beretta that Tanner had given her, which was now tucked into the waistband of her shorts beneath her LAPD jacket.

"There's no chance you'll need this," Tanner had said.

"So why are you giving it to me?" she'd countered.

"Well, there's that old Murphy's Law business. Just take it, and keep the piece out of sight when you're in the bedroom."

The bedroom, yes—her private sanctuary, which had turned out not to be private at all. For a month she had slept here, worked on her exercise rig, showered, brushed her teeth, dressed and undressed, and because the curtains had been closed, she had thought she was unobserved.

Wrong. The curtains were closed now, but she knew that eyes watched her as she made a pretense of putting some laundry away. Gavin Treat's eyes, perhaps. The eyes of Detective Walsh and Detective Cellini and Deputy Tanner, certainly—they were observing her on a computer monitor in an unmarked car down the street. And other eyes—the eyes of strangers, visitors to the Web site, lonely men who spied on her in secrecy late at night.

Those eyes troubled her most of all. Possibly there were only a few dozen watchers of that sort, yet they were scattered across the country or around the world; they were faceless, nameless; they could be anyone, anywhere; and they had been in her bedroom, had invaded her *life*, just as surely as if any of them had come through her window wearing a ski mask.

A shiver ran through her. She felt the need to get out of the bedroom, if only for a minute or two.

She walked down the hall, past the spot where Adam had ambushed her and she'd dropped the knife—gone now, bagged and tagged by the evidence techs. Then into the living room, past the den where her computer was set up. The computer looked different to her now. It seemed vaguely menacing, and when she saw her reflection pass across the blank monitor, she felt her stomach twist.

Maybe from now on she would not haunt the online auction sites. Maybe she would just start going to garage sales—or find another hobby altogether. She had always liked using the computer, had liked the thought of connecting with the world through her telephone line, but now she knew that the same thread of wire could allow the world to connect with her.

Into the kitchen now. Looking out the window at the dark backyard. The Metro's D Platoon was out there—the SWAT team—concealed in the bushes, watching her as she watched the night.

Watchers everywhere.

Was Treat one of them? Had he seen her in the bedroom? Would he come?

He had to. Both of them had waited too long to play the deciding round of this contest.

They had to end it now.

On elbows and knees Gavin Treat wriggled through yards of dust and nets of spiderwebs. There were many fine arachnid specimens down here, enough to get him started on a new collection, but at the moment they held no interest for him.

Caitlin was all that mattered. Caitlin, home at last.

He had seen her on the laptop's screen, of course, Caitlin in her LAPD jacket—a borrowed jacket from the look of it, lent to her by some chivalrous member of the constabulary.

And of course, he had heard her too.

The construction of the bungalow was reasonably good, but the floorboards still creaked with every footstep.

Lying in the dark crawl space under the house, he had heard her enter, had traced her progress through the living room and down the hall, had known of her presence even before she entered the bedroom and became an image on a screen.

The crawl space had been his hiding place for the past two hours, ever since he quit his aimless driving and decided to hole up out of sight. He had come here, to Caitlin's house, partly in hopes of taking her by surprise when she returned, and partly on the principle so admirably set forth in that old short story by Poe—"The Purloined Letter," wasn't it? Hide in plain sight. Wherever the police might be looking for him, they would not think to check Caitlin's home.

It had been easy enough to pick the lock on the back door and slip inside, locking the door behind him. He had planned to stay above ground, naturally, but the living room and kitchen were no good—too many windows to be seen through. And the bedroom, too, was out. Although the drapes were closed, the Webcam was still running, and he could not afford to let his image go out on the Web. There was no reason to think the police knew of the Web site, but others did—Steven Gader and his like-minded subscribers to the site. He did not wish to be seen by them or by anyone.

By process of elimination, the laundry room had remained as the best place of concealment. It was windowless and not under surveillance. He had entered it, and then he had seen the trapdoor in the floor.

He had known at once that it led to a crawl space. The irony of it had pleased him immensely. She had hidden from him in a crawl space years ago. Now he would turn the tables.

He had waited, prone under the low subfloor, amid the rusty plumbing pipes and the scuttling bugs, with only the glow of his laptop's screen to light the darkness. The computer, wired into the AC, could run indefinitely. He was unaware of any hunger or impatience or discomfort. For him, there was only the soft glow of the screen, the creak of the house settling, the distant, steady beat of his heart.

He had passed the time by preparing for the kill.

He intended to take her in her bedroom. He did not want an audience.

His preparations had been nearly completed when she entered the house.

Now he bellied his way to the trapdoor and pushed it open slowly, wary of any sound that might give him away. Then he hoisted himself into the unlighted laundry room. Standing, he listened at the closed door to the hall. Footsteps passed by, diminishing.

She had gone back into the bedroom.

That was fine. That was perfect.

Treat opened the door and stepped into the hall.

61

"Something funny about the feed," Brand was saying.

Rawls squinted at the image of the empty bedroom. "What about it?"

"I don't know. Doesn't it look different to you?"

"Same room. Same lighting. Same camera angle."

"Yeah, but there's something . . ." Brand waved his hand, searching for the word. "Flicker. That's what."

"Streaming video always flickers."

"I'm not talking about that. I'm saying—oh, hell, maybe I'm just tired."

"I'll bet you are." Rawls swiveled his chair closer to the computer. "But that doesn't mean you're wrong." He started tapping the keyboard.

"What are you doing?"

"We know the user name and password for the remote sysadmin. We can get into the site's file manager, see if anybody's been monkeying with the video."

"It's probably nothing," Brand said. "Forget about it. I'm beat, that's all. Seeing things."

Rawls kept typing. He didn't answer.

* * *

The most difficult thing was not to look at the camera.

C. J. knew where it was. Detectives Walsh and Cellini had told her that it was most likely installed inside the curtain rod over her bedroom window. The rod was a hollow cylinder, large enough to hide a miniature camera, and it was painted dark brown, so dark that a tiny hole drilled in the surface would not be visible except on close inspection.

Treat must have entered her house when she was at work, planted the camera, and run the electrical wire through the rod and into the wall, tapping into the main circuitry.

She wished she could study the wall for signs of spackling and repainting, but she didn't dare. Anyway, she knew she would see nothing. Treat was a planner, not unlike Adam. He would leave nothing to chance. Most likely he had found the can of interior house paint she kept in the garage and had used it when painting over his handiwork. The color would match exactly.

He was smart. Had to be, if he'd eluded capture for more than two decades, an extraordinarily long run for any criminal, and unheard of for a serial killer. Then again, only the ones who got caught were known. How many other men like Gavin Treat were out there, moving from town to town, state to state, changing their MO and their selection of victims—killing children sometimes, then adults—using different methods, different strategies—leaving no clues? Was Treat an isolated freak, or was he only a single soldier in an unseen army, one among hundreds, thousands?

She paced the bedroom, then stopped. He might be watching her right now. She should not appear agitated. She had to act normal.

What would she normally do in her bedroom at ten minutes to two in the morning? Go to sleep, obviously. But she couldn't undress in front of that camera, not when she knew it was there.

Maybe she would just lie on the bed, fully clothed. Pretend to read or something. But to look natural, she had to take off the borrowed LAPD jacket. And that posed another problem—the Beretta in her waistband. Couldn't let the camera see that.

Casually she sidled up against the bureau, orienting herself so that her right hip, where the gun was hidden, would not be visible from the Webcam's vantage point. She slipped off the jacket and placed it in the top drawer of the bureau.

Now just take out the gun and slip it in the drawer also. No one would see.

She reached behind her right hip for the Beretta.

Another hand reached it first.

Plucked it free.

Him.

In her house, in her bedroom, directly behind her.

She tried to turn, but his arm—his taut, skeletal arm, all skin and bones—hooked her by the throat and yanked her backward against his chest.

"Got you, Caitlin Jean Osborn," he whispered in that voice she remembered from her nightmares, the voice that called to her when she lay in the crawl space so many years ago.

She wanted to speak, to say anything, but the pressure of his elbow on her throat was too strong.

"You shouldn't have come home." Gavin Treat's lips brushed her ear. "There's such a thing as pressing your luck."

62

"Where the hell is she?"

The voice on the radio belonged to Deputy Pardon, team leader of the Sheriff's SWAT squad.

Another voice—the D Platoon leader—answered him. "We were hoping you could tell us, Team Leader Two. We've lost visual. No sign of her in windows four or five."

"Nothing in window one," a voice said.

"Negative on windows two and three."

"All clear on window six."

"How about the camera?" the Metro SWAT leader asked.

"Negative." This was Tanner speaking, as he sat beside Walsh and Cellini in an undercover car a block down the street from C. J.'s bungalow. "She left the room five minutes ago, hasn't returned."

The computer resting on Tanner's lap showed an empty bedroom, lit by the nightstand lamp.

"She's disappeared," somebody said in the radio cross talk.

"All right, cut the chatter," Deputy Pardon ordered. "Stay alert. She'll resurface."

"She'd better," Cellini said in an undertone only Tanner could hear.

"Are there are any other rooms besides the bedroom where the curtains are closed?" Walsh asked.

Tanner shook his head. "The bedroom's the only one."

"Why don't we have infrared lenses trained on the house?"

"We do. On the front of the house anyway. But she's not showing up. No body heat."

"Then she's in the rear. There's nothing back there but the rear hall, the laundry room, and the bedroom."

"Well, she's not in the bedroom." Tanner tapped the computer screen for emphasis.

"Maybe she's doing her laundry," Cellini said, trying for humor. Nobody laughed.

"This is wrong." Walsh's face was set in deep lines of worry. "Maybe they should go in."

Tanner considered it. He wanted to agree, but he knew C. J. would be furious if they blew their cover in a misguided attempt to protect her. "Another minute or two," he said. "If we go in now, the game's up. We'll scare him off for sure."

Walsh frowned but nodded. "Minute or two. That's all."

Treat had the impression Caitlin wanted to speak. He had to admit to a certain curiosity over her final words. He eased the pressure on her throat incrementally.

"They'll see you," Caitlin whispered. "They're looking at you right now."

Treat almost smiled.

So it was a trap. They had known about the Webcam, the Web site, all of it. They had simply pretended to suspect nothing. Really, the authorities were more clever than he gave them credit for.

Still, all their cleverness would avail them nothing.

"I'm afraid, dear, I could hardly allow live video of a homicide to go out unedited over the Internet. Suppose impressionable young children were watching. I wouldn't want to warp their innocent minds."

"What . . ." She was trying to speak, but the words wouldn't come.

"No one can see us," he said more plainly. "We have the rarest luxury of all in this crowded, interconnected modern world. We have total privacy, Caitlin, just you and I."

He felt the tensing of her neck muscles and knew she was about to scream, but already his hand was on her mouth, forcing it shut, muffling her cry as he forced her away from the bureau.

"Bedtime, Caitlin," he breathed. "Rest in peace."

"Look at this."

Rawls had accessed the Web site's file manager and was studying the list of uploaded files. He pointed to the date next to one of the entries. Today's date.

"It was just updated," Brand said. The hour and minute were listed alongside the date. "Less than five minutes ago."

"Check out the filename. 'WebcamOne.avi.' "

"What the hell? That's not live video."

"Not anymore. He recorded three hundred K of the feed"—there were software programs that could capture a video stream as an .avi file—"and uploaded it to the file manager. He's got it linked to the Web page, so we think we're seeing a real-time shot when actually—"

"It's a goddamn loop," Brand finished. "That's why it looked wrong. Flickering—"

"Whenever the loop restarts." Rawls nodded. "Call Walsh. I'll try to get the live feed back."

Rawls figured the signal was still being sent. He simply had to relink it to the site.

He opened an editing program built into the file manager and brought up the Web page, which appeared as a clutter of HTML code. The link to the live video had been replaced by a link to the Web-camOne file.

"You remember the original link?" Brand asked as he flipped open Rawls's cell phone and punched redial. There was ringing on the other end of the line.

"I made note of it. Mind like a steel trap." Rawls deleted the new link, typed in the old one, and saved the changes, then pulled up the Web page and hit the Refresh button.

A live image of the bedroom appeared. Not empty anymore.

"Oh, Christ," Brand said, nearly dropping the phone.

C. J. Osborn was sprawled on her bed, a man on top of her, a tall man with sinewy arms, a man who was strangling her to death.

Walsh's cell phone was chirping at him. He groped for it in his pocket, still watching the laptop computer, and then the video image shivered and miraculously changed.

Cellini gasped.

Tanner was already on his feet, yelling into the microphone. "Code ninety-nine, she's down, *she's down!*"

On the screen, C. J. writhing as strong hands gripped her throat—the hands that had strangled Nikki Carter and Martha Eversol.

The phone was still ringing. Walsh grabbed it. "Yes?"

"This is Brand, FBI. You see it?"

Walsh took a breath. "We see it. SWAT's going in."

C. J. hadn't expected to die like this, spread-eagled on her back amid the tangled sheets, fingers on her throat, air cut off, vision dimming, until only his eyes remained clear and sharp in the descending darkness—eyes that cut through her, laser eyes, eyes that spoke of hatred and desperation and the singing joy of revenge.

Noise.

The boom of gunshots from the front and rear of the house.

Doors being blown open.

Rescue.

Treat heard it too. Released her throat and pivoted at the hips, still straddling her, and then the gun was in his hand, the Beretta he'd taken from her.

He fired three times at the bedroom doorway to hold off the assault.

And C. J. twisted on her side and reached out to her nightstand.

Treat swiveling to face her again.

The purse in her hand.

His gun tracing a slow arc toward her.

Her hand inside the purse, finding her off-duty gun, the Smith .38, her finger slipping inside the trigger guard.

Treat about to shoot, point-blank range, no way he could miss.

But she fired first.

Not aiming, just thrusting the purse in his direction and snapping the Smith's trigger, blowing the handbag to tatters as she fired again and again and again, each shot blossoming like a many-petaled rose on his chest, his neck, his belly, and his eyes still staring, not with hatred any longer, only with dazed surprise.

She emptied the gun, and Treat tottered, slumped, fell off the bed.

Over the ringing in her ears she heard the smack of his body on the floor, a sound as final as the thump of earth on a coffin lid.

Then SWAT was in the room, two teams, ten men or more, guns everywhere, and she was holding up her hands in a protective reflex, saying, "It's all right, guys. It's over. I got him. It's over."

It was too. Really.

The boogeyman was dead.

Epilogue

They called it "C. J."

To Adam, this was the bitterest irony. The Los Angeles County Central Jail, to which he had been transferred this morning after two months of reconstructive surgery on his right hand, was known to its inmates by those initials. In the echoing cell block where he had been installed during the pretrial period, he heard the other prisoners yelling and laughing and cursing, and every other breath out of their mouths was "C. J."

"Pissed off to be back in C. J., baby . . ."

"Hey, motherfucker, what you doing here in C. J.?"

"Food in C. J.'s pretty damn good compared with the shit I been eating."

"You fucking with me, man? Ain't nobody got nothing good to say about C. J. . . ."

He shut his eyes. Even here, he couldn't escape that name and the memories it stirred.

After a long time he found the courage to examine his cell. A commode in plain view. Two bunk beds. No window. Steel bars, cement walls painted green. The paint was layered so thick it felt spongy, like an encrustation of moss.

He sat on the floor, hands in his lap. His right hand had been repaired in a series of painful operations to knit bone and tendons and minimize the awful scarring. He had not regained full use of his hand—the fingers did not contract fully, and his fingertips were numb. He could barely hold a pencil. He would have to learn to write left-handed.

Write what? he wondered desolately. A résumé for my job search? An ad in the personals? Yeah, that would work.

Single White Professional Man, 30, currently incarcerated, awaiting trial for attempted murder of ex-wife, seeks college-educated female for friendship, dating, maybe more. Background in criminal law a plus.

Perfect.

In all his fantasies of killing C. J., he had not imagined this outcome. His worst expectation had been a dramatic standoff with police, ending in his glorious death. He had not conceived of this slow descent into degradation and despair.

His condo had been sold in an attempt to raise money for his legal defense, but he had so little equity in the property that the gesture was largely futile. His BMW, of course, had been trashed on the night of January 31. Under the circumstances, his insurance company had refused to cover the damages, not that he could blame them.

Brigham & Garner had fired him as soon as his name hit the papers. The only member of the firm to visit him in the hospital was good old Roger Eastman, and he had come not in friendship but in anger. Adam's "shenanigans"—that was the word Roger used—had bestowed unwanted publicity on Midvale Office Park, delaying plans to resume construction and jeopardizing Roger's investment. "The wife will kill me when she finds out how much money I stand to lose," Roger had said darkly. "Not if you kill her first," Adam replied, but Roger hadn't seen the humor in this riposte.

Well, what the hell. Being an attorney was boring anyway. And he could always be a jailhouse lawyer. Trade legal advice for cigarettes or something. Trouble was, he didn't smoke. Maybe he would start.

These thoughts ran through his brain, but most of his attention was occupied by his hulking, tattooed, buzz-cut cellmate, who had been introduced to him as Horse.

Why Horse? That was what Adam wanted to know. Throughout the morning, the question had assumed a strange urgency.

Was it because the man was as big as a horse? Or because he ate like a horse? Maybe he liked horse racing. Maybe his favorite movie was *A Man Called Horse*.

For hours Adam had worried over this riddle, while his cellmate sat on his bunk, stiff and silent. Finally he could endure the suspense no longer.

"Can I ask you something?" he said, meeting the man's eyes for the first time.

Horse grunted.

"Why do they call you that? You know . . . Horse?"

"Nickname."

"Yes, I gathered that much. But . . . why?"

Horse showed no expression. " 'Cause I got a big goddamn pecker, and when I pee, my homies say I piss like a fuckin' racehorse."

Well. Mystery solved.

"What are you in for?" Horse asked without stirring from his bunk.

"Awaiting trial. Can't raise the bail. They set it high."

"Don't care about that shit. Wanna know what you did."

"It's all allegations. Unproven."

"What they *say* you did."

Adam sighed. "Kidnapping, assault, battery, attempted murder, aiding and abetting . . ." That was for withholding knowledge of Bluebeard's Web site. "Couple counts of breaking and entering, possession of an unregistered firearm, other things."

"Lotta shit."

"It's all unproven." Adam clung to that word.

"You're innocent, right? Sure. Everybody's innocent. How long you goin' away for, if they nail you on all counts?"

"Life," Adam answered desolately.

Horse took this in without emotion. "You got money, I bet." He was looking at Adam's unlined face and the remnants of a stylish haircut.

"Not a lot."

"You was makin' money, on the outside."

"Yeah."

"Pullin' down big bucks."

"Getting there."

"And you throwed it all away. Was it worth it?"

Adam rallied. "Yes. It was worth it. I had to stand up for myself. I wouldn't let her walk all over me, you know?" He felt a man like Horse would understand. "She thought she could just sweep me out of her life, but I showed her. I taught her a damn lesson, at least. I let her know that nobody—*nobody*—fucks with me. Nobody makes me their bitch."

Horse sat very still, absorbing this tirade. Then he said, "You might be wrong about that last part, bro."

Adam saw that Horse was smiling.

And that smile made it real to him, all of it—this cell and the tattooed inmate and the shape of his life for the rest of his days.

C. J. met Walsh and Cellini for lunch at a coffee shop in Santa Monica, across the street from the palm-lined palisades. The topic of Gavin Treat was avoided for most of the meal. They talked of safe subjects—new departmental regulations that uniforms like C. J. didn't like, Walsh's fondness for *Columbo* and other cop shows, Cellini's time on patrol, C. J.'s hobby of collecting antiques. Rick Tanner's name came up. "I'm still seeing him," C. J. said with a smile. "He can be a little bit of a jerk sometimes, but . . . I guess I don't mind."

"All men are jerks sometimes," Cellini opined, drawing a protest from Walsh—a futile protest, since he was outvoted two to one.

When they were sipping coffee at the end of the meal, Walsh mentioned Treat for the first time. "You told us he gained access to your parents' house through a doggy door. The Sheriff's people in Riverside County have had a look at that door. It's only fifteen inches wide."

C. J. shrugged. "Even so, he must have used it."

"He did. He had Marfan syndrome—it causes loose limbs, you know, double-jointedness. People with that condition can sometimes pop their shoulders in and out of their sockets at will. That's how he got in."

"Dislocated his shoulders?"

"Evidently—one shoulder at a time. It would have hurt like hell for a minute or two, but I guess he had a high threshold of pain."

"Or a high degree of motivation. He lived to kill, didn't he? It was the only thing that mattered to him. No home, no friends, no long-term career. Just the body count."

"And his spiders," Walsh said.

Silence for a few moments, broken by Cellini.

"The car he got away in—at first we thought it was stolen. Turns out it's his. He registered it under a phony name. His getaway wheels. Know what we found in the trunk?"

"Let me guess. Fake ID, cash, a disguise?"

"Right on the money. He would have become Mr. Allan Holt. New social security number, birth certificate, driver's license—a New Mexico license, by the way. Two grand in bills of various denominations. Hair-coloring kit, glasses, change of clothes in a carry-on bag."

"So he could have made a clean break, started over."

Walsh nodded, picking up the story. "If you hadn't gone home that night, he might have decided to book. We wouldn't have caught him. He'd be killing again. You saved a lot of lives, C. J. You were right to take the risk, and I was wrong to try to talk you out of it."

"Thanks. But I wasn't as altruistic as you think. I did it for myself. I had to finish things. I'd lived with the fear too long. I had to get rid of it—exorcise it—once and for all."

They didn't say much after that. The check came, and Walsh paid, insisting that it was his prerogative as the highest-ranking officer present, the oldest person among them, and most important, the only man at the table. Cellini and C. J. reaffirmed their earlier vote, but they let Walsh pay anyway.

Then Walsh and Cellini drove off in a department-issue Caprice, and C. J. crossed the street to walk in Palisades Park.

The day was clear, and leaning on the railing at the edge of the high bluff, she could see Santa Monica Pier to the south, the haze of Malibu to the north, and before her, a great spread of blue sea. It was a great distance she had traveled—from the Mojave to the Pacific, from childhood to adulthood—yet Gavin Treat had found her.

She'd noticed that neither Walsh nor Cellini had asked if her exorcism had worked, if the fear was gone now. Well, of course they hadn't asked. Like her, they were cops—and they knew that while an old fear might fade, there would always be a new fear to take its place.

The world was full of darkness—they saw it every night and day—and where there was one Adam Nolan, one Gavin Treat, there would be others. The crawl space was always there, just below the surface of things, and this pleasant day, with its blue sky and sea breeze, was only a thin subfloor over a darker place.

She would be in the dark again—tomorrow perhaps, or next week or next year. There was no way to know.

But not today, she thought.

She lifted her head to the sun, holding that thought as a shield against all the unknowns in her future, against all the things she knew enough to fear. They were out there still, and they would find her.

Let them come, but not today.

Author's Note

First, let me invite any reader with Internet access to visit my Web site at http://michaelprescott.freeservers.com/. The site features book excerpts, information on my upcoming projects, and other neat stuff.

Second, I want to thank the many people who helped me at every stage of the writing and publication of *Last Breath*: my longtime editor Joseph Pittman, who worked with me to develop the idea; Doug Grad, Senior Editor at New American Library, who provided me with valuable feedback and perceptive critiques as he saw the project through to completion; Carolyn Nichols, Editorial Director of NAL, who has been highly supportive of all my books; Louise Burke, NAL's President and Publisher, whose enthusiasm and encouragement have made my job more rewarding than I ever thought it could be; Miriam Goderich, who offered me her customarily insightful suggestions on the manuscript; and Jane Dystel, my literary agent, who's always looking out for me.

Thanks, one and all!

NOVELS

On the Verge
Roland J. Green

Danger and intrigue explode in the Verge as Arist, a frozen world on the borders of known space, erupts into a war between weren and human colonists. When Concord Marines charge in to prevent the conflict from escalating off-world, but they soon discover that even darker forces are at work on Arist.

Available December 1998.

Starfall
Edited by Martin H. Greenberg and Mark Sehestedt

Contributors include Diane Duane, Kristine Katherine Rusch, Robert Silverberg and Karen Haber, Dean Wesley Smith, and Michael A. Stackpole. A collection of short stories detailing the adventure, the mystery, and the unending wonder in the Verge!

Available April 1999.

Zero Point
Richard Baker

Peter Sokolov, a bounty hunter and cybernetic killer for hire, is caught up in a deadly struggle for power and supremacy in the black abyss between the stars.

Available June 1999.

First in the past.
First in the future.

Fill out and mail with your payment to this address:

Amazing® Stories

Wizards of the Coast, Inc. • P.O. Box 469107 • Escondido, CA 92046-9107

Or for faster service, you may place credit card orders using the following methods:
Email: **amazing@pcspublink.com**   Call toll free: **1-800-395-7760**   Fax: **425-204-5928**

To U.S. addresses		
☐ 4 issues for $10.95	☐ 8 issues for $19.95	☐ 12 issues for $29.95
To Canadian addresses		
☐ 4 issues for $14.95	☐ 8 issues for $29.95	☐ 12 issues for $44.95

NAME (*please print*) _____

ADDRESS _____

CITY _____STATE/PROV_____

COUNTRY_____ZIP/POSTAL CODE _____

TELEPHONE(_____) _____EMAIL _____

Method of Payment
☐ CHECK (payable to *Amazing Stories*)   ☐ MONEY ORDER
☐ MASTERCARD   ☐ VISA   ☐ DISCOVER   ☐ BILL ME (*must be 18 or over*)

CREDIT CARD NUMBER _____

MC BANK NO. _____ EXPIRATION DATE_____

SIGNATURE _____DATE _____